U0504625

国学经典外译丛书（第一辑）

古诗文选英译

An Anthology of Ancient Chinese Poetry and Prose

孙大雨 ◎ 译

上海三联书店

“十三五”国家重点图书出版规划项目
国家出版基金资助项目

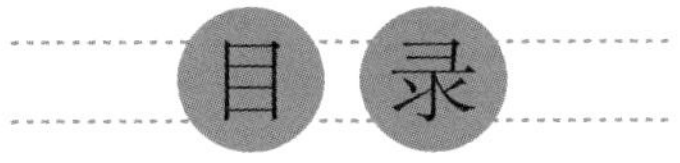

目录

增补篇

(92) 長相思　　李白

日色欲盡花含烟，月明如素愁不眠。趙瑟初停鳳凰柱，蜀琴欲奏鴛鴦弦。此曲有意無人傳，願隨春風寄燕然。憶君迢迢隔青天：昔時橫波目，今作流淚泉。不信妾腸斷，歸來看取明鏡前。

Long Drawn Yearning ☼ by Lih Bai

[The droop|ing dusk | is fad|ing fast | away |
And the flow	ers seem	to issue	a smok	y blue.
The moon	beams dazzle	like silk	of the pur	est white
As I	remain	awake	in pen	sive rue.
While the zith	er of Tsau	hath just stopt	on its Phœ	nix frets,
The hep	ta chord	Zud soon sound	eth its	Aix chords.
Since this song	of cherish	ing thoughts	can reach not	my good man,
I wish	it fol	low the spring	breeze to Yien-	ren's※ swards.
Remem	bering thee	so far off	beyond	the sky,
With dot	ing eyes	of love cast	on thee	in the past,
Today	I stream	them as tear	ful springs	and sigh.
If thou	believe	not my bow	els to pie	ces riven,
Come home	to see	'fore the mirror with	thine own eyen.

☼ This poem of conjugal love supposed to be written by a woman for her husband has nothing to do with the previous piece; they are unrelated and independent of each other.

※ Yien-ren (燕然) is a mountain called Hang-ai Mount (杭愛山) today, in the middle part of San-yin-noh-yan-khan (三音諾顏汗) of Outer Mongolia. In the first year of the Yung-yuan Period (永元元年), 89 A.D. in the Late Han Dynasty, General Dur Hsien (竇憲) defeated North Sen-yü (北單于) and ascended Yien-ren Mount to erect a monumental stone tablet to memorize his victory, before his triumphal march home. It is hinted by the poet that this poem was supposed to be written by the wife of the general, or one of the generals, in this expedition against the Huns.

September 14, 1982.

无名氏

击壤歌

日出而作，
日入而息；
凿井而饮，
耕田而食。
帝力于我何有哉？

Anonymous

Song of Clog-throwing[1]

Work at sunrise,
Rest at sundown.
Dig wells for drinking,
Till fields for eating.
Di's power, though great;
What's it to me and us?

［楚］ 宋玉

（前 *290*？—前 *222*）

神女赋

楚襄王与宋玉游于云梦之浦，使玉赋高唐之事。其夜玉寝，梦与神女遇，其状甚丽。玉异之，明日以白王。王曰："其梦若何？"玉对曰："晡夕之后，精神恍忽，若有所喜，纷纷扰扰，不知何意。目色仿佛，乍若有记，见一妇人，状甚奇异。寐而梦之，寤不自识，罔兮不乐，怅然失志。于是抚心定气，复见所梦。"王曰："状何如也？"玉曰：

Song Yu

(Chu, 290? —222 B. C.)

A Fu on the Divine Lady[2]

King Xiang of the state Chu, in company with his counsellor Song Yu, went on an excursion to the water-side of Yunmeng and bade him to compose a *fu* on the affair of Gaotang. That night, Yu slept and dreamt of meeting the Divine Lady who was so debonair. Being surprised, he told the king about it the next day. The king asked, "How was thy dream?" Yu replied, "After the middle of yester afternoon,

My senses were confused,
  I seemed to be glad whereat,
As if perturbed, perplexed,
  I did not know what was that.
Mine eyesight was not so sure, —
  Now I recall I had seen
A lady on a sudden, —
  Wonderful was her mien.
I went to sleep and dreamt,
  Getting, as I woke, no clue
Why I was so distressed, —
  My mood had been so blue.

Then, laying mine hand on the heart and fixing my wits, I saw again what I dreamt." The king asked, "How did she look like?" Yu replied,

“茂矣美矣，诸好备矣；盛矣丽矣，难测究矣；上古既无，世所未见，瑰姿玮态，不可胜赞。其始来也，耀乎若白日初出照屋梁，其少进也，皎若明月舒其光；须臾之间，美貌横生，晔兮如花，温乎如莹，五色并驰，不可殚形。详而视之，夺人目精。其盛饰也，则罗纨绮缋，盛文章，极服妙，

"Beauteous and excelling,
  The centre and peak of delight;
Splendent and happily rare,
  Inscrutable graces her dight.
There was none such of old,
  Nor is there any today;
Her ease and elegance,
  Praises can never display.

When she came at first, she irradiated like the white sun just up, on the roof beam shining. After a short while, she shone as the bright moon casteth its lighting.

In but a few moments,
  Her beauties diffused their sheen;
Flushing like a flower in bloom,
  Like gem or pearl was her mien;
Her favours multi-tinged,
  It is in vain to write;
When I looked at her closely,
  Dazzled became mine eyesight.

Her rich dressing embraced brocade, taffeta, tissue variegated and camlet,

Full of gloss and features gay,
  The acme of vestures fine,
In colours of sprightly ray.
  She shook her broidered clothes, —

彩照万方，振绣衣，被袿裳，秾不短，纤不长，步裔裔兮曜殿堂。忽兮改容，宛若游龙，乘云翔，嫷被服，侻薄装，沐兰泽，含若芳，性和适，宜侍旁，顺序卑，调心肠。”王曰：“若此盛矣，试为寡人赋之。”玉曰“唯唯”。夫何神女之姣丽兮，含阴阳之渥饰，被华藻之可好兮，若翡翠之奋翼。其象无双，其美无极：毛嫱鄣袂，不足程式；西施掩面，比之

Of garments upper and nether,
The heavier not too short,
Nor somewhat long the lighter;
Her gait was buoyantly free
As to lighten up the hall.
Abruptly she changed her manners,
Like a dragon swirling all
Round, hovering in clouds,
In such of her raiment fair,
In habit light so well meet.
Anointed with eupatory unguent,
She also spread the scent of pollia sweet.
In nature gentle and bland,
It is good to have her beside;
She fared in bearing suave,
Any one near, weal betide."

The king said, "Since she was so beautiful, thou mayst as well try to compose a *fu* on her for *me*." "Aye, my lord," replied Yu,

"How beauteous is she, the Lady Divine,
Adorned with, of Light and Shade(3), the occult pith!
Like the bright halcyon flapping its wings,
The garb of beau-ideal she is clothed with.
There is no match for her under the sun.
Tip-top, excelleth she over and above all.
With a sleeve would Mao Qiang(4) shadow her face,
Knowing she herself would far below fall.
Xishi(5) would hide her celebrated visage,

无色。近之既妖，远之有望，骨法多奇，应君之相；视之盈目，孰者克尚；私心独悦，乐之无量；交希恩疏，不可尽畅；他人莫睹，玉览其状。其状峨峨，何可极言？貌丰盈以庄姝兮，苞温润之玉颜；眸子炯其精朗兮，瞭多美而可观；眉联娟以蛾扬兮，朱唇的其若丹。素质干之醲实兮，志解泰而体闲。既姽婳于幽静兮，又婆娑乎人间。宜高殿以广意兮，

For fear she could have no hope of a score.
Looked at closely, she is dearly bewitching;
Afar, one gazeth at her but to adore.
Her carriage and demeanour inspire wonder,
Of a style befitting a sceptred, crowned head,
Full to the view of the beholder meek,
That wondereth who could share her marriage bed.
I was solely glad at heart,
Immeasurable in delight;
Being unfamiliar with her,
I might not feast much my sight.
Yet others could not see her,
While I alone had this right.
Her splendour is so gracious;
How could it be painted quite?
Ample is her face fresh, and soberly fair,
Of a complexion gem-like, warmly lucid;
The pupils of her eyes like crystals sparkle,
Their lustre twinkling with a charm splendid;
Her eye-brows are curved softly, sweetly waving;
Her scarlet lips, like minium, brightly shine.
In calibre of mind, plain, richly endowed,
She is full of candour, broad and mild in line.
Keeping herself serene in solitude high,
She hustleth yet amongst our mundane kind.
A great hall she shouldeth have to live in,

翼放纵而绰宽。动雾縠以徐步兮,拂墀声之珊珊。望余帷而延视兮,若流波之将澜。奋长袖以正衽兮,立踯躅而不安。澹清静其愔嫕兮,性沈详而不烦。时容与以微动兮,志未可乎得原。意似近而既远兮,若将来而复旋。褰余帱而请御兮,愿尽心之惓惓。怀贞亮之洁清兮,卒与我乎相难。陈嘉辞而云对兮,吐芬芳其若兰。精交接以来往兮,心凯康以乐欢。神独亨而未结兮,魂茕茕以无端,含然诺其不分兮,喟扬音而哀叹。頩薄怒以自持兮,曾不

For giving freedom and room to her large mind.
Crossing the door-step and tinkling her jadestones,
Her gentle gait rustleth her tiffany skirts.
Casting distant glances at my draperies,
Her look seemeth like a wave raising its crest.
Tossing her long sleeves to adjust her gown-fold,
She standth demurring as if in wait.
Mild like a rippling stream thoroughly limpid,
She is self-possessed and unruffled in trait.
Most often placid, seldom with slight stirrings,
Her mind could not be sounded to its root.
Her thoughts, seemingly near, reaching yet far,
Are supposed to concur, but really stay moot.
Lifting my coach curtain to ask for a drive,
She wisheth to be obliging in earnest.
With sheer uprightness of heart, pure and clear,
Suddenly she differeth from me in test.
Giving good reasons of her view in reply,
Her words are scentful like the eupatory.
Her spirit cometh and goeth in its flights;
Her heart is contented and calm in glory.
A soul solitary and unconnected,
She fareth alone in a boundless domain.
With her aye and promise not yet given,
She sometimes heaveth a sigh to plain.
Showing slight anger for keeping her pride,

可乎犯干。于是摇珮饰，鸣玉鸾，整衣服，敛容颜，顾女师，命太傅，欢情未接，将辞而去，迁延引身，不可亲附，似逝未行，中若相首，目略微眄，精彩相授，志态横出，不可胜记。

She could not brook infringement and still remain.
So then, she shaketh her wearing ornament,
Clinketh her phoenix of chalcedony;
Setteth to order her fine array,
Changeth her features to gravity;
Signaleth at her tutoress,
Ordereth her elderly maid for a thing:
With the tendrils of joy not conjoined,
Thus, she is set upon departing.
Pacing to and fro and turning about,
She mayeth not be closed with and talked to;
About to leave but not yet gone,
She seemeth to regard her white-hoofed colt;
Eyeing askance a little the while,
She hath her good will pledged understood.
Diverse are her expressions winsome;
I could not depict them all, so good.

意离未绝,神志怖覆,礼不遑讫,辞不及究,愿假须臾,神女称遽,徊肠伤气,颠倒失据。罔然而冥,忽不知处。情独私怀,谁者可语?惆怅垂涕,求之至曙。

Although intent to leave, yet having not broken,
  She still wisheth to guard from harm and fear.
Since it canneth not end ceremoniously,
  I say, and there is no time to make words clear,
Mayeth she allow me a few moments perhaps?
  The Lady sayeth she must rush along.
I become thereon helpless and defeated,
  Swept clean off my feet and turned upside down.
And then, in a trice, she vanisheth from sight;
  I could not find where she is, though hard I try.
The matter is confined to myself alone;
  Whomsoever could I let it be shared by?
With streaming eyes and a dismayed, hard struck heart,

Tr. September 18, 1974.

宋玉

高唐赋

昔者楚襄王与宋玉游于云梦之台,望高唐之观,其上独有云气,崪兮直上,忽兮改容,须臾之间,变化无穷。王问玉曰:“此何气也?”玉对曰:“所谓朝云者也。”王曰:“何谓朝云?”玉曰:“昔者先王尝游高唐,怠而昼寝,梦见一妇人,曰:‘妾巫山之女也,为高唐之客,闻君游高唐,愿荐枕席。’王因幸之。去而辞曰:‘妾在巫山之阳。高邱之岨,旦为朝云,莫为行雨,朝朝莫莫,阳台之下。’旦朝视之,如言,故为立庙,号曰朝云。”

Song Yu[8]

A Fu[6] on Gaotang[7]

Years ago king Xiang of Chu took a trip with 〔his favorite courtiers〕 Song Yu to the Elevation of Yunmeng[9]. They looked 〔in the distance〕 at the Temple of Gaotang, over which just hung a canopy of vapour.

Up and up it did rise;
Suddenly it changed its guise;
Moments but few had flitted by;
Multiplex was its wise.

The king asked Yu, "What vapour is that?" Yu replied, "That is the so-called Morning Clouds." The king asked, "What is meant by 'the Morning Clouds'?" Yu said, "Years ago the late king had once taken a trip to Gaotang. Being tired, he took a nap. In his dream he saw a lady, telling him, 'I am the daughter of the Wu Mountains and now a visitor to Gaotang; having heard that thou hast taken a trip hither, I wish to serve thee upon the pillow and the mat.' The king thereupon favoured her. While leaving, she said, 'I am in the south of the Wu Mountains and on the pinnacle rock of the highland; at dawn I am the morning clouds and towards sunset I become the showering rain; be it after daybreak or be it before dusk, I am always there below the Southern Elevation'. Latter, when observed early in the morning, she was indeed there as she had said. So a temple was erected for her, named

王曰:“朝云始出,然若何也?”玉对曰:“其始出也,晰兮若松榯,其少进也,晰兮若姣姬,扬袂鄣日,而望所思;忽兮改容,偈兮若驾驷马,建羽旗;湫兮如风;凄兮如雨;风止雨霁,云无处所。”王曰:“寡人方今可以游乎?”玉曰:“可。”王曰:“其何如矣?”玉曰:“高矣显矣,临望远矣;广矣普矣,万物祖矣;上属于

'Morning Clouds'." The king then asked, "When she, the Morning Clouds, appears at first, how does she look like?" Yu answered,

"When she first appears, she looks like a cluster of luxuriant
pines upright sheer;
After a short while, she becomes lustrous like a fair damsel,
Raising her long sleeve to shade the glowing sun and show her
cheer
To the one in her mind [far beyond that blue fell]
All of a sudden she changes her shape and [gentle] manners,
Turning swiftly into scores of quadrigæ and a host of plume-
woven banners;
Soon it becomes like cool gusts of wind blowing and cold rain
drizzling all around;
And then these would stop and cease and the clouds are no-
where to be found."

The king asked, "Could I go there now?" Yu said, "Aye, my lord." The king then asked, "How would she be like now?" Yu said,

"Oh, high! ah, resplendent! she is;
[hail, yet hail!]
The more ye look at her, the farther
she recedes [towering tall];
The wider she expands and arches
out in the blue,
The more she dominates and lords
it over all.
She changes into anything which
belongs to the heaven and [earth]

天，下见于渊，珍怪奇伟，不可称论。”王曰：“试为寡人赋之。”

玉曰：“唯唯。”

惟高唐之大体兮，殊无物类之可仪；比巫山赫其无畴兮，道互折而曾累。登巉岩而下望兮，临大阺之稸水。遇天雨之新霁兮，观百谷之俱集。濞汹汹其无声兮，溃淡淡而并入。滂洋洋而四施兮，蓊湛湛而不止。长风至而波起兮，若丽山之孤亩。势薄岸而相击兮，隘交引而却会。崪中怒而特高兮，若浮海而望碣石。砾碨磥而相摩兮，

Or is found in the depths of rivers,
lakes and the sea,
Into anything rare and strange,
wonderful and magnificent,
Ye canst not speak of, praise
or discuss them amply."

The king said, "Try to compose a *fu* on her for me." Yu said, "Aye, my liege.[(10)]

Take Gaotang all in all, there is nothing whatsoever with it to compare.
For the Wu Mountains have no match, the ways to them intertwine and accumulate.
Rising on the precipices and looking down, one sees the water collected in the huge hollow there
When it turns fair after raining, one overlooks streams converging from a hundred vales late.
The body of water heaves noiselessly as the overflow from all sides feeds it higher and higher still;
The flood swells and grabbles, extending its expanse and volume to wax and fill.
When a gale blows and waves rise, it is like the wondrous rock beds of the Beauteous Islet;
Holding the narrow banks between them yet dashing against one another, they join the ridges high;
Gathering their force and upheaving, they look like Jie-shi[(11)] seen on the billows.

嶒震天之礚礚。巨石溺溺之瀺灂兮,沫潼潼而高厉。水澹澹而盘纡兮,洪波淫淫之溶滴。奔扬踊而相击兮,云兴声之霈霈。猛兽惊而跳骇兮,妄奔走而驰迈。虎豹豺兕,失气恐喙;雕鹗鹰鹞,飞扬伏窜;股战胁息,安敢妄挚?于是水虫尽暴,乘渚之阳;鼋鼍鳣鲔,交积纵横,振鳞奋翼,蜲蜲蜿蜿。中阪遥望,玄木冬荣,煌煌荧荧,夺人目精,

Gigantic rocks uprooted by water crash each against each and
fall, rocking the sky[12];
Colossal masses clashing the water and sinking, splash aloft with
them froths and foams;
The mountain lakelet shaking and whirling, its flowing waves
flux far off tossing about;
Their rushing at one another gives out cloudy spray that sends
rain-drops big pattering.[13]
Wild beasts, panic-stricken, jump and run wildly, in trampling,
tumultuous rout:
Tigers, leopards, *chai*-wolves and unicorns,
Cowering, lose their voice to roar or yelp;
Buzzards, king pandions, eagles and vultures
Fly up, crouch hidden or escape sans help:
Shivering with fear and holding their breaths,
How dare they still be as fierce as of old?
Then the denizens of water all appear,
South of a small islet in numbers untold:
Chelones, *tuó*-dragons[14], sturgeons and tunnies,
Gather and shoal, skip and romp all at once,
Stirring their scales and shaking their fins,
Swimming along like serpents and dragons[15].
Seen distantly from the middle of a slope,
Deep woods grow in their winter luxuriance;
They send out lustre and glory in the sun,
Dazzling the eyesight with their brilliance;

烂兮若列星，曾不可殚形。榛林郁盛，葩华复盖；双椅垂房，杊枝还会；徙靡澹淡，随波闇蔼；东西施翼，猗狔丰沛。绿叶紫裹，朱茎白蒂；纤条悲鸣，声似竽籁。清浊相和，五变四会；感心动耳，回肠伤气。孤子寡妇，寒心酸鼻；长吏隳官，贤士失志，愁思无已，叹息垂泪。登高远望，使人心瘁！

Their sheen shoots like darting sparks of the stars,
Of which it is vain to describe the radiance.
The forests spread out their tall erect lengths,
Covered with dense foliage and flowers;
The polycarpous trees hang their ovaries,
Bending the boughs downward to form bowers;
Their branches wave and the water ripples below,
The pictures become blurred and dim anon;
On all sides around the greenery prospers, —
It is so benign to be in this verdant throng.
Their leaves are full green and ovaries purple,
Vermilion trunks they have and peduncles white;
Their slender twigs sing sadly in the wind,
Like the pipings of the big *yu*-reeds[16] quite,
The clear tones in unison with the heavy,
The five variables and the accords four, —
These touch the heart and move the ears sorely,
Turn the soft bowels and wound the soul to its core[17].
The orphan son and the widowed woman,
Hearing this, have their hearts chilled and hopes shorn;
The state official out of his used post,
The virtuous scholar alone and lorn,
Heaving heavy groans and shedding salty drops,
Are daily by melancholy thoughts outworn[18].
Climbing higher up and looking far off,
One is made sick at heart indeed betimes!

盘岸巑岏，裖陈硙硙。盘石险峻，倾崎崖隤；岩岖参差，纵横相追；陬互横牾，背穴偃蹠。交加累积，重叠增益，状若砥柱，在巫山之下。仰视山颠，肃何芊芊，炫耀虹蜺；俯视崝嵘，窐寥窈冥，不见其底：虚闻松声，倾耳洋洋。立而熊经，久而不去，足尽汗出，悠悠忽忽。怊怅自失，使

Winding round, precipitous, rise the sharp cliffs,
Spreading in unprecedented lofty climes.
The immense rocks rise up and run like wild,
Slant, stoop, protrude, veer, uplift and let fall;
They stand towering and extend zigzag,
Chase one another, then crouch and sprawl;
They come together athwart and criss-cross,
Or go apart, back to back, as if with gall.
Overlapping and aggregated become they,
Multiplicate to an astounding state,
Till they come to the foot of the Wu Mountains,
Where there is a multitude of Giant Pillars[19]
Casting looks upward at the tops of these,
They are covered with rich herbage one sees,
With a couple of rainbows[20] arching on high;
Looking back and down, it is so sheer and steep,
Empty and profound, infinitely deep,
Nothing like the bottom is anywhere nigh:
Only the distant roarings of the pines
Are heard from the hundreds of heights around.
One stands still calmly to inhale and exhale,
Fixedly at one spot, unbent and unbound,
So that he perspires at his two feet and
Feels in body as in mind at ease and sound.
Then one becomes suddenly perplexed and lost,
The heart is fluttered unwittingly with main,

人心动,无故自恐;贲育之断,不能为勇。卒愕异物,不知所生:縰縰莘莘,若生于鬼,若生于神;状似走兽,或像飞禽;谲诡奇伟,不可究陈。上至观侧,地盖底平,箕踵漫衍,芳草罗生。秋兰茝蕙,江蓠载菁。青荃射干,揭车苞并。薄草靡靡,联延夭夭;越香掩掩,众雀嗷嗷;雌雄相

A strange fear assails from within anon,
For in spite of oneself, it would be in vain
To quell it though one be brave as Ben and Yu[21]
The outcome is the shock at seeing strange things,
For it is unknown where they could come from, —
Such a big crowd of monstrous devilkins,
As if they were born of spirits weird and wild,
Or owe their lives to some wayward godlings,
They seem to be [bobbing, bolting, troting] brutes,
Or of the [hopping, bipenate,] feathered tribe,
Odd and queer, fantastical and grotesque,
It is impossible in full to describe[22].

Rising up unto the side of the temple,
One finds the ground level and plane, sans a stone,
The horse-shoe shaped ridge opens its bottom wide,
With odorous herbs and trees all overgrown.
Autumn eupatories[23], thymes, coumarous,
Thickets of scenting umbellets in full blow,
Green kingly *quan*, purple fleur-de-lis in glory,
Jie-che sweet, one and all they bloom and grow.
Unbroken, interminate, in a lusty state,
The grass-green herbage thrives closely together;
The rues spread their perfumes all around them,
And birds flock here, of fair songs and fine feather.
Some of these, having missed their mates in flight,
Are crying sadly for the missed to gather.

失，哀鸣相号。王雎鹂黄，正冥楚鸠；姊归思妇，垂鸡高巢。其鸣喈喈，当年遨游，更唱迭和，赴曲随流。有方之士羡门高，谿上成，郁林公，乐聚谷，进纯牺，祷璇室，醮诸神，礼太一。传祝已具，言辞已毕，王乃乘玉舆，驷苍螭，垂旒旌，旆合谐，䌷大弦，而雅声流冽，风过而增悲哀。

The constant osprays, the singing orioles,
The throstles joyous*, the soft plaintive turtle doves,
The cuckoos whose cries are like a lone wife's,
The pheasants of long tail plume(24) nesting above:
They chant with sweet harmonious accord,
At the prime of their lives, in wanderlust;
They intonate and respond each to the others,
As they should in one song and in common gust.
With the man of fair parts Xian-men Gao(25)
Who turned fairy by a mountain brooklet,
And another one, the Yulin Elder,(26)
Who likes to gather grains, to serve at the rites,
Offerings have been given fine and pure,
Prayers made in the ruby-decorated hall,
To all the deities divine honours paid
And homage done the star of the supreme god(27).
When all the prayers are said, all wishes laid,
The king leaves riding in a carriage of jade,
A quadriga drawn by four dragonets blue,
With oriflammes and hanging flags round about;
Then, the streamers flutter in one direction,
The chord of strings grows mellifluous and stout,
And the note of *ya*(28) flows with a chilly strain,
So that, as the winds blow past, it sounds mournful.

---

* I have not the faintest idea of what the original 正冥 means here.

于是调讴令人惏悷憯凄,胁息增欷。于是乃纵猎者,基址如星。传言羽猎,衔枚无声。弓弩不发,罘罕不倾。涉漭漭,驰苹苹。飞鸟未及起,走兽未及发。弭节奄忽,蹏足洒血。举功先得,获车已实。王将欲往见之,必先斋戒,差时择日,简舆玄服,建云旆,蜺为旌,翠为盖,风起雨止,

The tune then becomes plaintive and grieving,
It catches one's breath and makes one doleful.
Now, hunters are to be let loose in the wild,
Which, seen afar, is spangled with town walls like stars.
The word is said that soldiers should go to hunt,
And they should keep strictly quiet in their tasks.
As yet no arrows have been shot from the bows,
But the snares and nets are filled enow soon.
Far and wide has been the crossing of water,
As the galloping on the grassy plain boon.
The flying race has thus far no time to rise,
The hoofed beasts are not yet ready to fleet.
While the chase takes its course slowly or apace,
The games are caught before they could retreat.
Those who get the spoils first are preferred for merits,
As the carts are already loaded with deers meet(29).

Thenceforth, when the king wants to visit the temple,
He will keep a three-day's fast beforehand,
Choose his day and moment of departure first,
Select his carriage and dress in sober black,
Erect his standards of clouds, rainbow colours
And the cover(30) made of the king-fisher's plumes,
When the wind has risen and rain has stopped,
Ere he takes this voyage of a thousand *li*.

千里而逝。盖发蒙往，自会思，万方忧，国害开，贤圣辅不逮，九窍通郁，精神察滞，延年益寿千万岁！

For by clearing the hazy thoughts of the past,
Our lord is bound to be keen in wits and sight;
He will be anxious for the good of all people;
Thus the harms to the state would be set aright;
The virtuous and sage would lend timely help;
His nine vents[31] would be free from stoppers that choke,
His spirits aware of where the stickings lie:
And then, let long life come to him for aye!"[32]

Tr. Angust 14, 1974.

［汉］ 司马迁

（约前 *145* 或 *135*—?）

淳于髡讽齐威王

（节选自《史记·滑稽列传》）

威王八年，楚大发兵加齐。齐王使淳于髡之赵请救兵，赍金百斤，车马十驷。淳于髡仰天大笑，冠缨索绝。王曰："先生少之乎?"髡曰："何敢?"王曰："笑岂有说乎?"髡曰："今者臣从东方来，见道旁有禳田者，操一豚蹄，酒一盂，祝曰：'瓯窭满篝，汙邪满车，五谷蕃熟，穰穰满家。'臣见其所持者狭，而所欲者奢，故笑之。"于是齐威王乃益赍黄金千镒，白璧十双，车马百驷。髡辞而行，至赵。赵王与之精兵十万，革车千乘。楚闻之，夜引兵而去。

Sima Qian

(Han, 145 or 135—? B. C)

Chunyu Kun's[33] Indirect Counsel to King Wei of Qi

(Selected from lives of the Comedians of The Records of the Historian)

In the eighth year of King Wei's reign, the state of Chu dispatched a large expeditionary force against Qi. The king of Qi sent Chunyu Kun to the state of Zhao to ask for relief troops, who was to take along with him a hundred-weight of gold and ten quadrigæ. [On hearing the king's request to him in person,] Chunyu Kun faced heavenward and laughed so uproariously that the cord of his hat snapped. The king asked him, "Sire, do you take these as too little?" Chunyu said, "How dare I?" The King said, "Do you have anything to say about your laughing?" Chunyu answered, "Your humble servant has just come from the east and has seen some one by the wayside offering sacrifice to ask blessing on his farm, with a pig's leg and a tankard of wine in his hands. The man said, 'I pray Thou wouldst make my narrow high fields reap me a plentiful harvest; I pray Thou wouldst make my low marshy lands also yield me a bountiful crop; let my five grains[34] all grow luxuriantly; let cereals fill my house'. I saw he offered little and asked for much, and so I laughed." Then King Wei increased his gifts to Zhao to ten hundred-weights of gold, ten pairs of white bi[35] and a hundred quadrigae. Chunyu bade adieu to the King and went forthwith to Zhao. The king of Zhao gave him shock troops of one hundred thousand strong and a thousand war chariots. On hearing this, Chu withdrew its besiegers in the night.

威王大说，置酒后宫，召髡赐之酒，问曰："先生能饮几何而醉？"髡对曰："巨饮一斗亦醉，一石亦醉。"威王曰："先生饮一斗而醉，恶能饮一石哉！其说可得闻乎？"髡曰："赐酒大王之前，执法在旁，御史在后，髡恐惧俯伏而饮，不过一斗径醉矣。若亲有严客，髡帣鞲鞠䐶，侍酒于前，时赐余沥，奉觞上寿数起，饮不过二斗径醉矣。若朋友交游，久不相见，卒然相睹，欢然道故，私情相语，饮可五六斗径醉矣。若乃州闾之会，男女杂坐，行酒稽留，六博投壶，相引为曹，握手无罚，目眙不禁，前有堕珥，后有遗簪。髡窃乐此，饮可八斗而醉二参。日暮酒阑，合尊促坐，

King Wei was overjoyed by the success. He ordered a festive carousal in his palace and bade Chunyu to partake of his royal favour, asking him at the moment, "Sire, how much could you drink to be intoxicated?" Chunyu said, "Your humble servant will be drunk after taking a *dou*[36] and will also be drunk after taking a *shi*." King Wei then said, "If you will be drunk, Sire, after taking a *dou*, how can you take a *shi*? Could you explain to me what you have just said?" Chunyu answered, "When Your Majesty favours me with royal drinks before your regal presence, with the executor of law at my side and the chancellor of royal decrees behind, I, crouching on all fours in fear, could drink but a *dou* and would be overcome with intoxication. If my father were to entertain some august guests and I, folding back my sleeves, bending my body and kneeling beside to attend on them, — meanwhile they would often propose bumpers to me and I would be told to drink health to them in a number of beakers, — I would then become drunk after having two *dou* only. If friends of mine whom I have not seen for a long time meet me on the sudden and we speak of our good old days and warm our feelings for one another, then I could take five or six *dou* to be drunk. If it were at a gathering of the neighbourhood, men and women sit together at random, wine is served to detain the attendants, games of mutually surrounding multi-checker and of pitching arrows[37] into bottles would attract parties, holding one another's hands would not be punished and gazing at each other is not forbidden, there may be fallen [pearl] ear-rings in the front or [jade] hair-pins left over behind, I confess I take delight in such a company and could quench my thirst up to eight *dou* as I get drunk from evening till morning. When dusk falls and the carousal waxes

男女同席,履舄交错,杯盘狼藉,堂上烛灭,主人留髡而送客,罗襦襟解,微闻芗泽。当此之时,髡心最欢,能饮一石。故曰酒极则乱,乐极则悲,万事尽然。言不可极,极之而衰。以讽谏焉。”齐王曰:“善!”乃罢长夜之饮,以髡为诸侯主客。宗室置酒,髡尝在侧。

late, beakers are taken to one table and scattered seats moved closer, men and women sit side by side, pairs of shoes larger as well as smaller are near to one another, the cups and plates look unseemly, the candles in the hall are snuffed out, the host asks me to remain and sees other guests off home, — at that moment a silken doublet is unloosened and I faintly smell a breath of fragrance. Right then my heart is merriest and I could drink a *shi*. Therefore, it can be said that overdrinking of wine would lead to misdemeanour and excessive joy would end in sorrow, which teaches us that all things in life are like this, that one should not go to extremes which could only breed grief — so, this might be taken as an indirect counsel."

The king then said, "Very well," and put an end to his night-long revels thereafter. He made Chunyu Kun the chief guest whenever he gave audience to his vassals from then on. When members of his royal family offered drinking feasts, Chunyu Kun was often invited to attend.

［晋］ 刘伶

（？—？）

酒德颂

有大人先生，以天地为一朝，万期为须臾，日月为扃牖，八荒为庭衢。行无辙迹，居无室庐，幕天席地，纵意所如。止则操卮执觚，动则挈榼提壶，惟酒是务，焉知其余？有贵介公子，搢绅处士，闻吾风声，议其所以。乃奋袂攘襟，

Liu Lin[39]

(*Jin*, ? —?)

In Praise of the Quality of Drinking[38]

There is a gentleman of high virtue and the night way[40]
Who takes the heaven and earth as of one morning
And ten millenniums a mere wink of a day,
The sun and the moon his portal and casement
And the eight expanses[41] his courtyard and highway.
He comes and goes without a track of his vehicle,
Puts up in no room or house wherein to stay,
Using the sky as his tent and the ground his mat,
Doing whatever seeming to him pleasant and gay.
When he stops anywhere, he holds his vase and mug;
When he moves on, he takes along his beaker and jug;
Wine is the thing always and uppermost in his mind;
What else does he care for but to finger, of a flagon or a pot the
lug?
There are grand nobles and princes true blue
As well as courtiers high in rank and untitled celebrities too,
Who, hearing of my sough of how he behaves himself,
Talk of him and the things he deems fit to do.
Tossing the long sleeves and shaking the collar folds of their
gowns,

怒目切齿，陈说礼法，是非锋起。先生于是方捧罂承槽，衔杯漱醪，奋髯箕踞，枕麴籍糟，无思无虑，其乐陶陶，兀然而醉，豁然而醒，静听不闻雷霆之声，熟视不睹泰山之形，不觉寒暑之切肌，利欲之感情。俯视万物扰扰焉，如江汉之载浮萍，二豪侍侧焉，如蜾蠃之与螟蛉。

Throwing angry looks left and right and setting their teeth,
They preach manners and stand for the regular order,
With arguments rife as bristling swords out of sheath.
Just then our good sire is holding his pot to fill from a cistern,
Then imbibes at his stoup and parts the settled lees from his wine.
Puffs up his whiskers while squatting upon his hams,
Treads the waste dregs but pillows his barm loaves fine.
Free from all cumbrous thoughts and nipping cares,
Cheerily enjoying his breezy buoyancy under a vine,
Now he is overcome with sousing at a sudden stroke,
And then, recovering wide-awake, is in spirits divine;
He hears not the thunderclaps though listening in quiet,
And looking steadily, sees not Tai Shan's[42] towering majesty in the sunshine;
He feels not the furies of burning heat and biting cold,
Either the lust of desires, or the greed for gain malign.
He overlooks the ten thousand puddering things of the world
As the Long and the Han Rivers bearing up the tiny "floating disks,"[43]
And the two mighty ones[44] waiting on him by the side,
As the black bee[45], carrying on its back the "ming-ling",[46] that frisks.

Tr. July 16, 1974.

[晋] 潘岳

(247—300)

秋兴赋

晋十有四年,余春秋三十有二,始见二毛。以太尉掾兼虎贲中郎将,寓直于散骑之省。高阁连云,阳景罕曜。珥蝉冕而袭纨绮之士,此焉游处。仆野人也,偃息不过茅屋茂林之下,谈话不过农夫田父之客。摄官承乏,猥厕朝列,夙兴晏寝,匪遑底宁。譬犹池鱼笼鸟,有江湖山薮之思。于是染翰操纸,慨然而赋。于时秋也,故以"秋兴"名篇,其辞曰:

Pan Yue

(Jin, 247—300)

A Fu[47] on Autumn Feelings

In the fourteenth year of Jin[49], having attained the age of thirty-two, I begin fo find white hairs on my top. As one of the subordinate knights of the Lord of War[50] and at the same time a lieutenant general of the "Warriors of Tigerish Dash",[51] I serve concurrently as an Imperial Attendant of the Department of Court Affairs. High mansions and pavilions touch the clouds; splendid spectacles shine brilliantly in the sun. Gentlemen wearing coronets decorated with jade cicadae[52] and clothed with taffetas and tiffanies frequent this place. I am a countryman, lying at rest in the past only under a thatched roof and in the luxuriant woods, holding converse formerly but with farmers and tillers of the soil. Taking charge of the official posts to fill up the vacancies, I stand in the ranks of the court; rising early in the morning and retiring late at night, I find no occasion for tranquil repose of heart and mind. It is like fishes in the pond or birds in cages longing for rivers and lakes, marshes and mountains. So I stain my brush and spread paper to compose a *fu* for giving expression to my thoughts at this time of the autumn, calling it thus *Autumn Feelings*, which runs like this:

四运忽其代序兮，万物纷以回薄。览花莳之时育兮，察盛衰之所托。感冬索而春敷兮，嗟夏茂而秋落。虽末士之荣悴兮，伊人情之美恶。善乎宋玉之言曰："悲哉秋之为气也，萧瑟兮草木摇落而变衰；憀慄兮若在远行，登山临水送将归。"夫送归怀慕徒之恋兮，远行有羁旅之愤。临川感流以叹逝兮，登山怀远而悼近。彼四戚之疚心兮，

51

Pan Yue

The turnings of the seasons pass speedily, taking place one by one in order;
All things shake and avoid one another in ways manifold.
I see the blooms and the sprouts growing in their time,
And observe the flourish and decline of things by them told.
Feeling the desolation of winter and the richness of spring,
I sigh at summer's luxuriance and autumn's leaves russet and gold.
From the humble scholar's favourable or depressed state,
Could be gathered the high or low spirits people in general hold.
Well it is said by Song Yu(53):
Saddening, ah, is the breath of autumn, lonely and astringent;
Shaken by it, grass and woods shed leaves and become enervate;
Grieving and cheerless it is as one leaving for a distant land,
Or one going up hills and down to the water-side to bid adieu, returning late.
For seeing off and returning, trudging and pining for the one who is gone;
Embarking on a long voyage, alone among strangers, sad and forlorn;
Standing beside a stream to muse on its flow and grieve over the fleeting of time;
And climbing up mounts to yearn for a distant one, and a near one to mourn:
These four grievous burdens weigh down heavily people's hearts,

遭一涂而难忍。嗟秋日之可哀兮,谅无愁而不尽。野有归燕,隰有翔隼。游氛朝兴,槁叶夕陨。于是乃屏轻箑,释纤絺,藉莞蒻,御袷衣。庭树槭以洒落兮,劲风戾而吹帷。蝉嘒嘒以寒吟兮,雁飘飘而南飞。天晃朗以弥高兮,日悠扬而浸微。何微阳之短晷兮,觉凉夜之方永。月曈胧以含光兮,露凄清以凝冷。熠耀粲于阶闼兮,蟋蟀鸣乎轩屏。听离鸿之晨吟兮,望流火之余景。宵耿介而不寐兮,独展

Any single one of which would be hard enough to bear;
The autumnal days of theirs are so laden with sorrows,
That no sort of sadness, say, has not become their share.
Over the wilds fly the homing swallows;
Above the lowland hovers the marsh falcon
A floating haze rises in the morning;
In the evening drop the leaves fallen.
So then, I lay aside the light fan
And put away clothes of gauzy lawn,
Sit and lie on mats of fine weave
And wear my lined gown.
Trees in my yard rustle and let fall their leaves;
Gusts of winds blow on the curtains with might;
The cicadæ sing in a subdued tone in the cool air;
Wild-geese fly in rows southward in flapping flight.
The sky shines more brightly and ever higher does as appear;
The livelong daylight gets shorter every day;
How the dwindling light shortens the daytime!
The cooler night is felt to be much longer in its way.
The moon shines in its luminescent rotundity;
The dews in clear translucence fix the cold of the night sky;
Beams immaculate spread on the steps and doorway;
Crickets sing at the paneled partition in the corridor nearby.
I listen to the morning moans of the departing wild ansers,
And look at the remaining twinkles of the vanishing Flame. (54)
I stay up all night, unlike others, all alone,

转乎华省。悟时岁之遒尽兮,慨俯首而自省。斑鬓髟以承弁兮,素发飒以垂领。仰群俊之逸轨兮,攀云汉以游骋。登春台之熙熙兮,珥金貂之炯炯。苟趣舍之殊途兮,庸讵识其躁静。闻至人之休风兮,齐天地于一指。彼知安而忘危兮,固出生而入死。行投趾于容迹兮,殆不践而获底。阙侧足以及泉兮,虽猴猿而不履。龟祀骨于宗祧兮,思反身于绿水。且敛衽以归来兮,忽投绂以高厉。

Ruminating over a host of things, so diverse, never the same.
I ponder on the ending of the year and my spent time,
Lowering my head feelingly to examine doings of mine;
Gray tufts round my ears grow long to signify ashes of the past,
Hoary hairs hang down my collar bespeaking decline.
I think of those clever and capable setting aside the rule,
Clambering up above the clouds to soar in the sky;
They succeed in rising upon the spring platform of pleasaunce,
Pitching their coronets with gold drops and marten tails of the high.
If one aims at striking a new path for himself,
How could he see the fitness of following suit or otherwise?
I have heard of the excellent way of the supreme man,
Who regards all things from heaven to earth as of the same size. (55)
Those people have come to know security, forgetting danger,
Unaware that they have left life to build their own mound(56).
Being ashamed of what they have been as they are,
They think they could be erect without standing on the ground;
For side-stepping to get to the spring of a bubbling well,
Even a monkey would not play such a poor game;
The tortoise, before he is burnt for lot-casting in a temple,
Always wishes to return to the green water wherefrom it came.
So, let me in all solemnity get back home,
Throwing off my official burden to stay aloof, carefree in mind(57),

耕东皋之沃壤兮,输黍稷之余税。泉涌湍于石涧兮,菊扬芳于崖澨。濯秋水之涓涓兮,玩游儵之潎潎。逍遥乎山川之阿,放旷乎人间之世。优哉游哉,聊以卒岁。

To till the rich loam of the eastern upland,
And pay my portion of taxes of corn and millet in kind.
The fountain gushes forth its currents among the rocks;
The chrysanthemums spread their fairness;
I wish to bathe myself in the ripples of the antumnal stream on
the hillside and in the meadows,
And watch the swift darting, in water, of the white min-
nows.[58]
Thus, I may wander freely by the sides of mountains and rivers,
Be at large to do what pleases me in this wide human world,
Taking ease to the top of my bent,
Passing the end of the year, full well content.

[晋] 王羲之

（*321—379* 或 *303—361* 或 *307—365*）

兰亭集序

永和九年，岁在癸丑，暮春之初，会于会稽山阴之兰亭，修禊事也。群贤毕至，少长咸集。此地有崇山峻岭，茂林修竹。又有清流激湍，映带左右，引以为流觞曲水，列坐其次，虽无丝竹管弦之盛，一觞一咏，亦足以畅叙幽情。

是日也，天朗气清，惠风和畅。仰观宇宙之大，俯察品类之盛。所以游目骋怀，足以极视听之娱，信可乐也。夫人之相与，俯仰一世，或取诸怀抱。晤言一室之内；

王羲之　兰亭序（冯承素摹本）

Wang Xizhi

(Jin, 321? —379? or 303—361 or 307—365)

A Sketch of the Gathering at Orchid Arbour

At the beginning of late spring in the ninth year of Yong-he when the primordial signs of the calendar combine as *Gui-chou*, we meet at Orchid Arbour in the *xian* Shanyin of Guiji *fu* for washing off ill luck. All the virtuous come to meet here, the youthful as well as the elderly. Here there are noble mountains and precipitous cliffs, dense forests and tall bamboo groves, with limpid streams and torrential rapids flashing on the right and left. To sit by the side of the tortuous currents and empty the beakers, even though without the sounding of musical instruments, a mere drinking accompanied by the composition of poetry would be enough to exchange and interfuse our heartfelt feelings for one another.

On this day, the sky is resplendent and the air serene, the beneficent breezes are graciously temperate. Looking ahead aloft, one sees the macrocosm of the universe and gazing downward, observes the multiplicity of the earthly existence, thus to extend one's eyesight, and quicken one's imagination for heightening to the top limit one's wits: what bounteous delight this is!

For what men have to do with their fellows during their lifetimes, either fetched from their bosoms and discussed with others in certain rooms or taken from their apprehension and cast abroad far beyond

或因寄所托,放浪形骸之外。虽取舍万殊,静躁不同,当其欣于所遇,暂得于己,快然自足,曾不知老之将至。及其所之既倦,情随事迁,感慨系之矣。向之所欣,俯仰之间,已为陈迹,犹不能不以之兴怀。况修短随化,终期于尽。古人云:“死生亦大矣”,岂不痛哉。

每览昔人兴感之由,若合一契,未尝不临文嗟悼,不能喻之于怀。固知一死生为虚诞,齐彭殇为妄作。后之视今,亦犹今之视昔,悲夫!故列叙时人,录其所述,虽世殊事异,所以兴怀,其致一也。后之览者,亦将有感于斯文。

their corporeal frames, although what they adopt or reject are multifariously divergent, being variously different in quietude and tumult, — so when they are glad of what they have come across, well-contented with their state of being so far, living happily in their good fortune, without knowing that old age would soon descend upon them; and when they are tired of the past, their feelings undergo a metamorphosis as the result of the changed state of affairs and sentient responses are produced thereof.

What was acclaimed in the past has become during one's looking ahead up and down things of bygone days; yet one could not help being deeply moved in feelings while touching them in reality. What is more, the length and shortness of life depend on Nature's decree; they would sooner or later reach finality. As the ancient saying (by Confucius) has it — momentous is the matter of life and death: how awfully painful it is! Whenever we examine the occasion on which notable people of the past heaved their feelings in one accord, we cannot but notice that never one of them but was full of sighs and lamentations on the subject and could not set it free from their inmost parts. Thence it could be concluded that to identify life and death is sheer nonsense and to equalize Peng Zu and a dead stripling is a sorry jest. Our succeeding generations would look on us as we do on the past, alas! Therefore, we delineate the participants of our gathering and note down their compositions at this juncture. Though the world of our succeeding generations would be different from ours and their affairs unlike ours, their sentiments about life and death would be the same as those we cherish. The future readers of this sketch would be sentient of this brief piece.

Tr. February 1, 1981.

［晋］ 陶渊明

(*365* 或 *372* 或 *376—427*)

归去来辞

归去来兮,田园将芜胡不归！既自以心为形役,奚惆怅而独悲?悟已往之不谏,知来者之可追。实迷途其未远,觉今是而昨非。舟遥遥以轻飏,风飘飘而吹衣。问征夫以前路,恨晨光之熹微。乃瞻衡宇,载欣载奔,僮仆欢迎,稚子候门。三径就荒,松菊犹存。携幼入室,有酒盈樽,引壶觞以自酌,眄庭柯以怡颜;倚南窗以寄傲,审容膝

Tao Yuanming

(Jin, 365 or 372 or 376—427)

Retracing My Way Home

— a prose poem —

Let me retrace my steps home! My fields and garden would be grown over with weeds apace; why do I not wend my way home? Since I have subjected my heart to serve my body, wherefore do I become dejected and choked with grief? Realizing my past to be lacking in counsel, I know my future is yet within the bounds of my pursuit. Having indeed lost my way but not long, I feel I am right at present and was wrong yesterday.

The barque swung gently on the waves afar, and gusts of wind afluttering my athwart clothes. Asking the travellers coming my path about the way stretching ahead, I deplored that the dawn dusk was still dimly gray. Catching sight of the cross plank door of my house, I felt glad on a sudden and fell to running... My errand boy and men greeted me cheerfully, and my children were waiting at the entrance. The by ways and paths of my garden began to look desolate, but the pines and the chrysanthemums were still there. Holding the little dear by the hand and going into the palour, I found an earthen pot full of wine. Making use of a jug and a feathered beaker to drink by myself, I gazed at the trees in the yard to lighten my face. Leaning against the southern window in airing my pride, I mused on the reposing of my legs in the nook as a token of my quietude.

之易安。园日涉以成趣,门虽设而常关。策扶老以流憩,时矫首而遐观。云无心以出岫,鸟倦飞而知还。景翳翳以将入,抚孤松而盘桓。

归去来兮,请息交以绝游。世与我而相违,复驾言兮焉求!悦亲戚之情话,乐琴书以消忧。农人告余以春及,将有事于西畴。或命巾车,或棹孤舟;既窈窕以寻壑,亦崎岖而经丘。木欣欣以向荣,泉涓涓而始流;善万物之得时,感吾生之行休。

已矣乎,寓形宇内复几时,曷不委心任去留。胡为遑

Roving daily in the garden becomes my favourite practice; the hedge-door, though it stands there, is usually closed. With a cane to rely upon for supporting my years and helping me to pace on or to pause, I often lift my head to command a fair view of the distance. The clouds with a vacant heart float forth from the cliffs; the birds tiring of flight know when to return to their nests. The landscape looks blurred as I am to retire under the roof, resting my hand on a solitary pine to linger for a while. Thus I have retraced my way home, and am going to end my intercourse with the world. Since it runs counter to my bents, for what should I venture forth to it with words conveyed in vain? Pleased with the feeling words of my kin and friends, I also find good cheer in the table heptachord and tomes of books for dispelling my gloom.

Farmers told me spring has come here and they would be busy at the western suburb. I take to a draped cart or row a solitary boat to look for caves and caverns that seem so quaint and unearthly, and climb across heights steep and ramble over hillocks rather low. The trees shoot out joyously in new glory; the springs bubble merrily and begin to overflow. Being glad that all living things are in the heyday of their youth, I am passing my life in contented rest.

Let it come then as it would! Remaining in this world for I know not how long, why do I not set my mind at ease in thinking of whether to leave or to remain? Why should I be in a hurry to get to I know not

遑欲何之？富贵非吾愿，帝乡不可期。怀良辰以孤往，或植杖而耘耔。登东皋以舒啸，临清流而赋诗。聊乘化以归尽，乐夫天命复奚疑！

whither? To be wealthy and to be high in rank are not what I wish; to be in the celestial city is not what I expect. I may wish to go somewhere on a fair day alone, or to weed and manure the soil, sticking my cane nearby in the clay. Or I may wish to rise on the eastern bank to halloo in easing my heart, or to compose poetry by the side of a limpid stream. In such wise, I may merge into Nature and come to my end, delighting in the decree of Heaven and doubting nought.

Tr. 15 April, 1974.

陶渊明

桃花源记

晋太元中,武陵人捕鱼为业,缘溪行,忘路之远近。忽逢桃花林,夹岸数百步,中无杂树,芳草鲜美,落英缤纷。渔人甚异之。复前行,欲穷其林。林尽水源,便得一山。山有小口,仿佛若有光,便舍船从口入。初极狭,才通人。复行数十步。豁然开朗,土地平旷,屋舍俨然。有良田美池桑竹之属。阡陌交通,鸡犬相闻。其中往来种作,男女衣着,悉如外人。黄发垂髫,并怡然自乐。见渔人,乃大惊。问所从来,具答之。便要还家,以设酒杀鸡作食。

Tao Yuanming

The Peach Blossom Visionary Land

During the Tai-yuan years of the dynasty Jin, a fisherman from the county of Wuling strolled on the bank of a stream, forgetting the distance of his track, into a grove of blossoming peach trees all at once. For several hundred steps along the bank side, there were no other trees; the sward was freshly green and fallen petals of the peach blooms were scattered on the grass verdure. The fisherman, surprised by the sight, walked on to see where the grove would end. It ended at the source of the stream, where there was a mountain. An aperture opened on the mount, from which light seemed to be emitted.

The man abandoned his boat and entered the opening. It was narrow at first, just enough to pass through. After several tens of steps, the way led to vast spaciousness. The land was level and expanded, houses were spread out in good order; goodly farms, fair ponds and mulberry and bamboo thickets were to be seen everywhere. The ways and cross roads were stretched out far and wide. Cocks' crew and dogs' barking were heard here and there. The men and women coming and going in their tilling and handicraft work were dressed all like people outside. The aged with hair of light beige and children with cut hair fringing their foreheads all looked gay and contented. Seeing the fisherman, people were greatly surprised, asking him whence he came from and being replied to. They then invited him to their homes, offering wine

村中闻有此人，咸来问讯。自云先世避秦时乱，率妻子邑人，来此绝境，不复出焉，遂与外人间隔。问今是何世，乃不知有汉，无论魏晋。此人一一为具言，所闻皆叹惋。余人各复延至其家，皆出酒食。停数日，辞去。此中人语云：“不足为外人道也。”

既出，得其船，便扶向路，处处志之。及郡下，诣太守说如此。太守即遣人随其往，寻向所志，遂迷不复得路。

南阳刘子骥，高尚士也。闻之，欣然亲往，未果，寻病终。后遂无问津者。

and killing chickens for entertainment. When it was generally known in the village that there was this man, more people came to see and ask questions of him. They all said that their forefathers, fleeing from turmoils during the Qin Dynasty, led their families and villagers hither to this isolated district to stay, and so being separated from the outside world. They asked what time it was then, knowing not there was any dynasty Han, to say nothing of those of Wei and Jin. The man answered them all in details, whereon they heaved sighs and exclamations. All the others also invited him severally to their homes for hospitality. After many a day, he made his departure. They told him not to publicize his sojourn there.

When out, he sought out his boat and noted closely the way leading to the aperture of the mount. After his return to the chief town of the county, he went to the alderman and made a report of his out-landish excursion. The county official dispatched a man to follow him whereto he would lead. But he could not find the spots he had noted on his way back and so lost the whereabouts of the grove of blossoming peach trees. Liu Ziji of Nanyang, a scholar of high repute, hearing of the story sought to find out the place. He fell sick and died, before his attempted trial. Thereafter, no one ever ventured the visionary deed.

Tr. August 14, 1980.

陶渊明

五柳先生传

先生不知何许人也，亦不详其姓字。宅边有五柳树，因以为号焉。闲静少言，不慕荣利。好读书，不求甚解；每有会意，便欣然忘食。性嗜酒，家贫不能常得；亲旧知其如此，或置酒而招之。造饮辄尽，期在必醉。既醉而退，曾不吝去留。环堵萧然，不蔽风日；短褐穿结，箪瓢屡空：晏如也。常著文自娱，颇示己志。忘怀得失，以此自终，

Tao Yuan-ming

The Life of the Sire of Five Willows*

No one knows whence the Sire hails, nor are people told of his name. As there are five willows beside his abode, he has called himself by such a title. Living quietly in solitude and spare of speech, he covets not rank nor wealth. He takes delight in books, but is not enmeshed in mere words; whenever illumined in his reading, he jovially forgets his meals. Fond of wine, he is too poor to resort to it often; knowing this, his kin and friends would invite him to bumpers. Deeply would he quench his thirst then, intent upon being drunk. When intoxicated, he retires or stays on in good humour. Bare walls enclose his quarters, defending him not from blustering winds and hot sunshine; his short coats of coarse fabric are patched and knotted, his reed cereal case and gourd shell for liquid food are often empty: but he takes such at his ease. Many a time he writes articles to please himself and show his bent. Regardless of worldly gain or loss, he whiles away his time till the end.

---

* This is a spiritual self-portrait of the poet Tao Yuanming.

赞曰:黔娄有言:“不戚戚于贫贱,不汲汲于富贵。”味其言,兹若人之俦乎?衔觞赋诗,以乐其志。无怀氏之民欤?葛天氏之民欤?

The epiphonema runs thus:

It was said by the celebrated recluse Qian Lou: "Be not depressed by poverty and humbleness and be not obsessed by wealth and power." Doesn't this dictum suit well those of his kind? He quaffs at his beaker and chants his poems to find happiness in his sublimating will. Isn't he a free, blissful subject of our legendary kings at the dawn of the world, the One of Care-free Rule and the One of Heavenly Grace?

Tr. August, 1980.

陶渊明

饮酒

结庐在人境，
而无车马喧。
问君何能尔？
心远地自偏。
采菊东篱下，
悠然见南山。
山气日夕佳，
飞鸟日与还。
此中有真意，
欲辨已忘言。

Tao Yuanming

Drinking

I set up my cottage in the world of men,
Away from the hubbub of horses and carriages.
Being asked how it could be thus, I reply,
"My heart stays apart, so secluded must be the spot."
In plucking chrysanthemums beneath the east hedge,
I vacantly see the southern mountains afar;
The mountain aura hovereth fair morn and eve,
The birds fly from and back to their nests early and late.
There is the pith of truth in all this sight;
When I am about to say how, I forget my words.

Tr. August 26, 1981.

[唐] 孙过庭

(*648—703*)

书谱[*][①]

夫自古之善书者,汉、魏有钟、张之绝,晋末称二王之妙。

王羲之云:“顷寻诸名书,钟、张信为绝伦,其余不足观。”可谓钟、张云没,而羲、献继之。又云:“吾书比之钟、张,钟当抗行,或谓过之。张草犹当雁行,然张精熟,池水尽墨,假令寡人耽之若此,未必谢之。”此乃推张迈钟之意也。

考其专擅,虽未果于前规;摭以兼通,故无惭于即事。

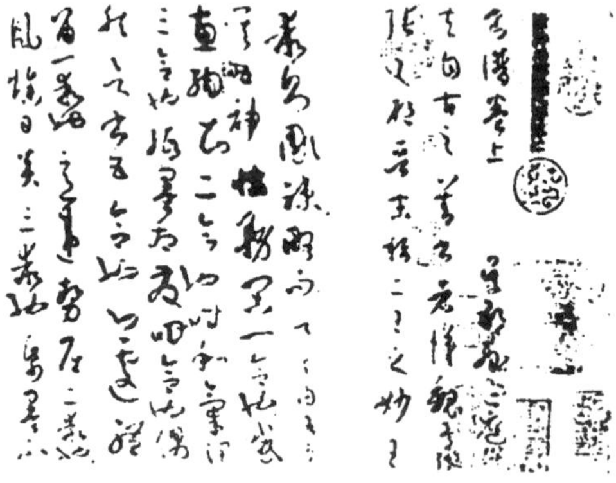

孙过庭书谱

---

* 墨迹本,纸本,草书,高27.2厘米,长892.24厘米,三百五十一行,凡三千五百余言。现藏台北故宫博物院。——编者

Sun Guoting

(*Tang*, *648—703*)

On the Fine Art of Chinese Calligraphy*

Since olden times, for names great in *shu-fa*, the Dynasties Han and Wei have given us Zhong and Zhang, and the later years of Jin, the two Wangs, father and son. "Delving into the past masters," declared Wang Xizhi, "I find Zhong and Zhang matchless indeed, but as to all the rest, I can see nothing of great value in them." Thus, after those two had passed on, Xizhi and Xianzhi continued in the tradition. To quote the elder Wang again: "My *shu* makes a fair rival to the works of Zhong and Zhang, or, as some would say, even surpasses theirs. The *cao shu* of Boying I consider, indeed, as an even match to that of mine, but that is because he had thoroughly given himself to it, so that, it was told, the pond whereby he practised his art became wholly darkened, by constant use, with his ink: had I cherished that style as dearly as he did, I don't see why I should not take the lead of him in it too" — meaning this, as is obvious, to be a compliment to Zhang as contrasted to his light dismissal of Zhong. For truly, in their own particular fields Xizhi might not be the equal of these earlier masters, yet in range and variety he bows to no one either in the past or in

---

* The introduction to a lost essay of six chapters, in two parts, on *Shu-fa*(书法), the fine art of Chinese calligraphy, the original title being *Shu-bu*(书谱).

评者云:“彼之四贤,古今特绝;而今不逮古,古质而今妍。”

夫质以代兴,妍因俗易。虽书契之作,适以记言;而淳醨一迁,质文三变,驰骛沿革,物理常然。贵能古不乖时,今不同弊,所谓“文质彬彬,然后君子”。何必易雕宫于穴处,反玉辂于椎轮者乎!

又云:“子敬之不及逸少,犹逸少之不及钟、张。”意者以为评得其纲纪,而未详其始卒也。

且元常专工于隶书,伯英尤精于草体;彼之二美,而

recent times.

There are critics who say that those four masters have encountered as yet no peer throughout the ages; but that among themselves, the earlier ones, moving in their lonely simplicity, are superior to the later two, who are after, and are thus hampered by variety and elegance. That is hardly true. For simplicity arises only with the dawn of an epoch, and variety evolves after an age of practice: both are born naturally of Time, but neither can be regarded as an artistic criterion. Indeed, characters were devised in the beginning simply to record men's speech, and not for proving or illustrating a theory. Yet under-neath the flux of all things, the law of change rules supreme, causing all and every one of them to pass through a number of stages — commencing with a simple nativity and ending in a profuse death — until in each case a full cycle is completed; why then, should *shu-fa* not obey this universal law? Rarely, if ever, do we succeed in being as artless as the ancients without losing the spirit of the age, or as modern as can be and yet be free from the faults of the time. This is aptly put by the saying that the ideal of perfection consists in the successful fusing of the rich and the simple into a confluent harmony. For we need not, in our effort to be plain, give up palaces of choice carving in favour of dingy dens of mud, or go back from wheels of fine jade to heavy wooden ones.

Again, there are critics who say that Xianzhi falls behind Xizhi just as the latter trails after Zhong and Zhang. Such comments are not without some truth, but they do not tell the whole story. True it is Zhong has approached well-nigh the impossible with his *li shu* and Zhang with his *cao*; but then, Xizhi steers his way through in both

逸少兼之:拟草则余真,比真则长草,虽专工小劣,而博涉多优。总其终始,匪无乖互。

谢安素善尺椟,而轻子敬之书。子敬尝作佳书与之,谓必存录,安辄题后答之。甚以为恨。

安尝问敬:“卿书何如右军?”答云:“故当胜。”安云:“物论殊不尔。”子敬又答:“时人那得知!”敬虽权以此辞,折安所鉴,自称胜父,不亦过乎!

且立身扬名,事资尊显。“胜母”之里,曾参不入。以子敬之豪翰[*],绍右军之笔札,虽复粗传楷则,实恐未克箕

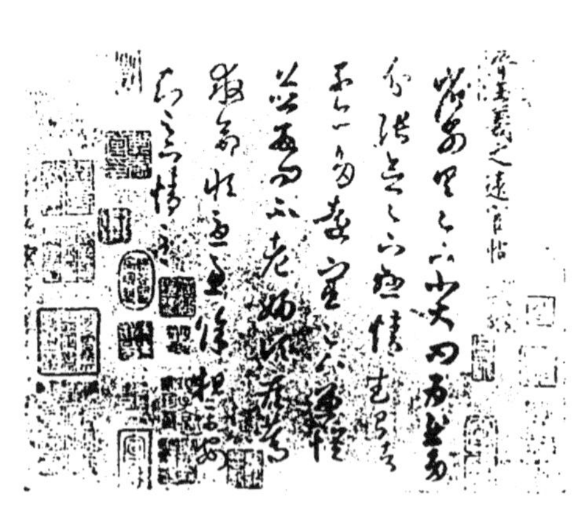

王羲之远宧帖

王羲之鸭头丸帖

* 豪翰:豪古通毫,豪翰就是毛笔。

styles with equal ease. So, compared to either Zhong or Zhang with their mastery in a single style, the elder Wang wins always by one more stake. And even though he does not claim to be a specialist (perhaps not by blind accident, but out of careful choice), one must, taking the whole affair into account, admit that his versatile genius is worth much more than the narrow gifts of either one of the others.

Xie An, also a master of this art, was known to hold little respect for Xianzhi's work. Many a time letters were sent to him by Xianzhi when the writer had them well done, in the hope that Xie would keep them for their excellence. To the utter disappointment of Xianzhi, they were invariably sent back with scribbled replies upon them. Xie An once asked him, "How does your *shu* compare with your father's?" "Better," was the answer. Xie An said, "People think rather differently." The other again replied, "They know nothing of what they are talking about." Cleverly did Xianzhi snub Xie into silence, but his pretension to knowing more of this art than even his distinguished father no doubt passes all reasonable bounds.

The shortest way for a man to set himself on his feet and spread a fair name, so goes the saying, lies in properly revering the sovereign and raising his own parents into prominence. Possibly the pages of Xianzhi do betray here and there gleams of his father's revealing beauty in some diminished degree, but one can scarcely believe that his brush-work has ever approached the sustained level of Xizhi's. Moreover, he loved to affiliate himself with the blessed spirits of the upper world. This and his reluctance to respect his father not only raise him to nowhere in people's esteem, but on the contrary, only remind one of

裘。况乃假托神仙,耻崇家范,以斯成学,孰愈面墙!

后羲之往都,临行题壁。子敬密拭除之,辄书易其处,私谓不恶。羲之还见,乃叹曰:“吾去时真大醉也。”敬乃内惭。

是知逸少之比钟、张,则专博斯别;子敬之不及逸少,无或疑焉。

余志学之年,留心翰墨,味钟、张之余烈,挹羲、献之前规,极虑专精,时逾二纪,有乖入木之术,无间临池之志。

观夫悬针垂露之异,奔雷坠石之奇,鸿飞兽骇之资,鸾舞蛇惊之态,绝岸颓峰之势,临危据槁之形;或重若崩

the old saying that the proper cure for a noisy braggadocio is a few years of silent learning. To illustrate my point convincingly, let me relate an incident that happened between the father and his son. Once, before leaving the capital, Xizhi brushed something on the wall in memory of his trip. His son scraped off the characters in secret and put down his own instead, thinking them no worse than the original. On his return, Xizhi exclaimed: "How sorely intoxicated must I have been before I left here." Xianzhi then felt ashamed in his heart. This clearly proves my notion that while Xizhi is distinguished from Zhong and Zhang in his range and variety, the difference between the father and the son is one altogether between wealth and poverty.

When I was fifteen, I began to take great pleasure in this art, drinking in the divine fragrance of Zhong and Zhang and observing the beautiful law in the wake of Xi and Xian. I breathed and lived in this wondrous art for more than two decades, ever with hopes of improving my hand by ceaseless practice, albeit not to the extent of excelling that master of masters, Wang Xizhi. Of the wonders of *shu-fa*, I have seen many and many a one. Here, a drop of crystal dew hangs its ear on the tip of a needle; there, the rumbling of thunder hails down a shower of stones. I have seen flocks of queen-swans floating on their stately wings, or a frantic stampede rushing off at terrific speed. Sometimes in the lines a flaming phoenix dances a lordly dance, or a sinuous serpent wriggles with speckled fright. And I have seen sunken peaks plunging headlong down the precipices, or a person clinging to a dry vine while the whole silent valley yawns below. Some strokes seem as heavy as the falling banks of clouds, others as light as the wings of a cicada. A

云,或轻如蝉翼;导之则泉注,顿之则山安;纤纤乎似初月之出天崖,落落乎犹众星之列河汉;同自然之妙有,非力运之能成;信可谓智巧兼优,心手双畅:翰不虚动,下必有由。一画之间,变起伏于峰杪,一点之内,殊衄挫于豪*芒。

况云积其点画,乃成其字。曾不傍窥尺牍,俯习寸阴;引班超以为辞,援项籍而自满;任笔为体,聚墨成形;心昏拟效之方,手迷挥运之理:求其妍妙,不亦谬哉!

然君子立身,务修其本。扬雄谓诗赋小道,壮夫不

---

* 豪:古通毫。

little conducting and a fountain bubbles forth, a little halting and a mountain settles down in peace. Tenderly, a new moon beams on the horizon; or, as the style becomes solemn, a river of stars, luminous and large, descends down the solitary expanse of night. All these seem as wonderful as Nature herself and almost beyond the power of man, though they all the more glorify the union between ingenuity and artistry, and reflect the delight of the artist when his hand moves at his heart's desire. The brush never touches the paper but with a purpose — the miens and tones of the strokes and the dots all lying in wait, as it were, at the command of the tip of the brush.

To the ardent student it has become ever more acutely a source of anxiety, that this subtle art should be so badly neglected these later days. Many are those I have come across, declaring themselves Ban Cao reborn — Ban Cao who, early in youth, having flung away his brush to follow the army, rounded an eventful life by establishing himself among the few immortal generals of this land — and others quoting as their eloquent example Xiang Ji, who, as a wild youngster, started his career by selling his books to buy himself a sword, and ended as an ever-victorious hero and warrior trailing fire through history. They neither take pains to study the works of old masters, nor bother themselves with industrious practice. Knowing no rules of their own making, nor fine examples to model upon, they let the brush go wild to form its own random styles, and trust the ink with daubing shapes at its own free will. It seems quite absurd to expect good works from students like these.

Ideal manhood is realized, it is said, primarily through perfection of one's self. Yang Xiong declared that poetry is a trivial thing, not a

为;况复溺思豪厘,沦精翰墨者也。

夫潜神对奕,犹标坐隐之名;乐志垂纶,尚体行藏之趣。

讵若功宣礼乐,妙拟神仙,犹埏埴之罔穷,与工炉而并运。好异尚奇之士,翫体势之多方;穷微测妙之夫,得推移之奥赜。著述者假其糟粕,藻鉴者挹其菁华,固义理之会归,信贤达之兼善者矣。存精寓赏,岂徒然与!

而东晋士人,互相陶染。至于王、谢之族,郗、庾之伦,纵不尽其神奇,咸亦挹其风味。去之滋永,斯道愈微。

石鼓文(篆书)

张迁碑(隶书)

fit object for manly occupation. If such be the estate of poetry, what lot would fall on *shu-fa* and its dear students, those who weave their cares around the brush and think of nothing, all day long, but this apparently slight affair of ink and paper? Nevertheless, there is little cause for anxiety. For even to sit in leisurely attention playing chess is considered a virtue of the hermit. And in casting baits amidst the silence of the water and the woods, one may feel with sweet content the purity of one's own soul, now that one has chosen to sail over and above the tumultuous ways of the world because the world is unworthy of one. Besides these occupations, there are those of rectifying ceremonies and of composing music. And some even live in complete detachment from this busy world, or rather on the plane of the immortals and the blessed of heaven, doing nothing at all for a living. For the occupations serve only as media: it is for the individuals to make them emit shadows or shine with individual glory — just as potters mould clay in sundry ways and smiths tame metals differently. So *shu-fa* itself is not in the least the cause for blame. What is more, fortunately, the world does not lack men engaged in this pursuit: so that lovers of the quaint and the novel can enjoy a multitude of forms and designs and philosophers and critics have something to occupy their analytical minds with, writers may use it as a tool for self-expression and connoisseurs dip their cup into it for nectar. It is then to be studied by the virtuous and the wise alike. How can an appreciation of it be regarded as vain?

As a cult, in fact, it won the hearts of all the cultured people of Eastern Jin. In the families of Wang and Xie and among the circles of Xi and Yu, the splendours of this art might not have reached the highest pitch, but the atmosphere then was certainly permeated with it. As

方复闻疑称疑，得末行末；古今阻绝，无所质问；设有所会，缄秘已深；遂令学者茫然，莫知领要，徒见成功之美，不悟所致之由。

或乃就分布于累年，向规矩而犹远，图真不悟，习草将迷。假令薄解草书，粗传隶法，则好溺偏固，自阙通规。讵知心手会归，若同源而异派；转用之术，犹共树而分条者乎？加以趋变适时，行书为要；题勒方富，真乃居先。草不兼真，殆于专谨；真不通草，殊非翰札。真以点画为形质，使转为情性；草以点画为情性，使转为形质。草乖使转，不能成字；真亏点画，犹可记文。回互虽殊，大体相涉。

（传）钟繇宣示表（真书）

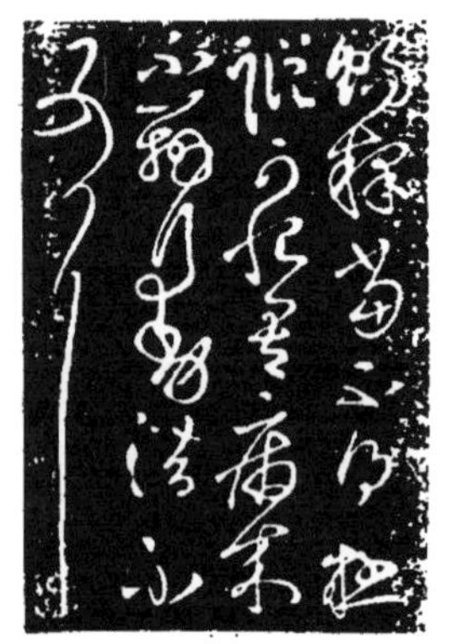

（传）张芝草书

（选自淳化阁帖）

time goes by, its practice vanishes too. And since questions cannot be asked across time and discoveries have been jealously kept secret, doubts remain as doubts and defects, once they have come, stay on. Thus, the beginner is bewildered as to what he should learn, seeing only the beauty of success but not the way beauty has come to pass. People spend years to get acquainted with the different styles, only to run farther and farther away from where they aim. They either fail on the threshold of *zhen shu*, or become mazed in the labyrinths of *cao*. In case they happen to know a little of either *cao* or *li*, ofttimes they develop a narrow interest in one of them instead of advancing at an even speed on both wheels. They do not understand that in artistic matters one's wish and ability should flow from one and the same source: the co-operation of the two depending upon the masterly synthesis of a fertile experience.

Truly, the sundry styles perform different functions in spite of their close relations: thus *xing shu*, due to its pliancy, serves best for daily use, while *zhen* is preferred for monumental purposes, to be hung up on high or carved on stones. But on the other hand, the various styles are too closely related in structure to allow isolated treatments: thus *cao* exclusive of *zhen* lacks caution and sobriety, *zhen* devoid of *cao* becomes too stiff for personal use; *zhen* uses dots and strokes as substance, drives and twists as expressions, *cao* employs dots and strokes as expressions and drives and twists as substance. *Cao* failing at drives and twists looks no more like characters, while *zhen* missing a stroke or two still conveys the sense. So, however dissimilar the styles may appear in details, the motive power that pulsates in all styles and lends them an enchantment does not have to pass through any hard

故亦傍通二篆，俯贯八分，包括篇章，涵泳飞白。若豪厘不察，则胡越殊风者焉。

至如钟繇隶奇，张芝草圣，此乃专精一体，以至绝伦。伯英不真，而点画狼藉；元常不草，使转纵横。自兹已降，不能兼善者，有所不逮，非专精也。

虽篆、隶、草、章，工用多变；济成厥美，各有攸宜：篆尚婉而通，隶欲精而密，草贵流而畅，章务检而便。

然后凛之以风神，温之以妍润，鼓之以枯劲，和之以闲雅。故可达其情性，形其哀乐。验燥湿之殊节，千古依然；体老壮之异时，百龄俄顷。嗟乎，不及其门，讵窥其奥者也！

王羲之行书

（选自集王字圣教序）

cleavage or insuperable wall. A master must, to be brief, subdue the two *zhuans*, bring *ba fen* and *zhang cao* into manageable terms, and reduce the gigantic *fei bai* into complete subservience. In all these, a trifling oversight often brings about a divergence greater than that of the clashing customs of two peoples.

It is true, as we have seen, that Zhong and Zhang have scaled un-approachable heights each in his one and only way — the former in *li shu* and the latter in *cao*. In any realm other than their own, they are equally helpless: the *zhen shu* of Boying is confused with unruly dots and strokes, and the *cao shu* of Yuanchang stagnates with clumsy drives and twists. But after these two, one must be able to handle several styles to excel in any one field, without being, of course, the crest and crown in them all. Just as the four major styles meet different needs, so do they point to different standards of perfection. At the best, then, *zhuan shu* looks complaisant and mild, *li* comes in tight-fitted units, *cao* flows and goes on forever, *zhen* is succinct and neat. Having fulfilled these conditions, one proceeds to make one's work breathe and smile, so to speak, sweeten it with softness and moisture, strengthen it with astute dry vigour, and finally tranquillize the whole matter into peace as if no effort, no art at all, has been applied. Not till then are one's sentiments fully expressed and one's joys and sorrows fixed, on the paper. And thus, the intrinsic values are preserved for a thousand years, and the secret of beauty, once secured on the paper, blooms on forever. Alas! if one does not probe deep into the heart, all these would seem no better than dreams that have never occurred to the dreamer.

又一时而书,有乖有合,合则流媚,乖则雕疏。略言其由,各有其五:神怡务闲,一合也;感惠徇知,二合也;时和气润,三合也;纸墨相发,四合也;偶然欲书,五合也。心遽体留,一乖也;意违势屈,二乖也;风燥日炎,三乖也;纸墨不称,四乖也;情怠手阑,五乖也。乖合之际,优劣互差。得时不如得器,得器不如得志。若五乖同萃,思遏手蒙;五合交臻,神融笔畅。畅无不知,蒙无所从。当仁者得意忘言,罕陈其要;企学者希风叙妙,虽述犹疏。徒立其工,未敷厥旨,不揆庸昧,辄效所明,庶欲弘既往之风规,导将来之器识,除繁去滥,睹迹明心者焉。

And then occasion, too, comes into play. Sometimes one pursues one's work without any great difficulty, at other times with overwhelming troubles. In the former case, one's work moves on gracefully; in the latter, it remains broken and bare. To be brief, five causes account for either state. They are these and the reverse: calm and leisureliness of the moment, thankful or gracious state of the artist's mind, temperateness and serenity of the weather, agreeableness between ink and paper, and an inspired wish for brushing. Among the favours and disfavours enumerated, some are more preferable and others less desired. Proper moments are not as helpful as fine tools, which again are less courted than the right moods or states of mind. If the five disfavours converge together, thoughts coagulate and the hand wavers; if the five favours flow in concert, imagination melts and streams down through one's fingers. In the former instance, the brush is at a loss where to follow; in the latter, wherever it goes, it goes with ease. Unfortunately, those having the qualification forget to narrate their adventures out of delight; others just embarking on the journey relate copiously what is not worth the telling. And so the real methods of this art remain a secret.

The present writer has already described in brief the conditions and consequences, but has as yet hardly touched upon the procedure, of this art. Without shying at my own incompetence, I venture to set forth what little I have learned through years of study: so that the river of Tradition may roll on with full force to gladden the resounding shores of Futurity.

代有《笔阵图》七行，中画执笔三手，图貌乖舛，点画湮讹。顷见南北流传，疑是右军所制。虽则未详真伪，尚可发启童蒙。既常俗所存，不藉编录。

至于诸家势评，多涉浮华，莫不外状其形，内迷其理，今之所撰，亦无取焉。

若乃师宜官之高名，徒彰史牒；邯郸淳之令范，空著缣缃。暨乎崔、杜以来，萧、羊已往，代祀绵远，名氏滋繁。或藉甚不渝，人亡业显：或凭附增价，身谢道衰。加以糜蠹不传，搜秘将尽，偶逢缄赏，时亦罕窥，优劣纷纭，殆难覼缕。其有显闻当代，遗迹见存，无俟抑扬，自标先后。

In the course of writing this, I have unsparingly discarded materials that seem to me of doubtful value. There is current a picture giving three poses of holding the brush with seven lines of explanatory text. The figures are all out of shape and the characters ill written. Yet it is supposed all over the country to be based on a work of Wang Xizhi. While its authenticity is still to be proved, it is good enough for opening up the minds of youngsters. But as it has already become the property of the public, I am not going to make use of it once more in my treatise. As to the comments by various critics, I can see them all merely pecking at the surface. The appearance is discussed in full while the cause is left in haziness. These, too, I have skipped over. Neither have I been benefited by Shi Yiguan whose loud fame echoes only in history, or by Handan Chun whose splendid works have long vanished together with their bodies of brocade. From Cui and Du to Xiao and Yang, the intervening years have indeed produced a prodigious number of notables. Some of them won fame after they had ceased to be, or else became popular simply because of their death. Their works have suffered either the ravage of moths or the covetousness of collectors. Those that have survived the two and happened to have come to my notice may not be accessible to the public. Since their qualities vary extensively and thus defy enumeration, and enumeration, even if possible, would not serve our purpose in any case, I have altogether refrained from naming them in the present work. Concerning the others who enjoyed reputation during their lifetimes, I deem it unnecessary to laud or criticize them any more; for all these years of appraisal have long fitted them into the niches where they properly belong, and further comments are bound to be idle or futile. And then, there are the ‘six

且六爻之作，肇自轩辕；八体之兴，始于嬴政。其来尚矣，厥用斯弘。但今古不同，妍质悬隔，既非所习，又亦略诸。

复有龙蛇云露之流，龟鹤花英之类，乍图真于率尔，或写瑞于当年，巧涉丹青，工亏翰墨，异夫楷式，非所详焉。

代传羲之《与子敬笔势论》十章，文鄙理疏，意乖言拙，详其旨趣，殊非右军。且右军位重才高，调清词雅，声尘未泯，翰椟仍存。观夫致一书、陈一事，造次之际，稽古斯在；岂有贻谋令嗣，道叶义方，章则顿亏，一至于此！又云与张伯英同学，斯乃更彰虚诞。若指汉末伯英，时代全不相接；必有晋人同号，史传何其寂寥！非训非经，宜从弃掷。

yao' traceable to Emperor Xuan Yuan and the ' eight *di*' begun during Shi Huang-*di*, the Great. These, springing from illustrious origins, were indeed widely in use in olden times. But their forms are too simple and antiquated for us. As I am, besides, unlearned in them, they are left out too. In regard to hieroglyphics, our Muse before her coming of age, I have seen symbols such as a dragon in flight, clouds in flux, or a snowy crane dimpling the water on one foot, flowers freeing their fragrance in the breeze. The figures may be the footprints of a few flimsy moments, or images left by some gorgeous episodes of history. No matter which, they are drawings of some sort and belong, therefore, rather to the art of painting than to that of *shu-fa*. Last of all, I have also ignored a tract of ten chapters on brush-work said to be written by Wang Xizhi expressly for his son Xianzhi. Of this work, the style is so cracked, the logic so crabbed and the conception as a whole so crooked that no one with any semblance of judgment would believe in its authorship. Xizhi has long been reputed for his high position and superb talent, his clear cadence and elevated diction. Not only is his fame still fresh in the air, but his writings, both formal and personal, too, are well preserved. Even a short note or a letter of his written in haste sheds a cool light of quietude. How can a lesson to his offspring, a lesson he must have believed for the highest good of his son, be embodied in such broken language? The tract refers to Zhang Boying as the writer's fellow pupil, thus supplying an excellent piece of internal evidence as to its falsity. If the Boying of late Han were meant to be the person, the times of Wang and of him are hundreds of years apart. If he were a Jin contemporary of Xizhi, why are histories and chronicles silent about him? In short, the tract teaches nothing and commands

夫心之所达,不易尽于名言;言之所通,尚难形于纸墨。粗可仿佛其状,纲纪其辞。冀酌希夷,取会佳境。阙而未逮,请俟将来。

今撰执、使、转、用之由,以祛未悟:执,谓深浅长短之类是也;使,谓纵横牵掣之类是也;转,谓钩镮盘纡之类是也;用,谓点画向背之类是也。方复会其数法,归于一途;编列众工,错综群妙;举前人之未及,启后学于成规;窥其根源,析其枝派。贵使文约理赡,迹显心通;披卷可明,下笔无滞。诡辞异说,非所详焉。

然今之所陈,务裨学者。但右军之书,代多称习,良可据为宗匠,取立指归。岂唯会古通今,亦乃情深调合,

naught and so should be thrown away.

Now in this my own work, I do not pretend to attempt the impossible. For what one's thoughts have dimly in store is not easily made clear by eloquent words, and what the latter can only barely convey is still harder for the dull brush to put down. In other words, I do not profess to set forth the ideal state we are striving after, a state which seems to me to lie, like the highest flight of music, on the fringe of sight and hearing, slowly deepening into an outlandish dream. If any such thing as fixing a goal for *shu-fa* is to be attempted, it will be in the future. To do justice to my theme, I want merely to study the various methods by which a character is duly attacked. These go under four headings: the proportional length and width of the character, the drives and restraints of the straight lines, the curves and hooks of the twisted lines, and the balance binding all the dots and strokes into a unit. After expounding these in full, I shall conduct the sundry approaches into one channel and pool the various methods together, and tell what has been left untold by past masters and guide the new-comers to the vantage grounds of old. The sources are to be traced and the tributaries waded through. And the language is to be simple and the meaning clear, so that the reader understands it offhand and will there-after be hindered by no doubt while employing his hand. As to strange tales and eccentric ways, I see no need to dabble with them here.

The works of Wang Xizhi have for generations been the model for students, and I think they well deserve the honour. In addition to a thorough grasp of the past as well as the contemporary practice of the art, they betray a uniqueness of sentiments and style. The rubbings of

致使摹拓日广，研习岁滋；先后著名，多从散落；历代孤绍，非其效与？

试言其由，略陈数意：止如《乐毅论》、《黄庭经》、《东方朔画赞》、《太师箴》、《兰亭集序》、《告誓文》，斯并代俗所传、真行绝致者也。

写《乐毅》则情多怫郁，书《画赞》则意涉瓌奇；《黄庭经》则怡怿虚无；《太师箴》又纵横争折；暨乎兰亭兴集，思逸神超；私门诫誓，情拘志惨。所谓涉乐方笑，言哀已叹。岂惟驻想流波，将贻啴嗳之奏；驰神睢涣，方思藻绘之文。虽其目击道存，尚或心迷议舛。莫不强名为体，共习分区。岂知情动形言，取会风骚之意；阳舒阴惨，本乎天地

王羲之乐毅论

王羲之黄庭经

them from marble inscriptions have long been distributed all over the country, yet the interest students take in copying them is still increasing steadily. The eminent works of those before or after him are laid aside and forgotten and lost: a few solitary exceptions that have escaped oblivion are of course no match for him. The reason for this is obvious enough. Works of the master such as these: *An Essay on Le Yi*, *Huang Ting Jing*, *Eulogizing a Portrait Painting of Dongfang Shuo*, *An Address Exhorting the Imperial Tutor*, *A Sketch of the Gathering at Orchid Arbour*, *A Pledge of Faith* — one and all, they test *zhen shu* and *xing shu* to the utmost; yet at the same time, each unfolds a style of its own to heighten the literary mood. Thus, the *Essay* wears a darkling despondency and the *Jing* a veil of blissful solitude; the *Eulogium* has a wandering, will-o'-the-wisp air, while the *Address* blazes out a white path through a jungle of arguments. When it comes to the *Sketch* in memory of that celebrated gathering, radiant thoughts simply come floating by and fleeting away, wings after wings, into a world of divine ideality. As the subject turns on family faith and blood bondage, tears gleam and pathos flows deep and mute. All these indicate clearly a power to laugh on the brink of joy and to sigh ere a word of grief is whispered. For one should be thinking of lapping waves even before his fingers caress a soft melody, and one who has no feeling for winding waterways rarely patterns his brushings with curving grace.

There are plenty of those who, frozen in sentiments and benumbed in sensibility, would be puzzled in the very face of immaculate beauty. Yet in one way or another, without failure they put on some artificial manner which I hesitate to call style. Poetry is nothing, one may safely say, but genuine feeling clothed in words, and the mutability of the

之心。既失其情，理乖其实，原夫所致，安有体哉！

夫运用之方，虽由己出，规模所设，信属目前。差之一毫，失之千里。苟知其术，适可兼通。心不厌精，手不忘熟。若运用尽于精熟，规矩暗于胸襟，自然容与徘徊，意先笔后，潇洒流落，翰逸神飞。亦犹弘羊之心，豫乎无际；庖丁之目，不见全牛。尝有好事，就吾求习，吾乃粗举纲要，随而授之，无不心悟手从，言忘意得；纵未穷于众术，断可极于所诣矣。

若思通楷则，少不如老；学成规矩，老不如少。思则老而逾妙，学乃少而可勉。勉之不已，抑有三时；时然一

year proceeds only from the heart of Nature. Likewise, this principle holds, I think, true in *shu-fa*; for without feeling as the source, where-from issues the style? However, though the application of the various rules rests entirely with the individual, they are not to be flouted or dispensed with altogether; the negligence of a hair's breadth in their use often brings about miles of mistakes; only when they are thoroughly under control can the hand enjoy perfect freedom. Nor is this all. For there is still that passion for perfection to be kept perpetually burning, and what has already been learned must every moment be vigilantly protected from rust and mould. After that, the style simply goes like a barque sailing on a gentle sea: thoughts unfurl while onward speeds the brush; what is brushed, then dips and bows unwittingly from billow to billow; while up the masts and down the poles, flags flash and flutter in unison, greeting hilariously the briny breeze and the incandescent noon-day peace.

I have been asked on several occasions to give tuition. After instructing them in principles, I have found my pupils able to carry out their wishes invariably with success — forgetting the heavy words while under the lifting influence of the idea. Although they do not claim sovereignty in all, they are at least tolerable masters of their own chosen styles. I have also found that it is more suitable for youth than for old age to learn the rudiments and easier for old age than for youth to master this art. That is because thinking, as implied in the former, is the fruit of maturity, and endeavour, as required in the latter, is the seed for the young to sow. Endeavour must pass three stages in

变,极其分矣。至如初学分布,但求平正;既知平正,务追险绝;既能险绝,复归平正。初谓未及,中则过之,后乃通会,通会之际,人书俱老。

仲尼云:五十知命也,七十从心。故以达夷险之情,体权变之道。亦犹谋而后动,动不失宜;时然后言,言必中理矣。是以右军之书,末年多妙,当缘思虑通审,志气和平,不激不厉,而风规自远,子敬以下,莫不鼓努为力,标置成体,岂独工用不侔,亦乃神情悬隔者也。

或有鄙其所作,或乃矜其所运。自矜者将穷性域,绝于诱进之途;自鄙者尚屈情涯,必有可通之理。嗟乎,盖有学而不能,未有不学而能者也。考之即事,断可明焉。

succession to prove its full virtue. So the beginner should first aim at confomity and moderation, after which he goes upon perilous ways, and later comes to moderation and conformity once more. During the first stage, he does not reach high enough to the point; during the second, he hits above it; but at last, the arrow sticks tremblingly in the bull's-eye. When the artist enters upon the last stage, both himself and his art become silvered with age. Confucius said: "At fifty I began to perceive the will of heaven; from seventy onwards, I do whatever I please without trespass." Then is the time to be free and easy with life without having to guard against misdeeds. That is why a plan must precede a move if the move is to be successful or why thinking should be the begetter of meaningful words.

For the same reason, the works of Xizhi during his declining years are rich with wonders. They reflect the meditative calm, the pellucid wisdom, and in the absence of any conscious effort, the great depth and age of the composed mind behind. Since Xianzhi and his kind, everyone sweats and fumes for a style, only to fail pitifully, not in mere details, but in the general spirit or atmosphere. Some of them cherish little confidence in their own works; others crimson all over with pride. The humble ones need some expansion of the heart, but will live up to their expectations some day. The haughty ones have fenced up their visions and will stay cut away from the royal road to perfection. Alas! I have heard of people studying hard without being able to learn, but do not yet know that one can learn other than by study — evidences to which abound everywhere.

然消息多方，性情不一，乍刚柔以合体，忽劳逸而分驱：或恬澹雍容，内涵筋骨；或折挫槎枿，外曜峰芒。察之者尚精，拟之者贵似。况拟不能似，察不能精；分布犹疏，形骸未检；跃泉之态未睹其妍，窥井之谈已闻其丑。纵欲唐突羲、献，诬罔钟、张，安能掩当年之目，杜将来之口！慕习之辈，尤宜慎诸。

至有未悟淹留，偏追劲疾；不能迅速，翻效迟重。夫劲速者，超逸之机；迟留者，赏会之致。将反其速，行臻会美之方；

专溺于迟，终爽绝伦之妙。能速不速，所谓淹留；因迟就迟，讵名赏会！非其心闲手敏，难以兼通者焉。

The first lesson the beginner should take is to look into the particular traits of each style, for works of the same style by different artists usually show marked departures and works by the same artist at different times are by no means the same either. Sometimes strength and sinuosity are coiled up in one stroke, or they may be bodied forth separately; or an apparent smoothness may be the guise over bones and sinews, or else a burly vigour throbs and beats simply on the surface. In any case, the student should plunge deep into his subject, and if starting with imitation, he must copy his model without respite. When he does neither one of these — when on account of his absence of mind and reluctance to copy, the distribution of strokes falls out of order and the structure of the body appears loose in shape — then, to what is splendid and to what are the pitfalls in this art he is equally a stranger, and as such he will remain. And then, whatever be the reasons he ignores Zhong and Zhang and neglects Xi and Xian, how could he cover the eyes of his time and stop the mouths of posterity? Of this, the beginner should especially be careful.

As regards the common faults, there is not such a great variety of them as a wide prevalence of two or three. Some let loose a running hand because they do not know how to linger; others pause and loiter because they are helpless in assuming the right speed. In their ideal state, speed is the flash of inspiration and lingering the food of enjoyment. To hurry away between intervals only, is the secret of perfection; but to be slow in any circumstance whatsoever is to renounce all possibilities of achieving the extraordinary. Hastening not when the occasion demands haste is to dawdle; lingering merely out of a sluggish nature has nothing to do with enjoyment. Unless the mind is set at ease and

假令众妙攸归，务存骨气；骨既存矣，而遒润加之。亦犹枝干扶疏，凌霜雪而弥劲；花叶鲜茂，与云日而相晖。如其骨力偏多，遒丽盖少，则若枯槎架险，巨石当路，虽妍媚云阙，而体质存焉。若遒丽居优，骨气将劣，譬夫芳林落蕊，空照灼而无依；兰沼漂蘋，徒青翠而奚托。是知偏工易就，尽善难求。

虽学宗一家，而变成多体，莫不随其性欲，便以为姿：质直者则径侹不遒；刚很者又倔强无润；矜敛者弊于拘束；脱易者失于规矩；温柔者伤于软缓；躁勇者过于剽迫；狐疑者溺于滞涩；迟重者终于蹇钝；轻琐者染于俗吏。斯皆独行之士，偏玩所乖。

《易》曰："观乎天文，以察时变；观乎人文，以化成天

the hand is alert in response, the two qualities of speed and leisureliness rarely favour one person. Having attained the mastery of when to stay and when to dash on, one proceeds to erect his *shu* on bony structures; and after that, polish and decoration follow in due course. If the bones and sinews are abundant and decoration appears meagre, it is like a bold twig bridging over thousands of feet, or like a gigantic rock blocking up the passage on a road: although the appearance does not please, yet the structure inspires security. But if decoration overflows and the structure is weak, then it resembles a forest full of fallen petals — gaudy for one moment and desolate the next; or is like green duckweeds drifted along by water, never getting anywhere in spite of their greenness.

Thus, it is easier to excel in one than in many ways. People who follow at first the same master will develop different styles later: their own traits will finally emerge and substitute those of the master. Those who are straightforward write with austerity and with rigour; others defiant in nature soon become harsh and unpleasant. Reserved persons carry along a stiff and stilted manner; and an undisciplined character will violate alike the rules that can be and those that cannot be violated. Gentleness unseasoned will prove to be effeminate; excessive courage certainly results in harshness. And then, there are the suspicious ones who hesitate to move along and thus become stale, the dull ones who are weighed down by their own clumsiness, and the trite and the vulgar who will appear as they really are. Such, in brief, are the maladies of the untalented. It is said in *Yi Jing*: "Observe the stars to detect the mutations of the times; observe the make-up of human nature to be lord and master of one and all under heaven." Likewise, the

下。”况书之为妙，近取诸身。假令运用未周，尚亏工于秘奥；而波澜之际，已浚发于灵台。必能傍通点画之情，博究始终之理，熔铸虫篆，陶均草隶。体五材之并用，仪形不极；像八音之迭起，感会无方。

至若数画并施，其形各异；众点齐列，为体互乖。一点成一字之规，一字乃终篇之准。违而不犯，和而不同；留不常迟，遣不恒疾；带燥方润，将浓遂枯；泯规矩于方圆，遁钩绳之曲直；乍显乍晦，若行若藏；穷变态于豪端，合情调于纸上；无间心手，忘怀楷则；自可背羲、献而无失，违钟、张而尚工。

secret of *shu-fa* does not lie within itself alone: if something is amiss in the work of art, the fault must come from the artist; if the work flushes and inspires, it is doubtless the flowering of the man.

The perfect artist is expected to control unflinchingly the forces that work between the dots and the strokes, and to start and halt a character with acid precision and pitiless power; he should fuse the hieroglyphic methods with those of *zhuan shu* and merge the principles of *cao* and *li*: until at last it seems as if the 'five elements' are mixed in various components to produce the thousand and one substances, and the *eight instruments* are played together to soften the rock and tame the tiger. Though at times several dots or strokes are brushed side by side, each is unlike any other. A dot gives a start to the character, which in turn becomes the discipline and rule on the entire sheet of paper. To be variegated yet not conflicting, harmonious but not methodized; to be lingering yet not static, moving but not always at full speed; to fluctuate with thythmic but not regular frequency from the dry to the moist back and forth; to be square or round as if the rule or the compass has been applied, to be straight or crooked like a string or a hook; to appear metallic and flinty and then wistful and fleecy; to come out unexpectedly and to glide away mysteriously: in a word, the brush must exhaust all the possible changes and lay bare every thought and feeling on the paper. And of course, the hand as well as the heart should be leisurely yet attentive, and the technique seemingly forgotten and all traces of obvious labour purged away. Then, even if one disagrees with Xi and Xian and ignores Zhong and Zhang, he still has his own merits to stand on and his own laws to obey. The two celebrated

譬夫绛树青琴,殊姿共艳;隋珠和璧,异质同妍。何必刻鹤图龙,竞惭真体;得鱼获兔,犹恡筌蹄。

闻夫家有南威之容,乃可论于淑媛;有龙泉之利,然后议于断割。语过其分,实累枢机。

吾尝尽思作书,谓为甚合,时称识者,辄以引示:其中巧丽,曾不留目;或有误失,翻被嗟赏。既昧所见,尤喻所闻。或以年职自高,轻致陵诮。余乃假之以缃缥,题之以古目:则贤者改观,愚夫继声,竞赏豪末之奇,罕议峰端之失;犹惠侯之好伪,似叶公之惧真。是知伯子之息流波,

beauties *Scarlet Maple* and *Green Lute* were both ravishing but each in her own way; the *Pearl of Sui* and the *Jade of He* are equally valuable though unlike in quality. Good works of a later date may share glory with earlier masterpieces without doing one another injury: it is quite unnecessary to carve a flamingo in the image of a dragon. For after all, imitation is but a means to bring out personal qualities.

I heard it said, one should have a Nan Wei home to sing in public praises of his fair lady, or a Long Quan by his side to speak of any miracle his sword can do; for misstatements and exaggeration always convert words into fountain-heads of laughter. Years ago I brushed some pieces of *shu*, I think, to the best of my power, and have therefrom won a little reputation. To my surprise, when the professors of *shu-fa* came to air their comments, merits were as a rule hushed over with neglect while defects were unanimously hailed with applause. The amateurs, not bold enough to say anything of their own, readily borrowed their ideas from gossip. On the other hand, there were plenty of those who spat abuses lightly because they happened to fill high positions, or simply because their long life had consumed a great many years. I then bound my works in silks of light lemon and titled them with lovely antique names. Almost at once, popular opinion turned its course: the quick-witted changed their tones and the slow ones echoed in chorus. Everyone then deluged my work with praises, scarcely aware that it is not altogether free from casual slips. Such ironical acceptance reminds one of the Baron of Hui, the reputed admirer and champion of whatever is fictitious, or of the Duke of Ye, who was said to be afraid of hearing any truth uttered, be it ever so delectable to others. No wonder, therefore, that Bo-ya abandoned his heptachord when Zhong Ziqi

盖有由矣。

夫蔡邕,不谬赏,孙阳不妄顾者,以其玄鉴精通,故不滞于耳目也。向使奇音在爨,庸听惊其妙响;逸足伏枥,凡识知其绝群,则伯喈不足称,良乐未可尚也。

至若老姥遇题扇,初怨而后请;门生获书几,父削而子懊;知与不知也。夫士,屈于不知己,而申于知己;彼不知也,曷足怪乎!

故庄子曰:“朝菌不知晦朔,蟪蛄不知春秋。”老子云:

was dead, for except his dear friend no person in his time could appreciate the subtle notes that flowed from his watery strings. Cai Yong and Sun Yang did not command anything unworthy of appreciation for the simple reason that their judgments were based on profound knowledge and not on the fickle senses. Cai saved a half-burned log from an oven fire when he heard an unusual crackling afar, and made out of the remnant wood the sounding board of a famous table lyre. Sun picked a ragged horse from a train of pack animals and reared thereof a renowned stallion. If every dull person could discern the rare among the ordinary as easily as those two, the rare would instantly lose their quality and become the ordinary.

The incidents about Wang Xizhi may be related here to sum up this part of the essay. Once coming upon a poor old woman, our great master took pity on her and brushed a fan for her. Not knowing who he was, she grieved that the gift had not been greater, only to discover later that his work was much coveted and commanded a large fortune. Another time, the master paid a visit to one of his followers and, in the absence of the host, left a lengthy note upon the surface of a new-made tea-table. When the pupil's father discovered the note, without knowing whom it was by, he quickly planed off the surface and with it all the priceless remains. These instances signify full well the blundering ignorance of the common people. A wise and learned man lives happily only among those who can fully appreciate him, but is bound to be blocked and frustrated in every way among persons who do not understand. Zhuang-*zi* said: "Mushrooms of one morning do not know that there are waxings and wanings of the moon. Crickets do not live to see the turning of spring into autumn." Lao-*zi* said: "A man with half a

"下士闻道,大笑之;不笑之则不足以为道也。"岂可执冰而咎夏虫哉!

自汉、魏已来,论书者多矣。妍蚩杂糅,条目纠纷;或重述旧章,了不殊于既往;或苟兴新说,竟无益于将来;徒使繁者弥繁,阙者仍阙。今撰为六篇,分成两卷,第其工用,名曰《书谱》。庶使一家后进,奉以规模;四海知音,或存观省;缄秘之旨,余无取焉。

垂拱三年写记

---

① 1929 年大雨先生二十四岁时译就此文,于 1935 年首次发表于《天下》月刊。当时他曾就该刊选用之示范书法发表不同看法并提出"四体为篆、隶、真、草,行在真与草之间……篆可以石鼓文及李斯示范,隶用张迁碑,真取钟繇《宣示表》,草取张芝书,行采王羲之为宜,真书示范应摄制宋《淳化阁帖》中之钟繇书。"现特选上述诸书法示范,以尊重大雨先生一家之说。

——编者

grain of wisdom laughs uproariously at the mention of any vital truth." We should not, of course, deride the insects of one summer with a piece of ice in our hands. Nor should we deplore the folly of the small man, without whose merriment the truth would cease to be truth to the master mind.

Witten in the third
year of Wu Zhao, Queen
Dowager's reign on Chui-gong(垂拱三年),
687*A. D.*

Tr. Autumn and Winter, 1929.

① 最后一段,译文原缺——编者

［唐］　陈子昂[*]

(*661—702*)

登幽州台歌

前不见古人，
后不见来者。
念天地之悠悠，
独怆然而涕下。

* 陈子昂有《感遇》诗三十首(今存十五)，张九龄有《感遇》九首，本原同出阮嗣宗。沈德潜《唐诗别裁》注陈子昂《感遇》诗云“感于心，因于遇，犹《庄子》之寓也，与感知遇意自别。”雨按：感知遇系感知遇之恩，陈、张二子意不在此，而在自表其立身行事之出乎本心(天性)，因各自之际遇而发，非所以取悦于朝庭，求媚于人生，俯仰皆可者也。易言之，系各自人格之表露。

Chen Zi'ang

(*Tang*, *661—702*)

Song on Ascending the Youzhou Terrace

Descrying nor the ancients of long yore,
Nor those that are to come in the future far,
I muse on the eternity of heaven and earth,
And, all alone, grieve mutely with tears for my lorn star.

Tr. July 1, 1983.

[唐] 贺知章

(659—约744)

回乡偶书

少小离家老大回*,
乡音无改鬓毛衰。
儿童相见不相识,
笑问客从何处来。

---

* 少小离家(一作:乡)老大回。

He Zhizhang

(*Tang*, *659—744?*)

Random Lines on Home-coming

Parting from home a stripling still
And coming back old already,
I keep my local speech tone unchanged,
With temple locks grizzled and scanty.
Village boys knowing me not at sight
As a wayfaring trekker,
Laughingly ask where from doth hail
The elderly stranger.

Tr. April 15, 1981.

［唐］ 张九龄*

（678—740）

感遇**

一

兰叶春葳蕤，
桂华秋皎洁。
欣欣此生意，
自尔为佳节。
谁知林栖者，
闻风坐相悦。
草木有本心，
何求美人折？

* 张九龄受屈原的影响很深，他为人品格极高，这首诗使人想起屈原的《橘颂》。他《感遇》九首中有“江南有丹橘”这一首为证。本诗的含意是说，他自己的人格品质是芳香的，犹如秋兰（非兰花）和桂花，玄宗重用他可以治国，由玄宗去做出决定，他自己是不变的这样一个存在。这种尽其为我的淡泊襟怀是非常可贵的。王维很钦佩他。

** 见 P. 120 脚注。

Zhang Jiuling

(*Tang*, *678—740*)

Feelings on My State

1

The eupatory leaves grow lush in spring;
The osmanthus sprigs in autumn bloom pure and sweet.
Luxuriant doth wax their rest of life,
To make both seasons festive occasions meet.
Who knoweth the forest-dweller smelling the breeze
Diffused with fragrant odours loveth them with delight?
The plants bear natural qualities of their own;
Why need the Beauteous One pluck them himself to bedight?

Tr. September 21, 1981.

二

江南有丹橘，
经冬犹绿林。
岂伊地气暖，
自有岁寒心。
可以荐佳客，
奈何阻重深。
运命唯所遇，
循环不可寻。
徒言树桃李，
此木岂无阴？

2

To the south of the River the cinnabar orange doth thrive;
In the winter it still is in shrubbery of virgin green.
Tis not only the earth cherishing its roots is mild and gentle,
But the vigour to stand severe cold in the plant lieth supreme.
The mature radiant fruit is fit to be offered to fair guests,
Had there been not hindrances cumbrous and rampant to ob-
struct. *
One's destiny could only be put up with sufferance dumb;
The dubious rule of vicissitudes cannot be traced before.
It is said timely planting of peach and plum trees giveth shade;
How is this goodly shrub not rewarded with both shade and fruit?

---

* This and the following two lines allude to his fine statesmanship being put to naught by the trust of the emperor Xuan-*zong*(玄宗) laid on his adversary as premier, the vicious Li Linfu(李林甫).

［唐］　王之涣

（*688—742*）

登鹳雀楼

白日依山尽，
黄河入海流。
欲穷千里目，
更上一层楼。

Wang Zhihuan

(*Tang*, *688—742*)

Ascending the Stork Tower

Behind the mounts day light doth glow and fail,
The Luteous River to the sea doth flow.
The view of a thousand *li* to command,
Up a storey higher thou shouldst now go.

Tr. March 28, 1981.

王之涣

凉州词*

黄河远上白云间，
一片孤城万仞**山。
羌笛何须怨《杨柳》？***
春风不度玉门关。

---

* 《凉州词》为唐乐府《凉州歌》的唱词。凉州在今甘肃省武威县。

** 仞，古代的长短量度，长古尺七尺。

*** 羌笛，古代西北域外一少数民族的一种乐器，后来常用作军乐。“杨柳”为古代一支歌曲，名“折杨柳”。后两句说羌笛何必去吹“折杨柳”，以幽怨的声调怪春光来迟呢？须知春风是吹不到玉门关外的啊，意朝廷对远戍者冷漠无情。

雍正八年刊本李安溪所定《榕村诗选》此诗句首作“黄河直上白云间”，第四句作“春光不度玉门关”。

1981年4月18日

Wang Zhihuan

Liang County Song[60]

The Luteous River glares heavenwards to the white clouds,
And a lorn pile lies by a mount a hundred furlongs high.
Why need the Qiang flute plain in a song of *Plucking Willows*?
Spring breezes would not be wafted out of the Jade Gate Pass.

Tr. April 18, 1981.

［唐］ 孟浩然

(*689—740*)

春晓

春眠不觉晓，
处处闻啼鸟。
夜来风雨声，
花落知多少？

Meng Haoran

(*Tang*, *689—740*)

Spring Dawn

Feeling not when cometh th' peep of spring dawn,
Everywhere birds' songs I hear in my slumber.
Through the sounds of wind and rain all th' night long,
Know I not how many th' flowers fall in number.

Tr. August 14, 1981.

［唐］ 李颀

（690—751）

听安万善吹觱篥歌

南山截竹为觱篥，
此乐本自龟兹出。
流传汉地曲转奇，
凉州胡人为我吹。
傍邻闻者多叹息，
远客思乡皆泪垂。
世人解听不解赏，
长飙风中自来往。
枯桑老柏寒飕飕，
九雏鸣凤乱啾啾。
龙吟虎啸一时发，
万籁百泉相与秋。
忽然更作《渔阳掺》，
黄云萧条白日暗。

Li Qi

(Tang, 690—751)

A Song on Listening to An Wanshan Playing the Bi-li Pipe

Cutting bamboo from the South Mount, a *bi-li* pipe[(61)] is made by;
Qiuci the Hu state is where its bizzare music cometh from.
Growing current in the Celestial Empire, it turneth weird;
My Hu friend from Liangzhou doth upon it for me perform.
Neighbours of mine listening to it cannot but utter sighs,
Far-away wanderers thinking of home become tearful all.
People at large like to hear it without sounding its tune motif,
Hurricane wild cometh and goeth freely in its swift call.
Mulberry withered and cypress old seemeth its ringing sound;
A chirping phoenix with nine small chicks nestling against her down;
A dragon groaning or a tiger roaring loud[(62)] all at once,
And soon springs bubble forth, gusts of wind are rising and blow along,
All of a sudden then burst out the drum beats in a hail storm[(63)],
Dull dun clouds cover the sky to make day light darken with gloom.

变调如闻《杨柳》春，
上林繁花照眼新。
岁夜高堂列明烛，
美酒一杯声一曲。

The pipe tune turneth its note to *Spring Breeze Breathing on the Willows*:

Imperial garden flowers are all blazing in full bloom.

On new years eve, in a high hall is lighted a host of candles;

One beaker of deep-delved wine with one *bi-li* pipe song to boom.

［唐］ 王维

（701？—761）

送别

下马饮君酒，
问君何所之？
君言不得意，
归隐南山陲*。
但去莫复问，
白云无尽时。

* 归隐（一作：卧）南山陲。

Wang Wei

(*Tang*, *701? —761*)

Bidding Adieu to a Friend*

As thou alight from thy horse,
I greet thee with a stoup of wine,
And ask thee whither thou wouldst tend.
Thy answer thou givest disheartened
Saying thou wouldst go to retire
As a recluse by the South Mount.
Go but thither without a query;
White clouds are there at all times.

Tr. August 16, 1981.

* These lines were written by the poet to his friend Meng Haoran(孟浩然), also a friend of Li Bai(李白), and South Mount was the South Xian Mountain(南岘山) of Xiangyang(襄阳), now in Hubei Province(湖北).

王维

青溪

言入黄花川，
每逐青溪水。
随山将万转，
趣途无百里。
声喧乱石中，
色静深松里。
漾漾泛菱荇，
澄澄映葭苇。
我心素已闲，
清川澹如此。
请留磐石上，
垂钓将已矣。

Wang Wei

Blue Runnel

In boating to the Yellow Flower Stream,
One should go coursing on the Blue Runnel down.
To cover the distance short of a houndred *li*,
The route windth round some ten thousand along.
The water roareth among a chaos of rocks,
The hills lie quiet beneath the thick pine trees.
Afloat on the waves are trapas and nymphaeas,
Reflected clearly are clumps of rushes and sedges.
Mine heart hath long been used to peace and calm; *
How this limpid stream is tranquil and pleasing!
I wish to remain here on this massive rock,
To spend my placid days in peace and angling.

---

* This and the line following indicate the harmony of the poet's state of mind as a recluse with the natural surroundings.

王维

栾家濑

飒飒秋雨中，
浅浅石溜泻。
跳波自相溅，
白鹭惊复下。

Wang Wei

Luan-jia Rapids

Amidst the spattering showers autumnal,
The dashing rapids on the rocky bank froth.
The leaping breakers splash 'gainst one another,
As an immaculate egret timidly steps forth.

Tr. December, 12, 1980.

王维

竹里馆

独坐幽篁里，
弹琴复长啸。
深林人不知，
明月来相照。

Wang Wei

Bamboo Grove Cabin

Sitting alone in the thickset bamboo grove,
I plucked the heptachord to haloo and croon.
The thicket hidden being withdrawn from men,
I was shone on by the full luminous moon.

Tr. December 18, 1980
Rev. November 24, 1985

王维

鸟鸣涧

人闲桂花落，
夜静春山空。
月出惊山鸟，
时鸣春涧中。

Wang Wei

Bird-Chirping Hollow

The light beams of the moon on the earth softly rain,
The night is quiet, the spring mount empty,
The moon's up-rise the birds doth frighten
To cry now and then in the springtide hollow.

Tr. April 20, 1981.

王维

杂诗

君自故乡来，
应知故乡事。
来日绮窗前，
寒梅著花未？

Wang Wei

Lines

Hailing from our good old homeland,
Thou ought to have tidings there from.
'Fore the caved windows thou passed that day,
Had the plum tree burst into blossom?

Tr. Fabruary 18, 1982.

王维

渭川田家

斜阳照墟落，
穷巷牛羊归。
野老念牧童，
倚杖候荆扉。
雉雊麦苗秀，
蚕眠桑叶稀。
田夫荷锄至，
相见语依依。
即此羡闲逸，
怅然吟《式微》。

Wang Wei

Smallholders' Homes by the Wei Stream

When slanting sunbeams shine on the village scene,
To the lanes retreated return all cattle and sheep.
Some rustics aged expecting the shepherd boys
Are waiting with their staffs at the brushwood doors.
He-pheasants clang and wheat stalks come to ear,
The mulberry leaves grow scant as silk worms sleep.
Farm hands now come up with their hoes on shoulders,
Seeing one another, fall they to talk with cheer.
In the air of all such leisurely good humour,
I yearn for a quiet hermit's life free and dear.

Tr. August 15, 1981.

王维

九月九日忆山东兄弟

独在异乡为异客，
每逢佳节倍思亲。
遥知兄弟登高处，
遍插茱萸少一人。

Wang Wei

Remembering My Brothers East of the Mountain on the Ninth Day of the Ninth Moon

Being a stranger all alone
  In a strange land far away,
I think of my parents all the more
  On a fair festival day.
I know full well my brothers all
  Would climb up the heights of a mount!
Inserting cornus shoots in their hair,
They'd all miss one in their count.

Tr. May 7, 1981.

王维

送元二使安西
（渭城曲）

渭城朝雨浥轻尘，
客舍青青柳色新。
劝君更尽一杯酒，
西出阳关无故人。

Wang Wei

Bidding Adieu to Yuan Junior in His Missoin to Anxi

(Song of the Town of Wei)

The fall of morning drops in this Town of Wei
  Its dust light doth moisten,
Tenderly green are the new willow sprouts
  Of this spring-adorned tavern.
I pray thee to quench once more full to the brim
  This farewell cup of wine,
For after thy departure from this western-most pass,
  Thou will have no old friend of thine.

Tr. December 16, 1980.

［唐］ 李白

（701—762）

远别离

远别离，古有皇英之二女，乃在洞庭之南，潇湘之浦。海水直下万里深，谁人不言此离苦？日惨惨兮云冥冥，猩猩啼烟兮鬼啸雨。我纵言之将何补？皇穹窃恐不照余之忠诚：雷凭凭兮欲吼怒；尧舜当之亦禅禹。君失臣兮龙为

Li Bai

(*Tang*, *701—762*)

Far Departed

Far departed, in days of distant yore,
There were the sisters Ehuang and Nüying[65],
From their common dearlord Zhonghua,
South of the wide expanse of Lake Dongting
At the Limpid Xiang Stream's water margin.
Sad like huge waves surging
Bottomlessly in deep sea,
Who could say this life-forsaking
Severance is not heart-wringing?
Drearily shineth the sun, with
Murky clouds enshrouding;
Hear, oh hear! the chimpanzees are screeching
Smoke, and lo! the spirits weird are squirting
Raindrops fine and mistily thick.
What availeth though I speak of it?[66]
I do fear Divine Heaven cast not His splendour
On my sworn allegiance of fealty:[67]
Thunder-claps would crash down roaring
Through the masses of racks momently;
E'en Yao[68] and Shun would be dethroned to give place
To Yu. Sovereigns would lose their inferiors,

鱼,权归臣兮鼠变虎。或云尧幽囚,舜野死。九嶷联绵皆相似,重瞳孤坟竟何是?帝子泣兮绿云间,随风波兮去无还,恸哭兮远望,见苍梧之深山。苍梧山崩湘水绝,竹上之泪乃可灭。

Dragons turn to finny soles, and power
Would be relegated to followers
As rats metamorphose into tigers. [69]
Some times people would quoth Yao was imprisoned in his time
And Shun died a lorn death in the wild;
On the Nine-peaked Dubious,
All tops alike and continuous,
Where doth lie the tomb lone
Of the duo-pupiled one?[70]
The bereaved princesses wept to mourn
In the green clouds of bamboo groves,
Waiting sore, while vanishing in the winds and
Looking far towards high mounts of Cangwu broad plain;
Unless the high Cangwu Mounts topple down all,
Their tear stains would keep fast on the verdant poles tall. [71]

Tr. March 17, 1983.

李白

蜀道难

噫吁嚱，危乎高哉！蜀道之难，难于上青天！蚕丛及鱼凫，开国何茫然！尔来四万八千岁，不与秦塞通人烟。西当太白有鸟道，可以横绝峨嵋巅。地崩山摧壮士死，然后天梯石栈相钩连。上有六龙回日之高标，下有冲波逆折之回川。黄鹄之飞尚不得过，猿猱欲度愁攀援。青泥

Li Bai

Difficult Is the Way to Shu — A Pindaric Ode

— The Poem in Triple-syllabic Measures —

Yi-Xu-xi!
How dangerously high and steep, the way to Shu
Is more difficult than ascending the blue sky!
Can-cong and Yu-fu[(72)], it is mysteriously unknown how
They began to found their remotely ancient state.
Since then for forty-eight millenia
It had been separated from the Qin terrain.
In the west, it connecteth Noble White Alp[(73)] with a bird's
Flight route, and joineth with the topmost peak of E-mei.
The earth yawned, the mountain crumbled, the five giants[(74)]
died;
And then heavenward steps and rock-hewn flights of stairs are
thus conjoined.
Up above there is the highest clift for Xihe[(75)]
To drive and turn his six dragons of the sun-chariot round,
And down below there are the clashing currents of the whirling
stream.
Yellow storks[(76)] could not fly over that and gibbons and hapales
Would be troubled by trying to climb up over it.
The Blue Sod Alps[(77)] twist and turn in winding about;

何盘盘，百步九折萦岩峦。扪参历井仰胁息，以手抚膺坐长叹。问君西游何时还，畏途巉岩不可攀。但见悲鸟号古木，雄飞雌从绕林间。又闻子规啼夜月，愁空山。蜀道之难，难于上青天！使人听此凋朱颜！连峰去天不盈尺，枯松倒挂倚绝壁。飞湍瀑流争喧豗，砯崖转石万壑雷。其险也若此，嗟尔远道之人，胡为乎来哉！剑阁峥嵘而崔嵬，

They twine round nine times to form peaks and pinnacles while whirling forth.
They pierce into the sky; on them you could touch the brilliant stars
While holding your breath and pressing a palm against your breast for heaving sighs.
Let me ask you when you would turn back from journeying westwards:
The fearful way and the sheer precipitous clifts are impassable and insurmountable.
You would only see sad birds crying on old trees;
The males followed by their females round the forests .
You would hear the cuckoos wailing at the moon, gasping out their griefs on bare mountain crests;
The way to Shu[(78)] is more difficult than ascending the azure sky;
The sad cries of the cuckoos[(79)] would make their hearers hasten to become old.
The chain of sharp peaks and pinnacles leaves the sky not a foot;
Withered pines hang beside the precipitous crags.
Flying rapids and dashing cataracts vie in their roarings;
The clashing of water against the rocks reverberates thunderbolts in ten thousands of hollows.
Such are the dangers, alas! why do you distant travellers come hither!
The Sword steeple[(80)] towereth high up over dizzy flights of steps:

一夫当关,万夫莫开。所守或匪亲,化为狼与豺。朝避猛虎,夕避长蛇,磨牙吮血,杀人如麻。锦城虽云乐,不如早还家。蜀道之难,难于上青天!侧身西望长咨嗟。

Let one valiant man block the pass, and ten thousand others cannot go through.

If the keeper is not an imperial kin, he might turn out to be a wolf or a hyena.

At morn, beware of tigers fierce; at dusk, look out for gigantic serpents!

They would grind their teeth and swallow blood, and butcher people like mowing down hemp .

Although the city of officials robed in gold-threaded brocade is a city pleasurable,

It is better to forgo it for your own homes.

The way to Shu is more difficult than ascending the blue;

One turning to look west ward could but heave long sighs.

Tr. August 7, 1981.

Li Bai

Difficult Is the Way to Shu — A Pindaric Ode

— The prose version —

Ah-hah ho! how dangerously high and steep, the way to Shu is more difficult than ascending the azure sky! Cancong and Yufu it is mysteriously unknown how they began to found their state. Since then for forty-eight thousand years, it had been separated from the Qin terrain. In the west, it connecteth the Noble White Alp with but a birds flight route, and is joined with the topmost peak of Emei. The earth yawned, the mountain crumbled, the fire giants died; and then heaven-ward steps and rock-hewn flights of stairs were conjoined. Up above there is the highest clift for Xihe to drive and turn his six dragons of the Sun-chariot around, and down below there are the clashing currents of the whirling stream. Yellow storks could not fly over that and gibbons and hapales would be worried by trying to climb up it. The Blue Sod Alps twist and turn in winding about; they twine round nine times to form peaks and pinnacles while whirling forward. They pierce into the sky; on them you could touch the bright stars while holding your breath and pressing a palm against your breast and heaving sighs. Let me ask you when you would turn back from journeying westwards: the fearful way and the precipitous clifts are impassable and insurmountable. You could only see sad birds crying on the old trees; the male ones followed by their females round the forests. You would hear the cuckoos wailing at the moon, gasping out their griefs on bare mountain crests; the way to Shu is more difficult than ascending the blue sky; the sad cries of the cuckoos would make their hearers hasten to become old. The chain of sharp peaks and pinnacles leaveth the sky not a foot; withered pines hang beside the precipitous crags. Flying rapids and dashing cataracts vie in their roarings; the clashing of water against the rocks produceth thunderbolts in ten thousand hollows. Such are the dangers, alas! Why do you distant travellers come hither! The Sword Steeple towereth aloft: Let one valiant man block the pass, and ten thousand others could not go through it. If the keeper is not an imperial kin, he might turn to be a wolf or a hyena. At morn, beware of tigers fierce; at dusk, look out for giant serpents! They would grind their teeth and swallow blood, and butcher people like mowing down hemp. Although the city of officials robed in gold-threaded brocade is a city of pleasure, it is better to give it up for home. The way to Shu is more difficult than ascending the blue sky; One turning to look westward could but heave long sighs.

Tr. August 3, 1981.

李白

乌夜啼

黄云城边乌欲栖，
归飞哑哑枝上啼。
机中织锦秦川女，
碧纱如烟隔窗语。
停梭怅然忆远人，
独宿孤房泪如雨。

Li Bai

Crows Croaking at Dusk[81]

By the town bulwalk, neath the sandy clouds,
   The crows are setting down for the night.
Returning to nests and croaking one and all,
   On branches of trees they come to alight.
To weave by hand her taffeta piece,[82]
   The Qin Stream young dame plieth her loom
While speaking alone by herself at the window screen
   Of smoky blue, of her drear doom .
She pauseth her shuttle to pine on her far-off lord;
   All alone in her room, raineth tears in accord.

Tr. October 17, 1982.

李白

乌栖曲

姑苏台上乌栖时，
吴王宫里醉西施。
吴歌楚舞欢未毕，
青山欲衔半边日。
银箭金壶漏水多，
起看秋月坠江波。
东方渐高奈乐何！

Li Bai

A Tune of Crow Roosting ’fore the Eve

When crows for nests are roosting ’fore the eve
on Gusu Mount beside the Gusu Terrace(83),
The Wu state(84) king’s enamoured belle Xishi
Is the carousal’s darling of the Palace.
Before the Wu-toned songs and Chu-mode steps
Are sung and danced to the end with joy and fun,
The verdant mount above the east horizon
Is about to mouth some half a piece of the sun.
The silver arrow telleth the golden case
Of clepsydra hath dript its water enow(85);
Arise, see how the autumnal moon’s sinking low
On the eastward flushing waves of the river flow;
The eastern sky is rising high, alas O!

李白

将进酒

君不见黄河之水天上来，
奔流到海不复回？
君不见高堂明镜悲白发，
朝如青丝暮成雪？
人生得意须尽欢，
莫使金樽空对月。
天生我材必有用，
千金散尽还复来。
烹羊宰牛且为乐，
会须一饮三百杯。
岑夫子，
丹丘生，
将进酒，
君莫停，
与君歌一曲，
请君为我倾耳听。
钟鼓馔玉不足贵，
但愿长醉不复醒。
古来圣贤皆寂寞，
惟有饮者留其名。

Li Bai

Carouse, Please

Seest thou not
the waters of the Luteous River rush down from the sky,
And roll off to the sea forevermore not to come back?
Seest thou not
White locks are wailed at before bright mirrors in halls high,
For turning at dusk into snowflakes from their morning's jet black?
Seize the moments of content in life and make full mirth of them;
Let not your golden beakers stay empty to glint at the moon.
Heaven hath endowed me with talents certes for good use;
A thousand pieces of gold being scattered 'll come back soon.
Let mutton and beef be broiled for making merry;
We should drain three hundred bumpers at one carouse.
My friends sire Cen and good Danqiu, pause not in drinking,
Let me sing a ditty for you, let me your kind ears arouse.
Banquets with bell-strikings and drum-beats are not by me prized,
But I wish to drink deep always, ne'er sadly sober remain.
Since olden times, saints and sages have all been solitary,
While drinkers throughout the ages their renown do retain.

陈王昔时宴平乐，
斗酒十千恣欢谑。
主人何为言少钱?
径须沽取对君酌。
五花马，
千金裘，
呼儿将出换美酒，
与尔同销万古愁。

175

Li Bai

When King Chenzhi of literary fame feasted at Pingle
Ten thousand coins were spent for each dipper of rare old vintage.
Why doth our taverner say there is any lack of cash?
We should not lack means to get wine your mind to assuage.
My mottled steed and the fur-lined robe of a thousand crowns,
Let my boy lead and fetch out to barter for drinks divine,
In order to banish with ye both our griefs eternal trine.

Tr. May 31, 1980.
Rev. July 20, 1981.
Rev. April 20, 1983.

李白

日出入行

日出东方隈，
似从地底来。
历天又入海，
六龙所舍安在哉？
其始与终古不息；
人非元气，
安得与之久徘徊？
草不谢荣于春风，
木不怨落于秋天。
谁挥鞭策驱四运？
万物兴歇皆自然。
羲和羲和，汝奚汩没于荒淫之波？
鲁阳何德，
驻景挥戈？
逆道违天，
矫诬实多。
吾将囊括大块，
浩然与溟涬同科。

Li Bai

The Lay of the Sun Arising and Sinking

The sun ariseth from the eastern bourn,
As though deep down out of the bowels of earth,
Athwart the sky to sink again in the sea.
Where do the Six Dragons[(86)] have their night berth?
The race beginneth from the dawn of time;
Since man is not the cosmic force,
How could we match its perpetual course?
As grass doth not feel grateful to spring winds for its lush growth,
So nor do the woods bear spite to autumn for their fall of leaves.
Who wieldeth the whip to lash on the run of the seasons!
The rise and fall of all beings are but natural.
Xihe, Xihe[(87)], why are ye sunk in the expanse of wanton waves?[(88)]
What virtue was at Lu-yang's[(89)] behest his lance to sway,
To make the setting Sun retrace its steps and delay?
It's against heaven's rule to practise trickery for law,
And to massacre the innocent to vaunt brute power[(90)].
I would enfold the macrocosm all in all,
Superbly 'neath my mind's one lofty pall.[(91)]

李白

塞下曲

一

塞虏乘秋下，
天兵出汉家。
将军分虎竹，
战士卧龙沙。
边月随弓影，
胡霜拂剑花。
玉关殊未入，
少妇莫长嗟！

Li Bai

Frontier Tunes

1

The frontier foes descend in autumnal raids;
Our celestial troops march forth to guard these Han lands.
Our chiefs insignias hold of tiger and bamboo;
Our infantry men lie on the Dragon Sands.
The border moon is curved like a bent bow;
The Hun sky frost on blades of our swords doth fall.
Our Jade Gate Pass hath not been crossed by me,
Young wife of mine, heave thee no sighs at all!

Tr. July 22, 1983.

二

五月*天山雪，
无花只有寒。
笛中闻《折柳》，
春色未曾看。
晓战随金鼓，
宵眠抱玉鞍。
愿将腰下剑，
直为斩楼兰。

* 英译为六月，系阳历计。——编者

2

In June* on Mount Tian-shan there's naught but snow;
  No flowers could be seen, still tarrieth the cold.
Mid tunes of flutes is heard The Plucking of Willow,
  The vernal hues of Spring are yet to behold
The battles at dawn ensure from drums and gongs,
  In nocturnal slumbers I doze off in saddle-hugging,
I would this flashing sword here by my loin,
  Be thrust forth straight for the foe Lou-lan's head-cutting.

Tr. July 24, 1983.

* The word in the original text is "May", according to the Chinese lunar calendar; "June" in the English version is so translated according to the Gregorian calendan. —Ed.

李白

玉阶怨

玉阶生白露，
夜久侵罗袜。
却下水晶帘，
玲珑望秋月。

Li Bai

Plaint on Gem Steps

Dew drops on the gem steps fall'n cool
Through her flimsy silken socks seep;
Stepping down through the screen of crystal beads
She at the sparkling autumnal moon doth peep.

Tr. April 17, 1982.

李白

清平调词

云想衣裳花想容，
春风拂槛露华浓。
若非群玉山头见，
会向瑶台月下逢。

一枝红艳露凝香，
云雨巫山枉断肠。
借问汉宫谁得似，
可怜飞燕倚新装。

Li Bai

For Qing-ping Tunes[92]

Tinged cloudlets are likened unto her raiment
And the flowers unto her mien.
Spring zephyrs along the balustrade
Gently brush the crystal dew's sheen.
If not seen on the wondrous Mount of Gems
At some enchanted strand,
She could be met with on the Magic Tower
In the moonlit fairyland.

Tr. July 5, 1981.

A spray of fresh pink beauty[93] sparkleth
With dews full of scents sweet;
The clouds and showers of Mount Wu's Belle[94]
Remain today a mere legend.
If it be asked who in the Han palace
Could ever be named as her like,
The answer is "The Flitting Swallow"[95]
In her newly sewn skirt of gauze.

Tr. July 6, 1981.

名花倾国两相欢，
长得君王带笑看。
解释春风无限恨，
沉香亭北倚阑干。

187

Li Bai

The Flower famed and the Beauty renowned
   Rejoice in each other's note.
They are both smiled upon tenderly
   With love by our sovereign lord,
To banish his grief and cares in plenty
   From state affairs in the spring breeze,
As they two incline by the balustrade
   North of the aloes-wood arbour.

Tr. July 7, 1981.

李白

静夜思

床前明月光，
疑是地上霜。
举头望山月，*
低头思故乡。

* 举头望山月(一作:明月)

Li Bai

Thoughts in a Still Night

The luminous moonshine before my bed,
Is thought to be the frost fallen on the ground.
I lift my head to gaze at the cliff moon,
And then bow down to muse on my distant home.

Tr. May, 1980.

李白

春思

燕草如碧丝，
秦桑低绿枝。
当君怀归日，
是妾断肠时。
春风不相识，
何事入罗帏？

Li Bai

Spring Thoughts

When the grasses of Yan[96] are like tufts of green silk in the
breeze,
The luxuriant mulberry leaves of Qing[97] hang low on trees.
As thou think of the day when thou wouldst come home from
way-faring,
I am pining away broken-hearted while lorn fits me seize.
The spring breeze is a stranger altogether unknown to me;
What hast it to do with blowing into my silk curtain piece?

Tr. October 9, 1981.

李白

子夜吴歌

长安一片月，
万户捣衣声。
秋风吹不尽，
总是月关情。
何日平胡虏，
良人罢远征？

Li Bai

Ziye's Wu Song[98]

With moonshine flooding all Chang'an City,
Ten thousand households are clubbing their laundry.
Autumnal winds are blowing all this while,
With yearnings for the Pass of Gem Gateway.
"When could the Huns be subdued for good and aye,
So my goodman could be back from draft far away?"

Tr. December 31, 1918.

李白

长相思

长相思，在长安。
络纬秋啼金井阑，
微霜凄凄簟色寒。
孤灯不明思欲绝，
卷帷望月空长叹。
美人如花隔云端。
上有青冥之长天，*
下有渌水之波澜。
天长地远魂飞苦，**
梦魂不到关山难，
长相思，
摧心肝！

---

* 上有青冥之长(一作:高)天。
** 天长地(一作:路)远魂飞苦。

Li Bai

Long Drawn Yearning[99]

Ah! long drawn yearning, thither for Chang'an Town!
The katydid is chirping its fall time song
By the well-curb of marble in bas-relief,
While thin frost falleth and mats show warm clime is gone.
The lone and flickering light waneth dim in burning
And my forlorn and dazed thoughts run out nigh;
I turn the lowly hung down curtain up,
To gaze at the moon and heave in vain my sigh.
The Beauteous One[100], like a flower beyond the clouds,
Is vaulted above by the empyrean azure,
And by the expanse of clear waves upborne below[101].
The skyey distance stretching thus far doth allure
My poor soul to strive so hard in attaining my goal
In its dreams to reach the Border Defile Mount[102]!
Ah! long drawn yearning; it gnaweth my heart, — the dole!

Tr. September 9, 1982.

李白

江上吟

木兰之枻沙棠舟，
玉箫金管坐两头。
美酒樽中置千斛，
载妓随波任去留。
仙人有待乘黄鹤；
海客无心随白鸥。
屈平辞赋悬日月；
楚王台榭空山丘。
兴酣落笔摇五岳，
诗成啸傲凌沧洲。*

* 诗成啸（一作：笑）傲凌沧洲。

Li Bai

Chant Over the Stream

Aboard a sand pyrus(103) barge with magnolia oars,
Gay players of jade pipes and golden flutes
Mellifluously attune their melodies
At the bow and stern with liquid chords of lutes.
The barque full laden with vintage old and rare,
Along doth bear sonorous belles debonair
To drift wherever listeth the flow of waves.
The fairy flied down through the azure air(104)
By means of riding astride a yellow crane(105).
The seaboard farer free from wiles his care
Could banish by fixing eyes on the gulls in flight(106).
The radiant odes of Qu Ping's hang ever bright
Throughout the ages to vie with the sun and moon(107),
But terraces, and arbours built thereon,
Of the kings of Chu(108) could hardly last very long.
When mine ethereal, high mood is on me,
I could wield my brush to shake the Five Noble Mounts,
And as a masterly poem is brought to finish,
I would become elated in spirit to stride
Beyond my hermitage by the waterside.

功名富贵若长在，
汉水亦应西北流。

199

Li Bai

If worldly glamour were to last forever,
The Stream of Han south-eastwards in its flow
Should turn the course north-westerly to go.

李白

横江词

横江馆前津吏迎，
向余东指海云生。
“郎今欲渡缘何事？
如何风波不可行！”

Li Bai

River-crossing Tune

'Fore the ferry pavilion the quay-guard greeteth me;
To the east he pointeth to the sea-side clouds rising.
For what would you, Master, the river cross?
With such blasts and waves there could be no ferrying.

Tr. April 27, 1982.

李白

金陵城西楼月下吟

金陵夜寂凉风发，
独上高楼望吴越。
白云映水摇空城，
白露垂珠滴秋月。
月下沉吟久不归，
古来相接眼中稀。
解道澄江静如练，
令人长忆谢玄晖。

Li Bai

Humming under the Moon atop the West Tower in Jinling City

Mid the silent night in Jin-ling rising a cool blast,
Up the tower climb I, of Wu and Yue to command my view.
White clouds flashing light on water shake the empty town;
On the autumnal moonshine fall drops of pearly clear dew.
Hum I under the moon, into the depth of the night.
Since the days of old, things are seldom noticed eye to eye.
It is seen the limpid River is calm like tiffany,
Thus reminding one how Xie Tiao(109) his verse doth beautify.

Tr. May 25, 1982.

李白

峨眉山月歌

峨眉山月半轮秋，
影入平羌江水流。
夜发青溪向三峡，
思君不见下渝州。

Li Bai

Song of the Emei Mount Peaks Moon

Half a disc of that autumnal moon o'er Emei[110] peaks,
Throws its bright image into the streams of Pingqiang.[111]
Leaving Qingxi[112] for the Three Gorges[113] by night,
I think of, seeing not thee, all the way down to Yuzhou.[114]

Tr. July 1, 1981.

李白

赠汪伦

李白乘舟将欲行，
忽闻岸上踏歌声。
桃花潭水深千尺，
不及汪伦送我情。

Li Bai

To Wang Lun

Li Bai embarking, just about to depart,
　On a sudden heareth tramping and songs on the strand.
The Peach Bloom Deep, a thousand feet in depth,
　Runneth not so deep as Wang Lun's thoughts for me command.

Tr. April 24, 1982.

李白

山中问答

问余何意栖碧山，
笑而不答心自闲。
桃花流水窅然去，
别有天地非人间。

Li Bai

Question and Answer in the Mounts

Being asked why I retire to the green mounts,
Smiling I reply not with my heart vacant.
Peach blooms and a flowing stream receding far,
Strange are heaven and earth, — a new birth verdant.

Tr. April 25, 1982.

李白

庐山谣寄卢侍御虚舟

我本楚狂人，
凤歌笑孔丘。
手持绿玉杖，
朝别黄鹤楼。
五岳寻仙不辞远，
一生好入名山游。
庐山秀出南斗旁，
屏风九叠云锦张，
影落明湖青黛光。
金阙前开二峰长，
银河倒挂三石梁。
香炉瀑布遥相望，
回崖沓嶂凌苍苍。
翠影红霞映朝日，
鸟飞不到吴天长。
登高壮观天地间，

Li Bai

Ballad of Mount Lu,[115]
Sent to Lord Attendant[116] Lu Xuzhou

The lunatic of Chu[117] I am in fact,
Laughing at Confucius[118] with my Phoenix Song.
The Yellow Crane Tower[119] I left at morn,
A fairy's cane of green jade[120] taking along.
Not minding the distances to the Five Mounts[121] fairies to seek,
I all my Life like mounts renowned to climb and roam eke.
Mount Lu raiseth its sheer heights fair by the Little Bear[122],
Like nine-folded screens[123] enshrouded in gorgeous clouds of brocade,
Its image in the Lake[124] bright beaming a turquoise rare.
The Two High Cliffs[125] 'fore the Golden Portal Peak[126] tower;
The Silvery Triple Stream[127] from the Three Rock Beams is hung.
The Incense Burner Cataract falleth afar in shower;
Steep crests and folded summits are 'gainst the azure flung.
The rising sun doth its glow on blue tops and scarlet clouds throw;
The flight of birds could not through all the Wu Sky[128] go.
Ascending heights to command a broad view of the earth and sky,

大江茫茫去不还。
黄云万里动风色，
白波九道流雪山。
好为庐山谣，
兴因庐山发。
闲窥石镜清我心，
谢公行处苍苔没。
早服还丹无世情，
琴心三叠道初成。
遥见仙人彩云里，
手把芙蓉朝玉京。
先期汗漫九垓上，
愿接卢敖游太清。

I see the great torrential River go on forever.
Sometimes dark clouds for thousands of *li* are ruffled up high,
With snowy waves like heaving hills in nine streams[129] astir.
I like to sing aloud this Mount Lu Ballad;
My feelings for the Mount have risen right glad.
Looking at the Stone Mirror clarifieth my heart;
The whereabouts Sire Xie[130] once loitered is grown with moss.
Taking doses of cinnabar restored[131] in good time.
Would purge my mortality, paying bliss rare with cheap loss;
With utmost peace of mind[132], I fairyhood would win,
Espying then fairies floating high up in vermeil clouds,
With lotus blooms in their arms paying homage up the Sacred
    Mount[133].
I would expect you in advance in the ninth heaven[134],
Greeting you and in your company rove the empyrean.

Tr. February 28, 1982.

李白

梦游天姥吟留别

海客谈瀛洲，
烟涛微茫信难求。
越人语天姥，
云霞明灭或可睹。
天姥连天向天横，
势拔五岳掩赤城。
天台一万八千丈，
对此欲倒东南倾。
我欲因之梦吴越，
一夜飞度镜湖月。
湖月照我影，
送我至剡溪。
谢公宿处今尚在，
渌水荡漾清猿啼。

Li Bai

A Song for Some Friends[135], on a Dream Trip to Mount Tianmu[136]

Mariners speak of the legendary Islands of the Blest[137], ——
Amongst the blown spumes of smoky waves, hard of reach they are true.
Yue People speaking of Mount Tianmu are apt to have it thus:
'Neath clouds bedimmed or aglow, it is flashily looming blue.
Tianmu is rolling up sky-high, then running level with it;
It towereth above the Five Great Mounts[138] and the Crimson Town[139].
Mount Tiantai[140] known to be one hundred eighty thousand feet high,
Stretching by this, seemeth to be falling southeasterly down.
I would I could through dreaming probe deep into the realm of Yue,
In one night fly past the Mirror Lake's[141] reflected lustrous moon.
    The lake moon beameth on mine image[142],
    Watching me flit to the Shan Brook[143] soon.
There I see Sire Xie's[144] night hut standing upright still,
Where clear streams flow and flush, and I hear gibbons scream.

脚著谢公屐，
身登青云梯。
半壁见海日，
空中闻天鸡。
千岩万转路不定，
迷花倚石忽已暝。
熊咆龙吟殷岩泉，
慄深林兮惊层巅。
云青青兮欲雨，
水澹澹兮生烟。
列缺霹雳，
丘峦崩摧。
洞天石扉，
訇然中开。
青冥浩荡不见底，
日月照耀金银台。
霓为衣兮风为马，
云之君兮纷纷而来下。
虎鼓瑟兮鸾回车，
仙之人兮列如麻。

Wearing Sire Xie's Mountaineering clogs,
I climb flights of steps steep in th' extreme.
Looking eastwards from a crag at the sun on the heaving sea,
I hear the heaven's chanticleer[145] crowing aloud cock-a-doodle-doo.
Thousands of peaks with innumerable turns I find hard to trace;
Hosts of stray flowers by the rocks I glimpse as dusk falleth to coo.
Bears' growlings and dragon's groanings reverberate through rock dell springs
Tremors of fear shake the forests dark and cliffs precipitous.
Clouds bluish are about to sprinkle drops of rain down,
Water is rippling gently as smoke wreatheth soft.
Flash off the lightning jags;
Crash up the thunder-claps;
Pinnacle tops topple headlong;
Avalanches of rocks fall.
A Taoist cave's stone portal is thrown open with a loud bang.
An azure depth yawneth in the bottomless void;
Sun and moon are shooting their splendour on gold and silver spires;
With rainbow gowns and swift blasts as their steeds skyey,
Kinglings of clouds come severally flocking down.
Tigers are plucking in concert on harps heavenly;
Phoenixes are turning round vehicles light and airy.
A host of fairies descendeth all o'er the sky sublimely.

忽魂悸以魄动，
恍惊起而长嗟。
惟觉时之枕席，
失向来之烟霞。
世间行乐亦如此，
古来万事东流水。
别君去兮何时还？
且放白鹿青崖间，
须行即骑访名山。
安能摧眉折腰事权贵，
使我不得开心颜？

All of a sudden my spirit is quivering, tingling quick[(146)].
Lost and forlorn, I am frightened out of my dream sighs to heave.
Conscious on my pillow and bedding as I now have come round,
I have lost all those magnificent mountains and plains and lakes.
To fill one's life with rejoicings and jollity is just so;
All things from ancient days are no more than east-flowing water.
Leaving your company fair, when shall I come back north again?
Let my white deer freely graze in the green valleys.
If need be, I would ride it when I feel like to visit renowned mountains.
How could I wrinkle up my forehead and bend my waist to wait on those in power,
Making myself crest-fallen for nought?

Tr. December 17, 1981.

李白

金陵酒肆留别

风吹柳花满店香，
吴姬压酒劝客尝。
金陵子弟来相送，
欲行不行各尽觞。
请君试问东流水，
别意与之谁短长？

Li Bai

Parting Thoughts at a Jinling Tavern

Spring breeze with willow fluff is filling
The shop with the new brew's sweet odour;
The barmaids fair of Wu are pressing
Fresh wine to urge the guests to savour;
Bright youths of Jinling in twos and threes
Are coming as one to bid me adieu.
The one departing and those who remain,
All drain their stoups for love in lieu.
I beg thee please put questions to
The east-flowing water of the River,
Our farewell yearnings and the stream's,
Which of their cares of parting are stronger?

Tr. November 27, 1981.

李白

黄鹤楼送孟浩然之广陵

故人西辞黄鹤楼，
烟花三月下扬州。
孤帆远影碧空尽，
唯见长江天际流。

Li Bai

Seeing Meng Haoran Off to Guangling[147] on the Yellow Crane Tower[148]

Mine old friend leaveth the West
  From the Yellow Grane Tower.
In this flowery April[149] clime
  For thickly peopled[150] Yangzhou.
A solitary sail's distant speck
  Vanisheth in the clear blue:
What could be seen heavenward
  Flowing is but the Long River[151].

Tr. June 25, 1981.

李白

送友人

青山横北郭，
白水绕东城。
此地一为别，
孤蓬万里征。
浮云游子意；
落日故人情。
挥手自兹别，*
萧萧班马鸣。

---

* 挥手自兹别(一作:去)。

Li Bai

Bidding Adieu to a Friend

Across the north suburbs the mounts lie blue,
Around the town's east the stream windeth white.
We are to bid each other here our adieus,
And ye would wander far away ere this night.
Like floating clouds appear the wayfarer's thoughts,
Our friendly fleelings seem the sunset glow.
With waves of hands we bid our farewell now.
"Whinny!" doth neigh the departing colt to go.

Tr. July 19, 1983.

李白

宣州谢朓楼饯别校书叔云

弃我去者昨日之日不可留，
乱我心者今日之日多烦忧。
长风万里送秋雁，
对此可以酣高楼。
蓬莱文章建安骨，
中间小谢又清发。
俱怀逸兴壮思飞，
欲上青天揽明月。
抽刀断水水更流，
举杯销愁愁更愁。

Li Bai

Bidding Farewell with Feast to Decreed Editor Uncle Yun on Xie Tiao Tower in County Xuan

The days having left me, in all those yesterdays
  Could not be retained at all;
The days confusing me of-times nowadays
  Are full of worries and gall.
The winds that drive for thousands of li
  Send autumn's greylags south;
Commanding such a view well suiteth
  To drink deep atop this tower.
Your mind is illumed with fairy tracts and classics
  Of clairvoyant, happy strain(152),
My thoughts are lit up with glows of poetry afire
  With beauty of dazzling vein.
Both you and I are full of buoyant mood
  And spirits elevate,
Wishing to fly away ascending the blue
  To watch the moon looming great.
One slashing water with the blade of one's sword,
  It floweth on all the more;
One raiseth one's goblet to drown one's dolour deep,
  And it waxeth doubly sore.

人生在世不称意，
明朝散发弄扁舟。

229

Li Bai

Our life in this insensate, wretched world
　Is running counter to our bent;
Tomorrow let's hang up our hats of office[153],
　Take to boats on streams in content.

Tr. April 1, 1982.

李白

把酒问月

青天有月来几时？
我今停杯一问之。
人攀明月不可得，
月行却与人相随。
皎如飞镜临丹阙，
绿烟灭尽清辉发。
但见宵从海山来，
宁知晓向云间没？
白兔捣药秋复春，
姮娥孤栖与谁邻？
令人不见古时月，
今月曾经照古人。
古人今人若流水，
共看明月皆如此。
惟愿当歌对酒时，
月光长照金樽里。

Li Bai

Holding Drink to Ask the Moon[154]

"When doth the moon to the blue come?"
I stop my beaker to put the question
We could not lead or draw on the moon,
Though it moveth along with us to run.
It sparkleth like a flying mirror
O'erlooking the portal cinnabar[155].
The evening haze having subsided,
An ethereal radiance gloweth afar.
We see its rise from the sea at night;
Who knoweth its flight to the clouds at dawn?
The rabbit blanch[156] on the elixir of life
Keepeth on pounding, year in, year out.
With whom doth the fairy lonely dame[157]
As neighbour keep her companion boon?
Our men see not the ancient moon.
Today's moon hath on the ancients shone.
Men ancient and of today like water
That floweth, see the moon thus all.
I would when we sing holding our drink,
The moon its beams to our beakers let fall.

Tr. April 7, 1982.

李白

登金陵凤凰台

凤凰台上凤凰游，
凤去台空江自流。
吴宫花草埋幽径，
晋代衣冠成古丘。
三山半落青天外。
二水中分白鹭洲。*
总为浮云能蔽日，
长安不见使人愁。

* 二(一作:一)水中分白鹭洲。

Li Bai

Ascending the Phoenix Terrace[158] of Jinling City

On the Phoenix Terrace, phoenixes alighted to play;
They flew off, leaving the empty terrace to overlook
the well-nigh boundless River flowing by itself away.
Wu Palace's[159] flowers and grass have buried the covert paths;
The celebrated courtiers of Jin[160] are entombed in clay.
The Tri-peaked Mount[161] is half pointed through the azure sky;
The dual stream[162] the Egret Ait[163] doth fork to splay.
It's all because the floating clouds[164] could cover the sun;
The Imperial City hid from sight[165] doth one dismay.

李白

望庐山瀑布

日照香炉生紫烟，
遥看瀑布挂前川。
飞流直下三千尺，
疑是银河落九天。

Li Bai

Sighting the Cataract of Mount Lu

The sun shining on the Incense-burner Peak
  Issueth purple smoke to wreathe round,
Seen afar the cataract seemeth hung from the cliff top
  To the water front of the Mount.
The flying torrent for three thousand feet
  Ceaselessly dashing down headlong.
Is taken to be the Silvery Stream* falling from
  The ninth heaven to the ground.

Tr. April 21, 1981.

* Silvery Stream: The Milky Way in Chinese.

李白

秋登宣城谢朓北楼

江城如画里，
山晚望晴空。
两水夹明镜，
双桥落彩虹。
人烟寒橘柚；
秋色老梧桐。
谁念北楼上，
临风怀谢公？

Li Bai

Ascending Xie Tiao's North Tower[166] at Xuan Cheng in Autumn

The River town like a painted landscape doth shine,
With mountains beaming late in a fair day.
The two entwining streams[167] as mirrors sparkle,
While the pair of bridges[168] like rainbows arch over gay.
With wreaths of cooking smoke arising in the air,
The tangerines and oranges[169] hang in red gold;
All tinges of the scene show fall is far advanced,
As platane leaves look sear and yellow in the cold[170],
Who that ascendeth pensively the North Tower
Doth 'gainst the wind Sire Xie our poet remember[171]?

Tr. September 21, 1982.

李白

早发白帝城

朝辞白帝彩云间，
千里江陵一日还。
两岸猿声啼不住，
轻舟已过万重山。

Li Bai

Embarking from Baidi Town[172] at Early Morn

Leaving Baidi on high at dawn
  Among the clouds in blaze gay,
A thousand li to Jiangling City[173]
  I sped within a day.
Unceasingly the gibbons screeched
  On both banks of the River,
As my light skiff shot through the folds
  Of mounts ten thousand with a whirr.

Tr. April 10, 1981.

李白

越中览古

越王勾践破吴归，
战士还家尽锦衣。*
宫女如花满春殿，
只今惟有鹧鸪飞。

* 战(一作:义)士还家尽锦衣。

Li Bai

Looking Back to Olden Times in Yue*

When Goujian King of Yue, had crushed his state foe Wu,
His homing warriors were dressed in brocade all.
Then beauties held captive, lush like flowers, thronged the spring court;
Now only partridges are flying and each to each call.

Tr. April 19, 1982.

* The poet(701—762) in this quatrain is thinking of the crushing defeat dealt by King Goujian of Yue(越王勾践) on his mortal foe Fucha(夫差) and his kingdom of Wu(吴), which was annexed in the year 473 B. C.

李白

月下独酌

花间一壶酒，
独酌无相亲。
举杯邀明月，
对影成三人。
月既不解饮，
影徒随我身。
暂伴月将影，
行乐须及春。
我歌月徘徊，
我舞影零乱。
醒时同交欢，
醉后各分散。
永结无情游，
相期邈云汉。

Li Bai

Drinking Alone under the Moon

With a jug of wine among the flowers,
I drink alone sans company.
To the moon aloft I raise my cup,
With my shadow to form a group of three.
As the moon doth not drinking ken,
And shadow mine followeth my body,
I keep company with them twain,
While spring is here to make myself merry.
The moon here lingereth while I sing,
I dance and my shadow spreadeth in rout.
When sober I am, we jolly remain,
When drunk I become, we scatter all about.
Let's knit our carefree tie of the good old day;
We may meet above sometime at the milky way.

Tr. February 7, 1981.

李白

独坐敬亭山*

众鸟高飞尽，
孤云独去闲。
相看两不厌，
只有敬亭山。

* 敬亭山，一名昭亭山，在安徽宣城县北，“东临宛溪，南俯城闉，烟市风帆，极目如画。”

Li Bai

Sitting in Repose Alone on Jingting Hill

All birds have flown up high and far away,
A lonely cloud floated off leisurely.
We gaze at each other to our both fill,
I myself and my hearty Jingting Hill.

Tr. April 16, 1982.

李白

访戴天山道士不遇

犬吠水声中，
桃花带雨浓。*
树深时见鹿，
溪午不闻钟。
野竹分青霭，
飞泉挂碧峰。
无人知所去，
愁倚两三松。

* 桃花带雨（一作：露）浓。

Li Bai

A Visit to the Taoist Priest of Daitian Mount without Meeting Him

A dog is barking mid the splash of water,
The rain-besprinkled peach blooms appear a pink gay.
Mongst thickset trees are often sighted deers,
By the runnel, silent are the bells of noonday.
The wild bamboos divide the verdant hue,
A flying spring hangeth down from a green peak.
No one could tell his whereabouts just now,
Nonplussed, I wonder where I could him seek.

Tr. July 20, 1983

李白

劳劳亭[*]

天下伤心处，
劳劳送客亭。
春风知别苦，
不遣柳条青。

* 劳劳亭，一名临沧观，又名望远楼，吴时建，故址在今南京江宁西南，古时送别之所。

Li Bai

Sad, Sad Arbour

The grievous spot beneath the sky,
Is the Sad, Sad Arbour for bidding adieu.
The spring breeze knowing farewell's pain,
Giveth not the willow strips a green hue.

Tr. April 18, 1982.

李白

关山月

明月出天山，
苍茫云海间。
长风几万里，
吹度玉门关。
汉下白登道，
胡窥青海湾。
由来征战地，
不见有人还。
戍客望边邑，
思归多苦颜。
高楼当此夜，
叹息未应闲。

Li Bai

Moonlight on the Mount of Borderland Pass

The lustrous moon hast risen o'er Mount Sky,
Shedding its sheen midst the sea of clouds up high.
For thousands of *li* wind blasts are being blown,
To drive past the Gem Cateway Pass 'neath the sky.
Han troops were sent to battle on the Bai-deng ways,
The Huns off dared about the Blue Sea banks to pry.
Since olden times from this age-old battle ground,
No one hath been seen to get back home by.
All levied men looking at frontier spots,
Would bitterly pine for home with faces wry.
Their mates in storeyed chambers in such nights,
Would not e'er cease to heave a sigh after a sigh.

Tr. December 28, 1981.

李白

幽涧泉

拂彼白石，
弹吾素琴。
幽涧愀兮流泉深。
善手明徽，
高张清心。
寂历如千古松，
飕飗兮万寻。
中见愁猿吊影而危处兮，
叫秋木而长吟。
客有哀时失志而听者，
泪淋浪以沾襟。
乃缉商缀羽，潺湲成音。
吾但写声发情于妙指，
殊不知此曲之古今。
幽涧泉，
鸣深林。

Li Bai

Secluded Gorge Spring

Let me wipe that slab of white stone
With the sleeve folds of my loose flowing gown;
I'm to pluck my heptachord plain
By the side of a fresh spring bubbling deep down
In this secluded gorge 'tween mounts twain.
Fair-toned pluckings of fingers deft and apt,
Well directed by my lucid mind and vacant;
Solitary as if lasting a thousand years long,
Like the subdued roarings of a sea of pine foliage
Six score furlongs thick to form a dense throng,
Midst which are to be seen the gibbons sadly shrieking
Self-pityingly, jumping about and clambering
Along precariously atop autumnal trees.
There is one forlorn of hope and bewailing
The times, hearing woe-begone cries such as these,
Who doth flush tears his lapels to drench through.
Thereupon I summon tuneful notes in a gentle flow,
Toning at my finger tips with feelings the melody,
Knowing not, albeit, the sonata thus performed by me
Be ancient or modern. Ah, Secluded Gorge Spring,
In the depth of the forest, it doth sparkle and clearly sing.

Tr. July 14, 1983.

李白

公无渡河

黄河西来决昆仑，
咆哮万里触龙门。
波滔天，
尧咨嗟。
大禹治百川，
儿啼不窥家。
杀湍堙洪水，
九州始蚕麻。
其害乃去，
茫然风沙。
披发之叟狂而痴，
清晨临流欲奚为？
旁人不惜妻止之，
“公无渡河苦渡之。
虎可搏，
河难冯，
公果溺死流海湄。
有长鲸白齿若雪山，

Li Bai

Goodman, Cross Ye Not the River[174]

The Luteous River[175] coming from the west
Doth break forth at the foot of Mount Kunlun
To roar for thousands of *li*,
And dash 'gainst the Gate of Dragon[176].
Its waves ran tossing their white crests at the skies,
To make *Di* Yao in grieving heave his sighs.
Thereupon Great Yu conducted hundreds of streams
To flush to the east in their tumultuous flow
(He by-passed thrice his home in thirteen years)[177],
Subduing cataracts, suppressing the flood,
For the Nine States to settle down to till and sow[178]
When the calamitous deluge was over,
There still remain the stormy sand gusts to blow.
A wild-miened madman, spreading his hoary hair
In the blasts, what would he do, in face of the river?
The onlookers would heed not what he doeth.
But his own mate up steppeth to stop her man:
"My goodman, cross ye not the river, refrain!
Ye might as well go with a tiger to grapple,
But wade ye not the river torrents main;
If ye be drowned and drifted to some far-off shore,
There'd be giant whales with white teeth like snowy peaks;

公乎公乎挂罥于其间。
箜篌所悲竟不还！”

My goodmam, ye'd be wound up high o'er there.
Just as the zither's plaint sore, — home, no more!"

Tr. June 18, 1983.

李白

春夜宴从弟桃花园序

夫天地者，万物之逆旅也。光阴者，百代之过客也。而浮生若梦，为欢几何！古人秉烛夜游，良有以也。况阳春召我以烟景，大块假我以文章。会桃花之芳园，序天伦之乐事；群季俊秀，皆为惠连；吾人咏歌，独惭康乐。幽赏未已。高谈转清。开琼筵以坐花，飞羽觞而醉月。不有佳咏，何申雅怀？如诗不成，罚依金谷酒数。

Li Bai

Epistolet Inviting My Cousins to a Spring Night Banquet in the Garden of Peach Blossoms

As heaven and earth form the caravansary * of all beings, so one's span of mortality is a transient guest of millenniums. Our floating life is like a dream: how scanty are its joys! That is the reason why there were men of old lighting lanterns to illuminate their night ramblings. Moreover, Spring summons us with her splendid landscape and Nature lends us his brave** masterpiece. Gathering in the fair garden of peach blossoms to exchange our natural brotherly love, we would make a boon company of talented youths. The songs you will sing actuated by your superior gifts would put me your elder cousin to shame. Before the appreciative epithets of the scene would cease, our elevated converse*** would rise to a pure (tenored Lao-Zhuang) metaphysical discourse. Superb banquet would be spread while we sit at the table enjoying the flowers, and winged beakers would be given flight to between one another in sousing while we gaze at the moon. Without subtile writings, how could we express our exquisite feelings? If any one of us fail to compose a poem, three bumpers would fall to his lot by enforcement.

---

* Caravansary: inn with a large inner courtyard where caravans put up in Eastern countries; Khan.

** brave: excellent; splendid.

*** converse: conversation (old use).

李白

金陵歌送别范宣

石头巉岩如虎踞，
凌波欲过沧江去。
钟山龙盘走势来，
秀色横分历阳树。
四十余帝三百秋，
功名事迹随东流。
白马小儿谁家子？
泰清之岁来关囚。
金陵昔时何壮哉！
席卷英豪天下来。
冠盖散为烟雾尽，
金舆玉座成寒灰。
扣剑悲吟空咄嗟，
梁陈白骨乱如麻。
天子龙沉景阳井，
谁歌《玉树后庭花》？
此地伤心不能道，
目下离离长春草。
送尔长江万里心，
他年来访南山皓。

Li Bai

Song of Farewell Sung in Jinling for Fan Xuan

The Rocky Mount its cliffs like a squating tiger[179] doth rear,
O'erlooking the waves as for to cross the river blue.
The chain of Zhong Heights windeth up twisting as a dragon,
To share with the trees of Liyang in their verdant hue.
For autumns three hundred, o'er forty ruling *di*[180],
Their events and glories have all ebbed with the east flowing stream.
The boy astride a white horse tall, — what could he be?[181]
The yielder-rebel in Tai-qing years, of crime extreme.
How fame and honour redound to Jingling's splendid past!
All the renowned and heroic had come to its demesne old.
Now all the lordly and notable are turned into smoke and fog,
Quadrigas golden and chairs of gem have become ashes cold,
I sigh and shout in vain, while striking my sword blade:
Skeletons of Liang and Chen were rank like heaps of cut broom.
The Emperor had sunk down the Jingyang court well[182];
Who was to sing the *Palace Rear Yard Jade-tree Bloom*?
This place is heart-wringing beyond the saying of words;
It is now grown with hanging down, tall weeds of spring;
I see thee off with regret like this River of thousands of *li*;
Let some future year, to see a Hoary Recluse[183], back thee bring.

李白

下终南山过斛斯山人宿置酒

暮从碧山下，
山月随人归。
却顾所来径，
苍苍横翠微。
相携及田家，
童稚开荆扉。
绿竹入幽径，
青萝拂行衣。
欢言得所憩，
美酒聊共挥。
长歌吟松风，
曲尽河星稀。
我醉君复乐，
陶然共忘机。

Li Bai

Descending from Mount Zhongnan[184], Putting Up at the Mountaineer[185] Husi's Lodging and Being Entertained with Drinking

Towards the dusk as I come down from the verdant heights,
The mountain moon is following me closely along.
When I look backwards at the trail just passed through now,
How emerald green beams the mountain-side's sloping lawn!
Encountering my host, I am led to his rustic home;
His youngsters open the brushwood doors with cheer smiling,
The bamboo grove unfoldeth a shade secluded path;
The hanging usnea whorls rustle against the pedestrians'clothing.
With kindly words, I am given bed and offered good fares,
As well as mellow wine in bumpers for toast to raise.
We sing the *Song of Winds into the Pine Forest Blown*;[186]
When we finish, stars in the Silvery Stream[187] grow dim in their gaze.
I become drunk and you go talkative and boon,
We both are set quite free from the bounded ego of our own.

Tr. October 5, 1981.

［唐］ 崔颢

（？—754）

黄鹤楼

昔人已乘黄鹤去，
此地空余黄鹤楼。
黄鹤一去不复返，
白云千载空悠悠。
晴川历历汉阳树，
芳草萋萋鹦鹉洲。
日暮乡关何处是？
烟波江上使人愁。

Cui Hao

(*Tang*, ? —754)

Yellow Crane Tower[188]

The man of fairy lore hath gone
By riding a yellow crane,
So here is but left the tower called
The Yellow Crane by name.
The yellow crane hath flied away
Not to come back again,
For a thousand years there are white clouds
Floating in the blue void main.
The sun on the fair-day river shineth
And on trees of Hanyang Town[189]
The sweet verdure on the Parrot Isle[190]
Is beaming a lush, fresh lawn.
In the setting sun's light where could be
The native pass of the borough?
The smoky spumes on the River's surface
Fill the onlookers with sorrow.

Tr. September 13, 1981.

［唐］ 杜甫

（712—770）

望岳

岱宗夫如何？
齐鲁青未了。
造化钟神秀；
阴阳割昏晓。
荡胸生曾云；
决眥入归鸟。
会当凌绝顶，
一览众山小。

Du Fu

(*Tang*, *712—770*)

Sighting the Great Mount Dai

How is the magnificent Mount Dai[191]?
A boundless mass of green peaks and cliffs
Towering over the states Qi and Lu.
Nature doth summon here Wondrous Beauty;
Thus Light and Shade[192] could divide and part.
The cumulus doth broaden one's breast;
'T would split one's eyelids to watch homing birds.
Some day I must climb up to the top,
To look down viewing all the peaks small.

杜甫

房兵曹胡马

胡马大宛名，
锋棱瘦骨成。
竹批双耳峻，
风入四蹄轻。
所向无空阔，
真堪托死生。
骁腾有如此，
万里可横行。

Du Fu

Chief of Corps Fang's Steed of the Huns

The Hun clans steed of Dayuan fame
    Is stalwart, spare in build,
With ears like whittled bamboo flukes sharp,
    And hoofs wind-bome and -filled.
Where'er it fareth, there's no breadth;
    Your life and death may entrust to it ye,
As, brave and dauntless is it thus,
    Ten thousand *li* it speedeth in a spree.

Tr. May 24, 1984.

杜甫

画鹰

素练风霜起，
苍鹰画作殊。
攫身思狡兔，
侧目似愁胡。
绦镟光堪擿，
轩楹势可呼。
何当击凡鸟，
毛血洒平芜。

Du Fu

A Hawk Portrayed

Frosty winds arise from the sheet of silk white;
Drawn, a hawk is nonpareil, vivacious, true,
Heaving up in perch, with thoughts of hares wild,
Turning eyes aslant, like an ape in deep rue.
Silken cords and metal frame both shine bright,
At the hall pillar whereon the picture is hung.
Would these talons were to thrash ill, vile fowls,
To make their sickly blood and feathers on sod flung.

Tr. May 28, 1984.

杜甫

兵车行

车辚辚，
马萧萧，
行人弓箭各在腰。
耶娘妻子走相送，
尘埃不见咸阳桥。
牵衣顿足拦道哭，
哭声直上干云霄。
道旁过者问行人，
行人但云点行频。
或从十五北防河，
便至四十西营田。
去时里正与裹头，
归来头白还戍边。
边庭流血成海水，
武皇开边意未已。
君不闻汉家山东二百州，
千村万落生荆杞。
纵有健妇把锄犁，
禾生陇亩无东西。
况复秦兵耐苦战，
被驱不异犬与鸡。
长者虽有问，

Du Fu

The Rime of the War-chariots

Rumble the chariots, neigh and snort the horses,
Men of arms with bows and arrows all hung
Dazzlingly athwart their both flanks and hips,
March alongside with parents, wires and children;
Dusts are trampled up, the Xianyang Bridge from sight hid.
Dragging clothes and stamping feet, the files they clutter,
Cries and clamours rising skyward they utter.
Passers-by ask the marching men of their condition;
The raw recruits say incessant is the conscription.
Some from fifteen are drafted north the River to fend,
Till at forty they are sent west border farms to tend.
When departing, ward leaders wound turbans round their heads,
Coming back hoary, they are sent to the borderland.
On the frontiers bloodshed flusheth to form seas of gore;
Emperor Wu yet aimeth his domain to expand.
See you not in the two hundred Han counties east of the Mount,
Thousands of villages and hamlets are choked with brambles and
thorns?
Though there be hardy women to wield the hoes and ploughs,
Corn groweth scattered on plots and in fields devoid of rows.
Since we Qing recruits are inured to hard fought battles,
We are driven to fight like cocks and dogs amain.
Though you elders are concerned to question us,

役夫敢申恨？
且如今年冬，
未休关西卒。
县官急索租，
租税从何出？
信知生男恶，
反是生女好。
生女犹得嫁比邻，
生男埋没随百草。
君不见青海头，
古来白骨无人收。
新鬼烦冤旧鬼哭，
天阴雨湿风啾啾。

How do we conscript men dare to show our bile vain?
Take for instance what is happening this winter.
Not at all is enlisting west of the Passlet free.
Magistrates are pressing for taxes in kind hard;
Where should they come from? What are they to be?
Plain it is, giving birth to boys is a curse,
Not comparable to bearing daughters at all.
Daughters could be married to some neighbours,
Sons would only lie buried under the grasses tall.
See you not on the distant shores of the Blue Sea,
Bones of those who fell down long ago lie bleaching,
New ghosts wail in company with those of old,
Under a dreary sky, rain drizzling and wind screeching.

杜甫

饮中八仙歌

知章骑马似乘船，
眼花落井水底眠。
汝阳三斗始朝天，
道逢曲车口流涎，
恨不移封向酒泉。
左相日兴费万钱，
饮如长鲸吸百川，
衔杯乐圣称避贤。
宗之潇洒美少年，
举觞白眼望青天，
皎如玉树临风前。
苏晋长斋绣佛前，
醉中往往爱逃禅。
李白一斗诗百篇，
长安市上酒家眠，
天子呼来不上船，
自称臣是酒中仙。

Du Fu

Song on the Eight Faeries in Drinking[193]

Zhizhang[194] rideth his horse like sitting aboard on tossing waves;
Dazed in sight and fallen down a well, he dozeth on.
The Prince of Ruyang[195] would attend his Sovereign's morning court
Only after taking three big bumpers of drinks strong;
Meeting wheeled tanks of liquors on the way, saliva would he flow,
Grieved that he is not ordained the fief of Wine Spring.
Li the Left Chancellor[196], spending ten thousand coins daily,
Draweth scores of streams like a giant whale in his drinking,
Relishing cups in these sage times, giving place to Virtue.
Zongzhi[197], lively, refined, the flower of youthful manliness,
Raiseth stoups with his pupils white glinting at the gross common[198],
Turning his sight to the radiant azure, graceful, matchless,
Splendid like a jade tree waving in spree fore heaven's winds.
Su Jin[199] the vegetarian, facing Buddha's portrait,
Oft his dyhana vigils faileth to keep when drunk he be.
Li Bai[200] poureth forth a hundred poems after a quart's weight,
Falling asleep in a public house in Chang'an the chief town,
Waving aside th' Son of Heavens summons to appear,
Saying he himself is a faery in th'realm of spirits.

张旭三杯草圣传，
脱帽露顶王公前，
挥毫落纸如云烟。
焦遂五斗方卓然，
高谈雄辩惊四筵。

Zhang Xu[201], famed as th'*cao* mode calligraphic art's seer,
Taking off his hat after three huge mugs fore th'king and lords,
Waveth brushes across scrolls like flights of smoke and cloud.
Jiao Sui[202] beameth bright after five full horns of liquid fire,
Talking, arguing fervidly, with wonder his company cloth
shroud.

Tr. September 20, 1884.

杜甫

丽人行

三月三日天气新，
长安水边多丽人。
态浓意远淑且真，
肌理细腻骨肉匀。
绣罗衣裳照暮春，
蹙金孔雀银麒麟。
头上何所有？
翠薇盍叶垂鬓唇。
背后何所见？
珠压腰衱稳称身。
就中云幕椒房亲，
赐名大国虢与秦。
紫驼之峰出翠釜，
水精之盘行素鳞。
犀箸餍饫久未下，
鸾刀缕切空纷纶。
黄门飞鞚不动尘，
御厨络绎送八珍。
箫鼓哀吟感鬼神，
宾从杂沓实要津。
后来鞍马何逡巡！
当轩下马入锦茵。

Du Fu

The Lay of the Belles[203]

On the Third Moon's Third Day[204], while fresh is the clime,
On Chang'an's bund, there belles are a good many,
Of graces rich and rare, in virtue, chaste, pure[205],
In flesh and bones, well matched, in aspect, dainty.
Their broidered taffeta vestures shine in late spring,
With gold-thread phoenixes[206] and unicorns[207] in silver.
And what are decked on their comely heads?
With emerald gems, down to temples, of multi-layer[208].
And what are espied behind their backs?
With pearl-studded bands[209], around their waist lines curving.
Amongst them are the doted-on One's sisters fair,
Entitled the State Queens of Han and Guo and Qing[210].
For victuals, they choose camel hump stew in sapphrine jugs,
And shining fish fresh steamed on crystal platters.
Being satiated, they keep held back for long
Their chopsticks of thinoceros's horn, as cutters
Of their maids with tinkling bells[211] bustle about in vain.
The eunuchs let fly their reins without stirring up dust,
The imperial kitchen sending the choice eight with silk nets.
All the pipes and tabours play in concord with gust,
While guests and attendants hustle to their noted alcoves.
And last, up cometh a wavering, saddled horse[212],
Its rider, dismounting at the platform, stalketh

杨花雪落覆白苹，
青鸟飞去衔红巾。
炙手可热势绝伦，
慎莫近前丞相嗔！

By a short front path through the lush shrubs of gorse,
Direct [via the hall] to the brocade-cushioned parlour.
The willow catkins on the marsileas white
Are falling thick; blue birds are making flight
With kerchiefs red in their bills to show amour's troth[213],
His mighty power's hot air could your hands sear;
Beware, come not near, the Chancellor would be wroth.

杜甫

渼陂行

岑参兄弟皆好奇，
携我远来游渼陂。
天地黤惨忽异色，
波涛万里堆琉璃。
琉璃漫汗泛舟入，
事殊兴极忧思集，
鼍作鲸吞不复知，
恶风白浪何嗟及？
主人锦帆相为开，
舟子喜甚无氛埃。
凫鹥散乱棹讴发，
丝管啁啾空翠来。
沉竿续缦深莫测，
菱叶荷花净如拭。
宛在中流渤澥清，
下归无极终南黑。
半陂已南纯浸山，
动影袅窕冲融间。
船舷暝戛云际寺，
水面月出蓝田关。
此时骊龙亦吐珠，

Du Fu

The Lay of Meipi

Fond of wonders are the Cen Shen[(214)] brothers,
Taking me afar for this trip to Meipi[(215)].
Of a sudden heaven and earth their colours change;
Waves torrential heave on th' expanse of a glazy sea.
Boundless swells our barque is tossed by and buoyed up on;
Strange 'tis, grieved am I[(216)] while full excited too:
Alligators in craze and whales in gulp fits
Heed I not; wild gusts, foamy heaves, with me nor ado.
All at once, the chief boatman hoisteth his silken sails,
Right glad is the crew, as blown o'er is the squall,
Scattered are the water fowls, while the boat songs
Ring out loud, the strings and flutes aboard enthrall
All the emerald of the hillsides wide around.
Deep is probed the sounding pole to test in vain;
Leaves of trapa and lotus flowers seem washed clean.
While in midstream, limpid blue is it like the main,
Down 'neath Zhongnan's foot, its mass loometh jet black.
In the southern half of Mei pi is steeped
Deep the shadowed south mount, its wavering image
Silhouetted and fluctuating 'gainst white clouds heaped.
Th' shallop bow, reflected, hitteth th' bonzary
Cloud-girt; a mirrored moon ariseth up Blue Field Pass.
Thereon, ebon dragons spew forth their pearls,

冯夷击鼓群龙趋。
湘妃汉女出歌舞，
金支翠旗光有无。
咫尺但愁雷雨至，
苍茫不晓神灵意，
少壮几时奈老何，
向来哀乐何其多。

As Fengyi, God of Luteous River, his drum of brass
Beateth, to summon them; Xiang queens and Han sprites all appear
Singing and dancing, while golden boughs and green flags
Plumed with king-fisher's feather flash and darken clear.
Swiftly, fear-stricken, I were caught in a thunder-storm:
Unpredictable is the will of divinity.
How could youth retard the approach of old age?
Joy and sorrow fill the sack of infinity!

Tr. March 17, 1984.

杜甫

月夜

今夜鄜州月，
闺中只独看。
遥怜小儿女，
未解忆长安。
香雾云鬟湿，
清辉玉臂寒。
何时依虚幌，
双照泪痕干？

Du Fu

A Moonlight Night[217]

The moon tonight at Fuzhou
Is but seen alone in her chamber.
A pity 'tis to me, so far
Away here, to think our children
Not yet know how Chang'an to remember.
Her cloudy coiffure is moistened
By a mist of odorous flavour;
The moon's fair lustre is cooling
Her gem-hued arms to deliver
A shapely curvature.
I wonder when I'd stand with her
By the gauzy curtain drapery,
To let moon beams shine and quiver
On our teary stains to dry them
Off slowly both together.

Tr. October 30, 1983.

杜甫

春望

国破山河在，
城春草木深。
感时花溅泪，
恨别鸟惊心。
烽火连三月，
家书抵万金。
白头搔更短，
浑欲不胜簪。

Du Fu

Spring Prospects[218]

The state being broken up,
Its mounts and streams remain.
The capital in spring
Doth thickly plants contain.
Aggrieved by the times' events,
On flowers I shed my tears;
With regrets for enforced partings,
The birds' songs stir up my fears.
Midst flares of war for three moons,
Home letters seem a huge sum.
Mine hoary hair's scratched so thin,
This hair pin would slip through the thrum.

Tr. November 11, 1983.

杜甫

羌村三首

一

峥嵘赤云西，
日脚下平地。
柴门鸟雀噪，
归客千里至。
妻孥怪我在，
惊定还拭泪。
世乱遭飘荡，
生还偶然遂。
邻人满墙头，
感叹亦歔欷。
夜阑更秉烛，
相对如梦寐。

Du Fu

Qiang Village[219]

— three poems —

1

Like red cliffs, clouds are towering in the west;
The fiery feet of the sun are stepping on the plain.
On bramble doors the sparrows twitter loud;
The homeward wayfarer his trek's end doth gain.
My mate and young, surprised at my being alive,
Their tears all wipe after moment's daze and stun.
Amidst these turmoils, suffering such disasters,
I've come back; what a chance is this fateful one[220]!
Our neighbours gather crowding atop the walls[221],
Being struck, astounded, heaving sighs in plenty;
All night we spend in candle light till dawn,
Bemused, as each to each in dreams doth pry.

杜甫

二

晚岁迫偷生，
还家少欢趣。
娇儿不离膝，
畏我复却去。
忆昔好追凉，
故绕池边树。
萧萧北风劲，
抚事煎百虑。
赖知禾黍收，
已觉糟床注。
如今足斟酌，
且用慰迟暮。

2

Enforced to live as by stealth in these late years, [222]
I come back home without any much good humour.
My children dear their father's knees seldom leave,
For fear I would soon depart at some late hour.
I could recall how airing I liked in the past[223],
Being used to walk all round the trees by the pond,
While roaringly blew the gusts of northerly winds,
I brooded on all what had happened that made me despond
With hap, the grains are in good time reaped and threshed,
And the wine press is properly worked on for brew.
Now that there would be enough supply of drinks,
For me to console old age and with warmth endue.

杜甫

三

群鸡正乱叫，
客至鸡斗争。
驱鸡上树木，
始闻扣柴荆。
父老四五人，
问我久远行。
手中各有携，
倾榼浊复清。
莫辞酒味薄，
黍地无人耕。
兵革既未息，
儿童尽东征。
请为父老歌，
艰难愧深情。
歌罢仰天叹，
四座泪纵横。

3

On the guest's arrival, the fighting village cocks,[224]
Are crowing one and all in a wild uproar;
They are all driven up to roost on the trees[225],
And then is heard the knocking on the bramble door.
The village elders, four or five of them,
All come for my trek so far-off and long, me to cheer,
They take along with them severally one and all,
And pour out tankards of drinks or turbid or clear,
Apologizing[226] for the wine's sore lack of strength,
For the millet fields are lacking hands to till,
As the punitive draftings are yet continued on,
The boys[227] are all enlisted for the eastward drive still.
"Your kind dear thoughts for me do deeply touch me;
Please let me sing for you, village elders, dear."
When I have finished, facing the sky I heave sighs;
All round me, tears do flush, making all eyes blear.

杜甫

赠卫八处士

人生不相见，
动如参与商。
今夕复何夕，
共此灯烛光。
少壮能几时？
鬓发各已苍！
访旧半为鬼，
惊呼热中肠。
焉知二十载，
重上君子堂？
昔别君未婚，
儿女忽成行。
怡然敬父执，
问我来何方。
问答未及已，*
儿女罗酒浆。**
夜雨剪春韭，
新炊间黄粱。
主称会面难，
一举累十觞。

---

* 问答未及已（一作：乃未已）。
** 儿女（一作：驱儿）罗酒浆。

Du Fu

To the Eighth Wei Brother, the Anchorite

Two friends oft sighting not each other in life,
Are like the stars Antares and Betelgeuse[(228)].
What a night is this serene and gracious one
For us in the gentle candle sheen from cares to break loose!
How long could one remain still young and strong?
Our crown and temporal tufts are growing hoar,
And 'tis known some half of our old friends 've become ghosts,
Distressed and grieving, we exclaim both sore.
How could I know after all these twenty years
I come to visit again your lustrous hall?
When I saw you last, you were not married yet;
Today you are surrounded by girls and boys tall.
In blandness they regards to their elder pay,
Inquiring me whence I do hither hail.
Before the genial converse is drawn to a close,
Your boys and girls afford sweet drinks and cocktail.
Mid even drizzles, they cut odorous allium of spring,
The new-husked rice is cooked with millet choice.
Mine host laying stress on the difficulty of meeting,
Proposeth toasts full then on end to rejoice.

十觞亦不醉，
感子故意长。
明日隔山岳，
世事两茫茫。

301

Du Fu

With stoups full ten I am not yet at all drunk,
Still I thank you heartily for your old time zeal.
Tomorrow we shall be severed again by mount chains
And hosts of mundane matters noisy peal.

杜甫

新安吏

客行新安道，
喧呼闻点兵。
借问新安吏：
“县小更无丁？”
“府帖昨夜下，
次选中男行。”
“中男绝短小，
何以守王城？”
肥男有母送，
瘦男独伶俜。
白水暮东流，
青山犹哭声。
“莫自使眼枯，
收汝泪纵横。
眼枯即见骨，
天地终无情。
我军取相州，
日夕望其平。
岂意贼难料，
归军星散营。
就粮近故垒，
练卒依旧京。
掘壕不到水，

Du Fu

Xin'an Officer[229]

While trudging on the high way toward[230] Xin'an,
One heard the tumult of recruits' roll call.
The chief officer of Xin'an was thus asked:
"Is none of age[231], your district being small?"
"Ordaining that the middle class[232] be listed,
The draughting order yesternight came down."
"The middle ones are still too undersized;
How could they well defend the Royal Town[233]?"
Stout boys were taken leave of by their mothers;
Lean ones, beloved by none, departed alone[234].
As white the stream did eastward flow ere eve,
The verdant hills still echoed with dear ones' moan.[235]
"Let not your eyes be quite exhausted till shrunk;[236]
"Restrain your tears too flushed to over-brimming!
"Your eyes when shriveled would expose their sockets;
"Alack! that Heaven and Earth[237] are void of feeling!
"Our troops imperical aim to take Xiangzhou city;
"By morn or night, we look forth the campaign to win;
"But unexpected are the rebels 'tactics[238],
"And our men are not subject to one supreme discipline[239].
"Yet with food supplies not far away at the base[240],
"Their training center is quite near the capital late[241];
"They'd dig their ditches not deep enough to find water[242];

牧马役亦轻。
况乃王师顺，
抚养甚分明。
送行勿泣血，
仆射如父兄。”

"In grazing horses, their labour is also not great.
"What's more, the cause of our armed might is upright[243],
"Our officers in command are strict yet kind.
"Let those who see the recruits off be not sorely sad;
"The deputy chancellor[244] holdeth you all in his mind."

Tr. February 2, 1985.

杜甫

石壕吏

暮投石壕村，
有吏夜捉人。
老翁逾墙走，
老妇出门看。
吏呼一何怒，
妇啼一何苦！
听妇前致词：
“三男邺城戍，
一男附书至，
二男新战死。
存者且偷生，
死者长已矣。
室中更无人，
惟有乳下孙。
有孙母未去，
出入无完裙。
老妪力虽衰，
且从吏夜归。
急应河阳役，
犹得备晨炊。”
夜久语声绝，
如闻泣幽咽。

Du Fu

The Shihao Officers[245]

At dusk I put up at the hamlet Shihao[246]
Where officers were pressing men to enlist.
An old man fled by clambering the wall;
His wife went forth to answer the front door shouts.
How angry were the officer's mad howls!
How wretched were the woman's plaintive cries!
I heard then what she said in these her words:
"My three sons went to guard the city Ye[247]
Of whom, one sent his message some days ago:
The other two were killed few days before.
The live one is to lead his life by stealth;
The two dead ones are blotted out for good!
There is no one else in this ill-fated room,
But mine infantile, still-its-ma's-milk-sucking grandson,
With its ma staying with me to care for it;
So poor we are, she weareth her skirt in rags.
Although both weak and aged I am by now,
I may still go with you officers to serve,
At the Heyang[248] encounter forth-coming,
For getting ready the breakfast for our troops."
As deep the night grew, she was no more heard;
Beseemeth it that sobs and weeping did sound.

天明登前途，
独与老翁别。

At daybreak forging ahead for my forward trudge,
I bade adieu to the old man alone[249].

Tr. January 9, 1985.

杜甫

潼关吏

士卒何草草，
筑城潼关道。
大城铁不如，
小城万丈余。
借问潼关吏：
“修关还备胡？”
要我下马行，
为我指山隅：
“连云列战格，
飞鸟不能逾。
胡来但自守，
岂复忧西都！
丈人视要处，
窄狭容单车。
艰难奋长戟，
万古用一夫。”
“哀哉桃林战，
百万化为鱼。
请嘱防关将，
慎勿学哥舒！”

Du Fu

Tong Pass[250] Officer[251]

How weary do the rank and file appear,
While building walls along the way to Tong Pass!
The bulwark huge than iron is more stalwart;
The citadel small ten thousand feet doth surpass[252].
The Tong Pass Officer is queried by me:
"Is strengthening the Pass still[253] to ward off the Tartars?"
I am then asked to dismount and look around,
Being shown about the verge of the peaks sparse:
"Up high in the clouds are ranged the palisades[254],
Which fleeting birds cannot even fly across.
Whene'er the Tartars come, but keep on guard,
Be care free from the western capital's[255] loss
Look thither, Sir, at those strategic straits,
Precipitous and narrow, single cart's tracks;
By wielding a long-shafted halberd[256] strong,
A hardy warrior could repel all attacks."
"Alas! the calamitous Taolin defeat[257],
When our men, a million, earthworms to fish became.
Please charge our generals in guard of the Pass,
To follow Geshu's example, never aim!"

Tr. February 14, 1985.

杜甫

新婚别

兔丝附蓬麻，
引蔓故不长：
嫁女与征夫，
不如弃路旁。
结发为妻子，*
席不暖君床。
暮婚晨告别，
无乃太匆忙。
君行虽不远，
守边赴河阳。
妾身未分明，
何以拜姑嫜？
父母养我时，
日夜令我藏。
生女有所归，
鸡狗亦得将。
君今往死地，
沉痛迫中肠。
誓欲随君去，
形势反苍黄。
勿为新婚念，

* 结发为妻子（一作：君妻；又作子妻）。

Du Fu

Parting after Nuptials

The dodder cleaving to the raspberry
And flax[259], its tendrils cannot thus be long;
To marry off one's girls to wayfarers
Is worse than casting them off the wayside along.
To be thy mate and wife fore'er and aye,
I share with thee thy bed not till'tis warm.
Our nuptials erst by eve and parting at morn, ——
To our union, is it not like thunder and storm?
Although thou goeth away not very far,
To guard the border and at Heyang quite near,
My station[260] here at home is not yet plain;
How shall I hold my in-laws[261] to be mine dear?
My parents reared me with solicitous care,
Safe-guarding me from touch with tricks of ill fate[262].
A girl once born would finally home by her lot;
She hath to nestle on her wedlock ultimate[263].
Since thou art now on the way to peril of death,
Sore pain is wringing hard mine heart and bowels!
Though I swear to follow thee where thou art going,
The shape of things preventeth my wish with scowls.
So mind thee not our new, dear cherished wedding,

努力事戎行。
妇人在军中，
兵气恐不扬。
自嗟贫家女，
久致罗襦裳。
罗襦不复施，
对君洗红妆。
仰视百鸟飞，
大小必双翔。
人事多错迕，
与君永相望！

But pay good heed to the warfare going on.
To have in the camps enlistees feminine,
The troops' morale would perhaps be soddened down.
I sigh for being a girl of a family poor;
It taketh me long to sew these stuffed clothes silken;
But padded garments of silk I stop to wear,
And for thy sake, I rouge and powder shun.
In looking up, I see all birds that fly;
Those large and small must hover by twos and twos.
Our human affairs are often wretched, awry;
But I look forward to be with thee, my spouse[264]!

Tr. March 17, 1985.

杜甫

垂老别

四郊未宁静，
垂老不得安。
子孙阵亡尽，
焉用身独完？
投杖出门去，
同行为辛酸。
幸有牙齿存，
所悲骨髓干。
男儿既介胄，
长揖别上官。
老妻卧路啼，
岁暮衣裳单。
孰知是死别，
且复伤其寒。
此去必不归，
还闻劝加餐。
土门壁甚坚，
杏园度亦难。
势异邺城下，
纵死时犹宽。
人生有离合，
岂择盛衰端？
忆昔少壮日，

Du Fu

Parting during Declining Years[265]

The suburbia[266] from chaos not yet free,
A man thus cannot peace enjoy while old.
With offspring all in battles fallen and gone,
Why need a wretched man his life to hold?
In throwing off his staff and leaving home,
He hath his compeers all for him feel sorry.
Though being lucky to have his teeth intact,
He's sad his marrow hath been shrunk and dry.
Since the man hath put on helmet and coat-of-mail,
He hath to salute his superior and depart.
His old helpmate by road side doth lie and wail,
As the year is drawing to close and sore is her heart
He knoweth well this is their death –parting nonce,
And grieveth her clothes too thin for the sharp chill.
This parting will have certainly no return,
Yet he is told to increase his daily meals still.
The fort of Tu-men[267] hath been strongly built,
And Apricot Orchard Town[268] is hard to pass through,
As things are not like the City of Ye's break-up,
Though I'd end in death, yet that I'd go to slow.
When Fate hath destined a couple to go apart,
One cannot choose between or youth or age.
Recalling all those peace-blest days of yore,

迟回竟长叹。
万国尽征戍，
烽火被冈峦。
积尸草木腥，
流血川原丹。
何乡为乐土，
安敢尚盘桓！
弃绝蓬室居，
塌然摧肺肝。

One could but sigh and dote on that parted stage.
Now that encounter and fortressing are rampant,
War flames o'er all the chain of mounts are flaring.
The corpses have left grass lands and woods all rank,
The streams and plains are all dyed gory by bleeding
Ah! where is to be found the land of bliss?
Why should I hesitate and linger on!
So, let me give up this humble thatched cottage,
And torn asunder is my heart anon.

Tr. April 7, 1985.

杜甫

无家别

寂寞天宝后，
园庐但蒿藜。
我里百余家，
世乱各东西。
存者无消息，
死者为尘泥。
贱子因阵败，
归来寻旧蹊。
久行见空巷，
日瘦气惨凄。
但对狐与狸，
竖毛怒我啼！
四邻何所有？
一二老寡妻。
宿鸟恋本枝，
安辞且穷栖。
方春独荷锄，
日暮还灌畦。
县吏知我至，
召令习鼓鼙。
虽从本州役，
内顾无所携，

Du Fu

Parting sans a Home[269]

Lorn and blighted since the Tian-bao Period,
Gardens, cottages, all grow lush with wild weeds.
O'er a hundred families of my homeland
Have been scattered all about by the rebel deeds.
Those who are living are without tidings,
Others that are dead have become dust and clay.
Piteous, poor me, back from Xiangzhou's bad rout,
Come I here to trace mine used past life's way.
After a long walk, reaching an empty lane, where
Beams of the sun are scant, the air is dreary,
I see foxes two and three, all staring,
Bristling their hair in wrath and screeching at me.
What are there, in the neighbourhood all around thither?
One or two old wives now widowed, reft of hope.
Nestling birds all cherish twigs of their own nests;
People could not but choose to live in their used scope.
During this springtide tillage, I wield the hoe alone;
Toward sun down, I water the vegetable patch small.
Just then having heard of my returning home,
The *Xian* officer summoneth me with a call
To drill the draftees as their corporal drummer.
Though enlisted am I now locally in this state,
There is no one, nor a home for me to part from;

近行止一身，
远去终转迷。
家乡既荡尽，
远近理亦齐。
永痛长病母，
五年委沟溪。
生我不得力，
终身两酸嘶。
人生无家别，
何以为蒸黎！

Going far off, I hold no hope of homing late.
As home and native land are all wiped clean off,
There is no difference 'twixt what's far and what's near.
Ever heart-broke, mourn I my long ill mother,
Five years since, she died in poverty sheer.
Birth she did give me, yet to her 'tis of no avail,
To her, as to me, bitter it proveth ever.
Now that one hath not even a home to part from,
How could one the lot of a subject suffer?

Tr. April 18, 1985.

杜甫

佳人

绝代有佳人，
幽居在空谷。
自云良家子，
零落依草木。
关中昔丧乱，
兄弟遭杀戮。
官高何足论？
不得收骨肉。
世情恶衰歇，
万事随转烛。
夫婿轻薄儿，
新人美如玉。
合昏尚知时，
鸳鸯不独宿；
但见新人笑，
那闻旧人哭？
在山泉水清，
出山泉山浊。
侍婢卖珠回，
牵萝补茅屋。
摘花不插发，
采柏动盈掬。

Du Fu

The Beauty[270]

A peerless beauty there doth reside
In a solitary abode in a dell.
She sayeth she erst came of high birth,
But haplessly by the woods here doth dwell.
Within the Pass[271] there was unrest;
My brothers have been ruthlessly killed.
Their station high was of no avail;
Their mortal remains are not buried as willed.
The ways of the world dislike ill-luck;
All things decline and bear fate to hem.
My goodman is a light, fickle one;
His new mated bride is fair like a gem.
The rose mallows[272] their time all know;
The mandarin ducks roost not alone.
He seeth his new won bride's smile sweet,
But heareth not the old one's sad groan.
The mountain springs are clear and pure;
When they flow outward, turbid they grow.[273]
Her maid, returning from selling her pearls,
Is mending the thatch with ivy bough.
She plucketh flowers not to deck her hair,
But filleth cypress leaves her palms'scoops all.

天寒翠袖薄，
日暮倚修竹。

In this chill air with green sleeves thin,
She leaneth at dusk on a bamboo tall.

Tr. June 16, 1985.

杜甫

梦李白两首

一

死别已吞声，
生别长恻恻！
江南瘴疠地，
逐客无消息。
故人入我梦，
明我长相忆。
恐非平生魂，
路远不可测。
魂来枫林青，
魂返关塞黑。
君今在罗网，
何以有羽翼？
落月满屋梁，
犹疑照颜色。
水深波浪阔，
毋使蛟龙得。

Du Fu

Two Poems on Dreaming of Li Bai[274]

1

Severance by death is choking in sorrow;
Parting during lifetime grieveth one deep!
South of the River hath been pestilence stricken;
Exiles there are scanter of news than tide neap.
Mine old friend my dream did enter last night;
Plain it is for I thought of him in earnest.
Doubt I harbour, it be your soul ethereal;
Far off, I know not it is your spirit manifest.
Your soul cometh afar hither from where maples are green,
Whither you'd go back from here full of passes black.
Now that you are caught in coiled nets intricate,
How could you fly hither fleetly on wings with knack?
The setting moon's sheen is spread on the beams of my room;
Vivid mien of his seemeth still shined upon clear.
Deep is the flood and broadly the huge waves upheave;
Watch out, let not sharks and dragons to you come near.

杜甫

二

浮云终日行，
游子久不至。
三夜频梦君，
情亲见君意。
告归常局促，
苦道来不易。
江湖多风波，
舟楫恐失坠！
出门搔白首，
若负平生志。
冠盖满京华，
斯人独憔悴！
孰云网恢恢？
将老身反累。
千秋万岁名，
寂寞身后事。

2

Clouds afloat are drifting along all day long;
So our wanderer cometh not back us to see.
Dreams I had of you for three nights on end;
Plain it is how your feelings are for me.
So reluctant was your farewell bidding mode,
Saying how thus difficult 'twas for you to come:
Bodies of waters are oft swept by winds and squalls,
Boating trips are then too apt to be troublesome.
Scratching his hoary head the while, he my door left,
As if having failed to fulfill his cherished will.
Hatted high officials(275) throng the capital;
Such a fine man alone is wretched yet still!
Who sayeth Heaven's law of justice kindly be?
Verging to age, he's tormented yet by ill hap!
Fame immortal is to be his future lot;
Lonelily would he enjoy it across the eternal gap.

杜甫

赠李白

秋来相顾尚飘蓬，
未就丹砂愧葛洪。
痛饮狂歌空度日，
飞扬跋扈为谁雄？

Du Fu

For Li Bai[276]

Since the coming of autumn, we both do still wander in vain,
Availing ourselves nought with cinnabar to follow Gehong;
Why with drinkings hard and singings wild to spend days,
Do you fly defiant and haughty, for whom be so high-flown?

Tr. October 30, 1985.

杜甫

月夜忆舍弟

戍鼓断人行，
边秋一雁声。
露从今夜白，
月是故乡明。
有弟皆分散，
无家问死生。
寄书长不达，
况乃未收兵。

Du Fu

Longing for My Younger Brothers[277] in a Moolight Night

The garrison's curfew drums have cleared the streets;
An autumn brant is heard in its border-flight screams.
The crystal dews are chilling from tonight forth;
Our moon at home is solely brighter in its gleams.
My brothers all are scattered wide o'er the land;
I have no home now to know of their life and death.
All messages sent astray could reach them nought,
Whenas the campaign is still in its full breadth.

Tr. January 31, 1985.

杜甫

江村

清江一曲抱村流，
长夏江村事事幽。
自来自去堂上燕，*
相亲相近水中鸥。
老妻画纸为棋局，
稚子敲针作钓钩。
但有故人供禄米，**
微躯此外更何求？

* 自来自去堂（一作：梁）上燕。
** 但有故人供禄米（一作：多病所须惟药物）。

Du Fu

Riverside Village[278]

A curve of limpid stream embracing round doth flow;
   In this long summer day's bank village all is quiet.
The swallows come and go by themselves high up in my hall;
   The gulls on the water bill and coo with love beset.
Mine elderly mate draweth lines on paper for a checkerboard;
   Our little boy striketh a needle to make a fishing hook.
If there but be old friends to supply me their office rice,
   What doth my humble self care, for something else to look?

杜甫

狂夫

万里桥西一草堂，
百花潭水即沧浪。
风含翠筱娟娟净，
雨浥红蕖冉冉香。
厚禄故人书断绝，
恒饥稚子色凄凉。
欲填沟壑惟疏放，
自笑狂夫老更狂。

Du Fu

The Crazy Man[279]

A thatched cot lieth in th'west of Ten-thousand-*li* Bridge[280],
By th' Multiflorous Pond[281] that's my clear Canglang[282] Stream.
While breezes cherish dainty bamboo pipes green and cute,
The lotus blooms pink, imbued with sprinkles, scent sweet and gleam.
The letters of a friend with heavy sovran bestowals[283] cease to come;
Mine ever hungry children's faces grow drear and sad.
To be starved to death and be thrown to th'canyons, one should be defiant[284];
I laugh at myself while getting old being e'er more mad[285].

杜甫

客至

舍南舍北皆春水，
但见群鸥日日来。
花径不曾缘客扫，
蓬门今始为君开。
盘飧市远无兼味，
樽酒家贫只旧醅。
肯与邻翁相对饮？
隔篱呼取尽余杯。

Du Fu

Arrival of a Guest[286]

Enfolded in the north and south with spring bourns,
From my thatched hall I see the gulls* by day.
My flower paths have not been swept for guests;
These shrub-strung doors are opened first on your way.
My victuals are plain, for I stay away from town;
This stoup of wine, as I'm poor, is an old brew.
Care ye to drink with the good old neighbour of mine?
I'll ask him to come and share our residue.

Tr. September 8, 1983.

* See note (106) of Li Bai's poem *Song on the River*(《江上吟》)

杜甫

春夜喜雨

好雨知时节，
当春乃发生。
随风潜入夜，
润物细无声。
野径云俱黑，
江船火独明。
晓看红湿处，
花重锦官城。

Du Fu

Glad at Raining in a Spring Night

Gracious raining knoweth its timely season,
  Down it cometh promptly during springtide.
Following breezes it slinketh by at nightfall,
  Things to soothe, minutely, mutely to bide.
Topping wild paths, clouds amass to loom black.
  Lights on a river barque alone do shine bright.
Look ye by dawn wherever red and moistened,
  Flowers blow the Brocade-robed Officials' Town with delight.

Tr. November 18, 1983.

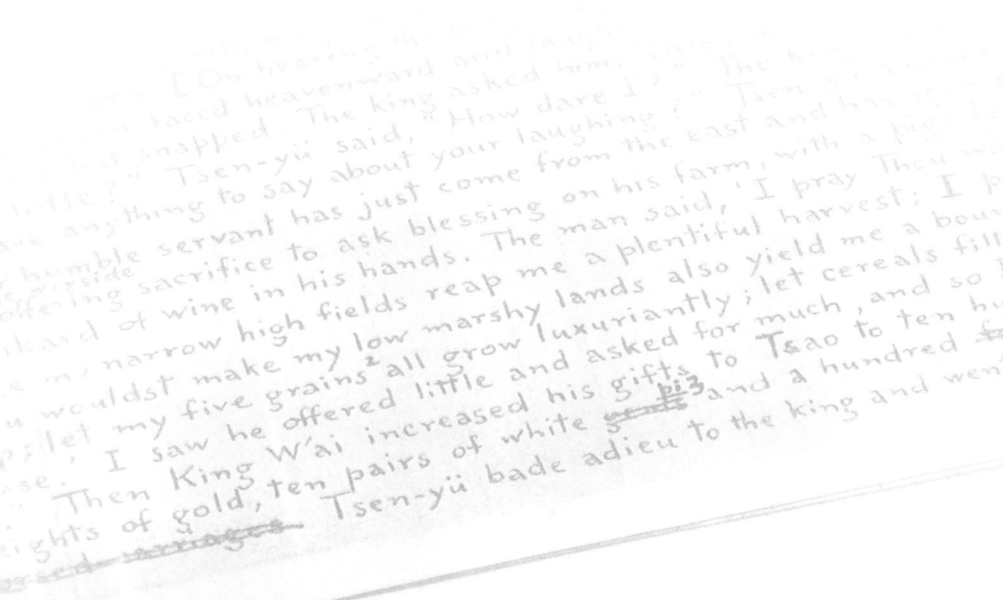

杜甫

茅屋为秋风所破歌

八月秋高风怒号，
卷我屋上三重茅。
茅飞渡江洒江郊，
高者挂罥长林梢，
下者飘转沉塘坳。
南村群童欺我老无力，
忍能对面为盗贼。
公然抱茅入竹去，
唇焦口燥呼不得，
归来倚杖自叹息。
俄顷风定云墨色，
秋天漠漠向昏黑。
布衾多年冷似铁，
娇儿恶卧踏里裂。

Du Fu

Song on My Cottage Being Broken by Autumnal Blasts[287]

The autumnal vault of heaven is arching high
  As September's blasts are roaring loud;
They blow away the three fold layers of reeds
  That the bulrush thatch of my house enshroud.
The reeds are blown across the river flow
  And scattered along the waterside;
Some masses hung up high as caught atop
  A number of brush wood brambles by the tide,
While others whirled and flung low down to float
  Or, submerged in ponds and stuck in mires, lay.
A pack of the southem village urchins taking
  Advantage of mine old age and decay,
Are brazen enough to play the brigands bold;
  They barefacedly snatch up and speed away
The bunches of reeds into the bamboo groves thick,
  Despite mine hoarse exhorting 'gainst their tricks;
So I could but come back to lean on my cane
  And heave vain sighs and cry alack!
Ere long the blasts are blown over and still,
  The blue dome is covered with clouds jet black.
My cloth bed quilt, after many years of use,
  Is cold and hard like an iron sheet,

床头屋漏无干处，
雨脚如麻未断绝。
自经丧乱少睡眠，
长夜沾湿何由彻？
安得广厦千万间，
大庇天下寒士俱欢颜，
风雨不动安如山！
呜呼，
何时眼前突兀见此屋，
吾庐独破受冻死亦足！

Being kicked and stamped to be full of holes by my boys
   In their naughtly sleep and dreams with feet.
On my bed the drips of rain leak down from the roof
   Like tufts of hemp incessant and fleet.
Ever since the rebel uprising, I have been
   Devoid of calm and restful sleep.
When would this chilly, wet and dolorous night
   Come to its end at a bright, fair peep?
How could there be great hosts of mansions broad
   To shelter and cheer up scholars all over,
Where they may live as calmly as mountain tops,
   With nor wind blasts nor drips to deter!
Alas!
If all of a sudden appeareth such a sight,
Then, mine hut be broken and I be frozen to death,
I would take that as of little concern and light.

Tr. October 20, 1983.

杜甫

三绝句

（选一）

殿前兵马虽骁雄，
纵暴略与羌浑同。
闻道杀人汉水上，
妇女多在官军中。

Du Fu

A Quatrain on the Crimes of the Court Brigades[288]

Although the warriors of the court are brave,
They ravage and debauch no less than our hated foes.
Well known to all are their murders on the Han Stream,
And women are rounded up by them as camp whores.

杜甫

绝句四首
（选一）

两个黄鹂鸣翠柳，
一行白鹭上青天。
窗含西岭千秋雪，
门泊东吴万里船。

Du Fu

A Quatrain

Two yellow orioles atop th' green willows sing,
A row of egrets white ascends the sky pale blue.
My casement frames th' west mounts capped with perennial snow,
Outdoors my house are moored ships thousands of *li* from East Wu.

Tr. April 13, 1981.

杜甫

绝句二首

一

迟日江山丽，
春风花草香。
泥融飞燕子，
沙暖睡鸳鸯。

Du Fu

Two Quatrains[289]

1

Under the slowly moving sun,
  The streams and hills with beauty abound;
As blown by breezes of the sparkling spring,
  All flowers and herbs sweet scents spread around.
The clay erst frozen waxing soft now,
  Is pecked by swallows their nests to make;
The sandy bank of the ait being warm,
  Along it paired mandarin ducks dozes take.

Tr. June 18, 1981.

二

江碧鸟愈白，
山青花欲然。
今春看又过，
何日是归年？

2 (A)

The river being blue, all the more
  The water fowls look dazzlingly white.
The hills lie verdant stretching along,
  The flowers on them are burning bright.
It seems this spring ere long would be gone,
  As the last several ones, once more;
Alas, what day would it be then,
  As I wish to be at home so sore?

2 (B)

— The variant version of this poem —

The River blue doth make the fowls look whiter;
The hillock green doth show its flowers burning.
This spring appeareth to have passed its prime;
When shall be the year I could go home, returning?

Tr. June 18, 1981.

杜甫

禹庙

禹庙空山里，
秋风落日斜。
荒庭垂橘柚，
古屋画龙蛇。
云气生虚壁，
江声走白沙。
早知乘四载，
疏凿控三巴。

Du Fu

Yu's Temple[290]

In Great Yu's temple up high in th' vacant mounts,
Autumnal wind on th' slanting sun's shine blows;
In its desolate court aloft hang citrus fruits;
On th'walls are spread the dragons and snakes frescoes.
While clouds are issuing out of hollowed crags,
Th' resounding river waves on th' white sands roll.
Well known it has been, he rode the four vehicles[291],
To conduct and dig, for the Three Ba's control.

Tr. November 30, 1983.

杜甫

秋兴八首

一

玉露凋伤枫树林，
巫山巫峡气萧森。
江间波浪兼天涌，
塞上风云接地阴。
丛菊两开他日泪，
孤舟一系故园心。
寒衣处处催刀尺，
白帝城高急暮砧。

二

夔府孤城落日斜，
每依北斗望京华。
听猿实下三声泪，
奉使虚随八月槎。
画省香炉违伏枕，
山楼粉堞隐悲笳。
请看石上藤萝月，
已映洲前芦荻花。

Du Fu

Eight Octaves on Autumnal Musings[292]

1[293]

Chill, crystal dews have seared the maple woods,
The aura of the Wu Mounts and Gorges is drear.
While waves of the flood upheave against the sky,
Dense wind –swept clouds unfurl to shroud the peaks sheer.
Chrysanthemums have bloomed twice with my tears of the past,
To a single boat are cleaving my thoughts nostalgic.
The need of winter garments is urgent all round,
In Bai Di aloft, the eve laundry clubbings sound thick.

2[294]

When the sun inclineth west at Kuizhou the lone town,
I use to yearn for the capital neath the Great Bear.
With tears bedewed at three sad wails of gibbons,
In vain I aim on the raft toward heaven to repair.
Prevented by illness the secretariat to attend,
By the Mountain tower's limed wall I list the pipe sorry.
Please look at the moon beams cast on the wisteria o'er the stones,
Reflecting their light on th'isle rush flowers hoary.

三

千家山郭静朝晖，
日日江楼坐翠微。
信宿渔人还泛泛，
清秋燕子故飞飞。
匡衡抗疏功名薄，
刘向传经心事违。
同学少年多不贱，
五陵衣马自轻肥。

四

闻道长安似弈棋，
百年世事不胜悲：
王侯第宅皆新主，
文武衣冠异昔时。
直北关山金鼓震，
征西车马羽书驰。
鱼龙寂寞秋江冷，
故国平居有所思。

3 (295)

In the thousand homes' mount town in morn sun calm,
For days I view aloft the rolling green;
While night after night the fishing boats float along,
To and fro autumn swallows flit about in the scene.
Like Kuang Heng, I dissented but thus fare ill;
Following Liu Xiang's example, I yet fail in mine aim:
As my fellow students of yore with joy do thrill,
Those favoured ones all prosper in wealth and fame.

4 (296)

I've heard that things in Chang'an are like chess games;
Its events these tens of years are seethed with sorrow.
The princely, noble mansions have new masters;
All civil and martial chiefs are none of years ago.
Right north from passes of mounts, reports of fights din;
The messages of westward campaigns in fights do flee. —
Like fish and dragons, neath autumn river cold,
I think of my native soil as an absentee.

五

蓬莱宫阙封南山，*
承露金茎霄汉间。
西望瑶池降王母，
东来紫气满函关。
云移雉尾开宫扇，
日绕龙鳞识圣颜。
一卧沧江惊岁晚，
几回青琐点朝班。

六

瞿塘峡口曲江头，
万里风烟接素秋。
花萼夹城通御气，
芙蓉小苑入边愁。
珠帘绣柱围黄鹄，
锦缆牙樯起白鸥。
回首可怜歌舞地，
秦中自古帝王州。

---

* 蓬莱宫阙封（一作：对）南山。

5[297]

The Penglai palatial mansions face the South Mounts;
A Golden Pillar riseth upright toward the sky.
High up from Gem Pool in the west, descendeth Dame Wang;
From th' east a purple aura the Han Pass doth sanctify.
Like clouds the fans of pheasant-tail plumes move to ope;
Dawn beams on the dragon robe reveal His mien. —
Lying by neath the flood, I am surprised 'tis so late;
How oft I was roll-called at the portal carved in green.

6[298]

The Jutang Gorge mouth and Zigzag River bank,
Though far apart, are joined in autumn's war fires.
From Flower-sepals Tower, led th' imperial path;
To Hibiscus Garden, went sad news of border pyres.
An alighting swan would be enclosed by towers;
While gulls in flight would be startled by masts and riggings.
But look back! what a pity is the site of dance and song;
This old terrain is from ages past the land of our kings.

七

昆明池水汉时功，
武帝旌旗在眼中。
织女机丝虚月夜，*
石鲸鳞甲动秋风。
波漂菰米沉云黑，
露冷莲房坠粉红。
关塞极天唯鸟道，
江湖满地一渔翁。

八

昆吾御宿自逶迤，
紫阁峰阴入渼陂。
香稻啄馀鹦鹉粒，
碧梧栖老凤凰枝。
佳人拾翠春相问，
仙侣同舟晚更移。
彩笔昔曾干气象，
白头吟望苦低垂。

* 织女机丝虚月夜(一作:夜月)。

7 (299)

The Kunming Lake's expanse was dug in Han;
Its flags and banners of Wu-*di* appear still waving.
That Shuttle Girl applieth not moonlit nights;
A jade whale its fins in autumn wind seem wafting.
The zizania fluttered by waves are dense like clouds;
The lotus cupules shivered by dews withered are. —
The clift pass so precipitous is but birds'path;
A fisherman lone and lorn, I have wandered far.

8 (300)

The way through Kunwu and Yusu circuitous is;
Via Purple Pavilion Peak's shade, one reacheth Meipi.
The grains of fragrant rice are by parrots' pecks left;
Firmiana branches green, long by phoenixes perched be.
Fair youths in springtide outing, gifts exchange;
Companions fairy share their boats till deep in night. —
In the past, my pictorial brush hath touched his Grandeur;
Expecting, sighing, now I bend my inclined head white.

杜甫

阁夜

岁暮阴阳催短景，
天涯霜雪霁寒宵。
五更鼓角声悲壮，
三峡星河影动摇。
野哭千家闻战伐，
夷歌数处起渔樵。
卧龙跃马终黄土，
人事音书漫寂寥。

Du Fu

Pavilion Night[301]

Toward th' close of th' year, the sun and moon
　Shorten the span of daylight high;
At the horizon, frost and snow
　Reflect their sheen on th' chill night sky.
Fore th' peep of dawn, the horns and drums
　Are sounding sad, heroic in air.
The starry Stream as mirrored in
　The Triple Gorges doth flutter and flare.
Thousands of families, mourning, wail
　In th' wild for th' loss of their dear and young.
The wood cutters and fishermen
　Of several parts, folk songs have sung.
The Lying Dragon, th' Galloping Horse,
　Are all now buried neath the soil;
With my relations and tidings severed,
　A shadow am I, a flimsy foil.

杜甫

登高

风急天高猿啸哀，
渚清沙白鸟飞回。
无边落木萧萧下，
不尽长江滚滚来。
万里悲秋常作客，
百年多病独登台。
艰难苦恨繁霜鬓，
潦倒新停浊酒杯。

Du Fu

Ascending a Height

Wind gusts blow fast, heaven's vault archeth high
  And the gibbons screech sadly to cry;
The ait looketh clear, the sands spread white
  And birds to and fro fly.
The boundless crop of autumnal leaves
  Are rustling ceaselessly down;
The endless streams of the Long River
  Are rolling forever on.
As a wanderer for ten thousand *li*
  I mourn these days of late fall;
Arising on this terrace all alone,
  I think of my sickly days livelong.
I hate these hard times increasing daily
  My temple locks of frost hoar.
I have just renounced my stoup, sodden
  With troubles and frailties sore.

Tr. August 9, 1981.

杜甫

观公孙大娘弟子舞剑器行

大历二年十月十九日，夔府别驾元持宅，见临颍李十二娘舞剑器，壮其蔚跂，问其所师，曰："余公孙大娘弟子也。"开元五载，余尚童稚，记于郾城观公孙氏舞剑器浑脱，浏漓顿挫，独出冠时，自高头宜春梨园二伎坊内人，洎外供奉，晓是舞者，圣文神武皇帝初，公孙一人而已。玉貌锦衣，况余白首，今兹弟子，亦匪盛颜。既辨其由来，知波澜莫二，抚事慷慨，聊为《剑器行》。往者吴人张旭，善草书

Du Fu

A Song on Watching Lady Gongsun's Disciple in Her "Rapier Thrusting and Fencing" Dance

Proem: — On the 19th of the tenth moon in the second year of Da-li, [302], at the mansion-house of Yuanchi, the deputy sheriff of Kuizhou [303], I saw the sword dance of Li the Twelfth Lady of Linying. Being struck by the magnificent spectacle, I asked her about the master of her art. She said, "I am Lady Gongsun's disciple." Early in the fifth year of Kai-yuan [304], I was still a child. Then, I remember, in the *xian* Yancheng, I had the hap to watch Gongsun's sword-pyrrhic dance, whirling, forceful and fraught with thythmical grace, quite out of the common; from the two inner-court dancing troupes Yichun and Liyuan [305] to the outer-court one. Among the *danseuses* and men-dancers conversant with this dance, during the early years of our Sage-artistic and Holy-militant Emperor [306], Gongsun was the sole select person. Reminiscent of her jade-like countenance and brocaded raiment, [I could not hope to see her again, while] I myself have become hoary-headed today; now even her disciple is no more like her then in the bloom of her youth. Tracing the source of my present spectacle, I see the mistress and her disciple are surprisingly equal in their impeccable arts. Dwelling feelingly on such foot-prints of Time, I compose herewith the song below on this unforgetable event. In the past, Zhang Xu [307] of Wu, noted for his *cao*

帖,数常于邺县见公孙大娘舞西河剑器,自此草书长进,豪荡感激,即公孙可知矣。

昔有佳人公孙氏,
一舞剑器动四方。
观者如山色沮丧,
天地为之久低昂。
㸌如羿射九日落,
矫如群帝骖龙翔。
来如雷霆收震怒,
罢如江海凝清光。
绛唇珠袖两寂寞,
晚有弟子传芬芳。
临颍美人在白帝,
妙舞此曲神扬扬。
与余问答既有以,
感时抚事增惋伤。
先帝侍女八千人,
公孙剑器初第一。
五十年间似反掌,
风尘澒洞昏王室。
梨园子弟散如烟,
女乐余姿映寒日。
金粟堆前木已拱,
瞿塘石城草萧瑟。

mode of calligraphy, having many a time observed in Ye *xian* Lady Gongsun perform the Xihe sword dance, became therefrom excelling in his callingraphic art. Since Zhang's mastery of his talents was due to the influence exerted on him by her dancing graces, the beauties of her art itself can readily be imagined.

There was a lady fair by the name of Congsun,
Whose wondrous "Fencing" dance spread her fame far and near.
Her spectators crowded round like mountain crags,
Astounded all while heaven and earth hailed with cheer.
Like Yi[(308)] in a flash having nine suns shot down,
Like godheads driving dragons swiftly along,
She cometh like thunder-claps withdrawing their wrath,
And pauseth like streams and seas with their glory on.
Her red-lipped songs and pearl-sleeved dances mute and still,
Of late her disciple continueth her splendid grace.
The spirited Linying beauty from Baidi Town
Performeth this song with dance her mistress to trace.
In our exchange of words having learnt the source,
I dwell on past events thoughtful of each case.
Among the hundreds of court troupe artistes fair,
Gongsun's "Fencing" dance ranked certes the very first.
For fifty years as in turning over one's palm,
The vast sand storm[(309)] hast on the ruling house burst.
The court troupe members have all dispersed like smoke,
But one bright star still sparkleth in the cold air.[(310)]
The mausoleum trees[(311)] have now grown tall,
In the stone-walled town[(312)] at Jutang the grasses are bare.

玳弦急管曲复终，
乐极哀来月东出。
老夫不知其所往，
足茧荒山转愁疾。

375

Du Fu

The strings and pipes with the song are ended and mute,
The rapture over as sadness bideth with the moon.
Being an aged man I know not where to wend,
As with foot corns and for tramping rocky paths
Of mountains wild, I grieve to leave too soon[313].

Tr. October 29, 1981

杜甫

登岳阳楼

昔闻洞庭水，
今上岳阳楼。
吴楚东南坼，
乾坤日夜浮。
亲朋无一字，
老病有孤舟。
戎马关山北，
凭轩涕泗流。

Du Fu

Ascending Yueyang Tower[314]

Th' expanse of Dongting's waters[315] long I've heard;
Today I ascend the Yueyang Tower to command.
The states Chu and Wu were here south-easterly split;
All heaven and earth by day and night seem its strand.
My kith and kin a single word send me not;
I feel both aged and ill on this sole boat.
Our border legions line up north of the Pass Mount[316];
By the tower window, my tears stream forth as by rote.

Tr. February 13, 1984.

杜甫

蜀相

丞相祠堂何处寻？
锦官城外柏森森。
映阶碧草自春色，
隔叶黄鹂空好音。
三顾频烦天下计，
两朝开济老臣心。
出师未捷身先死，
长使英雄泪满襟。

Du Fu

Chancellor of Shu[317]

The Memorial Hall of the Chancellor — where is its site to be found?
Beyond th' walls of Jinguan Town, a cedar old riseth there thickset and tall.
The fresh verdure of th' lawn reflecteth on the steps vernal hues by itself;
In the foliage chanteth in vain[318] the golden oriole's tuneful call.
Being visited thrice and then ofttimes conferred on affairs of statecraft,
In installing and propping up two reigns as their adamantine support,
You in person the state's corps dispatch led, but died before triumph could be won:
It doth make all our heroes, for mourning your noble cause, to tears e'er resort.

杜甫

对雪

战哭多新鬼，
愁吟独老翁。
乱云低薄暮，
急雪舞回风。
瓢弃樽无绿，
炉存火似红。
数州消息断，
愁坐正书空。

Du Fu

Facing Snowing[319]

Hosts of the ghosts of the fall'n in the battle are bewailed for;
Sadly doth sing all alone by himself an old wretched man.
Masses of the cloud bank are hanging low down o'er the rising dusk;
Rapidly drifted, the snow flakes are dancing and swirl as van.
Laid aside hath been my gourd shell and vacant my mug[320] remaineth;
Idle hath become the existing but sick stove as if in glow.
Several states are all severed in tidings[321] the meanwhile;
Sitting alone in lorn grief, I could but with "huh!" the air sow.

Tr. June 5, 1984.

杜甫

旅夜书怀

细草微风岸，
危樯独夜舟。
星垂平野阔，
月涌大江流。
名岂文章著？
官应老病休。
飘飘何所似？
天地一沙鸥。

Du Fu

Thoughts Durning My Night Travel[323]

Slim sedges are fluttered by a gentle breeze on the bank;
A mast ariseth sheer in my lone night barque.
The stars hang sparkling o'er the plain's broad expanse,
The moon is silvering the River's waves dark.
My name of note is not just to my letters[324] due.
Mine office relieved, for illness and old age dull.
To fluff now here, then there, what am I like?
'Twixt heaven and earth, a mere sandy beach gull.

［唐］ 岑参

（约 715—770）

碛中作

走马西来欲到天，
辞家见月两回圆。
今夜未知何处宿，*
平沙莽莽绝人烟。**

---

* 今夜未（一作：不）知何处宿。

** 平沙莽莽（一作：万里）绝人烟。

Cen Shen

(*Tang*, *715—770*)

Lines Written in the Desert

Riding ever westwards as if for the sky,
Twice I saw the moon wax full all along.
I know not where I shall put up for the night,
Ever and aye the sands extend and extend on.

Tr. April 24, 1981

[唐] 张继
(? —?)

枫桥夜泊

月落乌啼霜满天，
江村渔火对愁眠。*
姑苏城外寒山寺，
夜半钟声到客船。

* 江村(一作:枫)渔火对愁眠。

Zhang Ji

(*Tang* ? —?)

Night Mooring at Fengqiao Village

The moon is sinking; a crow croaks a-dreaming;
'Neath the night sky the frost casts a haze;
Few fishing-boat lights of th' river side village
Are dozing off in their mutual sad gaze.
From the Cold Hill Bonzary outside
The city wall of Gusu town,
The resounding bell is tolling its clangour
At midnight to the passenger ship down.

［唐］　韦应物

（约 737—约 791）

滁州西涧*

独怜幽草涧边生，
上有黄鹂深树鸣。
春潮带雨晚来急，
野渡无人舟自横。

* 这首诗很优美，但有一缺点，黄鹂不会在傍晚的雨中鸣唱。上两句不能同下两句连在一起。

Wei Yingwu

(*Tang*, 737? —791?)

The Mountain Stream in the West of Chuzhou*

Alone I fondly find rich meadow spread
On the bank of the mountain stream;
High up above an oriole is singing
In the tree's thick foliage;
Spring tide with rains flows fast before evening falls;
A boat alongside the ferry wild by itself lies.

* This poem is very beautiful. The defect, however, is that orioles never sing in the evening rains. The first two lines, therefore, are scarcely possible to form into one with the next two.

［唐］ 卢伦

（748—约799）

塞下曲二首

一

林暗草惊风，
将军夜引弓*。
平明寻白羽，
没在石棱中。

二

月黑雁飞高，**
单于夜遁逃。
欲将轻骑逐，
大雪满弓刀。

---

* 此句中将军指李广。汉文帝、景帝时人，击匈奴有功，善射。

** 塞下寒冬，雁早已南飞，何来高飞之雁？“雁飞高”三字应改为“朔风号”。

Lu Lun

(*Tang*, *748—799?*)

Borderland Tunes

1

In the forest dark the weeds by wild gusts were shocked;
The general* drew hard his mighty bow.
Early next morn the feathered arrow is found;
Stuck deep in a rock cleft on a boulder low.

2

The moon is hidden dark; The boreas roars.
The khan has fled windward in the night northwards.
We think of chasing him with a light mounted force;
Blinding snow falls all o'er our bows and swords.

Tr. February 13, 1981.

* The general alludes to Li Cuang(李广), who served the three dynasties of Wen-*di*(文帝), Jing-*di*(景帝) and Wu-*di*(武帝) of the Han Dynasty. He was a terror to the Hun renowned for his mighty, accurate shooting.

［唐］ 孟郊

(*751—814*)

游子吟

慈母手中线，
游子身上衣。
临行密密缝，
意恐迟迟归。
谁言寸草心，*
报得三春晖？

* 谁言寸草心（一作：谁知寸心草。）

Meng Jiao

(*Tang*, *751—814*)

The Wandering Son's Song

The thread from my dear mother's hand
Was sewn in the clothes of her wandering son.
For fear of my belated return,
Before my leave they were closely woven.
Who says mine heart like a blade of grass
Could repay her love's gentle beams of spring sun?

Tr. August 21, 1982.

[唐] 崔护
(? —831)

题都城南庄

去年今日此门中,
人面桃花相映红。
人面不知何处去,*
桃花依旧笑春风。

* 人面不知(一作:只今)何处去。

Cui Hu

(*Tang*, ? —*831*)

In the Capital's Southern Village

On this same day last year within this door, *
A comely face and peach blooms together did glow.
She I've admired has gone I know not where,
Th' peach blooms are smiling still in th' breeze to blow.

Tr. April 27, 1981.

* Brushed on a Cottage Door in the Capital's Southern Village.

［唐］ 常建

（？—？）

题破山寺后禅院

清晨入古寺，
初日照高林。
曲径通幽处，
禅房花木深。
山光悦鸟性，
潭影空人心。
万籁此俱寂，
惟余钟磬音。

Chang Jian

(*Tang*, ? —?)

On the Rear Dhyana[325] Hall of Po Shan Bonzary[326]

When at dawn I repaired[327] to the bonzary old,
The first beams of the rising sun shone on trees tall.
Winding paths led to covert[328], secluded[329] groves[330]
Where lush thicket and flowers enclosed th' dhyana hall.
The rare[331] aura[332] of the mount pleased the nature of the birds,
Images in rock pit pools freed one's mind's ups and downs.[333]
All the hubbubs[334] of men were hushed as by a spell:[335]
There was nothing left but the bell's and *qing*'s clangs[336].

Tr. May 24, 1980.

常建

宿王昌龄隐居

清溪深不测，
隐处唯孤云。
松际露微月，
清光犹为君。
茅亭宿花影，
药院滋苔纹。
余亦谢时去，
西山鸾鹤群。

Chang Jian

Putting Up at Wang Changling's Hermitage*

The limpid stream floweth unfathomably deep,
  In solitary clouds is enshrouded the quiet hut.
Through the dense pine leafage peepeth down the shaded moon,
  Whose crystalline beamings for thy pure sake illume.
By the bulrush-thatched arbour sleep the flower shadows,
  In the court where peonies bloom deep green moss groweth
    thick.
In this vacant air, I too become released from the world,
  Befriending phoenixes and storks of the western hills.

Tr. August 18, 1981.

* 此诗译者曾有意要修改,后因年事已高,未能如愿。——编者

［唐］ 韩愈

（763—824）

石鼓歌

张生手持石鼓文，
劝我试作石鼓歌。
少陵无人谪仙死，
才薄将奈石鼓何？
周纲陵迟四海沸，
宣王愤起挥天戈。
大开明堂受朝贺，
诸侯剑佩鸣相磨。
搜于岐阳骋雄俊，
万里禽兽皆遮罗。
镌功勒成告万世，
凿石作鼓隳嵯峨。
从臣才艺咸第一，
简选撰刻留山阿。
雨淋日炙野火烧，
鬼物守护烦撝呵。
公从何处得纸本？
毫发尽备无差讹。
辞严义密读难晓，
字体不类隶与蝌。

Han Yu

(*Tang*, *763—824*)

The Lay of the Stone Drums

With the inscription of the Stone Drums in his hand,
Sire Zhang urged me to make a song of them.
Du Fu is gone and the exiled faery[(337)] no more;
Being poor in gift, what could I do with the Drums?
The sceptre of Zhou sank low and chaos bore sway;
Xuan-*wang*[(338)] then arose to draw his heavenly sword.
He won and held court to receive homage and hurrah;
His vassals thronged, their sabers jostled and sang.
They gathered at Qiyang[(339)] to vie in splendour;
Games thousands of *li* around were hunted to repast.
Thus the feat was carved to tell all ages to come,
After stones were quarried from heights and these were hewn, —
Attendant courtiers, masters of letters and of art,
Were chosen to compose and brush the work, —
And thence ten blocks were left by the mountain side.
Rains drenched; the sun scorched and wild fire burned round them;
May spirits guard them all along from harm!
Where do you, Sire, get these paper rubbings from,
The gross and minutiae all here, full-formed and clear?
Bearing words strict and sense close, but hard to ken,
The type of character is not *li* nor *ke*[(340)].

年深岂免有缺画？
快剑斫断生蛟鼍。
鸾翔凤翥众仙下，
珊瑚碧树交枝柯。
金绳铁索锁钮壮，
古鼎跃水龙腾梭。
陋儒编诗不收入，
二雅褊迫无委蛇。
孔子西行不到秦，
掎摭星宿遗羲娥。
嗟余好古生苦晚。
对此涕泪双滂沱。
忆昔初蒙博士征，
其年始改称元和。
故人从军在右辅，
为我量度掘臼科。
濯冠沐浴告祭酒，
如此至宝存岂多？
毡包席裹可立致，
十鼓只载数骆驼。
荐诸太庙比郜鼎，
光价岂止百倍过？
圣恩若许留太学，
诸生讲解得切磋。
观经洪都尚填咽，
坐见举国来奔波。
剜苔剔藓露节角，
安置妥帖平不颇。

Old in years, might not the script lose some strokes now?
There, water-dragons[341] and hog-dragons are slashed;
Bright phoenixes hover round and faeries descend;
Green jade and coral trecs intertwining grow;
Gold rope with cord of iron twist to a knot;
A bronze tripodal vessel jumps out of water, …
Ignored by ribald scholars in garnering poetry,
The two *yas* included not poems of stately size[342].
Confucius traveling westward entered not Qin[343].
In raising stars to the sky he missed Xi and E?
Too late, alas! was I born an antiquary,
For this I must let flow two streams of tears,
I recall when I first donned the doctor's robe,
That year our lord had his reign named Yuan-he[344];
A friend commanding troops right of Chang'an[345],
Had thought of digging for me the precious remains.
I washed my hat and bathed to tell those in power.
Such priceless treasure does not exist often.
In felt and mat they could be quickly wrapped,
Ten Drums may be laden on not many camels.
Compared with trophies[346], in the Temple Imperial,
Exceeds not the worth of these a hundredfold?
If our good lord let them be laid in the College,
What fruits could pupils under tuition then reap!
To see the show of classics at Hongdu[347],
The whole country did rush to throng the town.
When scraped of moss and lichen, showing their tendons,
These could be securely placed, even on the ground;

大厦深檐与盖复，
经历久远期无佗。
中朝大官老于事，
讵肯感激徒媕婀。
牧童敲火牛砺角，
谁复著手为摩挲？
日销月铄就埋没，
六年西顾空吟哦。
羲之俗书趁姿媚，
数纸尚可博白鹅。
继周八代争战罢，
无人收拾理则那。
方今太平日无事，
柄任儒术崇丘轲。
安能以此上论列？
愿借辩口如悬河。
石鼓之歌止于此，
呜呼吾意其蹉跎！

'Neath gable-roof deep and held in structure big,
They will pass through long ages without mishap.
High officials old in dealing with the world,
Not thankful at all, prefer to hesitate.
Thus, cowboys strike for fire, horns oxen sharpen;
Who'd touch and rub them ever with loving care?
They daily, monthly, weather-worn, in clay sunk,
For six years I looked to the west and sighed to naught.
The common brush-work charming of Xizhi.
On a few sheets of paper could yet win him white geese(348).
When warfare for eight dynasties since Zhou stilled,
Why is it none cares to put these in goodly order?
Now peace has come to stay, nothing disturbs;
To the fore comes learning, revered are Qiu and Ke(349).
How could the reasons just named convince someone,
As to start an eloquent tongue flow river waves?
The Lay of the Stone Drums here draws to a close,
Alas! I fear time will be lost, but in vain.

Tr. April 27, 1974.

［唐］ 刘禹锡

（772—842）

陋室铭

山不在高，有仙则名；水不在深，有龙则灵。斯是陋室，惟吾德馨。苔痕上阶绿，草色入帘青。谈笑有鸿儒，往来无白丁。可以调素琴，阅金经。无丝竹之乱耳，无案牍之劳形。南阳诸葛庐，西蜀子云亭：孔子云，何陋之有？

Liu Yuxi

(*Tang*, *772—842*)

An Eulogium on a Humble Cell

A mount needs not be high; it becomes noted when on it fairies dwell.

A body of water needs not be deep; it would be ensouled, if a dragon makes it its resting whereabouts.

This hut of mine is a humble one, but I make it virtuously fragrant in repute.

The green moss creeping on the stepping stones and the verdure in the courtyard peeping through the screen do tell the presence of spring.

Here could be heard the table-talks and laughters of renowned scholars, but the rough and gross come not hither their wares to sell.

Here plain table-heptachord could be plucked and golden classics read the worldly cares to quell.

But there are without riotous strings and pipes to confuse the ears, and tedious official documents to ring quietude's knell.

Zhuge's recluse cottage at Nanyang and Yang Xiong's hermit arbour in West Shu, — according to Confucius, wherefore could either one of them be branded as a humble cell?

Tr. August 17, 1980.

刘禹锡

秋词

自古逢秋悲寂寥，
我言秋日胜春朝。
晴空一鹤排云上，
便引诗情到碧宵。

Liu Yuxi

Autumnal Song

Since of yore fall is grieved as lone and vacant,
Methinks autumnal days excel the spring morn.
A crane ascends through the clouds to the radiant sky,
Leading poetic thoughts to the boundless azure.

Tr. May 2, 1981.

刘禹锡

竹枝词

山桃红花满上头，
蜀江春水拍山流。
花红易衰似郎意，
水流无限似侬愁。

Liu Yuxi

Bamboo Twig Song

Peach blooms on the mountain slopes in full flush blow,
The River's spring streams along the rocky banks flow.
The flowers pink would easily fade like thy love,
The endless currents would rush on like my sorrow.

Tr. May 4, 1981.

刘禹锡

乌衣巷

朱雀桥边野草花，
乌衣巷口夕阳斜。
旧时王谢堂前燕，
飞入寻常百姓家。

Li Yuxi

Black Coat Lane[350]

Wild nameless flowers by the Cinnabar Bird Bridge
Are aglow in the last sun-beams in the Black Coat Lane.
The swallows 'fore the Wang and Xie noble mansions
Now fly into the nobodies' homestalls.

Tr. May 7, 1981.

刘禹锡

石头城

山围故国周遭在，
潮打空城寂寞回。
淮水东边旧时月，
夜深还过女墙来。

Liu Yuxi

Stone-walled City[351]

A chain of hills surrounds the capital old,
The tides the empty city beat and mutely ebb.
The old-time moon on the east side of the Huai Stream,
In the depth of night still crosses the low parapet.

Tr. May 5, 1981.

［唐］ 白居易

（772—846）

草

离离原上草，
一岁一枯荣。
野火烧不尽，
春风吹又生。
远芳侵古道，
晴翠接荒城。
又送王孙去，
萋萋满别情。

Bai Juyi

(*Tang*, *772—846*)

Grasses

Tall and hanging down, the grasses on the wide plain
Flourish and wither once in every year.
Wild fire could not burn them up to extirpate,
Springtide zephyrs blow and they come to life again.
Distant verdure overcometh ancient highways,
Fair-day emerald stretcheth away to waste cities.
Bidding farewell to wanderers going somewhither,
Lush-growing grasses waft in the breeze full of parting cares.

Tr. August 25, 1981.

［唐］ 柳宗元

（773—819）

与浩初上人同看山，寄京华亲友*

海畔尖山似剑芒，
秋来处处愁断肠。**
若为化得身千亿，
散上峰头望故乡。

* 寄京华亲友（一作：故）。

** 秋来处处愁断（一作：割愁）肠。

Liu Zongyuan

(*Tang*, *773—819*)

On Sighting the Mounts with the Bonze Haochu, Lines Written to My Kin and Friends in the Capital

Shrill, seaside peaks like poniards pointing skywards
In this fall day evevywhere my sad bowels pierce.
How could I be turned into a million selves
To be scattered on to those tops to descry my homeland?

Tr. April 26, 1981.

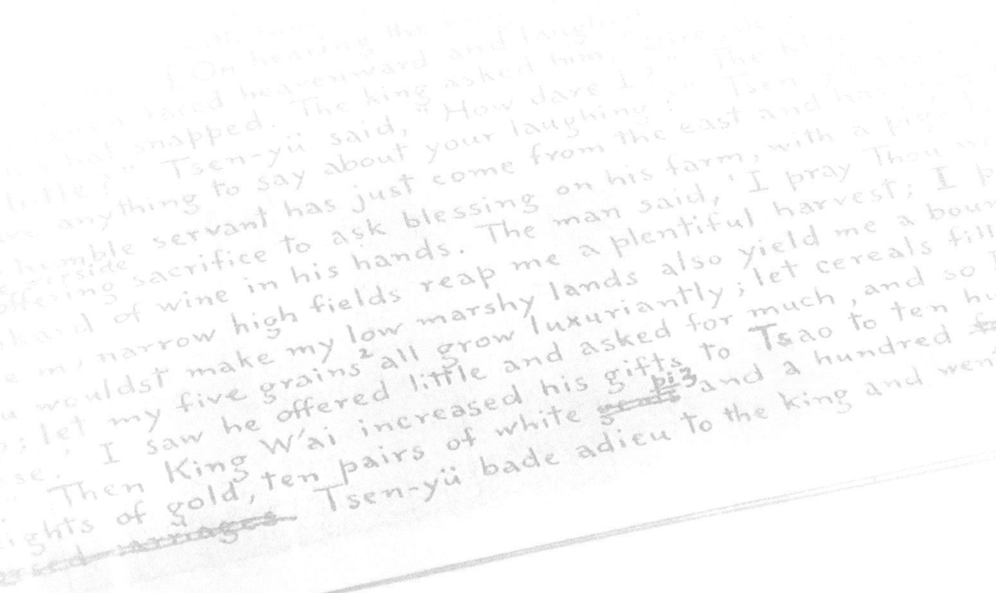

柳宗元

溪居

久为簪组累，
幸此南夷谪。
闲依农圃邻，
偶似山林客。
晓耕翻露草，
夜榜响溪石。
来往不逢人，
长歌楚天碧。

Liu Zongyuan

Abiding by the Runlet[352]

For long being entangled by ties of office,
I sense fine hap as an exile to the wild South.
In my leisurely sojourn with farming neighbours,
I feel I am somewhat like a mountain sylvan.
In daybreak tillage upturning dewy weeds,
In nightly row resounding oar strokes from bank rocks,
I come and go without meeting anyone,
And sing aloud 'neath the azure sky of Chu.

Tr. November 16, 1981.

柳宗元

江雪

千山鸟飞绝，
万径人踪灭。
孤舟蓑笠翁，
独钓寒江雪。

Liu Zongyuan

Snowing on the River[353]

Not a bird o'er the hundreds of peaks,
Not a man on the thousands of trails.
An old angler alone in a boat,
With his rod and line, in raining outfit,
Is fishing on the river midst th' snowdrift.

Tr. December 14, 1980.

柳宗元

渔翁

渔翁夜傍西岩宿，
晓汲清湘燃楚竹。
烟消日出不见人，
欸乃一声山水绿。
回看天际下中流，
岩上无心云相逐。

Liu Zongyuan

The Angler*

The angler passing his night by the West Mount,
Some limpid water from the Xiang Stream drawn,
Doth kindle bamboo stems verdant to heat at dawn,
The smoke being dispersed the sun arising,
He is seen not; the scull "*ai-nai*" doth sound, —
A green expanse show the water and the mount;
A skiff from above descendeth down the midstream;
About the crags the carefree clouds rush round.

Tr. November 25, 1981

* From the original 楚竹(bamboos of Chu), we know this poem was written during the poet's exile to Yongzhou(永州).

［唐］ 贾岛
(779—843)

寻隐者不遇

松下问童子，
言师采药去。
只在此山中，
云深不知处。

Jia Dao

(*Tang*, *779—843*)

A Call on the Recluse Who Is Just Out

I asked the boy beneath the pine tree,
  Who said, "The master's gone herbs to pick;
He must be some where around these clifts,
  Concealed unseen in the clouds thick".

Tr. May 27, 1981.

［唐］ 张祜

（约 785—约 852）

集灵台

虢国夫人承主恩，
平明骑马入宫门。
却嫌脂粉污颜色，
淡扫蛾眉朝至尊。

Zhang Hu

(*Tang*, *785*? —*852*?)

Jiling Terrace[354]

The fair State Queen of Guo, in favour supreme,
At full ope dawn doth ride in the palace gate;
For disliking rouge and powder to daub her beauty,
She leaveth her eyebrows light, to tend on the potentate.

Tr. February 23, 1985.

［唐］ 杜牧

(*803—853*)

山行

远上寒山石径斜，
白云生处有人家。
停车坐看枫林晚，
霜叶红于二月花。

Du Mu

(*Tang*, *803—853*)

Mountain Trip

Far up the mountainside the stone trail wound,
Where the clouds were thick, there stood some abodes.
I stopt my cart to watch the maple forest late
With frost-bitten leaves more crimson than spring blooms.

Tr. April 16, 1981.

杜牧

赠别

多情却似总无情，
唯觉樽前笑不成。
蜡烛有心还惜别，
替人垂泪到天明。

Du Mu

Lines in Bidding Adieu

Moved with lorn cares yet appearing placid,
We feel not like changing smiles at our stoups,
But the candle is thoughtful of our parting,
Shedding tears all night long till the peep of dawn.

Tr. June 18, 1981.

杜牧

清明

清明时节雨纷纷，
路上行人欲断魂。
借问酒家何处有，
牧童遥指杏花村。

Du Mu

The Clear-and-Bright Feast[355]

Upon the Clear-and-Bright Feast of spring
　The rain drizzleth down in spray.
Pedestrians on country-side ways
　In gloom are pining away.
When asked "Where a tavern fair for rest
　Is hereabouts to be found",
The shepherd boy the Apricot Bloom Vill
　Doth point to afar and say.

Tr. May 24, 1981.

杜牧

边上闻胡笳

何处吹笳薄暮天？
塞垣高鸟没狼烟。*
游人一听头堪白，
苏武曾经十九年。**

* 狼烟，烧狼粪的烟，即烽烟。据说这种烟直往上升，风吹不斜，所以被边塞地区用作报警信号。

** 苏武，汉武帝派往匈奴的使节，匈奴单于要他投降，他不屈服，被送到北海牧羊十九年。他历尽艰辛困苦，始终不忘自己是汉朝使者，表现出崇高的民族气节。诗人赞叹他的坚贞志节。

Du Mu

Hearing Tartar Clarinet on the Border

Whence is blown the clarinet at sunset?
Border mountain parapets 'neath a high bird
Hideth wolf dung smoke columns from one's sight.
Visitors hearing it would have their hair turned white.
For nineteen years all along, Su Wu had this heard!

［唐］ 温庭筠

（约 812—866）

瑶瑟怨

冰簟银床梦不成，
碧天如水夜云轻。
雁声远过潇湘去，
十二楼中月自明。

Wen Tingyun

(*Tang*, *812? —866*)

Plaints from the Gemmed Harp[356]

On the cool mat of woven bamboo strips,
　In a silver framed bed, dreamless I lie.
The azure sky is like flooding water
　And the clouds of night float lightly in the sky.
The cries of wild geese sound afar
　Toward the Xiao and Xiang Streams' valleys.
In the twelve Storeyed Houses of the faerie land[357]
　The moon shineth brightly [o'er the galleries].

［唐］ 李商隐

（约 813—约 858）

乐游原

向晚意不适，
驱车登古原。
夕阳无限好，
只是近黄昏。

Li Shangyin

(Tang, 813? —858?)

The Gladdening Upland[358]

Toward eve, troubled I feel,
So drive my cart to the Old Plain.
How wondrous looks the sundown!
What a pity 'tis nearing dusk.

Tr. June 28, 1981.

李商隐

夜雨寄北

君问归期未有期，
巴山夜雨涨秋池。
何当共剪西窗烛，
却话巴山夜雨时。

Li Shangyin

Lines Sent to the North Written during Night Rains[359]

Being asked for my home-coming date,
I tell thee I'm not sure when that'll be,
As night rains on the mounts of Ba fall
And autumn pools are brimmed from the lea.
Then we shall by the west window sit,
Clipping the candle wick in some night,
And talk of the night rains on th' Ba mounts,
When I think of thee with mute delight.

Tr. June 20, 1981.

李商隐

嫦娥

云母屏风烛影深，
长河渐落晓星沉。
嫦娥应悔偷灵药，
碧海青天夜夜心。

Li Shangyin

Chang'e[(360)]

High mica screens illumed in flashes
  By flickering lights of candles tall;
The Silvery Stream * beginning to fade
  And the Morning Star to fall.
Chang'e should now sorely regret
  For stealing the herb of fay,
So she hath to face all alone the blue sky
  And the sea immense night and day.

Tr. June 24, 1981.

* The Milky Way.

［唐］ 韩偓

（约 842—923）

自沙县抵龙溪县，值泉州军过后，村落皆空，因有一绝

水自潺湲日自斜，
尽无鸡犬有鸣鸦。
千村万落如寒食，
不见人烟空见花。

Han Wo

(*Tang*, *842*? —*923*)

Villages Deserted after the March of Troops

The streams still flush and the sun still slants,
All cocks and dogs are mute, but still croak the crows.
All the villages seem to keep the Cold Repast;[361]
No people could be seen, but merely flowers.

［宋］ 苏轼
（1037—1101）

前赤壁赋

壬戌之秋，七月既望，苏子与客泛舟游于赤壁之下。清风徐来，水波不兴。举酒属客，诵明月之诗，歌窈窕之章。少焉，月出于东山之上，徘徊于斗牛之间。白露横江，水光接天。纵一苇之所如，凌万顷之茫然。浩浩乎如冯虚御风，而不知其所止；飘飘乎如遗世独立，羽化而登仙。于是饮酒乐甚，扣舷而歌之。歌曰："桂棹兮兰桨，击空明兮溯流光，渺渺兮予怀，望美人兮天一方。"

Su Shi[362]

(Song, 1037—1101)

A Fu[363] on the Red Cliffs[364]
(The Fore Piece)

In the autumn of the year[365] Ren-xu, on the day after the seventh full moon, Su-*zi*[366] boated [on the River[367]] with some guests below the Red Cliffs. The zephyrs breathed softly, and the waves heaved not. He poured wine for his guests, reciting the poem *The Bright Moon*[368] and singing the stanzas of "Our virgin maid debonair".[369]

A little later, the moon rose above the eastern heights and loomed between the Dipper and the Ox. Translucent dews fell on the River; the reflection of water touched the sky. Let the board go afloat by itself, let it ride the ten thousand acres of waves [as far as to the horizon]; it was like going on the top of the void and giving the wind the reins to go whither they wish and one knows not whereto, fluttering, as it were, like having bidden farewell to this world and become a winged being of the faerie.[370] Then, taking a drink and being transported with joy, Su-*zi* tapped on the bow and sang a song which goes like this:

"Laurel boat and sandal-wood[371] oars
    Beat the empty light, pierce the sheen;
Shoot my feelings out of my bosom,
    Eye I the Beauty[372] across the serene."

客有吹洞箫者，倚歌而和之，其声呜呜然，如怨如慕，如泣如诉，余音嫋嫋，不绝如缕，舞幽壑之潜蛟，泣孤舟之嫠妇。

苏子愀然，正襟危坐而问客曰："何为其然也？"客曰："'月明星稀，乌鹊南飞'，此非曹孟德之诗乎？西望夏口，东望武昌，山川相缪，郁乎苍苍，此非孟德之困于周郎者乎？方其破荆州，下江陵，顺流而东也，舳舻千里，旌旗蔽空，酾酒临江，横槊赋诗，固一世之雄也。而今安在哉！况吾与子渔樵于江渚之上，侣鱼虾而友麋鹿，驾一叶之扁舟，举匏樽以相属；寄蜉蝣于天地，渺沧海之一粟，哀吾生

[Meanwhile,] one of the guests who, playing on the pipe in tune with the song, seemed to whistle sighs of complaining and yearning, moans and mutterings against wrongs, with a lingering note continuous like a thread. It was like a water-dragon, dancing in a deep dell, or a widow weeping in a solitary boat. Su-*zi*, changed in looks, setting a-right the fold of his gown and sitting bolt upright, asked him who sounded this tune(373), "How is it that it's like this?" The guest answered,

"'The moon is bright, the stars are sparse,
The ravens ebon are flying southerly.'(374)

Isn't this Cao Mengde's poem?

Looking westward, facing Xiakou(375),
Looking eastward, facing Wuchang(376), —
Round the mountains twists the River, —
One sees a deep blue haze is drawn.

Isn't this where Mengde got enmeshed by the young Zhou? When he broke through Jingzhou,(377) put off from Jiangling(378) and sailed east-ward down the stream, his gigantic arks trailed for a thousand *li*, his oriflammes and standards shaded the sunlight, he splashed libation onto the waves(379) [to the Spirit of the River] and laid athwart his tall lance to compose poetry. At that moment, he was indeed the lord of his time. But where is he now, oh, where? Furthermore, you and I cast nets and chop coppice on the islet, take fishes and shrimps as our companions and befriend the deer and the elk, ride on the waves in this leaf of a light boat and raise the pot to fill each other's stoup, and lead our beings like mites between heaven and earth, tiny as a grain of millet in the blue deep. I lament the transcience of our lives and

之须臾，羡长江之无穷，挟飞仙以遨游，抱明月而长终；知不可乎骤得，托遗响于悲风。”

苏子曰：“客亦知夫水与月乎？逝者如斯，而未尝往也；盈虚者如彼，而卒莫消长也。盖将自其变者而观之，则天地曾不能以一瞬，自其不变者而观之，则物与我皆无尽也，而又何羡乎！且夫天地之间，物各有主，苟非吾之所有，虽一毫而莫取。惟江上之清风，与山间之明月，耳得之而为声，目遇之而成色，取之无禁，用之不竭，是造物者之无尽藏也，而吾与子之所共适。”

客喜而笑，洗盏更酌。肴核既尽，杯盘狼藉。相与枕藉乎舟中，不知东方之既白。

admire the infinity of the River, wish to hold on the waist of a flying fairy to wander a-breast with him up and down the empyrean and to clasp the luminous moon in my bosom through all eternity, but knowing that such things could not be done at all in a trice, so I gave my residual tune an anguishing tone."[(380)]

Su-*zi* then said to him, "Does my guest know of the water and the moon? 'What is vanishing like this'[381] has not really gone at all. What waxes and wanes like that has actually increased or decreased not a whit. For if one looks into the heart of change, our heaven and earth cannot last a twinkle. If one looks into the soul of fixity, things and 'I myself' are all infinite. So, why should one admire [the River]? Besides, between heaven and earth, things all have their masters. If that something is not mine, not the least bit I would take of it. Only the clear winds on the River and the bright moon round the mountains, one's ears get them as sounds and one's eyes meet it as colour. One may take them as one lists, for there is no prohibition, or use them as one pleases, since they could not be exhausted. They are the boundless store of nature, and you and I are now enjoying them."[(382)]

The guest smiled in gladness [on hearing this], and the dishes[(383)] were washed for further drinking. The victuals, fruits and nuts were all eaten; the cups and plates looked unseemly. The company lay asleep pillowing one another in the boat, without knowing the dawn had become white in the east.

Tr. May 21, 1974.

苏轼

后赤壁赋

是岁十月之望，步自雪堂，将归于临皋，二客从予过黄泥之坂。霜露既降，木叶尽脱，人影在地，仰见明月；顾而乐之，行歌相答。已而叹曰："有客无酒，有酒无肴，月白风清，如此良夜何？"客曰："今者薄暮，举网得鱼，巨口细鳞，状似松江之鲈，顾安所得酒乎？"归而谋诸妇，妇曰："我有斗酒，藏之久矣，以待子不时之需。"于是携酒与鱼，复游于赤壁之下。江流有声，断岸千尺。山高月小，水落石出。曾日月之几何，而江山不可复识矣！

Su Shi

A Fu on the Red Cliffs
(The Hind Piece)

On the day of the tenth full moon that year, walking from Snow Hall[(384)] to retum to Lingao,[(385)] I crossed the Yellow Clay Incline[(386)] in company with two guests. Hoar frost had fallen down; leaves of the woods were all shed. Our shadows were cast on the ground; above, the moon was over the head. We were glad of the sight; hummed songs one another led.[(387)]

After a while, I sighed and said, "With guests and without wine, or with wine and without victuals, with the moon white and the winds clear, what is to be done with this excellent night." One of my guests said, "At dusk today we drew a net and got some fish, large in mouth and tiny in scale, looking like the perch of Song-*jiang*[(388)]. But where is wine to be got?" I went home to consult my spouse. She said, "I have a *dou* of wine stored up long ago, waiting for your untimely need." So, we took along our wine and fish to go aboating again beneath the Red Cliffs.

The River flow resounded with a noise; the broken banks were a thousand feet tall; the water fell low and rocks jutted out; the peaks were steep and the moon looked small. The days and months gone by had not been many, but the River and the mounts were beyond recognition.

予乃摄衣而上，履巉岩，披蒙茸，踞虎豹，登虬龙，攀栖鹘之危巢，俯冯夷之幽宫。盖二客不能从焉。划然长啸，草木震动，山鸣谷应，风起水涌。予亦悄然而悲，肃然而恐，凛乎其不可留也。反而登舟，放乎中流，听其所止而休焉。

时夜将半，四顾寂寥。适有孤鹤横江东来，翅如车轮，玄裳缟衣，戛然长鸣，掠予舟而西也。须臾客去，予亦就睡。梦一道士，羽衣蹁跹，过临皋之下，揖余而言曰："赤壁之游乐乎？"问其姓名，俯而不答。"呜呼！噫嘻！我知之矣！畴昔之夜，飞鸣而过我者，非子也耶？"道士顾笑，余亦惊寤。开户视之，不见其处。

I then hitched the folds of my drapery and trod on the precipice, pushed apart the weeds and briars, squatted on, rose above and clambered upon the dens [caves] and nests of tigers and leopards, horned dragons and vultures, and looked down into Fengyi's[(389)] deep palace, as my two guests could not follow me thither.[(390)] I uttered a yell far up above; trees and grass were shaken; the peaks rumbled and the valleys answered in echo; water gushed out and gusts of winds started to blow. I was also shaken by sadness and became gravely struck with terror, sensing the impossibility of remaining there.[(391)] I descended and returned to the boat; rowing to the midstream, I let it go by itself and to its rest float.[(392)]

That was about the middle of the night; there was nothing astir all around. Just then, a solitary crane crossed the River from the east, its wings like carriage wheels, white in upper and black in nether garments, shrieking out a long cry and flying over my boat westward. Not long after, my guests left me and I went to sleep. I dreamed a taoist priest in his robe of feathers[(393)] flapping past Lingao, holding out his hands locked in each other to extend a courtesy[(394)] to me, said, "Was your trip to the Red Cliffs pleasurable?" I asked his name; he stooped and did not reply. "A-ha, o-ho, I've known it!" said I, "The other night, was it not you who flied crying past me?" The taoist priest looked back and smiled, and I was wakened by surprise. Opening the door and looking for the man, I could not see him where he had been.

Tr. May 24, 1974.

［宋］ 叶绍翁

(*1225—1264*)

游园不值

应怜屐齿印苍苔，*
小扣柴扉久不开。
春色满园关不住，
一枝红杏出墙来。

* 此句中“屐”，古时本为木履，底有“齿”痕两条，一在前，一在后，是叠出的横条木纹，穿了去走泥滑的地面，可以防滑倒。汉元帝时黄门令史游在他的《急就篇》里说起它，唐颜师古在他的此书注解里这样解释。但王筠（南朝梁时人）的《说文句读》说，“屐有草有帛者，非止木也。”可见在唐以前的南北朝已不一定是木屐，虽然最早是木制的雨鞋。南宋理宗时的这位诗人叶绍翁在此诗中用此字，意思是在春雨初晴后访友游园。我们在这里用 clog(wooden-soled shoe)来译这个字，屐齿作 clog-teeth (jags, juts) prints，虽然也可以笼统译为 my clog-prints。

Ye Shaoweng

(*Song*, *1225—1264*)

Visiting a Garden When Its Master Is Out

I repine at pressing clog-teeth prints on the deep green moss;
The brushwood door when knocked as I wait long doth not ope
at all.
The ravishing beauties of the garden could not be contained:
A bough of glowing apricot blooms stretcheth out of the wall.

Tr. June 8, 1981.

增补篇

[汉] 司马迁

商君列传

（选自《史记》）

商君者，卫之诸庶孽公子也，名鞅，姓公孙氏，其祖本姬姓也。

鞅少好刑名之学，事魏相公叔痤为中庶子。公叔痤知其贤，未及进。会痤病，魏惠王亲往问病，曰："公叔病有如不可讳，将奈社稷何？"公叔曰："痤之中庶子公孙鞅，年虽少，有奇才，愿王举国而听之。"王嘿然。王且去，痤屏人言曰："王即不听用鞅，必杀之，无令出境。"王许诺而去。公叔痤召鞅谢曰："今者王问可以为相者，

Supplement

Sima Qian

The Life of Lord Shang

Lord Shang(商君), one of the several collateral or concubineborn princes of the state Wei(卫), bearing the name Yang (鞅) and the original surname Gongsun(公孙), was descended from Kang Shu(康叔), a brother of King Wu[1], Ji Fan(武王姬发), founder of the Zhou(周) Dynasty. In his youth he was fondly engrossed in studies of the theoretics of law, and later served under Gongshu Cuo(公叔痤), premier of the state Wei(魏), as his family steward. Gongshu Cuo knew he was brilliantly endowed, but did not happen to have recommended him formally to the king during his office. While Gongshu was laid up with fatal illness, however, King Hui of Wei(魏惠王), paying favour to his chief minister by seeing him in person, asked him, "In the event your illness falls to the condition which is unmentionable, what should be done to the state?" Gongshu replied, "My steward Gongsun Yang, though young in years, is unusually capable; it is my wish that Your Majesty would uplift him to prominence." The King kept mum. As he was rising to leave, Gongshu ordered his followers to retire and then said, "If Your Majesty do not mean to make use of his devotions, do kill him please, suffering him not to cross your boundaries. "This the King promised, and left. Gongshu Cuo then summoned

我言若，王色不许我，我方先君后臣，因谓王即弗用鞅，当杀之。王许我。汝可疾去矣，且见禽。”鞅曰：“彼王不能用君之言任臣，又安能用君之言杀臣乎？”卒不去。惠王既去，而谓左右曰：“公叔病甚，悲乎，欲令寡人以国听公孙鞅也，岂不悖哉！”

公叔既死，公孙鞅闻秦孝公下令国中求贤者，将修缪公之业，东复侵地，乃遂西入秦，因孝公宠臣景监以求见孝公。

Gongsun and asked pardon of him, adding, "Just now the king queried me who could succeed me as prime minister. I recommended you, but His Majesty did not look affirming. I must put the king's interests first and my private concern for you next, so I adviced him to kill you if he doesn't intend to make use of your abilities. The king promised me. So, you better dispatch in haste, lest you would be apprehended." Gongsun said in reply, "Since the king could not avail himself of your words by appointing me to that position, how could he do so by killing me?" So he desisted from leaving. King Hui left and said to those around him, "Gongshu is sorely ill, alas! he would have me put the reins of the state in Gongsun Yang's hands; how absurd it is!"

After Gongshu had died, Gongsun heard that Viscount Xiao (孝公)[(2)] of the state Qin (秦) ordered to find those renowned to be most capable in his domain and that the Viscount would restore his preeminent predecessor Viscount Mu's (缪公) glory (the viscount, also known as 秦穆公), who had lived some three hundred years earlier and had the foresight to appoint to premiership and other high posts Baili Xi, Jian Shu, You Yu (百里奚, 蹇叔, 由余) and others, defeated the state Jin (晋), annexed those of Liang and Rui (梁, 芮), turning westward to overcome many a petty state and absorbing them all, so as to become invincible in the Far West[(3)] by reoccupying the territory taken back by Jin when Jin was weakened by civil war and the former had become strong again. As Gongsun learned that the state of affairs in Jin was favourable to his self-promotion, he turned westward and entered the country, seeking to have an interview with viscount Xiao through the good offices of his favourite eunuch Jing (景监). When he was

孝公既见卫鞅,语事良久,孝公时时睡,弗听。罢而孝公怒景监曰:“子之客妄人耳,安足用邪!”景监以让卫鞅,卫鞅曰:“吾说公以帝道,其志不开悟矣。”后五日,复求见鞅。鞅复见孝公,益愈,然而未中旨。罢而孝公复让景监,景监亦让鞅。鞅曰:“吾说公以王道而未入也。请复见鞅。”鞅复见孝公,孝公善之而未用也。罢而去。孝公谓景监曰:“汝客善,可与语矣。”鞅曰:“吾说公以霸道,其意欲用之矣。诚复见我,我知之矣。”卫鞅复见孝公。公与语,不自知膝之前于席也。语数日不厌。景监曰:“子何以中吾君,吾君之欢甚也。”鞅曰:“吾说君以帝王之道比三代,而君曰:‘久远,吾不能

granted an interview with the viscount, he talked a long while, but the viscount fell asleep, listening not to him. The affair being over, viscount Xiao blamed the eunuch in displeasure, "Your friend is a madcap; how could he be of use!" Eunuch Jing blamed Gongsun in turn. Gongsun said, "I urged on the Viscount the beneficential ways and means of the Five Ancient Sagacious Emperors(4), but His Honour was not cognizant of what I said." Five days later, the viscount wanted to see Gongsun again. So he went to the viscount the second time, and spoke his fill, but to little avail. The viscount blamed eunuch Jing once more, who did the same to Gongsun in turn. He then said, "I offered the Viscount the kindly ways and means of the Three Gentle Kings(5) but he could not adopt them. Please let him see once more." So he was again granted an interview; the viscount was somewhat pleased with him this time, but he had not yet quite ingratiated himself into the viscount's good graces. The visit ended. Viscount Shao said to the eunuch, "Your friend is all right; I can speak with him now." Gongsun said, "I spoke to His Honour of the ways and means of the Five Magnificent Princes;(6) he seemed to be in the mood of accepting them. In case His Honour would give me still another chance, I know what to say to him." They were brought together. This time the viscount conversed with him in earnest, without knowing that his knees were getting closer and closer to the speaker on the mat(7). The converse went on for several days without sating. Eunuch Jing said, "How do you please my Lord? He is so glad!" Gongsun replied, "I spoke to His Honour of the munificent ways and means of the Three Illustrious Dynasties, Xia, Shang and Zhou(夏,商,周), and His Honour said, 'That's too far

待。且贤君者，各及其身显名天下，安能邑邑待数十百年以成帝王乎？'故吾以强国之术说君，君大悦之耳。然亦难以比德于殷周矣。"

孝公既用卫鞅，鞅欲变法，恐天下议己。卫鞅曰："疑行无名，疑事无功。且夫有高人之行者，固见非于世；有独知之虑者，必见敖于民。愚者闇于成事，知者见于未萌。民不可与虑始而可与乐成。论至德者不和于俗，成大功者不谋于众。是以圣人苟可以强国，不法其故；苟可以利民，不循其礼。"孝公曰："善。"甘龙曰："不然。圣人不易民而教，知者不变法而治。因民而教，不劳而成功；

away; I could not wait. Besides, a good king wishes his fair repute would spread all over the countries while he is yet living to enjoy it; how could he wait anxiously for tens and hundreds of years to become legerdary figures of yore?' So I spoke to him of the effective methods of strengthening the state, and pleased him to the utmost. But that is of-course not to be compared to the virtuous reigns of Yin[(8)] and Zhou (殷,周)."

When Viscount Xiao had put Gongsun at his post and the latter wanted to alter the laws, the Viscount wavered in anxiety lest the world might censure him. Gongsun then said, "One who vacillates between one's courses could reap no repute; one who doubts one's achievements could meet no success. Furthermore, one who exceeds the common run of men in what he does is bound to be disapproved by the vulgar; and one who is single in foresight is sure to be despised by the multitude. The foolish are ignorant of the way of success, while the wise could usually see ahead of the turn of events. People could not be trusted with in deliberating the ins and outs of what is to be done, but may enjoy the fruits of success when it is accomplished. Those who speak of the ultimate verities of things do not conform to the crowd, and the authors of great achievements do not consult the mass. Therefore, the sagacious, if certain measures could fortify the state, would not follow antiquated practices, and if such could benefit the people, would not stick to old rules." The Viscount said, "Very well." Gan Long (甘龙)[(9)] said, "Not so. The sagacious could not change a people for another one to teach them a new course, and the wise do not initiate a new set of laws to rule them. To teach a people according to what they are familiar with would succeed without too much strained efforts, and to govern

缘法而治者,吏习而民安之。"卫鞅曰:"龙之所言,世俗之言也。常人安于故俗,学者溺于所闻。以此两者居官守法可也,非所与论于法之外也。三代不同礼而王,五伯不同法而霸。智者作法,愚者制焉;贤者更礼,不肖者拘焉。"杜挚曰:"利不百,不变法;功不十,不易器。法古无过,循礼无邪。"卫鞅曰:"治世不一道,便国不法古。故汤武不循古而王,夏、殷不易礼而亡。反古者不可非,而循礼者不足多。"孝公曰:"善。"以卫鞅为左庶长,卒定变法之令。

along the path of statutes they are accustomed to, would make the officials feel used and the people undisturbed." Gongsun said, "Gan Long's words are those of the common mass. Ordinary people are used to old practices, and scholars are blinded by what they often hear. It would do well to stick to these two in holding official posts and living conventionally, but would not do at all to discuss matters wherewithal that are totally novel and out of the common rut. The Three Illustrious Dynasties achieved the state of Universal Peace with different codes of conduct, and the Five Magnificent States wrought for their might via different legislation. The wise formulate laws, the foolish stick to them; the sagacious renovate rules of conduct, those devoid of sense follow precedents blindly." Du Zhi(杜挚)[(10)] said, "If the benefits do not increase a hundredfold, laws are not altered in toto; if the profits are not tenfold, a machine is not displaced by another. There is no fault in following old practices, and no mistake in sticking to codes of conduct of the past." Gongsun said, "The way to govern a state is not confined to one hard and fast rule; if it is beneficial to the state, there is no necessity to conform to practices of bygone days. Thus, Tang and Wu, the two illustrious Kings of Shang and Zhou(商汤,周武), achieved their peaceful rules without resorting to precedants of old; Jie and Zou, the two violent tyrants of Xia and Yin(夏桀,殷纣), were undone and extinct without changing their used systems of conduct. To alter the ways and means of yore is not to be blamed, and to follow the codes of the past is not necessarily praiseworthy." "Very well," said Viscount Xiao. So he made Gongsun Yang his Left Chief Steward(左庶长), the tenth in rank of his ducal government, and set finally the decree for altering the statutes.

令民为什伍，而相牧司连坐。不告奸者腰斩，告奸者与斩敌首同赏，匿奸者与降敌同罚。民有二男以上不分异者，倍其赋。有军功者，各以率受上爵；为私斗者，各以轻重被刑大小。僇力本业，耕织致粟帛多者复其身。事末利及怠而贫者，举以为收孥。宗室非有军功论，不得为属籍。明尊卑爵秩等级，各以差次名田宅，臣妾衣

The new laws are in brief like this. The population is organized into adjoining groups of ten households and five; every household has the bounden duty to accuse and expose any other among the ten of a misdeed; if it is not done, all of them would be punished for hiding or conniving at the crime. Those that refrain from accusation are to be cut asunder at the waist(腰斩); those that accuse properly will be rewarded with state distinction as killing a state foe who is a commissioned officer by chopping off his head; hiding a criminal is punished like yielding to the enemy, the person guilty of this to be punished accordingly and his whole family becoming slaves male and female. A house-hold having two adult males living together would be doubly taxed. Those having achieved military distinction would be rewarded with state orders of merit according to there deserts. Those engaged in private clashes would be punished in relation to the size of the offence. Those who strain their efforts in farming, tilling the sail and weaving so as to produce large quantities of grain and cloth, are to be excused from their state duties of labour. Those who are employed in industrial and commercial pursuits or are lazy and thus become destitute are all to be reduced to be state slaves. Nobles of the main ducal lineage, other than the direct offsprings of the duke, are not regarded as within the family as its members, if they have not accomplished military distinction. Degree of bobility and the living appertaining to each man are to be redisposed according to such, and when so affirmed, such people would occupy their respective residences and own their relevant farms in graduated order, and possess fix numbers of slaves male and female, and could wear what modes of dresses fitting their dignity. Those

服以家次。有功者显荣,无功者虽富无所芬华。

令既具,未布,恐民之不信,已乃立三丈之木于国都市南门,募民有能徙置北门者予十金。民怪之,莫敢徙。复曰:“能徙者予五十金”。有一人徙之,辄予五十金,以明不欺。卒下令。

令行于民期年,秦民之国都言初令之不便者以千数。于是太子犯法。卫鞅曰:“法之不行,自上犯之。”将法太子。太子,君嗣也,不可施刑,刑其傅公子虔,黥其师公孙贾。明日,秦人皆趋令。行之十年,秦民大悦,道不拾遗,山无盗贼,家给人足。民勇于公

meritorious in military achievements are to be distinguished and glorified; others devoid of such distinction, though they may be wealthy, could not share such glory.

The decree was drawn up, but not yet promulgated, for fear the people might not believe in it. So a log of thirty feet was erected at the southern gate of the capital of the duchy, and it was proclaimed that anyone who could move it to the northern gate would be given ten pieces of gold. People were puzzled by this; none dared to move the log. It was again proclaimed: "The one who could move it would be given fifty pieces of gold." There was one man who moved it; he was immediately given the fifty pieces, to show that there was no nonsense. At last, the decree was promulgated.

A year after the decree was put in force, people all over the duchy came by thousands to the capital to say that the new laws were incommodious. And then the prince ducal committed an offence. Gongsun Yang said, "The new statutes could not be put into effect, for they are hindered from the top." He meant to punish the prince according to the new law. But the prince was the lineal successor of the viscount, and so could not be submitted to the barbs of law. Therefore, his tutor, Prince Qian(公子虔), was punished instead, and his teacher Gongsun Jia(公孙贾), defaced with knife incisings, dyed with black, on the forehead. The next day, the whole duchy yielded to the new laws without a rub. After the new statutes were put in force for ten years, the people of the duchy were greatly pleased; anything left by one on the roads and streets was not picked up by anyone else; there were no highwaymen in the mountains; families became affluent and men plentiful. People were brave in public warfare, but timid in private routs;

战，怯于私斗，乡邑大治。秦民初言令不便者有来言令便者，卫鞅曰："此皆乱化之民也。"尽迁之于边城。其后民莫敢议令。

于是以鞅为大良造，将兵围魏安邑，降之。

居三年，作为筑冀阙宫庭咸阳，秦自雍徙都之。而令民父子兄弟同室内息者为禁。而集小乡邑聚为县，置令、丞，凡三十一县。为田开阡陌封疆，而赋税平。平斗桶权衡丈尺。

行之四年，公子虔复犯约，劓之。

居五年，秦人富强，天子致胙于孝公，诸侯毕贺。

the countryside and cities and towns became very peaceful. A number of the dutchy's subjects who had said the new laws were incommodious now came and said they were quite commodious. Gongsun Yang said, "These are all disturbers and hindrances of the educational and cultural well-being of the duchy;" he ordered to have them all moved to the border towns. Thereafter, people dared not comment on any decree.

The viscount promoted Gongsun Yang to the position of Daliang-zao(大良造), which was equivalent to the post of premiership, but at the same time was the commander-in-chief of the state, subject only to the viscount. He then led troops to besiege Anyi(安邑), capital of the kingdom Wei(魏), and subjugated it. For three years, thereafter, he built court mansions and palaces at Xianyang(咸阳), to which the duchy Qin moved as its capital from the old one at Yong (雍). He issued the order that father and sons and brothers were forbidden to live together in one household. He delineated the countrysides, boroughs and villages into *xians*(县), thirty-one in number altogether, directly under the sway of the viscount, with magistrates and superintendants(令,丞) as their heads and assistants. To enlarge the areas of the cultivable land, he erased the barriers and boundaries of the field lots, thus equalizing the land tax. He unified the standards of measurement for capacity, weight and length. For four years he ruled thus, and Prince Qian(公子虔) infringed the law again; he ordered to have his nose cut off. At the end of five years Qin became rich and strong. His Majesty the King of Zhou sent portions of the cold meat, offerings to Heaven, Earth and the God of the Kingdom, as a great royal favour to Viscount Xiao, and his fellow vassals all

其明年，齐败魏兵于马陵，虏其太子申，杀将军庞涓。其明年，卫鞅说孝公曰：“秦之与魏，譬若人之有腹心疾，非魏并秦，秦即并魏。何者？魏居领阨之西，都安邑，与秦界河，而独擅山东之利。利则西侵秦，病则东收地。今以君之贤圣，国赖以盛。而魏往年大破于齐，诸侯畔之，可因此时伐魏。魏不支秦，必东徙。东徙，秦据河山之固，东乡以制诸侯，此帝王之业也。”孝公以为然，使卫鞅将而伐魏。魏使公子卬将而击之。军既相距，卫鞅遗魏将公子卬书曰：“吾始与公子欢，今俱为两国将，不忍相攻，可与公子面相见，

congratulated him.

Next year[11]. an army of the state Qi(齐) defeated the troops of Wei(魏) at Maling(马陵), took its prince royal Shen(太子申) captive and killed its general Pong Juan(庞涓). A year later, Gongsun Yang said to Duke Xiao, "Qin and Wei are like one's heart trouble to each other; if we are not overcome by Wei, we must annex Wei. Why? Wei is situated in the west of the mountainous key positions, with Anyi(安邑) as its capital, bordering Qin at the Yellow River and enjoying all by itself the riches of the east of the mountains. When conditions are favourable, it turns west ward to encroach on Qin; when unfavourable, it faces the east to prey on others. With Your Excellency to crown and adorn the state, our country prospers and waxes great. Wei was overcome by Qi last year; all its fellow vassals now rebel against it. We could take this opportunity to assail it now. Unable to stand against Qin, Wei would have to move its capital eastward. Then Qin could fortify itself with the security of the River and the Mountains to face east-ward to check all the other states. This is the enterprise of a sovereign, a king." Viscount Xiao approved of the plan and appointed Gongsun to head an army for attacking Wei. Wei sent Prince Ang(公子卬) as commander of its forces to ward off the attack. When the two armies were in sight of each other, Gongsun sent a letter to Prince Ang, saying "I have been most kindly disposed toward Your Honour for ever so long. Now that we are both generals of our respective state armies, I feel very much against my bent to launch an attack. Please let me propose to meet Your Honour face to face and convene for an alliance instead, and we shall drink health to each other and then both draw our

盟,乐饮而罢兵,以安秦魏。”魏公子卬以为然。会盟已,饮,而卫鞅伏甲士而袭虏魏公子卬,因攻其军,尽破之以归秦。魏惠王兵数破于齐秦,国内空,日以削,恐,乃使使割河西之地献于秦以和。而魏遂去安邑,徙都大梁。梁惠王曰:“寡人恨不用公叔痤之言也。”卫鞅既破魏还,秦封之於、商十五邑,号为商君。

商君相秦十年,宗室贵戚多怨望者。赵良见商君,商君曰:“鞅之得见也,从孟兰皋,今鞅请得交,可乎?”赵良曰:“仆弗敢愿也。孔丘有言曰:‘推贤而戴者进,聚不肖而王者退。’仆不肖,故不

men backward, to make the affair a peaceful one to Qin as well as to Wei." Prince Ang of Wei thought well of the proposal. So, after the convening, they drank. But Gongsun had laid an ambuscade in advance, He signaled his hidden warriors to attack and capture the prince, and then ordered a massed attack on the Wei army, overwhelmed it and had it surrender totally to Qin. Now, King Hui of Wei(魏惠王) had his troops smashed once and again by Qi and Qin, the defense of his country becoming almost vacant and its territory shrinking day by day; being struck with fear, he sent an envoy to cut and offer his territory west of the River to Qin to sue for peace. Then Wei moved its capital from Anyi(安邑) to Daliang(大梁). King Hui of Wei(魏惠王) said, "I do regret for not taking Congshu Cuo's counsel years ago!" When Gongsun Yang returned to Xianyang after he had beaten Wei, Qin granted him the fief of fifteen boroughs of Wu and Shang(於商十五邑), bestowing on him the title Lord of Shang(商君).

During the ten years while Lord Shang was holding the premiership of Qin, nobilities of the main ducal line as well as those related to it by marriage often laid blame on him and complained of him behind his back. Zao Liang(赵良), a Confucian scholar and a recluse, saw him once. Lord Shang said to him, "I have the honour and pleasure of seeing you through the introduction of Meng Langao(孟兰皋). Now, may I become a friend of yours?" Zao Liang replied, "I dare not wish it. Kong Qiu(孔丘)[12] once said, 'If you recommend the virtuous and men of merit, those who love the people would come close to you; if you befriend men of questionable nature, those of upright and fair qualities would avoid you.' I admit I am not good enough to

敢受命。仆闻之曰:‘非其位而居之曰贪位,非其名而有之曰贪名。’仆听君之义,则恐仆贪位贪名也。故不敢闻命。”商君曰:“子不说吾治秦与?”赵良曰:“反听之谓聪,内视之谓明,自胜之谓强。虞舜有言曰:‘自卑也尚矣。’君不若道虞舜之道,无为问仆矣。”商君曰:“始秦戎翟之教,父子无别,同室而居。今我更制其教,而为其男女之别,大筑冀阙,营如鲁卫矣。子观我治秦也,孰与五羖大夫贤?”赵良曰:“千羊之皮,不如一狐之腋;千人之诺诺,不如一士之谔谔。武王谔谔以昌,殷纣墨墨以亡。君若不非武王乎,则仆请终日正言而无诛,可乎?”商君曰:“语有之矣,貌言华也,至言实也,苦

accede to your order. I heard it said, 'To occupy a position not suitable to one is to be greedy of it; to bear the repute not deserving to one is to be greedy of the name.' If I were to accept your kindliness, I would be greedy of both the position and the name. Therefore, I dare not be your obedient servant." Lord Shang then asked, "Are you displeased with my governing Qin?" Zao Liang answered, "To reflect on oneself is to be wise; to examine oneself is to be clear-sighted; to restrain oneself is to be strong. Sun of the dynasty Yu(虞舜), one of the ancient Five Illustrious Emperors, had the saying, 'To be humble is a rare quality.' You might as well do according to Yu Sun's way, without having to ask my opinion." Lord Shang then said, "Formerly, Qin people lived like the Rong and Di (戎,翟) of the uncivilized Far West; fathers and sons lived in the same room. Now I have changed the custom by teaching people to distinguish between men and women. I have also built court mansions and palaces magnificent and spacious like those of Lu and Wei (鲁,卫). You can see how my ruling of Qin is to be compared with that of the Courtier of Five Black Sheepskins,(13) whether his or mine be the superior one." Zao Liang said, "A thousand pieces of sheepskin are not comparable to one suit of fox fur. A thousand people's humming yeas are not to be compared to the solitary upright words of a scholar. King Wu of Zhou(周武王) prospered in his reign because of such upright utterances; the reign of King Chou of Yin(殷纣) became extinct because of a deathly fit of fearful stillness. If you do not disapprove King Wu, I beg to be candid with you all day long without being blamed, may I?" Lord Shang said, "The proverbial saying has it that to speak what is obvious is vain, to speak heartily is

言药也，甘言疾也。夫子果肯终日正言，鞅之药也。鞅将事子，子又何辞焉！”赵良曰：“夫五羖大夫，荆之鄙人也。闻秦缪公之贤而愿望见，行而无资，自粥于秦客，被褐食牛。期年，缪公知之，举之牛口之下，而加之百姓之上，秦国莫敢望焉。相秦六七年，而东伐郑，三置晋国之君，一救荆国之祸。发教封内，而巴人致贡；施德诸侯，而八戎来服。由余闻之，款关请见。五羖大夫之相秦也，劳不坐乘，暑不张盖，行于国中，不从车乘，不操干戈，功名藏于府库，德

solid, to speak critically is medicinal and to speak sweetly is like illness. If you have the goodness to speak to me candidly all day long; you are my medicine. I would be at your service then; why should you decline friendship to me?" Zao Liang then said, "The 'Courtier of Five Black Sheepskins' was a countryman of Jin(荆). Hearing of the sterling worth of Viscount Mu of Qin(秦缪公), he wished to see him. But he was as poor as one could ever be. Without any means to travel, he sold himself as a bound slave to a subject of the duchy Qin; rudely dressed in short clothes of rough-woven cloth, he served his master as his cowboy. A year later, Viscount Mu(缪公) heard of the matter and elevated him from such a humble state by putting him above the Qin people as his prime minister, so that the whole duchy dared not behold in him one who had occupied such a low state. He governed Qin for some seven years, during which he sent an expedition eastward to march on Zheng(郑), helped to put three dukes as rulers of the duchy Jin(晋)[(14)] and once warded off the menace of Chu(楚) against Jin[(15)]. He taught and cultivated the Qin populace, and the people of Ba(巴) sent their emissary to offer tributes; he spread his beneficial influences to many a fellow state, and the Rong tribes(八戎) northwest of Qin all paid homage to his liege lord. Hearing of him, You Yu(由余)[(16)] knocked at his door to ask for his acquaintance. As the prime minister of Qin, the 'Courtier of Five Black Sheepskins' did not ride a carriage with a seat in it, had no covering for shade on it in the summer; wherever he went in the duchy, he had no escort vehicle, nor men of arms to guard him. His achievements and fair name are recorded in chronicles[(17)] deposited in the official storehouse, his virtuous deeds continue

行施于后世。五羖大夫死，秦国男女流涕，童子不歌谣，舂者不相杵。此五羖大夫之德也。今君之见秦王也，因嬖人景监以为主，非所以为名也。相秦不以百姓为事，而大筑冀阙，非所以为功也。刑黥太子之师傅，残伤民以骏刑，是积怨蓄祸也。教之化民也深于命，民之效上也捷于令。今君又左建外易，非所以为教也。君又南面而称寡人，日绳秦之贵公子。《诗》曰：‘相鼠有体，人而无礼；人而无礼，何不遄死。’以《诗》观之，非所以为寿也。公子虔杜门不出

to come down in all these generations. When the ' Courtier of Five Black Sheepskins' died, all men and women of the duchy Qin wept, boys and girls refrained from singing songs and ballads, labourers at their work in pounding grains ceased to hollo in unison. Such are the virtuous deeds of the ' Courtier of Five Black Sheepskins' and their effects. Now, in your case, you came to know the Prince of Qin through the introduction of his favourite eunuch Jin, which would serve ill for your fair name. Your holding the premiership does not aim at serving the people, but you have devoted yourself to the building of court mansions and palaces, which would not do as the accomplishment of a statesman. To punish and disfigure the tutor and the teacher of the prince ducal, to kill and hurt the people with inflictions of cruel punishments: these are acts for accumulating hatred and storing up ealamities. Teaching and cultivation will move the people more deeply than state decrees can ever do; they will act feelingly to redound upon their sovereign the more quickly. Now you have established your authority and refashioned the institutions by dubious means, but such is not the proper way to do the thing. Furthermore, you sit facing southward using the language of a monarch, subjecting the princes of the state daily to your will and discipline. *The Book of Odes* says:

The mouse of Xiang(18) is mannerly,
  Whereas a man kens not how to be so;
If a man kens not how to behave,
  Why not to death does he hurry to go?

According to *The Odes*, then, you are not acting for leading a long life. The Prince Qian has not crossed his threshold for eight years, and you

已八年矣，君又杀祝懽而黥公孙贾。《诗》曰：‘得人者兴，失人者崩。’此数事者，非所以得人也。君之出也，后车十数，从车载甲，多力而骈胁者为骖乘，持矛而操闟戟者旁车而趋。此一物不具，君固不出。《书》曰：‘恃德者昌，恃力者亡。’君之危若朝露，尚将欲延年益寿乎？则何不归十五都，灌园于鄙，劝秦王显岩穴之士，养老存孤，敬父兄，序有功，尊有德，可以少安。君尚将贪商于之富，宠秦国之教，畜百姓之怨，秦王一旦捐宾客而不立朝，秦国之所以收君者，岂其微哉？亡可翘足而待。”商君弗从。

have besides killed Zhu Huan(祝懽) and disfigured Gongsun Jia. *The Book of Odes* also says:

> Those who win people's hearts will flourish,
>
> Those who lose them will come to wrack[19].

These things I have just mentioned are not going to win people's hearts for you. When you go out, escort carts numbering over ten follow you, and loaded with armed men, mighty and muscular guards riding on your right, those holding lances and halberds rushing along beside your chariot. Without any one of these, you do not venture out. *Shu Jing*(《书经》) says, 'Those who depend on virtue prosper; those who depend on might fall to the ground'.[20] You are in danger like the morning dew, and yet do you still expect longevity? Then, why do you not return the fifteen boroughs to the Viscount, cultivate vegetables and water melons at certain distant countryside, urge the Viscount to elevate some hermits from a number of mountain cells, take care of the aged and subsidize those who are alone, pay respect to the fathers and elders, enroll in order those for encouragement of their good work done to the community and pay tributes to the virtuous? If you do all these, you may feel a little peaceful. If, on the contrary, you continue to feed jealously on the riches of Shang and Wu, to regard holding the power of teaching and cultivating the people of Qin as an honour and a favour of the Viscount, and to let the people's resentment against you grow, then, when one day His Excellency denies his appearance to his courtiers and guests, holding no more court, would this duchy be short of laying hands on you? Thus, obliteration would come in a trice." But to all these words, Lord Shang paid no heed at all.

后五月而秦孝公卒,太子立。公子虔之徒告商君欲反,发吏捕商君。商君亡至关下,欲舍客舍。客人不知其是商君也,曰:“商君之法,舍人无验者坐之。”商君喟然叹曰:“嗟乎,为法之敝一至此哉!”去之魏。魏人怨其欺公子卬而破魏师,弗受。商君欲之他国。魏人曰:“商君,秦之贼。秦强而贼入魏,弗归,不可。”遂内秦。商君既复入秦,走商邑,与其徒属发邑兵北出击郑。秦发兵攻商君,杀之于郑黾池。秦惠王车裂商君以徇,曰:“莫如商鞅反者!”遂灭商君之家。

太史公曰:商君,其天资刻薄人也。迹其欲干孝公以帝王

Five months later Viscount Xiao died, and the prince ducal Si (驷) was enthroned as King Hui of Qin(秦惠王). The followers of Prince Qian accused Lord Shang of plotting to rebel, and court corps were sent to apprehend him. Lord Shang escaped to a border pass, and wanted to put up in an inn for the night. The inn-keeper, not knowing his identity, said, "According to Lord Shang's law, a traveller without a document to identify him would be held for the violation." Lord Shang heaved a sigh of exclamation, "Alas! the fault of the laws should come to such a pass!" He went to Wei. The Wei people, hating him for his treachery to Prince Ang and the ensuing smashing defeat suffered by their troops, did not admit him. Lord Shang wanted to go to another country. The Wei people said, "Lord Shang is Qin's traitor now. Qin is strong and its traitor comes to Wei; if we do not send him back, it won't do." So they sent him back. When he returned to Qin, he went to his own borough of Shang and led its militia with his followers to strike from its northern outskirts the state of Zheng(郑). Qin sent soldiers to attack Lord Shang, killing him at Mianchi(黾池) of Zheng. King Hui of Qin(秦惠王) ordered to have Lord Shang pulled to pieces before the public with ox-carts tied to his head and limbs, saying, "Let none rebel as Shang Yang!" So, the whole family of Lord Shang was exterminated.

The Grand Curator of History says: Lord Shang is by nature a man of ruthless cruelty. Considering that he had at first offered to Viscount Xiao the ways and means of the Five Sagacious Emperors and those of the Three Gentle Kings for adoption, but in the end presented his wanton plot of atrocious might, we can make our conclusion

术,挟持浮说,非其质矣。且所因由嬖臣,及得用,刑公子虔,欺魏将印,不师赵良之言,亦足发明商君之少恩矣。余尝读商君开塞、耕战书,与其人行事相类。卒受恶名于秦,有以也夫!

① 在本书全稿付梓前夕,痛悉大雨教授谢世,其家属在整理教授遗墨时发现此译稿,现特作增补篇收入本集以表对大雨教授深切悼念之情,并使此译篇流传后世。

——编者

that his first proposals were not in his element, but his last one was. Moreover, he approached the viscount through the mediacy of his favourite eunuch. When he attained his ambition and power, he inflicted penalties on Prince Qian and Gongsun Jia, betrayed Prince Ang, commanding general of the kingdom Wei, with a nasty trick and did not take to lesson Zao Liang's words. All these go to prove how hardened a heart the man had[(20)]. I have read writings on Lord Shang's career like *Fortifying Key and Border Passes* and *Farming and Fighting*; they are in accord with his doings. It is not without cause that he got his wicked name in Qin.

Tr. March 1, 1974.

* On the eve when the manuscripts of this book were about to be sent to the press, we were distressed to learn of Prof. Sun Dayu's passing away. The English version of *The Life of Lord Shang* was found by his family in sorting out his works and therefore, collected here as an addition in memory of Prof. Sun so as to be handed down to future generations.

——Ed.

Notes

(1) Kangshu, meaning younger brother Kang, was given the state Wei as his fief by King Wu. In ancient times, people often took state names, official titles, fief names, nomenclatures of relations, etc. as family names.

(2) Viscount Xiao of Qin(秦孝公) ruled the viscounty from 361 to 338 B. C. He put Gongsun Yang, also known as Wei Yang (卫鞅) and finally called Shang Yang(商鞅), at his post to change the laws of Qin, thereby leading to intensity its ferosity and aggressiveness later on.

(3) This short parenthetical passage is apologetically inserted by the translator to elucidate the terse allusive original. Viscount Mu of the "Spring and Autumn" Period (770—477 B. C.) ruled Jin from 660 to 621 B. C.

(4) The Five Ancient Sagacious Emperors(五帝) are generally taken to be Huang-*di*, Zhuanxu, Di Ku, Tang Yao and Yu Sun(黄帝,颛顼,帝喾,唐尧,虞舜). They were all legendary sage rulers of the remote Golden Age. There are other variants of the names. The ways and means of these Sagacious Emperors and called the "Imperial Way"(帝道). It is superior to the "Kingly Way".

(5) The Three Gentle Kings(三王) mean the founding fathers of the Three Illustrious Dynasties, Yu of Xia, Tang of Shang and Wu of Zhou(夏禹,商汤,周武). The ways and means of the Three Gentle Kings are called the "Kingly Way"(王道). It is superior to the "Princely Way"(霸道) of the Five Princes.

(6) The Five Magnificent Princes(五霸) of the "Spring and Au-

tumn"(春秋) Period of the Zhou Dynasty were Marquis Huan of Qi(齐桓公), Duke Xiang of Song(宋襄公), Duke Wen of Jin(晋文公), Viscount Mu of Qin(秦穆公) and King Zhuang of Chu(楚庄王). Their ways and means are called the "Princely Way"(霸道). For better apprehension of the term, readers might as well bear in mind. Machiavelli's *The Prince*, as there are resembling traits between this and that Renaissance type of Italian political character of the western world.

(7) In ancient times people squatted on ground or floor mats indoors. They sat with legs in curvature and kneecaps protruding out in front. This sentence means that the duke was so much absorbed by what he heard that he did not know he was moving nearer and nearer to Gongsun.

(8) The dynasty Shang(商), founded by Chen Tang(成汤) after his revolution against Jie(桀) of Xia(夏), is also known as Yin(殷), because in the reign of Pan Gen(盘庚), he moved his capital to Yin(殷) and adopted it as his dynasty name in place of Shang.

(9) Gan Long and Du Zhi were Confucian scholars and attendant courtiers of the duke.

(10) 同(9)

(11) The twenty-first year of the reign of Viscount Xiao, 341 B. C.

(12) Confucius (551—478 B. C.)

(13) The Courtier of Five Black Sheepskins means Baili Xi(百里奚), a renowned statesman at the court of Viscount Mu of Qin (秦穆公) during the "Spring and Autumn"(春秋) Period. He had been a courtier of the state Yu(虞国) previously. When Yu went out of existence, he was taken captive to Jin

(晋), and then sent in the train of a Jin princess in her marriage as a follower courtier, to the court of Qin. Thence he left, went to the state Chu(楚), which was also called Jin (荆) in ancient times, and became a peasant in his native place. Hearing of the goodness of Viscount Mu of Qin, he sold himself in barter as a slave to a Qin merchant for five sheepskins of black rams in order to be near his future master. When the viscount heard of him, he was ransomed with the same barter and elevated to premiership at the age of being over seventy. In seven years, he made the duke one of the five noted "Princely rulers"(五霸) of the time.

(14) They were Duke Hui, Duke Huai and Duke Wen of Jin(晋惠公,晋怀公,晋文公). In the ninth year of Viscount Mu's reign in Qin (651 B. C.), Duke Xian of Jin(晋献公) died and civil war broke out in that country; Viscount Mu ordered Baili Xi (百里奚) to send Prince Yi Wu of Jin(晋公子夷吾) back to his state to become Duke Hui. In the twenty-second year of Viscount Mu's reign in Qin(638 B. C.), Prince Yu of Jin(晋公子圉) went back from Qin to Jin to wear his ducal coronet, becoming Duke Huai. In the twenty-fourth year of Viscount Mu's reign in Qin (636 B. C.), Prince Zhong Er of Jin(晋公子重耳), in exile in the state Chu(楚国), was sent back to become Duke Wen.

(15) In the twenty-eighth year of Viscount Mu's reign in Qin (632 B. C.), the combined forces of Qin, Jin, Qi. (齐) and Song (宋) beat back the troops of Chu(楚) at Chengpu(城濮), stopping its north-ward advance.

(16) You Yu(由余) was a prominent courtier of Qin in the Spring

and Autumn Period. His ancesters were originally subjects of Jin; escaping to the Rong(戎) tribes, he began to hold some official post there. Viscount Mu esteemed his abilities highly, and so contrived to alienate him from the Rongs. He came to Qin and was deeply entrusted by the viscount. Later, he helped Qin to wage war against the Rongs and conquered their twelve states.

(17) These were written with paint on bamboo strips of about two feet one inch long, the short ones half as long, linked breadthwise to one another, to form what was called 策 or 册, the individual strip being called 简.

(18) The xiang mouse(相鼠) could have its forefeet crossed as if to extend a courtesy or show respect.

(19) These two lines("得人者兴,失人者崩") are lost to the extant collection of the *Book of Odes*.

(20) These two sentences("恃德者昌,恃力者亡") are lost to the extant text of *Shang Shu*(《尚书》).

Notes

(1) According to The Records of Dis and Kings(《帝王世纪》) of Huangfu Mi(皇甫谧), in the times of Di Yao(帝尧) octogenarians and nonagenarians sang this song while throwing clogs for fun. Pieces of wood were shaped like clogs for foot wear, broad in front and tapering towards the round end, one piece being laid on the ground and the player taking another piece and walking away for thirty to forty steps to throw at the first piece. Those who could hit the first piece were the winners of the game.

(2) As related in the previous fu on Gaotang, the Divine Lady, now first called by such a title in this fu, was the daughter of the Wu Mountains and had a love affair, years ago, with Huai-*wang*(怀王), the late father of the present King Xiang of Chu(楚襄王), in a dream of the former, according to the now elderly courtier Song Yu. She did not appear in person in the last *fu*, which is mainly an account of the arduous excursion undertaken by the young king, in company with the poet, as a pleasure-seeking trip, but turning out to be a pilgrimage for the good of the new sovereign's mind, as seen by Song Yu, and a pleasurable journey full of natural beauty for the poet and his Worthy readers, though Xiang-*wang* was not one of them. He, with his miry mind, was keenly and merely in-

tent upon succeeding his father's amour with the legendary fairy lady! The Divine Lady, according to *The Taiping Wide Records*(《太平广记》),collected and written by Li Fang(李昉) and others under the imperial decree of Song *Tai-zong*(宋太宗) in the second year of his reign Tai-ping Xing-guo(太平兴国二年,977), was the 23rd daughter of Wang-*mu*(王母) named Yaoji(瑶姬), also called by the appellation the Lady of Cloud Flowers(云华夫人). lt is also said that her temple was below the Divine Lady Cliff(神女峰), the most acute and beautiful of twelve cliffs (they are, namely,望霞,翠屏,朝云 the Morning Clouds,松峦,集仙,聚鹤,净坛,上昇,起云,飞凤,登龙,聚泉) in the south-east of the present Wushan *xian*(巫山县), Sichuan Province. As for Wang-*mu* or Xi Wang-*mu*(西王母), the most noted fairy of female sex, stories about her are rife, into which we need not go here. In *The Life of King Mu* (of Chu reigning 1001—947 B. C.)(《穆天子传》), she is said to have invited the King as her guest on the Kunlun Mountains(昆仑山) when he led his far westward march. Although a note on that book by Guo Pu(郭璞) of Jin (晋) depicts her as a woman with teeth like those of a tigress, bushyhaired, wearing a (gold) hair ornament with crossed double lozenges and skilled at hallooing, she is generally represented in folklore, dramas, fiction tales, pictures and embroideries as a young lady of about twenty, of the most exquisite beauty, immortal and having already lived thousands of years. Yaoji, daughter of the Red Emperor(赤帝), according to one tradition, died Young and was buried in the south of the Wu Mountains. According to another, the Lady of Cloud

Flowers, Yaoji, passed the Wu Mountains where she met the Great Yu and taught him the three ways to expel the deluge from our land. To continue the thread of our comment on the main theme of these two *fu*, Xiang-*wang*, ignoring the exhortation given by our poet at the end of the last piece, is eagerly urging his liegeman to find out the wherewithal of his doted object of pursuit, at the beginning of this piece, as he is impatient for seeing her face to face. Under the circumstances, Song Yu, entirely at the mercy of his sovereign master in an absolute monarchy over twenty-two centuries ago, could only invent this fiction of his dream to coddle his lord into believing that he had indeed seen her the previous night and attempted to make a match between them, but for some reason unspecified in this fu though easily understood,

"With sheer uprightness of heart, pure and clear,

Suddenly she differeth from me in test."

In another word, the Divine Lady made up her mind, in a quick judgment, to give refusal, first, final and absolute, to the king's mad wishes. We are told that though she is

"In nature gentle and bland"

and

"Mild like a rippling stream thoroughly clear,"

yet

Showing slight anger for keeping her pride,

She could not brook infringement and still remain.

Her definite answer to the king's nonsense in an inalterable "No." With this result, our poet has tactfully ended Xiang-*wang's* wild goose chase without hurting himself. And as readers of his exquisite poetry, we are presented, by the way, with a glimpse of this enchanting immortal spirit.

(3) Shade(阴) and Light(阳) are the two primordial principles of the universe as well as of human life.

(4) Mao Qiang(毛嫱) was an ancient beauty, first mentioned in *Zhuang-zi*(《庄子》) together with Liji(丽姬).

(5) Xishi(西施), a beauty of the state Yue(越) during the Spring and Autumn Period(春秋,722—481 B. C.) of the Zhou Dynasty, was the daughter of a fire-wood vender. Goujian the king of Yue(越王勾践), was badly beaten by King Fucha of Wu(吴王夫差); he retired to Kuaiji(会稽) to plan for revenge. He knew Fu Cha was fond of women and so he intended to make a mess of his state affairs through his weakness. He searched his state and found Xishi and Zheng Dan(郑旦) for his purpose. For three years he had them taught and trained in manners and the trick of making a fool of his deadly foe. Then he ordered his chief counsellor and general Fan Li(范蠡) to offer the two pretty women to Fucha. The king of Wu was immensely pleased with them and had his politics indeed turned away. At last he was utterly beaten and the state Wu was annexed by Goujian.

(6) The *fu*(赋) is a type of Chinese classical *belle-lettres* in the nature of descriptive lyric poetry. The main part of Qu Yuan's (屈原) works, if not all of them, should come under this

heading, although none of them is called by it. The earliest specimens of this genre so named were written by Song Yu(宋玉), his disciple, — these two pieces, *Gaotang* and *The Divine Lady*, and *A Fu on the Wind*(《风赋》). The writings of Chu, Song, Jingcha(景差) and others were given the name Chu *ci*(楚辞) first by Liu Xiang(刘向) of the Han Dynasty (汉) in his collection of this type of writing. So the ci and the *fu*(辞赋) come to be mentioned together thereafter as closely related, since the latter has its very origin in the former. While Qu Yuan's *Suffering Throes*(《离骚》), *Nine Sylvae*(《九章》) and *Distant Wanderings Travels*(《远游》) and Song Yu's *Nine Clearings*(《九辩》) are strict poems, the *fu* since Song tends to be a confluence of poetry and prose after the manner of the former's *Diving to Know Where I Should Stay*(《卜居》) and the latter's three works mentioned above. It generally contains lines of thymed verse as well as short passages of prose more or less poetic, often in the form of a preamble. ln a great many cases after the Warring States Period (战国,403—221 B. C.) when these two protagonists lived, during the long years of Han, the Three Kingdoms, Jin, the Six Dynasties and Tang (汉,三国,晋,六朝,唐), the *fu* contains much euphuistic parallels of four-and-six-charactered statements(骈四俪六), prolific in imagery and vocabulary. One finds in it lines going in couplets, not so very free nor sometimes very strict, as a rule but not always graced with end rhymes. When its style becomes ornate to excess, the reader has a sense of being surfeited with sweetmeats or seeing a pretty woman over-rouged and-powdered, wearing a score of rings on her ten fingers. Thus, to say simply that it is prose poetry is not quite correct. As a type of literary expression, its source is traceable to one of the six elements (六义) of *Shi Jing* (《诗经》) — *The Book of Odes* of the dynasty Zhou (周), *viz. feng*, *ya*, *Song*, *fu*, *bi*, *xing* (风雅颂赋比兴), and is therefore a development of it. Well it is said by Ban Gu (班固), in the prelude to his *Fu on the Two Capitals* (《两都赋》), that the *fu* is the flow of ancient poetry.

(7) Gaotang, the Wu Mountains (巫山) and the Southern Elevation (阳台) have become proverbial in the Chinese language to mean the secret tryst of a man and a woman in love, while the phrase "clouds and rain" signifies their promiscuous intercourse.

(8) Song Yu, a subject of the state Chu (楚) during the Warring States Period, was a disciple of the great poet Qu Yuan (屈原). As a courtier of King Xiang (襄王), he composed his Nine Clearings to deplore his master's exile and clear him from the false charges laid against him. These two *fu*, *Gaotang* and *The Divine Lady*, were written by him for giving implied re-mon - strance to the young king. Xiang-*wang* was formally crowned in 298 B. C. when his father Huai-*wang* (怀王) had been trapped and taken captive by Zhao-*wang* of Qin (秦昭王) by means of a dirty trick and Qu Yuan had drowned himself the previous year. He proved himself a worse failure than his predecessor who had kept himself inaccessible to Qu Yuan, as a result of calumny, by repulsing his advances. The poet, well

versed in statecraft but prevented from putting his capabilities into practice, committed suicide in his banishment which was directly executed under the new ruler's order, again for libel, given between his father's captivity and his own coronation. His name has always been synonymous with one who knows nothing but fooling round with women.

(9) Yunmeng(云梦) was formerly an immense swamp in the south of the present Anlu *xian*(安陆县), Hubei Province(湖北省), some eight to nine hundred square *Li* in extent. It embraced two low expanses, one in the north of the River and the other in the south respectively called Yun and Meng in ancient days. During the centuries it has dried up into habitable land, though human efforts, interspersed with tens of lakelets.

(10) What goes before is the introduction to the main body of this *fu*. What follows is a descriptive account of the trailing made by the king in company with the poet toward the Temple of Gaotang.

(11) The latter half of this line in the original 若丽山之孤亩 seems to the translator to mean "like the unusual acres (of rock beds) of the Beauteous Islet Jieshi(碣石)". 亩 means 亩丘, acres of crags on the rocky islet explicitly mentioned two lines later and alluded to now. The islet is called 丽山 here, either because the poet gives this new name to Jieshi for its beauty or because it was in the vicinity of Licheng(骊成) by the seaside, 丽 being a simplification of 骊 and here used in its stead

(骊成之山). Instance of such simplification is not lacking in Chinese history and the language. Anyway, it was a cliff and an islet south-west of the old town Li-cheng, according to *The Geographical Annals of The Han Chronicles*(《汉书·地理志》), which site was in the south-west of Leting *xian*(乐亭县). According to *The Annotations to The Classic of Streams* (《水经注》) by Li Daoyuan(郦道元) of North Wei(北魏) durings the Six Dynasties (fl. 366—371), Jieshi Mountain had been in the south-east of Le'an-ting(乐安亭, which is the old town Le'an 乐安 in the north-east of the present Leting *xian*), *The Annotations* also says that the mountain had had several tens of *li* of ways walled by craggy rocks, and on the peak of the height, there had been huge rock pillars called Heaven Bridge Pillars. But this "seaside mountain" is, alas, actually nowhere to be found today. It did exist, however, in the chapter *Yu Gong*(《禹贡》), relating the deeds and measures of Great Yu(大禹), of the classic *The Book of the Past* (《尚书》— *Shang Shu*) written by Confucius himself, the greater part of which was burned by Yingzhen(嬴政), the Beginning Emperor of the Dynasty Qin(秦始皇) in Chinese history. It is said by Li that the mountain had been excavated by Yu in his Herculean efforts to conduct the deluge into the sea, so that the right part of it had later sunk into the Luteous River and the left part had been wrapped round and finally swallowed by the surges. Sima Qian in *The Life of Qin Shi-huang* of his *Chronicles*(司马迁《史记·秦始皇本纪》) says that Yingzhen, the monstrous Huge Dictator, visited Jieshi in 218 B.C., the third year after his conquest of the Six States(六国),

in his travels to the east. In a poem *Jieshi*(《碣石篇》) written for dancing by Cao Cao(曹操) and accompanied with Jin(晋) airs, the first of four stanzas is entitled *Looking at the Blue Sea* (《观沧海》), saying that the blue sea of the fairies is immense and the sun and moon rise from and sink into it. It is unlikely that Song Yu had personally visited the islet mountain, for the capital Ying(郢都) of Chu then, at present the old town Ying *xian*(郢县) in the south-east of Jiangling *xian*(江陵县), Hubei Province, was thousands of li from the spot and he had no occasion or necessity for such a long journey. The spectacular scenic beauty of this rocky islet must have been wide spread at the time of the poet, since he extols it in two lines not far apart, first allusively about looking downward and eastward from the peak and then literally about looking upward and westward from atop the sea waves.

(12) From *The Literary Selections* compiled by the Prince Imperial Zhaoming of the dynasty Liang(梁昭明太子《文选》), where the only comparably more reliable text of this *fu* exists, and from a Ming Dynasty block print edition copy of that book I once possessed, this version of mine should have been made. But I am forced to make this translation from a Dao Guang(道光) edition copy of Yao Nai's *Type Compilations of Old Literary Writings*(姚鼐《古文辞类纂》). There, this line reads 砾碨磥而相摩兮,巆震天之磕磕. There seems to be a corruption of the text in the first three characters, and the word 巆 is not to be found in the most comprehensive dictionary of the Chinese language, the *Kang-xi Dictionary*(《康熙字典》). Ac-

cording to that text in the edition just mentioned above, this line, when partially emendated, should be rendered thus "Gravels grind in their roughness while big rocks crash each against each, rocking the sky." 砾 is "gravels" and 硠礫 is the name of a mountain, which does not make sense and does not agree with the latter half of this line. On the other hand, 礌, I find, means big rocks or pushing rocks to fall down from a high place. Consequently, I make bold to translate in the present form.

(13) The foregoing lines since the last section give an account of the mountains, water and rocks.

(14) *Tuó*(鼍) or *tuódragon*(鼍龙), also called *lingtuó*(灵鼍), commonly known as hog-dragon(猪婆龙), is a reptile akin to the crocodile. It has four crawling claws and is covered all over the body with placoid scales, measuring from ten to twenty feet long. lt lived by the river-side of Yanngzi-*jiang* and Huai-*he*(长江,淮河) in ancient days. I do not know whether it is still existent or has become extinct. Its growls, like the beats of big drums, are noted in *Shi Jing*: "The *tuó*-drum beats sound 'von von'." In evenings and nights, it growled at regular intervals like keeping curfew drum beats. Fond of dozing and often closing its eyes, it was yet mighty in attacks. Its skin was used for covering big drums.

(15) The foregoing lines since the last section deal with the wild beasts, fowls and fishes, all fierce or gigantic.

(16) The *yu*-reeds(竽) was an ancient wind instrument of thirty-six reeds of graduated lengths fixedly arranged from one of the shortest two to two tallest ones and again to a shortest one in some half a large lagenaria(葫芦) shell, about 4½ feet tall. The *sheng*-reeds *or sheng*(笙) is a much smaller wind instrument of the same type with thirteen reeds, about a foot and a half tall. The latter is still in use, while the former has gone out of mode. They resemble the Pandean pipes.

(17) The original of this half a line has "cut short the breath."

(18) The preceding lines since the last section descibe the woods seen run across and passed on the way. Of course the depicture of the inanimate objects, animals and forests above is by no means a realistic one.

(19) Giant Pillars(砥柱). *The Annotations* of Li Daoyuan to *The Classic of Streams* by Sang Qin(桑钦) of the Han Dynasty says that 砥柱 was the name of mountains: in ancient times when Yu(禹) expelled the flood from our land, mountains and hills in the way of east flowing water were excavated by him; thus he dug apart a mountain in its middle, enabling the (Luteous) River to flow through the channel and wrap round both parts, so that as time passed, these were reduced to two giant pillars and then they were called by this proper name. Our poet means to say that there were a great many massive columns like such Giant Pillars at the foot of the Wu Mountains. There is a similar astonishing spectacle in the north of Ireland, which is

called the Giant's Causeway.

(20) The original 虹蜺, the same as 虹霓, means a couple of he and she-rainbows, — what are called the primary and secondary rainbows. The "male one" is full of splendour, while the "female one" is rather subdued in glory.

(21) Meng Ben(孟贲) and Xia Yu(夏育), the two ancient men of valour, are celebrated for their strength. Meng, a subject of the state Wei(卫) during the Warring States Period, has been known for raising a bronz *ding*(鼎) of thousands of catties over his head and for pulling out the horn of a live ox. Xia, a Zhou time man also of Wei, is noted for his strength to lift the weight of thirty thousand catties and pulling out the tail of an ox alive.

(22) The preceding lines since the last section tell of the king and the poet "climbing higher up and looking far off..." and then "casting looks upward at the tops of these...," what they saw and heard, felt and thought, till they came to the side of the Temple of Gaotang.

(23) These four lines and line seven mention eight aromatic herbs and fragrant flowers, and the few lines following name six birds of fine songs and fair feather. In Qu Yuan's *Suffering Throes* and other works, good birds and odorous herbs stand for loyal integrity or symbolize the fair personality of the poet. Due to my lack of knowledge in the fragrant herbs and fair

sweet flowers, I am afraid my rendering of the names is not wholly satisfactory. The original 秋兰 is, I believe, the eupatory or hemp agrimony(兰草,兰泽草,蕑,都梁香), called botanically Eupatorium cannabinum, three to four feet tall, which blows little flowers of light purple in late autumn and is sweet all over. It could also be 泽兰, which is arethusa, lightly fragrant, blowing purplish white flowers in August. Both of these grow in the wild or on mountains by the side of water. lt could not be the orchid(兰花) which belongs to the species Orchidaceae and blooms, some(墨兰,草兰) in early spring, others (蕙兰) in late spring and still others(建兰) in late summer and early autumn, The original 芷, or 白芷, botanically called Heracleum lanatum, belongs to the species Umbelliferae, over four feet all, and blows little white flowers in summer. Since it blooms aiso in umbellules like the 江蓠 in the next line and I am ignorant of its popular English name, I take the great liberty to substitute thyme(百里香) in its stead, which blows in late summer and early autumn little pink or white flowers and is sweet all over. The original 蕙, also called 薰草,零陵香, botanically named Coumarouna odorata, is the coumarou or tonka bean, flowering in the middle of August. The original 江蓠, also called 芎劳,蘼芜, botanically named Cnidium officinale, of the species Umbelliferae, is one to two feet tall, with leaves like those of the celery, blows in autumn little white flowers and is odorous all over. I am ignorant of its popular English name. The original 青荃, also called 荪, of which I am ignorant of the popular English name as well as its botanical one, I could only transliterate. It is said that it is an odoriferous herb standing for the king. The original 射干, botanically known as Belamcanda chinensis, of the species Iris, two to three feet tall, blows beautiful orange flowers with deep purple spots in autumn and is commonly called in the western world fleur-de-lis, lily of the valley or convallaria, which was the royal insignia of France. The original 揭车, the same as 藒车 or 藒车香, also called 䒗舆, of which I am ignorant of the popular English name as well as its botanical one, I could also only transliterate. It is said that it grew in Pengcheng(彭城), at present Tongshan *xian*(铜山县), Jiangsu, several feet tall, an aromatic herb blowing white flowers. The original 越香 in line 7 is inexplicable to me unless it means 越椒, the same as 茱萸. This plant has three varieties: 吴茱萸(Evodia rutaecarpa), 山茱萸(Cornus officinalis) and 食茱萸(Zanthoxylum ailanthoides). The fruits of the first two are for medical use and those of the last are an eatable spice; all these trees are ten to twenty feet tall. The first belongs to the Ruta family(芸香属), so too is the last, while the second bears the popular name of cornus. Although rue(芸香, Ruta grareolens) is an herb only two to three feet tall, — since I am unable to determine whether or not the poet means 越香 to be 越椒 and, if so, which one of the three trees he had in mind when he wrote this *fu*, I cannot help taking the arbitrary decision of rendering the original into the rue, which blossoms in June to July and is sweet all over.

(24) I think the original 垂鸡 means the pheasant of long tail plume.

(25) According to *The Book of Homage to Heaven and Earth* in Sima Qian's *The Chronicles*(司马迁《史记·封禅书》), the fairy was called Xianmeng Zigao(羡门子高). ln *The Life of Qing Shi-huang*(《秦始皇本纪》) by the Grand Curator of History(太史公), it is said that when that monstrous dictator visited Jieshi in his travels to the east in 218 B. C., the third year after he had annexed the Six States(六国), he sent a follower of his named Lu a native of Yan(燕人卢生), up the mountain to find Xianmeng Gaoshi(羡门高誓), the fairy. In the original of this *fu* and elsewhere, he is simply called Xianmeng Gao (羡门高).

(26) Yulin Elder(郁林公) was a fairy who lived on Yulin Mountain (郁林山), also called Yu Mountain(郁山) or Cangwu Mountain(苍梧山), now known as Yundai Mountain(云台山) in the north-east of Guanyun *xian*, Jiangsu Province(江苏省灌云县). With its steep, pointed cliffs deeply embedded in dense forests and clouds, the mountain was formerly on an islet called Yuzhou(郁洲), which is now joined with the mainland. As to why and how the fairy "likes to gather grains," I have no knowledge.

(27) The foregoing lines since the last section tell of what has been seen and heard by the side of the temple and the prayers made, homage done and rituals performed in the temple with the aid of two fairies.

(28) The *ya*(雅) was a large barrel-bellied wind instrument with

both ends quite small in size; if was some 6 feet high and its belly about 3½ feet in diameter. It is out of mode today.

(29) The foregoing lines since the last section tell of how, after the ceremony in the temple, the king gives word that there should be a royal chase of wild animals to celebrate the occasion, while he himself has already half turned a fairy and his progress in the air is accompanied by music and fluttering banners, as he rides in a jade carriage drawn by four blue dragonets.

(30) The ciborium(盖,华盖) is an umbrella-like affair, with its top flat and round and its circular hangings falling down deep. It was said to be first made by Huang-*di*(黄帝). The legend had it that when he fought Chiyou(蚩尤) in the wild of Zhuolu(涿鹿), there were multi-colour clouds and golden branches and jade leaves hovering over his head. Hence he made his cover in response to the happy angury.

(31) The nine vents(九窍) mean the small apertures of the human body, including the two eyes, the two ears, the two nostrils, the mouth and the two nether openings.

(32) Finally, the poet offers his implied remonstrance to the young sovereign that he is no more dashing and impulsive as formerly, but has become sober and thoughtful instead, being "anxious for the good of all people, And the harms to the state would be set aright, the virtuous and sage would lend timely help, …" In the end he congratulates the King with the good

wish "And then, let long life come to him for aye!" upon his expected transformation.

(33) Chunyu Kun(淳于髡) was a subject of the kingdom Qi(齐) during the Warring States Period(战国,403—247 B. C.) of Zhou(周). A contemporary of Mencius(孟轲) and Wei Yang (卫鞅, also known as Shang Yang, 商鞅), flourishing round the years, 360—340 B. C., he was a noted "humourist" and an eloquent speaker, being requested several times to act as special envoy of King Wei of Qin in diplomatic affairs with signal success.

(34) There are various classifications of the five grains. The most prevalent one includes rice, millet, Chinese corn, mai and bean(稻,黍,稷,麦,菽). Millet(黍) is also called 粟,小米, yielding little round grains of various colours — white, yellow, red and black; it is about 2½ feet tall in the fields. Chinese corn is a grain called high cereal(高粱), around 6½ feet tall, yielding small grains of red or white. *Mai* includes barley(大麦) and wheat(小麦).

(35) The *bi*(璧) is a gem ring or *rigol* nine inches (Zhou measure of length) in diameter, the rim three inches wide and the hole of the same length in diameter as the rim in width, according to *Er Ya*(《尔雅》), the earliest dictionary of the Chinese language, said to be first compiled by Zhou-*gong*(周公), added to by Confucius and his disciples and increased by the Han scholars(汉儒). It was annotated by Jin(晋), Song(宋) and

Qing(清) scholars. The Bi has a thickness of some eight or nine tenth of an inch and is bevelled at both edges on one side. It was only possessed by the royalties and nobilities.

(36) A *dou*(斗) is one tenth of a *shi*(石). An English gallon measures 0. 438783 modern *dou* in liquid capacity and an American gallon measures 0.365555 modern *dou* in the same. Therefore, a modern *dou* is equivalent to 2. 279 ×English gallons and a modern *shi* to 22.79 ×English gallons. Dou and *shi* in the Warring States Period might be somewhat different from their modern namesakes.

(37) Mutually surrounding multi-checker(今译为 the *wei*-chess,围棋) stands for the original 六博, which may also mean dice. It is related in Handan Chun's(邯郸淳) *A classic of the Arts* (《艺经》), which states that the game employs small, white and black checkers of 150 each and a checker-board marked by 17 lines lengthwise as well as crosswise of equi-distance. That was the prerequisite before and during the Tang Dynasty. From the Song Dynasty(宋), when Zhang Ni(张拟) stipulated it in his *Classic for Multi-checker*(《棋经》), downwards to the present, the number of lines is increased to 19 in each wise and that of multicheckers to 200 of each colour. The next game mentioned here, pitching arrows into bottles(投壶), was still played during the Ming Dynasty(明), but has become extinct to-day. The earthen or, later, the porcelain bottles used were specially modeled with two extra mouths each, one on either side, attached to the bottle's main mouth, smaller in size and

some three to four inches long, in the form of two rather large, short, tubular cavities. At banquets and carousals, the host and his guests would pitch arrows into the bottle mouths from a certain distance, the winner filling a bumper for the loser to drink. The game is ancient in origin, for *Li Ji*(《礼记》), — *The Book of Etiquette* of Zhou, devotes a chapter to it.

(May 3, 1974)

(38) The original 酒德 means the quality, nature or virtue of drinking.

(39) Liu Ling, a Jin(晋) subject, is well known in history as one of "the Virtuous Seven of the Bamboo Groves"(竹林七贤). He and his intimate friends Yuan Ji(阮籍) and Ji Kang(嵇康), all scholars and poets, were devotees to the philosophies of Lao-*zi*(老子) and Zhuang-*zi*(庄子) and bona fide companions in their recluse life. They were all fond of drinking, although not all of them were free from the taint of holding official posts. Liu is known for taking along large quantities of liquors in his carriage and having servants carrying pickaxes and spades to follow him, so that if he died of sousing, they could bury him on the instant. His wife remonstrated him strongly, but he listened not. He finished, however, his natural years. Yuan was noted for his habit of hallooing and singing poetry, his own or others', at the highest pitch and biggest volume of his voice and tuning the long, narrow, rectangular seven-chorded testudo(七弦琴)(Ji Kang was skilled in this too, besides being a calligrapher and a painter) whenever he felt inclined to

these, whether in company or by himself alone. He was even more used to riding in chaise than Liu; when there was no more way for it to proceed, he often wailed aloud to turn back. Liu did not leave any other work to posterity known to us than this *fu In Praise of the Quality of Drinking*; Yuan left to the world eighty odd poems entitled *Singings from the Bosom*(《咏怀诗》), *On the Way to Take Life*(《达生论》), *The Life of the Gentleman of Virtue and the Way*(《大人先生传》), etc. and Ji (who died of calumny a violent death) his *Collected Works*(《嵇中散集》). Their common bents and outlook of life could perhaps be attributed to the flagitious and malignant court politics which they, as literary men, had no power to cleanse or eradicate.

(40) The expression 大人 means originally a man of virtue. According to *Yi Jing* (《易经》), the virtue of 大人, literally "the great man" is one with that of the heaven and earth. *The Analects of Confucius* (《论语》) identifies "the great man" with the sage. Mencius(孟子) says, in the recorded sayings of his taken down by his disciples and entitled with his name, that "the great man" makes himself right, thereby causing things to right themselves. The original appellative 先生 connotes a man of the right way. According to *Explanations and Anecdotes Incident to The Book of Odes*(《韩诗外传》) by Han Ying(韩婴) of the Han Dynasty(汉), "In olden times, the man who knew the (right) way was called 先生, as if to say that he woke up early. It follows then that the man who does not know the way is ignorant of what is right and what is wrong; he is

not clear-sighted like a drunken man. Therefore, there are people who wake up early, others who wake up late and still others who wake up not at all." In *The Wei Strips* of *The Warring States Strips*(《战国策·卫策》), the term 先生 is used to mean a virtuous elder. Of course, both of these appellations have their later derivative meanings, which we need not go into here. In the light of the aforesaid, these two titles are hence rendered thus.

(41) The original 八方 means the distant places of the eight directions.

(42) Tai-shan(泰山) is a great range of mountains rising in the south-west of Jiaozhou Bay(胶州湾) in Shandong Province (山东省), running westward across the middle of the province and ending at the eastern bank of the Grand Canal. Its chief peak is in the north of Tai'an *xian*(泰安县). Being the most prominent one of the Five Great Ranges of Mountains (五岳) of old Cathay, it has ever been noted for its imposing majesty.

(43) "Floating disks" is a coinage of the translator for the original 浮萍, the botanical name of which is, I have learned, spirodela polyhiza, but the popular name I am ignorant of. They are very small water plants buoyed up on the surface or streams, lakes and ponds.

(44) "The two mighty ones"(二豪) are presumably the poet's two able-bodied hinds or farm-hands who helped him in his brew-

age.

(45) The original 蜾蠃 is called in entomology eumenes pomifomis, a wild bee of about half an inch long with a body bluish black in colour, building its hive on a tree branch or wall in the form of a bottle or ball, depositing in it the eggs or egg cells of "ming-ling" moths, mulberry pests, spiders, etc. after generation and sealing it, so that when the infant bees are hatched out, they could feed on the pest eggs.

(46) The *ming-ling* moth is entomologically called heliothis armiger-a, with a slender grayish yellow body of about half an inch long. Its eggs are called in Chinese 螟蛉 or their sons; when they grow up into larvae, they are light green in colour with yellow and black spots on every section of their bodies. They are harmful pests feeding on tobacco leaves, soy-bean, red-and green-beans, flax, etc., appearing in august. The bluish black bee often takes these eggs before they grow into larvae to feed its young. Our ancestors, not knowing the facts, thought erroneously the bees bearing these eggs with care on their backs to bring them up as their own offspring. Hence the name 螟蛉 in Chinese means foster-son or-daughter. In *The Book of Odes*, there is a poem which goes like this:

The *ming-ling* has its sons,
　The *guo-luo* bears 'em on the back;
Do teach and bring up your sons,
　So they be brought up well too.

It is amusing to think that if "the two mighty ones" were indeed to treat the poet as the bluish black bee has been doing with the "ming-ling" eggs, the story of Liu Ling would be very tragic.

(47) See the introductory remarks on the *fu* in my version of Song Yu's *A Fu on Gaotang*. This *fu* by Pan Yue is introduced here for it is the second of its kind after Song Yu's *Nine Clearings* (cf. its first, third and seventh sections) in China's poetic tradition on the subject of autumn feelings. In originality, it is much inferior to Song's work. Du Fu(杜甫) the great Tang poet has his well-known *Eight Octaves on Autumn Feelings* (《秋感八首》) and Ouyang Xiu(欧阳修) his *A Fu on Autumn Sounds*(《秋声赋》).

(48) Pan Yue, a Jin(晋) subject, was noted for his fine person in his own time and has been the paragon of masculine good looks ever since in China. It was said that when he appeared in Luoyang(洛阳), the capital of Jin, women meeting him on the ways often surrounded him by joining their hands and threw fresh fruits to him for their admiration. His writings have been known for their sweet choice of words and phrases, especially so are his elegiac poems. Being successful in his political career as Imperial Attendant in Matters of Writing(著作郎), Imperial Attendant at Riding(散骑侍郎) and Imperial Constant Attendant of the Department of Court Affairs(散骑常侍隶门下省), therefore called Pan of the Yellow Gate(潘黄门), he was, however, mean in character, flattering the court favourite of Emperor Wu of Jin(晋武帝) — Jia Mi(贾谧), to get what

he wanted. His whole family was exterminated for a false accusation, in an intrigue, of his hatching a plot of rebellion. The emperor himself, Sima Yan(司马炎), was a usurper of a usurping dynasty Wei(魏); so the court was bound to be saturated with villainy. Men like Yuan Ji, Ji Kang and Liu Ling (阮籍、嵇康、刘伶) fleered at politics and occupied themselves merely with poetry, wine and "pure talking". Tao Qian(陶潜), the great poet, "refusing to bend his waist for five *dou* of rice(不为五斗米折腰)", felt ashamed of himself after having been a *xian* magistrate for a short time and left his post to hurry back home, leaving to posterity his excelent *Retracing My way Home*(《归去来辞》).

(49) Or the fifth year of Emperor Wu's reign of Xian-ning(咸宁五年,279 A. D.)

(50) One of the subordinate knights of the Lord of War(太尉掾), whose position equaled the premier's. They were twenty-four in number.

(51) Lieutenant General of the "Wariors of Tigerish Dash"(虎贲中郎将)

(52) The Imperial Attendant at Riding and the Imperial Attendant in the Palace were high officials whose posts were instituted in the Qin Dynasty(秦), the latter going in and out of the palace to wait upon the emperor. In the Wei and Jin Dynasties(魏,晋), the two offices were combined into one and the official

was simply called the Imperial Attendant at Riding. Having attained a station higher than that, Pan Yue is speaking of his equals here. They wore ceremonial coronets at court, which, by no means a simple affair, consisted of a rectangular wooden board, tipped — lower before and higher behind, painted black on the top and red below, and a hat attached to it underneath, with strings of pearls and gems hanging down from the two narrower sides of the board in the front and at the back. The crown of an emperor had twelve strings of pearls and gems dangling fore and hind, his vassals coronets nine, his upper courtiers' also nine and lower courtiers' seven. The writer of this *fu* here speaks of his colleagues, like himself, "wearing coronets decorated with jade cicadae (and pitched with marten tails and gold drops)."

(53) These four lines are quoted from the first section of Song Yu's *Nine Clearings*.

(54) A line of *The Book of Odes* says, "The vanishing Flame of the seventh moon"(七月流火), meaning, according to the annotations, that the Star of Heart, the Great Flame, that appears on the southern horizon in the evenings of the sixth moon would dissappear at the end of the seventh moon.

(55) It is said in *Zhuang-zi*(《庄子》) that "All things are the same, be they long or short"(万物一齐,孰长孰短), and again that "Take life and death as of no difference, and yeas and nays as not contradictory"(以死生为一条,以可不可为一贯).

(56) This justifies the dictum that those who cry shame on others fully deserving it are not necessarily not fully deserving the shame cried on themselves by still others. Pan resorted to flattery in his sordid trick for promotion and power; he fell in a court intrigue equally infamous, failing to do what he says he would do in the concluding part of this *fu*. His "lowering my head feelingly to examine doings of mine" proved to be of no avail. Perhaps, his being a rustic, too young in age and therefore caught in the toils of his greed for affluence and rank and his lust for vainglory was his sole excuse for the sorry figure he cut himself.

(57) Literally translated, these two lines should be like this:

> So, let me set a-right the fold of my
>   gown and get back home,
> Throwing aside the silken cord of my
>   official seal to stay aloof and solemn.

(58) The literal rendering of these lines should be

> The chrysanthemums spread their fairness
>   on the hillside and by the stream.
> I wish to bathe myself in the ripples of
>   the autumnal water.
> And watch for fun the swift movements of the swimming
>   white minnows.

(59) Chen Bo-yu, with his common daily appellative as Zi'ang (661—702) was a native of Shehong County, Zizhou (pre-

fecture, ie, Sichuan Province today). He had been a courtier during Wu Zetian, Queen Dowager's reign of the Tang Dynasty. Based on his lofty ideals to attempt reforming the Tang Dynasty administration, he submitted many a recommendation for the benefit of the state and the people, which was, however, not deemed as acceptable. Being opposed to the decadent literary trends of the dynasties of Qi and Liang, he created a new Tang Dynasty poetic style with his powerful and bold works.

In 696, by order of Queen Wu Zetian, prince Wu Youyi commanded an expedition against Qidan (also Khitan, an ancient nationality in the northern part of China); Chen served as a staff officer in the army. A blue blood, Wu Youyi knew nothing about military affairs. Although Chen did work out ingenious stratagems for troop maneuvres, he again was set at naught. This poem was written at a time when he was frustrated at his efforts with the military. He seemed to feel that he had failed to come across heroic figures of ancient times like Yue Yi(乐毅) and King Zhao of the Yan Dynasty(燕昭王), neither would he be able to see those to come in the future, heaving, thus, his sighs of profound disappointment. The poem reflects the author's active spirit of trying to make contributions to his country.

(60) *Liang County Song* is the text for singing the *Liang County Tune* in the *Garner of Tunes* of the Tang Dynasty. Liang-zhou is, nowadays, Wuwei county, Gansu Province. The character "仞" represents a linear measure unit in ancient China of 7 ancient Chinese feet long. The Qiang flute was a wind instru-

ment of one of the minorities outside of the northwest regions of ancient China, later on often played in the military band. The "杨柳"(willow) refers to an ancient song named "Plucking Willows". The original locality of Jade Gate Pass lies in the north-west of Dun-huang county, Gansu Province. The last two lines say that why does someone have to play the "Plucking Willows" on the Qiang flute with its sullen note to complain of the latecoming of spring? People should learn that spring breeze would never reach farther on than the Jade Gate Pass. Between the lines, the lack of concern on the part of the imperial court for the frontier guards is insinuated.

(61) The *bi-li*(Written in Chinese as 觱篥,筚篥 or 悲篥) pipe was originated from Qiuci(龟兹), one of the thirty-six states of West Land(西域), now mainly lying in China's Xinjiang (meaning "New Territory") Province, whither the emperor Wu-*di* of Han(汉武帝) sent his great general Zhang Jian(张骞) in 122 B.C. as ambassador extraordinary to establish diplomatic relations and economic and cultural communications.

(62) It was commonly believed in ancient Cathay that a dragon's groaning would cause springs to bubble forth and a roaring tiger would provoke the winds blowing.

(63) The original《渔阳掺》also called《渔阳参挝》, was a drum tune stricken by the youthful and highly gifted scholar and poet *Mi Heng*(祢衡) of East Han(东汉) at a feast to which a great company of court officials were invited by Cao Cao(曹操) the

chancellor. Mi was ordered by Cao to beat on a big drum to amuse his guests as well as an insult to the young scholar for his arrogant attitude towards the overpowering courtier. Mi accepted the challenge and hit back by first undressing his gown and upper garment, then beating on the big drum a furiously rapid tune as a defiant protest to Cao and finally putting on his clothes to go away. According to Yu Xing's(庾信, fl. 540—560) poem *Listening to the Clubbing of Laundered Clothes at Night*(《夜听捣衣诗》), a line "Rapid clubbings sound like Yu-yang drum beats"(杵急渔阳掺) gives an inkling of the nature of this drum tune.

(64) The original "Willows"(杨柳) signifies the ancient song *Picking Willow Twigs*(《杨柳枝》) turning to a light, breezy new tune.

(65) Ehuang(娥皇) and Nüying(女英) were the two princesses of *Di* Yao(帝尧, fabled to have reigned from 2357 to 2257 B. C.) of Tao-tang(陶唐), given by him in marriage to Shun of Yu(虞舜, 2255—2207 B. C.), also named Zhonghua(重华), as his dual spouses. Legendary lore has it that *Di* Shun died in the wilds of Cangwu(苍梧之野) while leading his expedition against the rebellious Miao(苗) tribesmen. On hearing the tidings of his unexpected illness, they sped southward trying to succour him. But when they got to the Limpid Xiang Stream (潇湘), a furious squall overtook them and they were drowned without being able to catch sight of their dear lord, alive or dead. In Qu Yuan's(屈原, 345—286 B. C.) great

self-mourning ode *Summoning My Soul*(《招魂》), the last line says:

"魂兮归来哀江南!"

(Come back, oh my soul, to the south of Stream Ai!)

"'Ai' in the original means 'sorrow'. Stream Sorrow (哀江) is the section of Xiang Stream(湘水) called Limpid Xiang(潇湘) confluent with Miluo River(汨罗江), flowing northward into the Dongting Lake(洞庭湖). It has two islets called Great Sorrow and Small Sorrow(大小哀洲). Legend has it that Shun's two queens following in pursuit of, but failing to catch up with, him in his southern campaign, cried bitterly on these two islets, hence their names." — quoted from § 19 of Ⅶ, *Chü Yuan and His Works*, Introduction to my book *Selected Poems of Chü Yuan*.

This renowned poem of Li Bai in the manner of *Garner of Tunes* poems of Han and Wei(汉、魏《乐府》诗), with irregular measures and thymings like the Pindaric odes, makes use of the final, long departure of Shun from his dear queens, Yao's two princesses Ehuang and Nüying, as a tragic setting for the poet's feelings of alarm, indignation, sorrow and helplessness over the political mess made by Emperor Xuan-*zong* in his dotage. The theme and feelings are allusively and tersely, as well as discreetly and vaguely hinted at, to avoid wrathful persecution or fatal revenge from those the poet would certainly offend. *The Lay of the Sun Arising and Sinking* in the like vein and of the like matter is more hazy.

(66) The previous lines speak of Ehuang and Nüying's doomed de-

parting from their lord as tragic. Here, it is insinuated that the court debaucheries ("Wanton waves," see note to *The Lay of the Sun Arising and Sinking*) and Xuan-*zong's* blind trust of state affairs in Li Linfu and Yang Guozhong and that of military authority in An Lushan are bound for tragic and fatal outcome: the poet's counsel to the contrary would be of no avail.

(67) "I do fear Providence would not decree matters as I, cherishing my fidelity to the Emperor, wish things to happen."

(68) According to *The Chronicle of Bamboo Strips*(《竹书纪年》), unearthed from King Xiang of Wei's(魏襄王) mausoleum in the second year of the Tai-kang Period of Wu-*di* of Jin(晋武帝太康二年,281 A. D.) plundered by a Ji County(汲郡) Jsin subject called Bu Zhun(不准) in several tens of cart loads, *Di* Yao when advanced in age was banished to Pingyang(平阳) and imprisoned by Shun. This is contrary to *Di* Yao and *Di* Shun's traditionally good names and relations. To say Yao and Shun would have to abdicate to give place to Yu is simply an exaggeration to bring forth and foreshadow the following thoughts.

(69) These four lines may allude to Xuan-*zong's* entrusting of power in Li Linfu, Yang Guozhong, An Lushan and Geshu Han or these five and the next lines may allude to his prince Su-*zong's* (肃宗) coronation as emperor at Lingwu(灵武) and the latter's eunuch Li Fuguo(李辅国) faking his imperial decree to enforce the removal of Xuan-*zong's* living quarters to the

western part of the palace. Soon after this compulsory removal, Xuan-*zong* died of anger and grief.

(70) *Di* Shun was known to be duo-pupiled.

(71) There is a species of bamboo with sparse spots of mauve, traditionally said to be the tear stains of Ehuang and Nüying. Legendary lore has it that before the two sisters were drowned, they wailed bitterly facing the Plain of Cangwu; their tears sprinkled on the bamboo poles kept fast and last forever.

(72) Cancong and Yufu were ancient legendary kings who founded the state Shu over forty millennium years ago. It was isolated from the Middle Empire till its conquest by King Wei of Qin (秦惠王) in 316 B. C.

(73) Noble White Alp(太白山) lay in the west of the then capital Chang'an(长安) of the Dynasty Tang(唐), as it still does so in the west of the provincial chief city Xi'an(西安) of Shanxi Province(陕西) today. It was and is capped with snow all the year round, hence its name.

(74) It was said that King Wei of Qin sent five beautiful maidens to marry five princes of Shu. Shu dispatched five envoys of giant strength to greet the brides. On their way back to Zitong(梓潼), they came across a huge serpent entering its recess. They pulled its tail to drag it out. As a result the mountain crumbled, the five were all crashed to death and the five beauties

rose to a mountain top that was not undermined and were gorgonized.

(75) Xihe(羲和) is said to drive the chariot drawn by six dragons in which the God of Sun rides. When he drives to the highest cliff, he has to turn round his chariot to wind his way about.

(76) Yellow stocks are said to be of the highest flight.

(77) Blue Sod Alps(青泥岭), in Lüeyang *xian*(略阳县), Shanxi Province(陕西省) at present, is noted of its "twist and turn in winding about".

(78) Shu is in the southwest of Qin(秦).

(79) The cuckoos(子规,杜宇,杜鹃,望帝) are sad in their cries. One of the legends has it that Wang-*di*, the King of Shu, raped his premier's wife, felt ashamed of himself and escaped to turn himself into a bird sadly crying his own name to show regret.

(80) The Sword Steeple(剑阁) is between the Great Sword Mountain and the Small Sword Mountain in the northeast of the Sword Steeple *xian* of Sichuan Province today. It is the main passage or pass between Sichuan(四川) and Shanxi(陕西) Provinces, a part of the Southern Flight of Steps(南栈道).

(81) *Crows Craoking at Dusk* (《乌夜啼》) is an old traditional

theme and title in *The Garner of Tunes* poems. It was said to be first written by a certain Wang Yiqing(王义庆) during the Yuan-jia(元嘉) years(424—453) of the dynasty Liu Song(刘宋,420—470). In *The Garner of Tunes Anthology*(《乐府诗集》), there are eight poems so entitled. In the *Lives of Noted Women*(《列女传》) of the *Jin Dynasty Chronicle*(《晋书》), Dou Tao's(窦滔) wife Su Hui(苏蕙), when her husband was exiled to Liu Sha(流沙) by his king Fu Jian(苻坚) of Fore Qin(前秦), wove a series of palindromic and rondure poems on a broad piece of silk taffeta(织锦为回文旋图诗) and sent him it to show her commiserating love and devotion. It has been said that Li Bai probably used this traditional theme and title to voice his critical dissent from Emperor Xuan-*zong's*(唐玄宗) border expansion policy.

(82) The palindromic and rondure poem(回文诗,璇玑图诗) was ingeniously composed and then woven into such a pattern in a piece of taffeta that a host of variant versions of it could be read from the top down regularly to the end as well as from the end up reversely to the top and crosswise from the right to the left and then also from the left to the right in a number of roundabout ways. As the Chinese language consists of characters (in their written form, made up of strokes) each having a sound and a meaning of its own, unlike the western, Indo-European languages, which are all composed of words formed by combining alphabets to shape syllables and joining syllables to make words or particles, so it is possible in Chinese to join up two to three, four, five, six, seven or even eight characters to

make a phrase, clause, sentence or line of verse. In Su Hui's original palindromic and rondure poem, which is composed of 840 characters, woven in a piece of taffeta said to be 8 inches square, a Buddhist bonze by the name of Qi-*zong*(起宗) living at the turning of the Song(宋,960—1276) to the Yuan (元,1277—1367) Dynasties, found out 3752 poems of 3-charactered, 4-charactered, 5-charactered, 6-charactered and 7-charactered poems in these 840 characters. And a certain Kang Wanming(康万民) of the Ming Dynasty(1368—1643) added another "Xuanji" picture(璇玑图) and read out 4206 poems from Su Hui's original poem.

(83) Gusu Terrace(姑苏台) is on Gusu Mount(姑苏山), a range of hillocks thirty *li* south-west of the present Suzhou City(苏州市), which was anciently called Gu-su. The Terrace, also known as Xu Terrace(胥台), was first built by Fu Cha's father King He Lu of Wu(吴王阖庐). Fu Cha expanded the Terrace and spent three years to build the Spring Night Palace (春宵宫) for whole night carousals. Fu Cha's prince royal You(友) burnt down the palace when his defending troops were completely crushed by Gou Jian's invading legions.

(84) Fucha(夫差,? —473 B. C.), king of the state Wu(吴) at the end of the Spring and Autumn Period(春秋,770—476 B. C.) of the dynasty Zhou(周,1122—247 B. C.), overcame the armed forces of the state Yue(越) with a thrashing defeat and pierced into its capital Kuaiji(会稽). Goujian(勾践,? —465 B. C.), king of Yue, sued for peace, bribed Wu's chief

courtier Pi(太宰嚭) and knowing his enemy to be found of women, sent two exquisite beauties Xishi(西施) and Zheng Dan(郑旦), as human tributes of indemnity to pacify the victor. After twenty years of recuperation and incessant strengthening, Goujian, taking advantage of his enemy's, and leading all his hardened troops in person far away from the capital to attend a gathering of friendly state heads, forced a swift, resolute campaign to crush Wu and took over the control of its capital completely. Fucha committed suicide and Wu was annexed by Yue. Such is the political background of this poem.

This poem was not just a memorial lyric of historical events, according to the critic Zhan Ying(詹锳): it was an occult warning by our poet to his emperor Xuan-*zong* of Tang whose imperial concubine bore resemblance to Xishi in beauty as well as in the circumstances of her monarch's doting on her — Fucha lost his state and his life on account of Xishi, so Xuan-*zong* was going to lose his for Yang Yuhuan(杨玉环). Confer the notes on *The Lay of the Sun Arising and Sinking*.

(85) This was the copper-cased water-dripping timepiece the clepsydra(铜壶滴漏,or 漏壶), with a silverpin (attached to a bamboo float to buoy it up) to indicate how much water had been dripped for showing the passage of time, before the introduction of clocks and watches during the Ming Dynasty from Europe.

(May 20, 1983)

(86) According to *Huainan-zi*(《淮南子》), a work of legendary

lore and metaphysical strivings of the Lao-*zi*(老子) School of thought by Liu An(刘安,179—122 B. C.), the Sun rides a radiant chariot drawn by six flaming dragons.

(87) The driver of this solar chariot is Xihe(羲和).

(88) The original of this line 羲和,羲和,汝奚汩没于荒淫之波 is taken by me to allude to Emperor Xuan-*zong*'s(唐玄宗,685—672) being completely submerged in his enslaving infatuation for Yang Taizhen(杨太真), his undue trust of imperial affairs, political and military, in his malignant chancellor Li Linfu(李林甫), her three cousins, especially Yang Guozhong(杨国忠), her three brothers-in-law and his Hu general An Lushan(安禄山). The solar chariot at the time being driven by Xuan-*zong* is the dynasty Tang in Li Bai's imaginative, metaphorical vista, and the Sun signifies the *huang-di*, imperial or regal powers of all time. Yang Taizhen, the imperial concubine, was originally Prince Li Mao's(李瑁) wife and Xuan-*zong*'s daughter-in-law. After the decease of Xuan-*zong*'s favourite concubine Wu Hui-*fei*(武惠妃), Yang Taizhen was first ordained as a Taoist priestess to deceive the court's sense of decorum and then, in the fourth year of Tian-bao(天宝四年,755 A. D.), she was ceremonially appointed as his formal Imperial Concubine. Xuan-*zong* kept promiscuous relations with all her three sisters and she held similar secret affairs with her cousin Yang Guozhong and the Hu satrap general An Lushan, openly known as her foster son. Scholars and commentators have been silent during these thousand and two hundred odd years on

these points which are the hidden meaning of Xihe being "sunk in the expanse of wanton waves". In the 14th year of Tain-bao (天宝十四年,765 A. D.), the military governor An Lushan (安禄山), with his subordinate general Shi Siming(史思明) rebelled on account of the mutual jealousy between him and Yang Guozhong in their grasp for power and sexual promiscuities with Yang Taizheng. Luoyang(洛阳) and the then capital Chang'an(长安) fell to the foster son of the imperial concubine. Xuan-*zong* had to flee for his life to Shu(蜀,Sichuan today) before the fall of the capital; on his way of flight, he could not help having her strangled with a silk scarf and her cousin and paramour Yang Guozong beheaded, to pacify the commanders of the imperial guard at the Mawei Post Station (马嵬驿).

(89) According to *Huai Nan Zi*, Duke Luyang(鲁阳公) shook his lance at the sun when he was engaged in close fighting with the chief of Han(韩) as the sun was going to set; immediately, the setting sun bounced back from the north-western horizon for a distance of three *she*(三舍,ninety *li*), so that he could beat his antagonist in time. These four lines about monstrous Luyang's waving his lance at the sun seem to allude to An Lushan, Shi Siming and their fierce, marauding troops.

(90) An Lushan(安禄山) and Shi Siming's(史思明) Hu(胡) troops were notorious for their cruelty, massacre and ravage of civilians of Luoyang(洛阳), Chang'an(长安) the capital and thirteen counties of Jizhou(冀州), at present in Hebei(河北)

Province. The rebellion lasted for more than seven years and was exhausted by patricides and murders in the rebels' own camps; it petered out with the suicide of Shi Siming's son in the first year of the Guang-de Period (广德元年, 763 A. D.) of Dai-*zhong* (代宗), the grandson of Xuan-*zong*. Our poet died in the previous year; so too did, Xuan-*zong*, Li Bai's sovereign, and De-*zong* (德宗), Xuan-*zong* successor and Dai-*zong's* father.

(91) The last two lines of the original seem to mean the poet bearing all the calamities of Xuan-*zong's* reign with gloomy, distressing but patient resignation.

(92) Peonies were in glorious bloom in the imperial garden as the Emperor was enjoying their sight and fragrance, being attended by his doted concubine for the occasion. Ming Huang (明皇, formally known as Xuan-*zong* of Tang, 唐玄宗, 685—762, reigning from 712—756), sitting in the aloes-wood arbour and touched with winsome fancies musical and poetic, wished Li Bai to compose poems for accompanying the new tunes of melody. He said, "Enjoying these renowned flowers while facing my concubine, why should we resort to old tunes?" When the poet was summoned to appear opportunely for composing new verses, he was already quite drunk. Court attendants splashed water on his face and hand him his writing brush. Li Guinian (李龟年), the court tunes-composer, -singer and -performer, handed the gold-speckled silk scroll to Li Bai. Instantly, he composed three quatrains of exquisite beauty and brushed them

on the spread sheet (the stanza above being the first of them), members of the Court Singers and Players performed on strings and bamboo tubes, Li Guinian sang in accord and His Majesty attuned with a gem flute. Meanwhile, Yang Taizhen(杨太真) drank the West Liang(西凉) rare delicious port from a crystal chalice, wishing joy and longevity to her lord forever and aye.

—Taken from *Notable Happenings about Tang Poetry*(《唐诗纪事》) by Ji Yougong(计有功) of Song(宋).

(93) The spray of wood-stemmed peony with its pink flowers sprinkled with dews is compared to Yang Taizhen(杨太真) the imperial concubine graced with the Emperor's favours.

(94) The daughter of the Wu Mountains(巫山女神), as sung by Song Yu(宋玉) in his *A Fu on Gaotang*(《高唐赋》) "While leaving she said, 'I am in the south of the Wu Mountains and on the pinnacle rock of the highland; at dawn I am the morning clouds and towards sunset I become the showering rain; be it after daybreak or be it before dusk, I am always there below the southern Elevation.'" The favours and love bestowed on the daughter of the Wu Mountains by King Huai of Chu(楚怀王) were but a legendary tale, not to be compared to the grace and affection of Xuan-*zong* given her.

(95) Zhao Feiyan(赵飞燕), whose name means "the Flitting Swallow", was at first a maid of honour of Emperor Cheng of

Han's(汉成帝) princess Yang'e(阳阿公主). She was a beauty and a light-footed dancer; deeply beloved by the monarch, she was formally married as his empress. Years later, after the emperor's decease, she was debased as a common female subject for her sexual misdemeanour, whereupon she committed suicide.

As Xuan-*zong*(唐玄宗) and his imperial concubine were enjoying the flowering peonies in the aloes-wood arbour, our poet, as a member of the Court School of Literati(供奉翰林), was summoned to the feast and ordered to write poems for the occasion. He became part drunk and, having asked the attending chief eunuch Gao Lishi(高力士) to pull off his black silk high-heeled and thick-soled boots(靴), composed these three beautiful quatrains. The highly favoured eunuch resented the indignity and hit back by back-biting Li Bai as insinuating insults to the imperial concubine in his comparison of her to the Flitting Swallow and the daughter of the Wu Mountains. Our poet thus won the anger of the imperial concubine and the displeasure of the emperor.

(96) The climate of ancient Yan(燕), where the supposed poetess's husband is draughted for the armed forces, in the northern region of Hebei Province(河北省) and the south-west of Liaoning Province(辽宁省) today, is much colder than that of ancient Qin(秦) in the Shanxi Province today, where the supposed poetess is. So, when the grasses of Yan begin to turn verdant like tufts of green silk, the mulberry leaves of Qin are already thick and hanging low on the branches. When the hus-

band is touched by the approach of spring as he sees the grasses turning green, the wife has for more days been struck by the mulberry leaves growing thick and hanging low on the branches of the trees. The dear wife is so devoted to her beloved husband that she does not wish the spring breeze, a total stranger, to be wafted into her silk curtain piece.

(97) 同(96)

(98) This poem was supposed by the poet to be written by a Jin Dynasty(晋,265—419) dame of the state Wu(吴国) called Ziye thinking of her enlisted husband. Chang'an was the capital of the Tang(唐) Dynasty(618—906). Gem Gateway or Gem Pass was one of two ancient Passes, the other being called Yang Pass(阳关), the passage between the Tang Empire and West Domain(西域). It is the west of Dunhuang *xian*(敦煌县) in Gansu Province(甘肃省) today.

(99) *Long Drawn Yearning*《长相思》is the title of one of the songs of *The Garner of Tunes*《乐府》, which was originally named when the official organ was decreed to be set up by the emperor Wu-*di* of Han(汉武帝,140—87 B. C.), after the device of the suburb sacrificial rites in paying homage to Heaven and Earth, as the imperial institute for collecting folk songs and composing tunes for musical accompaniment("武帝定郊祀之礼,乃立乐府"). The song was at the very first one of the twenty-five songs of ancient plaints(《长相思》古怨思二十五曲之一), derived from a very ancient poem "Up above, long

drawn yearning is said; down below, long drawn parting is quothed"("本古诗'上言长相思,下言久别离'"). In old songs, therefore, this short snatch "Long drawn yearning" is often made use of for playing on dear rememberance. Li Bai also performs his tune on this age-long theme after the poets of Liang(梁) and Chen(陈) of the Six Dynasties(六朝).

(100) "The Beauteous One" in this imagined song of the supposed lady is meant by her to be her beloved mate.

(101) In the hallucination of the supposed poetess, her "Beauteous One" is seen by her at the horizon "vaulted above by the empyrean azure" and "by the expanse of clear waves upborne below".

(102) "The sky and earth where he is are thus far away that striving so hard as my soul doth, it cannot hope to reach there as the Mountain of the Jade Gate Pass(玉门关) — that is, the Border Defile Mount — is thousands of *li* away from me." The Jade Gate Pass, so renowned in the Tang poetry, in the county Dunhuang(敦煌郡) of Gansu Province(甘肃) today, was, according to Prince Zhanghuai(章怀太子), 3600 *li* from the imperial capital Chang'an (长安).

(103) Sand pyrus(沙棠) was said to be a highly buoyant wood growing on the Kunlun Mountains(昆仑山), the fruits of which when eaten by men would make them proof against being drowned.

(104) These four lines in the original, rendered into eight in the English version, occasion difficulties to a critic Zhu Jian(朱谏), who says they are irrelevant to their context as well as to themselves one another, and so the poem, he thinks, was probably composed by someone else who was, however, not a trifling poetaster, though not such an illustrious poet as Li Bai. A later critic Mei Dingzuo(梅鼎祚) dismisses this comment as a gross mistake. Wang Qi(王琦), the editor of the early Qian-long(乾隆) edition (1758) of Li Bai's *Complete Works*, opines that, the first two lines mean to say that to be intent upon becoming a fairy, one would not inevitably succeed in winning metamorphosis to fly heavenward, but to be free from wiles, forget one's identity and hive in consciousness with the gulls in their flights, one may attain spiritual freedom at the moment, while the next two lines mean to say that, to be intent upon poetic composition, one might in the end achieve immortal poetry such as Qu Yuan's, but to devote one's efforts to the establishment of worldly sights and visual glory such as the Chu(楚) kings' terraces and arbours, one could gain only transient satisfaction of the senses. The comparisons and contrasts between the first two instances and the second two would naturally give one the right choices. In short, the first two lines are related to the entertainment on the pyrus barge, while the second two are concerned with the lines following.

(105) To the west of ancient Ezhou(鄂州), called Wuchang(武昌) today, on the Yellow Crane *Ait*(黄鹄矶) in the Long

River(长江) or Yangzi-*jiang*(扬子江), there stands the Yellow Crane Tower(黄鹤楼). The structure, first built in the second year of the Huang-wu Period(黄武二年,223 A. D.) of Wu(吴) one of the Three Kingdoms(三国,220—280), was burnt down and rebuilt many times through the centuries. It derives its name from one of the three or all these legendary anecdotes: ① Fei Hui(费祎,? —253), the Grand General(大将军) of Han of Shu(蜀汉), after his metamorphosis into a fairy, once rode back in flying astride a yellow crance to rest for a while on the Tower; ② According to *The Tales of Strange Events*(《述异记》) by Zu Chongzhi(祖冲之,429—500,the great scientist of the South Dynasty,南朝,420—588), Xun Gui(荀瓌), once taking a rest on the Yellow Crane Tower in his trip to the east, noticed specks of something falling down in the south-western horizon, before long, they came as riders of yellow cranes and alighted by the Tower; the cranes stopped at the entrance and their riders shared a feast in doors; soon after their entertainment, they rode off astride the cranes and disappeared; ③ According to *Reliques of South Qi*(《南齐志》) now lost, quoted by *Geographical Scenic Spots of Notability*(《舆地纪胜》) *it is said that the fairy Wang Zi'an*(王子安) *often passed the Tower in his flights astride a yellow* crane.

(106) The chapter *Luteous Emperor* of *Lie-zi*(《列子·黄帝》) speaks of a seaboard farer who kept close company with the seagulls daily. The birds, not afraid of him, often flied near him and even stopped to perch on his shoulders and arms.

One day, his father said to him that he heard the birds were very familiar with him and so asked him to take one or two home to show them to himself. The next day when he went to the seaside, the gulls refrained from flying near him or stopping at his side.

(107) Qu Yuan(屈原,*circa* 345—286 B. C.), the greatest as well as the earliest renowned poet of ancient Cathay (and the greatest statesman and patriot of his time to boot), whose formal names are Ping(平) and Zhengze(正则), was a member of an anciently descended illustrious house closely related to the ruling royal family of the state Chu(楚). His great ode *Lee Sao*(《离骚》—*Suffering Throes*), *Nine Songs*(《九歌》), *A Sylva of Nine Pieces*(《九章》), *Sky-vaulting Queries*(《天问》), *Distant Wanderings*(《远游》) and *Hailing Home the Soul*(《招魂》) are the few extant works known to have descended to us from some twenty-three centuries ago.

(108) Wang Qi(王琦), the editor of the Qian-long edition of *Li Bai's Complete Works*, mentions two such terraces, the Zhanghua Terrace(章华台) said to be located in Jianli *xian*(监利县) of Hubei(湖北) Province today, and the Yunyang Terrace(云阳台), in the Yunyang County(云阳邑) of the state Chu(楚), now in Danyang *xian*(丹阳县) of Jiangsu(江苏) Province. They are probably non-existent now, or at most in ruins.

(109) Xie Tiao(谢朓,460?—496?), known also by his name of

daily use Xuan Hui(玄晖), an eminent poet of South Qi(南齐,479—502) of the Six Dynasties(六朝), has a poem *Ascending the Three-peaked Mount before Dusk and Looking Back at the Capital*(《晚登三山还望京邑》), with the lines:

Sunset clouds spread into taffeta,
The limpid River is like white tiffany.
(馀云散成绮,澄江净如练。)

(May 25, 1082)

(110) Two mounts facing each other like the antennae of a silkworm's moth in the remote distance are thus called Emei(峨眉); so the range of mountains is also called Emei(蛾眉), witten differently but pronounced the same, meaning the antennae of a silkworm's moth. The Buddhists called them the Luminous Mounts(光明山), while the Taoists named them the Empty Spiritualized Hollowed Heaven(虚灵洞天). The range is today in the south-west of the *xian* Emei(峨眉县) of Sichuan Province(四川省). It is a branch of the Min Mountains(岷山), rolling southward to the *xian* region and protruding in three mount peaks, called the Great *E*, the Middle *E* and the Small *E*(大峨、中峨、小峨).

(111) Pingqiang(平羌), a stream, also called Qingyi Stream(青衣水), in the east of Emei.

(112) The original 青溪 means the Qingxi Stream.

(113) The Three Gorges: those of the Long River(长江), Jutang

（瞿塘），Wu（巫）and Xiling（西陵），being narrow passages of the stream between high mountains on both banks.

（114） Yüzhou's（渝州）ancient domain is now the city of Chongqing（重庆）.

（115） Mount Lu（庐山）is in the south of the city Jiujiang（九江），Jiangxi（江西）Province today. According to legendary lore, during the reign of King Wu of Zhou（周武王，1122—1116 B. C.），there were seven brothers of the family Kuang（匡）thatching their cottages on the side of this mountain and hence it has been called Mount Kuang or Kuang Lu（Lu meaning "cottages"）.

（116） Lu Xuzhou（卢虚舟，the poet's friend to whom this poom was addressed），was Lord Attendant taking charge of insignia at court，Chief of the Guards and Security Warden of the Capital（殿中侍御史，掌殿廷仪卫及京城纠察）.

（117） According to the *Analects of Confucius*（《论语》），"The lunatic of Chu Jieyu（楚狂接舆）sang his song when he walked passing Confucius：'Phoenix，ah，Phoenix，how low hath virtue of the times sunk！'（凤兮凤兮，何德之衰！）And according to Huangfu Mi's（皇甫谧）*Lives of Men of High Virtues*（《高士传》），" Lu Tong（陆通），called also with his common，daily appellative（字）Jieyu（接舆），a subject of the state Chu（楚国），seeing the chaotic state of affairs in politics during the reign of King Zhao of Chu（楚昭王），affected to be a lunatic and declined to assume any office in the officialdom of his time. He counseled Confucius not to officiate for avoiding personal calamity.

(118) Here our poet, calling himself "the lunatic of Chu", compares his friend Lu Xuzhou to Confucius, by counselling him not to stay in office any longer, but to renounce the world and go with himself to visit the Five Renowned Mounts, seek out fairies, keep company with them and become fairies themselves.

(119) The original Yellow Crane Tower(黄鹤楼) was located on the Yellow Crane Ait(黄鹄矶) at Ezhou(鄂州) Town facing the Great River to the west. It was first built during the Three Kingdoms Period(三国) in the second year of Huang-wu(黄武二年) of Wu(吴,223 A. D.), being burnt down and rebuilt again and again through the centuries. According to one tradition, when Fei Hui(费祎,? —253) had been metamorphosed into a fairy, he rode off on and alighted from a yellow crane in this tower. Another legend has it that Xun Gui(荀瓌), once resting in the Tower, saw fairies coming astride cranes from the south-west and alighting there held their feast and flied away afterwards. A third folk tale says that the fairy known by the name Wang Zi'an(王子安) had passed the tower several times on the back of a crane.

(120) The cane of green jade was one used by a faery to prop himself or herself.

(121) The Five Mounts of the great Central Empire mean originally Tai, the East Mount(东岳泰山); Hua, the West Mount(西岳华山); Huo the South Mount(南岳霍山); Heng, the North Mount(北岳恒山) and Songgao the Central Mount(中岳嵩高). Here, however, they mean in general (at) the noted mountains of the land.

(122) By the side of the South Dipper(南斗星座) or the Little Bear (小熊星座) in contrast with the North Dipper(北斗) or the Great Bear(大熊星座).

(123) Folds of mountain ranges are involved like layers of screens wrapping around one another, all enshrouded in gorgeous clouds of brocade.

(124) Poyang Lake(鄱阳湖) which reflects a dark greenish-blue.

(125) The Incense Burner Cliff(香炉峰), and the Double Swords Cliffs(双剑峰).

(126) Golden Portal Peak(金阙岩), also called Rock Gate(石门), is in the south-west of the Incense Burner Cliff.

(127) The Silvery Stream(银河) means the Triple Waterfall(三叠泉) splashing down three-crooked over the Three Rock Beams(三石梁).

(128) The district of Mount Lu during the Spring and Autumn Peri-

od(春秋,722—481 B. C.) belonged to the Kingdom of Wu (吴国) of the Three Kingdoms(三国).

(129) In ancient geography, as the Great River flowed into Xunyang (浔阳) district, it branched off into nine streams.

(130) Xie Lingyun(谢灵运,390?—437?), a Six Dynasties poet whom Li Bai esteemed highly, in his poem *Entering the Mouth of Lake Pengli*(《入彭蠡湖口》) has a line "Climbing slopes to watch myself in the stone mirror." It was said that it could reflect human images.

(131) According to the occult art of metamorphosing oneself into a fairy, a proper quantity of mercury is to be transformed into cinnabar, which is changed back to mercury, then the mercury is restored into cinnabar. The process is repeated again and again, until the dosage fourth time restored to cinnabar. Then, swallowing the cinnabar would make one acquire fairyhood.

(132) The Chinese original 琴心三叠 means the complete composure of the mind as being totally free from lay thoughts. When one has reached that absolute quietude, one has obtained fairyhood.

(133) The newly initiated fairy, with a lotus bloom on his arm as a symbol, then goes on his pilgrimage up the Gem Capital Mount(玉京山) to pay homage to the Primeval Heavenly Di-

vinity(元始天尊).

(134) According to *Huainan-zi*(《淮南子》), a certain Lu Ao(卢敖), having roamed all over the land, came to Menggu Mountain(蒙谷山), where he saw a man of novel appearance whirling in the winds. Lu Ao requested him to keep his own company. That man laughed and said, "I expect to meet Han Man(汗漫, a fairy's name) on the outskirts of the Nineth Heaven, and so could not abide with you long". Saying this, he leapt into the clouds. It is known that Lu Ao was a doctor of the First Emperor of Qin(秦始皇时博士). Here, Li Bai calls his friend Lu Xuzhou Lu Ao and mean himself to be Han Man; he would expect to accompany his friend to rove the empyrean in the not distant future.

This poem was composed by Li Bai in the first year of Shang-yuan(上元元年,760) on Mount Lu, the year after he was pardoned by imperial decree from being suspected of implication in the murder of Emperor Su's(肃宗) brother King Yong(永王). The poet was then sixty years old. He had once taken a landscape-sighting trip to Mount Lu with Lu Xuzhou some years before. After being stricken in that untoward event with imprisonment and exile, he was then in his late years. Besides taking consolation in mountain sceneries, his interest in expecting to metamorphose himself into a fairy had gained on him. Some literary critics tend to say there are traces of his fairyhood in these lines. Two years later, Li Bai died. He had then purged his mortality and become an eternal spirit of poetry ever afterwards.

(135) Another title for this phantasmagoria given by the poet himself is *On Parting with Certain Gentle Friends of East Lu*(《别东鲁诸公》). The ancient state Lu, the dukedom given by King Wu(武王) of the Zhou(周) Dynasty as a fief to his younger brother Ji Dan(姬旦) in 1122 B. C., covering originaly 100 *li* square, lay in the southern part of our mordern Shandong (山东) Province and the northern fringes of today's Jiangsu (江苏) and Anhui(安徽) Provinces. This poem was written by Li Bai in the fourth year of the Tian-bao(天宝四年 745 A. D.) period of the emperor Xuan-*zong's*(玄宗) reign before he left east Lu for his journey to Yue. Although dynasties have passed away, large tract of land has been still known as Lu through the Tang Dynasty even to our modern times.

(136) Mount Tianmu is about 50 *li*(15.1 miles) east of Xinchang *xian*(新昌县) Zhejiang(浙江) Province today. According to legendary lore, it was so named on account of the singing of songs by an old heavenly lady heard by some one in remote antiquity. The mountain range regarded by the Taoists as their Sixteenth Region of Bliss(第十六福地), comes from the Kuocang(括苍) chain spreading over six *xian*. The poet Bai Jüyi(白居易) in his *Note on the Wozhou Mount Dhyana Hall* (《沃洲山禅院记》) says, "In the landscape of the Southeast, Yue(越) is the head, Shan(剡) the face and Tianmu of Wozhou(沃洲,in the east of Xinchang *xian*) the eyebrow and the eye."

(137) In ancient days, Penglai(蓬莱), Fangzhang(方丈) and

Yingzhou(瀛洲) were reputed to be the Three Fairy Island. In the West, fairies are conceived to be diminutive imaginary beings with supernatural powers, able to help or harm human beings. In China, they are supposed to be of ordinary human stature and to have their own supernatural existence and society.

(138) The Five Great Mounts: see the note on "the Great Mount Tai" in Du Fu's(杜甫) *Sighting the Great Mount Tai*(《望岳》).

(139) Crimson Town(赤城) is the southern-most mountain of the Tiantai Range. "Its rocks are red like glowing clouds during sunrise and sunset moments."

(140) Mount Tiantai(天台山): It is in the north of Tiantai *xian*(天台县) in Zhejiang Province. It is the eastern branch of the Xianxia Range(仙霞岭), connected in the southwest with the Kuocang and Yandang(雁荡) chains and in the northwest with the Siming(四明) and Jinghua(金华) mountains. Crimson Town is six *li* north of Tiantai *xian*. Mount Tianmu is in the north-west of Tiantai, overlooking Sheng *xian*(嵊县).

(141) Mirror Lake(镜湖,鉴湖) is in the city Shaoxing(绍兴市), Zhejiang Province.

(142) From this line on, the poem enters the poet's dream world.

(143) Shan Brook(剡溪) is a small stream in the south of Zhejiang's Sheng *xian*(嵊县); it is the upper stream of Cao'e River(曹娥江).

(144) Sire Xie's(谢公) night hut means the poet Xie Linyun's(谢灵运,380? —440?) transcient lodging place where he put up for a night before accending Tianmu Mount the next morning. Xie improved on the ancient clog for wear on raining days, which had two crosswise teeth or jags, one underneath the upper middle part of the sole and the other near the heel, by eliminating the front jag on the clog for ascending mountain tracks and eliminating the rear jag on the clog for descending mountain tracks. Clogs of such make were called Sire Xie's clogs.

(145) According to *Strange Tales*(《述异记》), "In the south-east, there is the Peach Capital Mountain(桃都山), on which grows the gigantic tree Peach Capital(桃都) with branches three thousand feet apart. The heaven's chanticleer crows when the sun shines on this tree, and then all cocks on this earth crow in response."

(146) In this line, the poet wakes up from his dream to "probe deep into the realm of Yue."

(147) In remote antiquity of Xia(夏,2205—1767 B. C.), Shang (商,1766—1123 B. C.) and Zhou(周,1122—247 B. C.), Yangzhou(扬州) was one of the Nine States(九州), embra-

cing the provinces Jiangsu(江苏), Anhui(安徽), Jiangxi(江西), Zhejiang(浙江) and Fujian(福建) at present. As time went on, its domain shrank considerably through the centuries. During the Tang Dynasty(唐,618—906 A. D.), the county Guangling(广陵郡) was also called Yangzhou(扬州). Today, the latter's namesake is in the middle of the province Jiangsu on the northern bank of Yangzi(扬子) the Long River(长江), as a mere city.

(148) The Yellow Crane Tower was a renowned structure in China's literary history. Its site is on the Yellow Crane Ait(黄鹄矶) of the Snake Hill(蛇山) by the northern bank of the city Wuchang(武昌). It was said to be first built in the second year of Huang-wu(黄武二年,223 A. D.) of Wu(吴), one of the Three Kingdoms(三国), Fei Hui(费祎), Wu's general, who lived at the turning of the 2nd to the 3rd centuries, becoming a fairy, was said to often rest the yellow crane he rode on the tower, hence its name. The tower was burnt and rebuilt many times in the nation's chronicle.

(149) The third moon of the lunar calendar is approximately corresponding to April of the Gregorian calendar.

(150) The original 烟花 has never been explained since the poet.

(151) As his dear friend has disappeared his feelings for him flush like the east-flowing torrents of the Long River.

(152) The original of these two and the following two lines 蓬莱文章建安骨,中间小谢又清发 is alluding to the philosophical and literary attainments of the poet's uncle Li Yun and the poetical talent of the poet himself. Li Bai means to say that his uncle Yun a decreed editor(校书郎), familiar with the philosophical works of Lao-*zi*(老子) and Zhuang-*zi*(庄子) has absorbed the deep, occult wisdom of these two fairy philosophers who have gone to live their eternal lives on the Five Fairy Islands Penglai(蓬莱), Fanghu(方壶), Yingzhou(瀛洲), Yuanqiao(员峤) and Daiyu(岱舆) and is well studied in the literary works of Cao Pi(曹丕), Wang Can(王粲), Chen Lin(陈琳), Xü Gan(徐干), Liu Zhen(刘桢), Ying Chang(应玚), Yuan Yu(阮瑀) and Cao Zhi(曹植), who lived during the Jian-an(建安) years(196—219) of Emperor Xian of Han(汉献帝,190—219). Speaking of himself, the poet says that his own endowments are comparable of those of Xie Tiao(谢朓,玄晖) of South Qi(南齐,479—501).

(153) In ancient China, a common man, usually a scholar, when given an office of some importance, would as a rule begin to wear an official hat at the ceremony of officiating until the end of his term. When he resigned, it was said that he hung up his hat (of office).

(154) The Poet's own note to this poem: "My old friend Jia Chun (贾淳) asks me to question the moon."

(155) The original of this, 丹阙, means "An imposing portal paint-

ed with cinnabar," that is a huge, imperial structure of stone blocks so coloured in the form of a gate, by ascending which one, usually an important personage, could command a view infinitely far and wide. The original of these two lines simply gives its reader the powerful but simple impression of the sparkling moon casting its beams upon himself who stands upright on a massive stone gateway of great importance.

(156) Legend has it that there is a white rabbit in the moon which keeps pounding on the elixir of life year in, year out.

(157) The ancient King Yi's(后羿) queen Heng'e(姮娥) has been said to have stolen the elixir of life given by the *Xi Wang-mu*, fairy Western Queen Mother(西王母) to the king and run away to the moon where she lives immortally in eternal loneliness.

(158) The Phoenix Terrace(凤凰台) was in the southwest of the chief town of the Jiangning County(江宁府), and is in the south-east of the city Jinling(金陵), now called Nanjing(南京). In the 16th year of the Yuan-jia Period(元嘉) of Wen-*di*(文帝) of Song(刘宋,439 A. D.) during the Six Dynasties(六朝), three multi-coloured birds like peacock with melodic chantings settled down on the hills, attended by a host of other birds. People called them phoenixes. They sojourned there for some time and flied away. A terrace was built to commemorate the occurrence.

(159) Wu Palaces mean those built by Sun Quan(孙权), the founder of the state Wu, one of the Three Kingdoms(220—280), at the beginning of his reign(221—252).

(160) The Jin Dynasty was divided into West Jin(西晋,265—316) and East Jin(东晋,317—420).

(161) The Tri-peaked Mount(三山) is fifty-seven *li* south-west of Jin-ling City, four *li* around and 290 Chinese feet high. It is actually a small hill, but is exaggerated by the poet to pierce "through the azure sky".

(162) There is a syntactic inversion of the original line 白鹭洲中分二水 into 二水中分白鹭洲 for the sake of rhyme. The Qinhuai River(秦淮河), the confluence of two streams flowing from the two mounts Jürong(句容) and Lishui(溧水), runs in union from Fangshan(方山) through the city Jingling westward into the River, where it dashes on the Egret Ait and is diverged into two currents wrapping round the Ait to run eastward.

(163) The Egret Ait is a little isle on which egrets in great numbers nested at that time.

(164) "The floating clouds" signify libels against the poet to the Emperor Xuan-*zong* of Tang(唐玄宗).

(165) He is prevented from the sight of the Imperial City; it makes

him sad.

(166) The Tower was built by Xie Tiao(460?—496?), High Sheriff of the Country Ning-guo-fu of South Qi(479—502,南齐宁国府太守谢朓). Li Bai cherished great admiration for Xie, as evidenced also in his another poem *Humming under the Moon atop the West Tower in Jinling City*(《金陵城西楼月下吟》), although we know he is a much greater poet.

(167) Two currents of water entwine around the town: they are the Wan(宛溪) and the Ju Streams(句溪).

(168) The pair of bridges called the Phoenix(凤凰) and the Jichuan (济川) arch over the Wan Stream. They were built across the water during the Kai-huang years(开皇,589—600) of the dynasty Sui(隋,589—617).

(169) The original 橘柚 (oranges and pomelos) should not be literally translated perhaps, for the latter, we know, would not bear fruit round Xuan Cheng, Anhui(安徽); it could only do so in Fujian(福建), Guangxi(广西), Guangdong(广东), Jiangxi(江西), Zhejiang(浙江), Hunan(湖南) and Sichuan(四川) Provinces, where the climate is much warmer. Here two Chinese characters must be employed by the poet: after 橘 there should be another one, to fill in the metre. The choices open to Li Bai were 柑(*gan*) and 橙(*cheng*), but he could use neither of them, for they are both of level tones(平声), while here only a character of uneven tone(仄声)

should be used, according to the rules of five-charactered *lü* verse(五言律诗) in the "late" prosody of classical Chinese poetry(今体诗)人烟寒橘柚(平平平仄仄);秋色老梧桐(平仄仄平平). So he was forced to pick out 柚 (*you*) (pomelos) to follow 桔 (*ju*) for the sake of tonal euphony.

(170) These two lines convey the sense and tone of the Chinese original 秋色老梧桐, which is a syntactic inversion of 梧桐秋色老 for the sake of rhyme, that is, the platane [leaves] show that the complexion of autumn is old — the fall season is far advanced — with the character 寒 (cold) of the previous original line removed to the end of these two lines in my rendition.

(171) The last two lines of the original as well as of my version consist of a question to be answered. The answer, not given in the poem, is understood: "It is I."

(172) This ancient peopled center high on the mountain-side originally called Fish Belly Town(鱼腹城), was in the east of the present Fengjie *xian*(奉节县) of Sichuan Province(四川省). Its name was changed into Baidi, meaning the Town of the White Emperor, by Gongsun Shu(公孙述,? B. C. —36) during early East Han(东汉,25—188 A. D.) who declared himself the supreme ruler bearing that tide for twelve years.

(173) From Baidi Town to Jiangling Prefecture(江陵府), a *xian* in Hubei(湖北) Province today, through the 700 *li* Three Gor-

ges(三峡) of the Long River(长江), the waterway bound by interminable cliffs, full of screeching gibbons, on both banks, known to be twelve hundred *li* in drift, was said to speed up a light boat in one day.

This masterly stroke of a seven-charactered *jue* quatrain(七绝) was written by Li Bai when he heard unexpectedly the message of his being pardoned by imperial decree at Bai *di* Town in the spring of the second year of the Qian-yuan Period (乾元二年,759) in Su-*zong*'s reign, on his way of exile to Yelang (夜郎) for his enforced involvement in the rebellion of Prince Yong(永王李璘). It breathes of great joy in the high speed of the skiff.

(174) According to Wang Qi(王琦), the editor of the Jian-Long (乾隆) edition of *Li Bai's Complete Works* (1758), the bonze Wang Qian's(王僧虔) *Records of Artistic Skill*(《技录》) mentions "*Goodman, Cross Ye Not the River*!"(《公无渡河》) as one of the thirty eight tunes or *The Tune of the Zither*(《箜篌引》). *Ancient and Present-day Notes*(《古今注》) has it thus: *The Tune of the Zizer* was composed by Li Yu(黎玉), the wife of the Korean quay guard Huoli Zigao (霍里子高). Zigao early one morning propelled his boat for washing himself. A white-haired madcap, holding a water pot and spreading his locks in the winds, attempted to wade the river; his wife ran after to stop him, but too late. The man was immediately drowned; his wife howled out a heart-breaking lament after him, and as soon as it was over, jumped into the river too. Zigao returned home to tell his wife the sight

and imitate the tones of the pathetic lament, whereupon, she, deeply moved, composed a tune of lament on the zizer after her husband's sad tale and mimicking. lt is said that all those who heard the tune could not help being touched to tears. Li Yu taught the tune to a neighbour's girl named Li Rong(丽容), calling it *The Tune of the zither*.

This poem is regarded by some critics such as Chen Hang (陈沆) and Zhan Ying(詹锳) to be packed with implications from contemporary political events of the poet's time, in which Li Bai himself was involved. When Xuan-*zong*'s imperial prince Li Lin(李璘), King Yong(永王), first moved his troops, he was expected by the poet to help putting down the rebellion while he appointed himself as his aide-de-camp (府僚佐), but seeing his attempt was but to harass the banks of the River(江) and Huai(淮), Li Bai ran away to Pengze (彭泽). When Li Lin was put down for his misdeed and being dealt with capital punishment, the poet was exiled to Yelang(夜郎) on account of the defamation that he aided Li Lin, but soon pardoned. "The Luteous River… to roar…" is taken to allude to An Lushan's rebellion. Yao in grief heaving his sighs is said to be compared to Xuan-*zong*'s anxiety over the revolt. Su-*zong*'s arduous efforts and his general's aid to suppress the uprising are supposed to be compared to great Yu's endearvour to overcome the deluge. Li Lin's harassing the banks of the River and Huai is thought to be compared to the old madman's folly in committing suicide and the whole poem is taken to be a metonymical elegy for Prince Li Lin. The web of analogy is spun too thin. So, the poem should rather be read simply as it seems to anyone without all these political implications.

(175) *Er Ya*(《尔雅》), the book of ancient naming and knowledge, consisting of twenty chapters in three volumes, said to be first compiled by Ji Dan, the Duke of Zhou(周公,姬旦,? —1104 B. C.) and successively ampliffied by Confucius(孔丘, 551—479 B. C.), Shusun Ton(叔孙通,260? — 90? B. C.). Some disciples of Confucius and Zheng Xuan(郑玄, 127—200) of East Han(东汉), and finally annotated by Guo Pu(郭璞,276—324) of Jin(晋) and Xing Bing(邢昺,932—1010) of Song, says the River gushes out from the north-west foot of Mount Kunlun(昆仑), at first in clear streams but becomes brownish yellow in colour midway and along its long course filled with a thousand seven hundred and one streams before flowing out into the sea.

(176) The Gate of Dragon(龙门), also called Yu's Gateway(禹门口) is first mentioned in *Yu's Proclamation of Taxes in Kind* (《禹贡》), a chapter of *Shang Shu*(《尚书》— *The Book of the Past*), the earliest book of history known to be written by Confucius. It is said in *the Record of Three Qins*(《三秦记》) that thousands of fishes and tortoises gather below the pass between two precipitous mountain crags without being able to dash up the down-pouring torrents; those that could do so would become dragons. The gate is in the north-west of Hejin *xian*(河津县) of Sanxi(山西) Province and the north-west of Hancheng *xian*(韩城县) of Shanxi(陕西) Province to-

day.

(177) The original of this line when literally rendered is "He bypassed his home, though he heard his child was crying(儿啼不窥家)." It is an age-old saying throughout the centuries that Great Yu conducting the deluge to the eastern sea for thirteen years passed his homestead three times without entering it. The cataclysm in Yao's reign ravaged the valleys of the Luteous River from 2286—2278 B. C.

(178) I take the liberty to translate the original 始蚕麻(to begin to plant hemp and raise silk-worm culture) into "to till and sow".

(179) Liu Bei(刘备), Emperor of Shu-Han(蜀汉) of the Three Kingdoms(三国), once sent his chancellor Zhuge Liang(诸葛亮) the great strategist to Jianye(建业), the capital of Wu(吴), of which the latter said after his observation of its geographical aspects: "The Zhong Heights wind and twist like a dragon and the Rocky Mount squats like a tiger."(钟山龙蟠,石头虎踞。)

(180) The Six Dynasties(六朝) founding their capitals in succession in Jianye(建业,建邺) — called Jiankang(建康) in East Jin(东晋) and Jinling(金陵) in Tang(唐), but commonly known as Nanjing(南京) today — were Wu(吴), East Jin(东晋), Song(宋), Qi(齐), Liang(梁) and Chen(陈) from 222 till 589 A. D., for 368 years: — after the extinction

of Wu in 280 till 316, there was a lapse of 36 years, so actually the city was the capitals of the states during the Six Dynasties for 332 years. In the late years of Da-tong(大同, the middle of the 540's), a boys' ballad prophesied: "〔Someone with〕Blue silk strings〔reins〕on a white horse from Shouyang(青丝白马寿阳来)." Not long later, Hou Jing(侯景) broke Danyang(丹阳) and appeared, riding a white horse and curbing it with blue reins.

(181) The original 白马小儿谁家子 shows the poet's contempt for Hou Jing(侯景). Hou was at first a subordinate to General Erzhu Rong(尔朱荣) of North Wei(北魏). Next, he took sides with Gao Huan(高欢) against Erzhu. Then he yielded to Liang(梁) in the first of Tai-qing(太清) years of Wu-*di* (武帝). Next year, he rebelled and broke down the city Jiankang. In the third year of Tai-qing(549), he overcame the inner capital town Taicheng(台城) and Wu-*di* died of hunger and sorrow. He ravaged with burning, massacre and sack Guangling(广陵), the county of Wu(吴郡), Wuxing (吴兴) and Kuaiji(会稽) by turns. Finally, he ascended the throne himself, but was defeated by several generals of Liang and killed by his own men.

(182) The Last Emperor of Chen(陈后生), hearing that the enemy soldiers of Sui(隋) had broken the defense of his capital, struggled with two of his courtiers, who tried to prevent him from getting into the Jingyang Palace(景阳殿) Court well, overcame them and got down with two of his favourite impe-

rial concubines Zhang(张贵妃) and Kong(孔贵嫔). However, they were salvaged out of the well by the Sui men as captives. The *Palace Rear Yard Jade-tree Bloom*(《玉树后庭花》) was one of the song composed by the Emperor himself and attuned to music.

(183) At the end of the Qin Dynasty(秦), there were Four Hoary Recluses(商山四皓), all octogenarians, living in seclusion in the Zhongnan Mountains(终南山), also called South Mountains(南山), which are known to have an extent of 800 *li* in length and breadth.

(184) Zhongnan Mountain(终南山) or the Qin range(秦岭) is situated in the south of the provincial chief city Xi'an(西安) of Shanxi(陕西) today, then the capital of the Tang(唐) Dynasty. At the time scholars not gone into the official arena mostly lived in their hermitages on this mountain.

(185) The mountaineer Husi(斛斯山人) was a recluse residing here. He was a descendant subject of North Zhou(北周), one of the Three North Dynasties(北朝), a member of the national minority Xian-bei(鲜卑).

(186) This is probably referring to the "Song" attuned to the heptachord strain so named, collected in the *Ancient Garner of Songs*(《古乐府》).

(187) The Milky Way in Chinese.

(188) Legendary tales have it that the fairy Wang Zi'an(王子安) often alighted on the Tower from his yellow crane as well as rode astride the bird from off it, hence its name. Actually, the tower was so named because it was built on the Yellow Crane Ait(黄鹤矶) by the side of the town Wuchang(武昌).

(189) Hanyang(汉阳) is in the west of Wuchang, on the northern bank of the Han Stream(汉水).

(190) The Parrot Isle(鹦鹉洲) is in the south-west of the tripartite city Wuhan(武汉), in the middle of the Yangzi(扬子) or Long River(长江).

(191) The Tai Mountain(泰山), also called Mount Dai(岱宗), sprawling across the ancient states Qi(齐) in the north and Lu(鲁) in the south, is in the present Shandong Province(山东省). The five great Mountains of the ancient empire are Tai, the great east mountain(东岳泰山); Hua, the great west mountain(西岳华山); Huo, the great south mountain(南岳霍山); Heng, the great north mountain(北岳恒山) and Song the great central mountain(中岳嵩山). Of them all, the Tai is the greatest, hence known as the chief of the five mountains the Noble Mount Dai(岱宗).

(192) The southern sides of the mountain exposed to the sunlight first, are light(阳) first and the northern sides of the mountain shone upon later are shaded(阴) at first.

(193) This poem was written in about the fifth year of the Tian-bao Period(天宝五载,746) during the dynasty Tang(唐,618—907) by the poet when he had arrived not long at the capital Chang'an(长安). It is known in history that Li Bai(李白) with He Zhizhang(贺知章). Li Shizhi(李适之), Li Jin(李琎), Cui Zongzhi(崔宗之), Su Jin(苏晋), Zhang Xu(张旭) and Jiao Sui(焦遂) were all eight of them noted drinkers, known as the "Eight Faeries in Drinking." Although all residing in Chang'an once, they did not do so at the same time. On the fact that they were drinkers alike, Du Fu based his relations. The poem in its verse structure is unusual: every line rhymes and all lines rhyme in concord; there is no begining, nor end; the lines describing the eight, the numbers of lines devoted to them are not equal, but at the begining and the end and in the middle, two lines are given to each person, in the fore and hind parts three or four lines are used, with order in variety. Among them all, He Zhizhang was the eldest, being forty-one years older than Li Bai (and fifty-two years' Du Fu's senior), so he is mentioned first of aIl. The others are named according to their official positions, from princedom through chancellorship to plain commonalty. The sketching of their drunken manners are characteristic individually, with a hidden strain of suppressed feelings.

The translator regrets for not rendering the original into English line by line and failing to use one all-embracing rhyme in all the lines. the Prince of Ruyang and Cui Zongzhi are each given one line: too many than in the original.

(194) He Zhizhang(贺知章), a native of Yongxing of the state Yue (越州永兴), known as Xiaoshan *xian* of Zhejiang Province (浙江省萧山县) today, was the Lord of the Secretariat(秘书监). He was noted for his carefree, unconventional manners, calling himself "the Madcap of Siming"(四明狂客). Having read some of Li Bai's masterly poems, he called his new acquaintance "the Exiled Fairy"(谪仙人); inviting the latter to a tavern, he untied a gold tortoise from his robe band to pay for their drinks for lack of enough ready cash.

(195) The Prince of Ruyang Li jin(汝阳王李琎) was Xuan-*zong's* nephew. It was his habitual practice to be thoroughly warmed up with strong drinks before he would attend the morning court of his uncle emperor. He was said to be so fond of alcholic liquors that he would his feudal estate were changed to Wine Spring(酒泉), a county called Jiuquan *xian*(酒泉县) today, in Gansu Province(甘肃省). It was said that under the county bulwark, there was actually a spring having the taste of wine.

(196) Li Shizhi(李适之) became the Left Chancellor(左相) of Xuan-*zong* in the eighth moon of the first year of the Tian-bao Period(天宝元年,742); in the fourth moon of the fifth year (746), he was pressured by Li Linfu(李林甫) off his office and in the seventh moon, demoted to Yichun(宜春) as the High Sheriff(太守) of that county. In the first moon of the next year, he committed suicide by taking poison. This poem of Du Fu was written sometime after Li was removed from his

chancellery and long before his poisoning himself. Whales were supposed in ancient days to be capable of sucking and spouting some hundred streams.

(197) Cui Zongzhi(崔宗之), son of the Lord of Imperial Personnel Department(吏部尚书) Cui Riyong(崔日用) and feudal successor to his father as the Duke of the State Qi(齐国公), was the Lord Attendant of the Imperial(侍御史) and a friend of Li Bai.

(198) Yuan Ji(阮籍,210—263), a noted scholar, poet, anchorite and drinker of Wei(魏,220—245) during the Three Kindoms (三国,220—280), reputed as one of "the Seven Sages of Bamboo Groves"(竹林七贤), was well known for his glinting with the white of his eyes at the vulgar lot to signify his contempt. Here, Cui Zongzhi is allusively sketched as looking down at the vulgar with sniffing pride.

(199) Su Jin(苏晋), one of the elect in an Imperial Examination during the early years of Xuan-*zong's* reign, was a devout believer in Buddhism and a vegetarian, but he often became drunk and forgot to observe his dhyana vigils. Buddhist faith prohibits the drinking of wine among its strict believers.

(200) Li Bai(李白,701—762) was well known for his prolific outpourings in poety after he had a quart fermented drinks. Once he was intoxicated in a tavern when he was summoned by Xuan-*zong* to appear before his imperial presence in an aloes-

wood arbour in the palace garden to compose poems for attuning with music. According to Fan Chuanzheng's(范传正) *New Tomb Tablet of Li Bai*(《李白新墓碑》), when Xuan-*zong* was once taking a barge on the White Lotus Pond(白莲池), he summoned Li Bai to write a tale on the occasion when the poet was already drunk at the Imperial Hall of Literati(翰林院); the emperor ordered Gao Lishi(高力士) the General (actually an eunuch) to help bearing the poet to his imperial presence. These incidents and his calling himself "a faery in the realm of spirits" before Xuan-*zong* show how he was in the emperor's high favour and how highly be bore himself.

(201) Zhang Xu(张旭) the eminent calligraphic artist, a native of the state Wu(吴), was called the sage of the *Cao* mode(草圣) of that art. When he was thoroughly drunken, he would take off his office hat even before princes and lords, howl and dash along, and then wield his brush on silk scrolls, hence known as Zhang the Lunatic(张颠).

(202) Jiao Sui(焦遂) of the commonalty, whose events are not well known, is said to be reputed for his sparkling eloquence. When he was thoroughly heated up with hard liquors, his companions at the table would be struck with wonder by his brilliant discourse.

(203) This descriptive lyrical ballad was presumably composed by Du Fu in the spring of the 12th year of the Tian-bao Period

(天宝十二年) during the reign of Xuan-*zong* of Tang(唐玄宗). In the eleventh moon of the previous year(天宝十一年, approximately 752 of the Gregorian calendar), Yang Guozhong(杨国忠), the so-called brother of the Imperial Concubine Yang Yuhuan(杨玉环) was decreed the Right Chancellor(右相) by imperial edict. The poem is a hidden satire on the court life with all its exquisite picturesque details. The crux of its sarcasm lies in the three lines (two in the original) "The willow catkins... to show amour's troth" towards the end. The butt of revulsion is named at the very end to be the big bogy — the new chancellor.

(204) In ancient times, the Celestial Stems(天干:甲、乙、丙、丁、戊、己、庚、辛、壬、癸) and twelve Terrestrial Branches(地支:子、丑、寅、卯、辰、巳、午、未、申、酉、戌、亥) were used as symbols matched in twos and progressing by rotation(甲子、乙丑、丙午、丁卯、戊辰、己巳、庚午……) to compute the periodic durations of the day, the days, the moons and the years till sixty of the pairs were completed to form a cycle and the process was repeated again and again. It is stated, nowadays, the lunar years are still named in this wise. In the *Ceremonial Records*(《礼仪志》) of *The Late Han Chronicles*(《后汉书》) that on the first Si day(巳日) of the year's third moon, officials and the commonalty all go to the eastern stream of Luoyang(洛阳) to purge themselves of dirt and illness. Since Wei(魏,220—266) and Jin(晋,266—420), the customary practice was fixed definitely on the third moon's third day of the lunar calendar. Among the great many beauties that came

to take a spring stroll on the bund of Zigzag River Pool(曲江池) south-east of Chang'an(长安) on the Third Day of the Third Moon, the most prominent were of course the notable sisters of the Imperial Concubine Yang Taizhen(杨太真).

(205) This is an inverted sarcasm.

(206) The original of Du Fu's poem has 蹙金孔雀 here. The four sacred animals of China's traditional lore are *qi-lin*(麒麟,unicorn of monoceros), *feng-huang*(凤凰,phoenix), *Shen-long*(神龙, divine dragon) and *ling-gui*(灵龟, prophetic tortoise), peacock being not among them. Although this poem of Du Fu belongs to the "Garner of Tunes" genre(乐府诗) and so need not conform to the prosodic pattern of meticulous distribution of level and uneven tones(平仄声) as it is necessary to do so in a "modern" *lii* or *jue* poem(今体律绝诗), yet to put the proper 凤凰 here would make the line's tones 仄平仄平平平平 altogether too unbalanced and noisy to its readers' ears; hence he chooses to substitute 孔雀(仄仄,peacock) instead for the sake of euphony. But in the translation, there is no necessity to render the original literally for no tonal redundancy is involved here, and peacock, in the West, often connotes the idea of vanity, while in China, there is no such allusive meaning. 蹙金 in the original means to embroider with gold thread curled or twisted tight, so as to make the embroidered surface slightly embossed.

(207) There is some difference between China's *qi-lin* and the uni-

corn or monoceros of the West. *Qi-lin* (specifically, *qi* is the male and *lin* the female) is a mythical animal like the elk in size, but having a single antler and a tail like that of an ox, with its hide covered all over by scales: it is noted for its kindness to other smaller creatures, as, very speedy in movement, it would not even step on ants. The unicorn or monoceros of the West is a fabled creature usually represented as a horse with a single spiraled horn projecting from its forehead and often with a goat's beard and a lion's tail; it is often symbolic of chastity or purity. *Feng-huang* in China (specifically, *feng* is the male bird and *huang* the female), also called *yan* (鶠) is the fabulous sovereign of birds. Collected in *Er Ya*(《尔雅》), the earliest lexicon of the world compiled in early Han(汉,202 B. C.—220 A. D.), *yan* or *feng-huang* is explained by its annotator to have the cock's head, the snake's neck, the swallow's chin, the tortoise's back and the fish's tail, with plumes of five hues and over six feet tall. When it appears, there would be universal peace. In the West, the phoenix is a fabulous Egyptian bird of great beauty too, but not so explicitly delineated; it is said to live five hundred years, to burn itself to death and to rise from its ashes in the freshness of youth, and live through another life cycle.

(208) With many-layered sparkling beryl gems strung and dropping down in folds from their raven hair to their temples.

(209) A variant, more common text has 腰衱 here, which means 裾

according to *Er Ya*(《尔雅》), and this is explained by its annotator Guo Pu(郭璞) as the back overlap of a robe(后裾). In the absence of North Song block print texts, it is more likely that the pearl-studded waist bands make their bodily curves shapely, rather than the back overlap or skirt of their gowns.

(210) According to the *Old Tang Chronicles*(《旧唐书》), the Imperial Concubine had three elder sisters, entitled the State Queens of Han(韩国夫人), of Guo(虢国夫人) and of Qin(秦国夫人), of whom only two are mentioned here in the original for metrical reasons. The State Queen of Han was her eldest sister, that of Guo, her third elder sister (and Yang Guozhong's mistress) and that of Qin, her eighth elder sister, all of whom were entitled in the seventh year of the Tian-bao Period(天宝七载,748). Before the State Queen of Guo was entitled, her husband had already died. The emperor Xuan*zong* had promiscuous relations with all of them, his most favoured one beside the Imperial Concubine being the State Queen of Guo, as evidenced by a noted quatrain entitled with her name(《虢国夫人》) written by the poet Zhang Hu(张祜). Priding herself on her natural beauty, she did not resort to cosmetics. Their easy virtue, especially the State Queen of Guo's cast a satirical light on the chaste, pure qualities of the belles mentioned in line 3, for the three State Queens are the chief ones of the belles, and Du Fu's satire is focused upon them.

(211) While the three Yang sisters, sated with delicacies, are reluctant to raise their chopsticks, their waiting maids keep on busily cutting threads, strips and slices of chickens, ducks, hams and the "choice eight" (八珍) with cutters of tinkling bells (鸾刀).

(212) The horse of Yang Guozhong seems to be hesitating because before and after him is his retinue of guards and attendants that retard its movement.

(213) These three lines (two in the original) mean obviously that when Yang Cuozhong has arrived, carriages and ridden horses are rife, for many are his attendants. The willow fluffs of late spring are spread by the uproarious disturbance to the surface of the Zigzag River Pool (曲江池) and partly settle on the white marsileas. Red hand-kerchiefs of the ladies promenading on the bund lost by them are left when dropped on the pathways. These are held between the bills of blue birds flying away. Insinuatingly, these lines mean the secret affair between Yang Guozhong and the State Queen of Guo, which was however known to all in the court, except perhaps the emperor Xuan-*zong* and even among his subjects. But Yang was the chancellor in power; our poet, for safety, could only hint with dubious suggestions. The willow fluffs, falling thick like snow and settling on the white marsileas, are compared to Yang Guozhong who is without a respectable parentage, depending on his disreputable relations with the State Queen of Guo who, in her turn, is the emperor's toy. Yang's birth and

personality are such a light stuff as the willow fluffs, for it was known that he was the son of Zhang Yizhi(张易之), the gigolo or kept underling paramour(面首) of the late Empress Wu Zhetian(武则天); he as a boy was taken by his mother to the Yang family and was considered a cousin of the Yang sisters. And furthermore, there had been a story of a certain courtier very close to the royal family of North Wei(北魏, 386—557) during the South and North Dynasties(420—589) bearing the name Yang Hua(杨华), which means willow fluff, who was forced by the mother queen of the ruler to copulate with her. Fearing that if the secret be known to the king, he would be executed for defaming the ruling house, the man fled to the southern state Liang(梁). The mother queen, pining for her beloved man, framed her *Song of White Willow Fluffs* (《杨白华歌》) to make her palace waiting maids sing in their dances, with snatches like "Willow fluffs are wafted by winds to settle down in a southern home" and "Be it wished that the willow fluffs are picked up by birds' bills to drop into nests", etc.

(May 16, 1984)

(214) Cen Shen(岑参, *circa* 714—770), a contemporary poet of Du Fu and his friend.

(215) Mei Pi(渼陂) was a lake five *li*(about 1.553 miles) in the west of Hu *xian*(鄠县) in Shanxi Province(陕西省) today, lying southwest of Chang'an(长安), the capital of the dynasty Tang(唐, 618—907). Its water came from Zhongnan

Mountain(终南山), with a bank of 14 *li*. At the end of the Yuan(元) Dynasty (1277—1368), the lake water was drawn dry by soldiers for catching all the fishes in it, and the dried Iake bed had become farms. Now, it has been restored to the original size.

(216) This poem is supposed by an annotator to be written by the poet in the 14th year of the Tian-bao Period(天宝十四年) of Xuan-*zong's*(玄宗) reign, 755 of the Gregorian calendar, when An Lushan(安禄山) the Hu(胡) satrap raised his revolt that lasted for seven years, hence《忧思集》(*Grieved Am I*) in the original.

(217) This poem was written by the poet in the eighth moon (September) of the 15th year of the Tian-bao Period(天宝十五年) or the first year of Zhi-de(至德元年, 756) not long after his stay at Fuzhou(鄜州), now called Fu *xian*(富县), all alone therefrom to Lingwu(灵武), the court in exile of Su-*zong* of Tang(唐肃宗), who ascended the throne there not long ago. On his way, he was captured by the rebel forces of An Lushan(安禄山) and Shi Siming(史思明) and taken as a prisoner to Chang'an(长安) the broken capital.

(218) This poem was written by Du Fu in the third moon (approx. April) of the second year of the Zhi-de Period(至德二年, 757) of De-*zong's*(德宗) reign (756—762), when the poet was a captive of the rebel forces of An Lushan(安禄山) and Shi Siming(史思明) in Chang'an(长安), the occupied cap-

ital.

The third and fourth lines of the original may be interpreted metaphorically; so, lines 4 to 8 of the English version should be rendered thus:

Ag̅griéved	bȳ thē tímes'	ēvénts,
Thē flów	er̄s tōo shéd	thēir teárs.
Rēgrét	ing̅ en̄fóre	cēd pártings,
E'en̄ birds	chánt sóngs wīth feárs.

(219) In the second year of the Zhi-de Period(至德二载,757) of Emperor Su-*zong's*(肃宗) reign (780—804), when Du Fu was holding the office "Left Gleaner"(左拾遗), i. e., the vice imperial admonisher of the court, Fang Guan(房馆) was dismissed from his chancellery for the smashing defeat of the imperial troops under his command by the rebel forces. Our poet, hoping to avert the decree by opining dissent, was actually banished for incurring the wroth of his sovereign from the court to his home at Qiang Village in the south of the state Fu(鄜州). These three poems were written during that period.

(220) "Turmoils"(世乱) in the previous line refers to the rebellion of An Lushan(安禄山) and Shi Siming(史思明) and the political and social chaos resulting therefrom; "disasters", or rather "driftings"(飘荡) to the poet's captivity by the rebel troops and his banishment by Su-*zong* from the court. During this calamitous turbulence of a rebellious war that had already lasted for over a year and while it seemed the Dynasty would be overthrown by the Hu satrap at any moment, our poet,

first captured by the rebel forces for less than a year and now that he was not wanted at the court, sees that he could still come back home alive, indeed what a fateful chance it was!

(221) In ancient times, the walls of a village house were quite low. His neighbours, wishing not to come into the house to incommode the family in its pathatic reunion of husband, wife and children, crowded on the walls to show their compassion and heave sighs.

(June 25, 1984)

(222) This second one of the three poems expresses the conflicting feelings of the writer: he is compelled by the emperor's order to come home for a visit against his own will during his old age; for this is meted out as a punishment to him for his ill proposed counsel to pardon the chancellor Fang Guan, Du Fu is much concerned with the well-being of the Empire; now that the rebellion is far from being suppressed, so his enforced stay at home seems to live by stealth to him.

(223) This is referring to the sixth and seventh moons of the previous year, the first one of the Zhi-de Period(至德元载,756), when Du Fu had already moved his family from Chang'an(长安) to Fuzhou(鄜州). In the eighth moon, he went alone for Linwu(灵武), Where he heard the prince royal had ascended the throne as Su-*zong*(肃宗); he was captured by the rebel troops on the way. In the summer of the next year(至德二载,757), he freed himself from captivity and went to the

court in exile at Feng-xiang(凤翔), where he was rewarded with the office of "Left Gleaner". His post as the secondary counsellor was not a big appointment, but he was near his sovereign. His advice to pardon the chancellor, however, soon met Su-*zong's* ire.

(June 30. 1984.)

(224) This last poem of the trio relates how the poet's neighbours taking along tankards of wine come to console him.

(225) Driving cocks and hens up to roost on trees was a common practice there and then.

(226) The village elders all earnestly beg pardon of the poet for their wine's lack of strength; it shows their warm feelings for him. This is due to the millet farms being not amply cultivated on account of the war of rebellion.

(227) For the supply of enlisted grown-up young men is insufficient, teen-aged boys are often pressed into military service.

(July 4, 1984)

(228) "Shen and Shang" in the orginal refer to two of the 28 constellations in ancient China, which are supposed not to be seen at the same time in the sky. The term is often used as a figure of speech to mean kinfolks or bosom friends yearning in vain for a reunion. Antares and Betelgeuse are assumed here to be the English equivalents.

(229) The poet's own note on this poem, a literary ballad, says: "Written after the recovery of the two capitals. Though they are recovered, the rebel's forces are still rife." The rebellion of An Lushan(安禄山,? —757), the Tartar satrap — who was murdered and succeeded by his own son An Qingxu(安庆绪,? —759) — and his subordinate general Shi Siming (史思明,? —761) — who broke the siege of Xiangzhou(相州) also called the city Ye(邺城), cordoned off by the Imperial army, and relieved An Qingxu in the second year of the Qian-yuan Period(乾元二年,759) of Su-*zong's*(肃宗) reign, but before long killed him — was carried on by Shi Chaoyi(史朝义,? —763), Shi Siming's son, who also murdered his own father in the second year of the Shang-yuan Period(上元二年,761) of Su-*zong's* reign, but committed suicide after his generals submitted to Tang, thus putting an end to the seven years odd rebellion.

In the winter of the first year of the Qian-yuan Period (乾元元年,758) of Su-*zong's*(肃宗) reign, the vast legions of the nine Viceroy Generals(节度使) Guo Ziyi(郭子仪), Li Guangbi(李光弼), Wang Sili(王思理) and others surrounded the city Ye(邺城), occupied by the rebel forces under An Qingxu. In the third moon next year, Shi Siming, who had once yielded to Tang, rebelled again, leading his men from Weizhou(魏州) to succor the city Ye, thus attacking the imperial army on both sides with Shi Chaoyi's men. There was no field marshal to give supreme command to the loyal troops and make concerted action. Six hundred thousand imperial soldiers were put to defeat. Guo Ziyi led his corps to break down the Heyang Bridge for defending Luoyang(洛阳) the old, eastern capital. But the situation quickly worsened. Luoyang and Tong Pass (潼关) soon became threatened. For averting the critical situation and strengthening the belligerent powers of the state, the Impernial government decreed compulsory enlistment everywhere to enlarge the supply of soldiery. All around Xin'an and Shǎn *xian*(陕县), all inhabitants, regardless of age and sex, were enforced to serve in the troops. The war brought great calamity to the people. Just then, Du Fu was returning to Huazhou(华州) via Luoyang(洛阳), seeing with his own eyes the people there, after the ravage of the rebel forces during the past two years, were now suffering from the compulsory enlistment and press into service by the Imperial army. So he wrote these six pieces *Xing'an Officer*, *Shihao Officer*, *Tong Pass Officer*, *Parting after Nuptials*, *Parting at Old Age and Parting without Home*; short narrative poems recording the sufferings of the people.

"*Xing'an Officer* gives an account of how the poet, while passing the town, just came upon the *xian* officers pressing enlistments hard. Those of age were already all enforced into military service; so the striplings were driven to the battlefields. The poet highly sympathised with them, but could only, while bearing pain, console and encourage them to augment their morale." — From Xiao Difei's comments.

(230) Xin'an is Xin'an *xian*(新安县) of Henan Province(河南省) today.

(231) According to Tang statute from the third year of the Tian-bao Period(天宝三载,744), a male person over eighteen years old was regarded a middle youth(中男) and one over twenty-three taken to be an adult(成丁).

(232) As all those having attained adulthood had been draughted, the class of middle youths was now next in order to be pressed into military service for increasing the size of the imperial army and to cope with the rebellious forces.

(233) The Royal Town means the Eastern Capital of Tang, which had been called the Royal Town during the Zhou Dynasty(周代,1122—256 B. C.).

(234) Those boys well taken care of by their mothers were fairly nourished and therefore thickset; they were taken leave off by their dear mothers who cried after they left; other boys who had no mothers, being wretchedly fed, were thus lean and short; they came alone, unaccompanied by mothers, and left alone, without mothers to grieve after their departure.

(235) As the draughted had disappeared eastward along the white water, the leave-taking mothers were still crying, with their groanings echoed by the green hills.

(236) From this line onward to the end, the words were all spoken by "One" of line 2 of this poem, that is, the poet himself. They are words of consolation, explanation and encourage-

ment.

(237) "Heaven and Earth" here alludes obscurely to the imperial court.

(238) According to *The Mirror for Achieving Civil Equity*(《资治通鉴》) by Sima Guang & others(司马光等 1084), Guo Ziyi (郭子仪) and eight other Viceroy Generals cordoned off the city Ye(邺城), while An Qingxu(安庆绪) held it vigilantly to wait for Shi Siming's(史思明) breaking the siege. As food supplies in the city were exhausted, horses' dung was eaten as food. But the imperial legions were not commanded by a marshal with concerted action. The long siege slackened the morale of the imperial troops. Shi selected his mounted ironsides to rush at the official beleaguerers day and night, sent herculean grapplers to steal the uniforms and insignias of the loyal forces and burned their food and fodder supplies. Thus, the official troops lacked staple and feed. Shi Siming then waved all his men forward for a decisive combat. As all the imperial corps were massed in the north of the river Anyang(安阳河) ... before they were marshalled in proper order, a terrific cyclone occurred, blasting everything and blackening all heaven and earth. Both armies were frightened, the official forces ran to the south and the rebel to the north. Guo Ziyi led his troops to break up the Heyang Bridge (河阳桥) for safeguarding Luoyang, the eastern capital.

(239) Bands of our beaten troops come back separately to their

camps scattered all about like stars. The trouble is that they are not under a single, unified and concerted command.

(240) This and the following lines consist of words of consolation and encouragement. At the time, there was a famine among the people, but Guo Ziyi's divisions obtained a huge food supply at the eastern capital.

(241) This line means that the new recruits are to be trained near Luoyang, the old capital.

(242) This signifies that their labour would not be heavy: the ditches dug by them would not ooze with water.

(243) The punitive expeditions against the rebellious forces are righteous.

(244) In the fifth moon of the second year of the Zhi-de Period(至德二载,757) of De-*zong's*(德宗) reign. Guo Ziyi(郭子仪, 697—781), concurrently a Viceroy General(节度使), for his failure to recover Chang'an(长安), the Western Capital (西京), begged his Emperor to depose himself from the Lordship of Construction(司空) to the post of Left of Deputy Chancellorship(左仆射). But by the time when Du Fu wrote this poem, Guo had already been elevated to the post of the Chief Lord of the Secretariat(中书令) or the Right Chancellorship(右相). Yet our poet still calls him here by his previous official post "the deputy chancellor", and says that he

would be kind to them the new recruits like a fatherly elder or an elder brother.

(245) This is the second piece of the poet's descriptive and narrative sketches of the Tang Imperial Army's pressing the populace to enlist for putting down the rebellion of An Lushan(安禄山) and Shi Siming(史思明). Du Fu shows his sympathy to the war-stricken public by relating what he saw on his way from Luoyang(洛阳) to Huazhou(华州). The poem is written in five-charactered unrhymed lines.

(246) Shihao hamlet(石壕村) is in the east of Shǎn *xian*(陕县) of He'nan Prorince(河南省).

(247) The City Ye(邺城), historically also known as Xiangzhou (相州), is the city Anyang(安阳市) of He'nan today.

(248) Heyang(河阳), now called Meng *xian*(孟县) in Henan Province, was where the imperial troops of Tang were massed against rebellious forces of An Lushan and Shi Siming.

(249) The poets bidding "adieu to the old man alone" shows that the old woman had been pressed into the imperial army for service.

(250) "Tong Pass was the inevitable narrow throat-like passage of strategic importance leading from Luoyang(洛阳), the eastern capital, to Chang'an(长安), the western one. In the

sixth moon of the 15th year of the Tian-bao Period(天宝十五载,756), when An Lushan's(安禄山) rebel forces attacked the pass, the old general Geshu Han(哥舒翰), commanding 200,000 imperial troops, blocked the Pass to resist. The drawn-out siege lasted for half a year, when Yang Guozhong (杨国忠), the Imperial Concubine's so-called cousin, pressed Geshu persistently to open the rampart and accept the challenge. The outcome was that the imperial army was completely smashed by the Tartar host and overwhelming numbers of the loyal men were drowned in the Luteous River (黄河)." — From notes and comments by Xiao Difei.

(251) The chief officer in change of keeping watch over the Tong Pass under the generals and superintending construction of the huge bulwark. Tong Pass is in Tong Pass *xian*(潼关县) today.

(252) These two lines are exaggerating statements.

(253) For the second time, for Geshu Han had lost the Pass before.

(254) Obstructive fence of pales of stakes set firmly in the ground for defence.

(255) The western capital means Chang'an(长安).

(256) The original 长戟 was a long-shafted weapon, a little different from a halberd, which in the 15 th and 16 th centuries in Eu-

rope was a combined spear and battle-axe; it was a long spear with a side prong near the top, not a battle axe.

(257) "Taolin(桃林) defeat" means the overwhelming defeat at the combat on the Dao-lin strategic terrain west of Lingbao *xian* (灵宝县) of He'nan Province(河南省) today to the Tong Pass(潼关).

(258) This is the first of the three *Partings* written by our poet to record the sufferings of the people during the rebellion of An Lushan and Shi Siming against the dynasty Tang. Early next morning after the nuptials the previous evening, the bride has to see her groom depart from her as a draftee. The poem is a monologue of the bride to her groom, regretting his enforced departure and yet exhorting him to fulfil his duty, and through her sad, complaining and painful assertions, portrays a good-natured, firm young woman of ill fortune in a feudalistic society.

(259) The stems and branches of raspberry and flax are short and slender; the dodder, clinging to them with tendrils in its growth, cannot thus be long. To marry off one's daughters to such wayfarers as the draftees is to court misfortune.

(260) According to Tang customs, on the third day after nuptials a bride would go with her groom to the cemeteries of his ancesters to do homage to them, then the matrimonial ceremony was considered to be fully accomplished. Now that the newly

wed couple had only stayed together for one night, the rites are not yet complete, and so her station is not yet clear.

(261) Father-in-law and mother-in-law.

(262) The original of these two lines means "my parents reared me by hiding me day and night from the sight of strangers" to conform to the rites of feudalistic moral code.

(263) In the male-centered ancient Chinese society, there was a saying that a girl married to a cock would have to follow the cock, and one married to a dog would have to follow the dog. Such is the literal sense of the original line.

(264) This last line expresses her love and devotion for her groom

(265) This poem gives an account of how an old man with his "offspring all in battles fallen and gone" responds to the drafting and his parting with his dear old mate whom he is not going to see again.

(266) The environs 100 *li* around the imperial city were called the "four suburbs". Here they mean the surrounding region of Luoyang(洛阳).

(267) Tumen(土门) is in the west of Zhuolu *xian*(涿鹿县) of Hebei Province(河北省) today.

(268) Apricot Orchard Town(杏园镇) is in Ji *xian*(汲县) of He'nan Province(河南省) today.

(269) The poem is the soliloquy of a homeless soldier scattered "from Xiangzhou's(相州) bad rout", coming back to his native place and levied once more to be the corporal drummer for training the new enlistees. His deserted homeland is covered with rank wild herbage; his village neighbours are all killed or dispersed elsewhere. After a circuitous walk, he finds out a certain lane, formerly familiar, now quite strange to him. There, the sunshine seems weak and the atomosphere is desolate. Before a shanty, he espies two or three foxes, which, seeing and staring at him, bristle their hair fiercely and screech at him. He encounters one or two aged widows. He takes up his hoe to till a little vegetable plot. And then he thinks of his mother who died of sore need in miserable poverty five years after the first uprising of An Lushan and Shi Siming's revolt in the 14th year (552) of the Tian-bao Period(天宝) of Xuan-*zong's*(玄宗) reign.

(270) This poem was written in the autumn of the second year of the Qian-yuan Period(乾元二年, 759) of De-*zong*(德宗)'s reign, when the rebellion of An Lushan(安禄山) and Shi Siming(史思明) had already broken out for more than four years. There was actually such a solitary beauty forsaken by her husband when her brothers had been slaughtered with others during the rebellious upheaval and their corpses were not even recovered to be properly buried. And she, though poor,

was virtuous and independant, living with her dear maid in a thatched cottage in a vale quite removed from town cooking cypress leaves for food. At the end of the poem, she is pictured as leaning against a tall bamboo in the cold breeze. But meanwhile, the poet has his own state of life and personality in mind in the poem, for some time earlier, he had resigned his official post at Huazhou(华州) and taking along his wife and children, crossed the Long Mounts(陇山) and came to live in poverty at Qinzhou(秦州), at present in Tianshui *xian* (天水县), in the east of Gansu(甘肃) Province bordering Shanxi(陕西) Province. There is close similarity between the state and mind of the solitary beauty and his own.

(271) West of Hangu Pass(函谷关以西) was called "Within the pass"(关中). In the sixth moon of the fifteenth year of the Tian-bao Period(天宝十五载六月) of Xuan-*zong*'s reign, An Lushan's uprising swept the regions of the Tang Empire West of the Hangu Pass.

(272) Rose mallow is a tall plant of the Hibiscus(木槿) family bearing rose-coloured of pink flowers, which blow at dawn and close at dusk.

(273) These two lines mean that though she is abandoned by her husband and living in pure poverty, she prefers to remain as she is in her present condition, not considering a second marriage with a well-to-do man of whatever state. This is of course in strict accord with the then current confucian ethics.

Reflecting on himself, Du Fu means to imply that, like this beauty, he would stick fast faithfully to the Tang regime in spite of its precarious pass at present.

(274) These two poems were written by Du Fu in the autumn of the second year of the Qian-yuan Period(乾元二年,759) of Su-*zong*'s(肃宗) reign, when the poet was staying at Qinzhou (秦州) in his travels. Since Li Bai and Du Fu parted from each other in the autumn of the fourth year of the Tian-bao Period(天宝四载,745) of Xuan-*zong*'s(玄宗) reign at Shimen(石门) of Yanzhou(兖州), now in the province Shandong(山东省), they had not ever seen, though having longed for, each other all along. In the second year of the Zhi-de Period(至德二载,757) of Su-*zong*'s reign, Li Bai, having been pressured into service by Prince Li Lin(永王李璘) while he stayed at Mount Lu(庐山) as a recluse, was imprisoned at Xunyang(浔阳), the modern River city Jiujiang(九江) of Jiangxi Province(江西省), for his affiliation with the prince's plot of rebellion. In the first year of the Qian-yuan Period(乾元元年,758), he was decreed to be exiled to Ye Lang(夜郎,Tongzi *xian* 桐梓县, of Guizhou, 贵州, Province today). In the second moon of the next year, he was pardoned on his way of exile at the Three Gorges(三峡) of the Yangzi River. Du Fu, staying at Qinzhou(秦州) in his travels, knew nothing of Li Bai's latest happenings. Pining for and sympathetic to his friend, he often dreamed of him and thus wrote these two poems.

(May 5, 1985)

(275) In ancient China from time immemorial, emperors, kings, nobilities, officials, scholars and their family members all wore special types of hats peculiar to their social positions. Peasants, labourers, artisans, common servants, theatre actors, merchants wore no distinct sort of hats. Officials, from the court chancellor and ministers down to the city and town sheriffs, alderman and village chiefs, all had their particular types of hats in accordance with their respective stations, and they all, down to a certain level, had accouterments such as the painted or laquered wooden badges signifying official status or titles, and metal (copper, brass or tin) signals mounted on painted poles, borne by their followers who walked by twos before their horse-drawn carriages or page-shouldered palanquins, as their pageants.

(May 13, 1985)

(276) In the fourth moon of the third year of the Tian-bao Period(天宝三载,744) in Xuan-*zong*'s(唐玄宗) reign, Du Fu made the acquaintance of Li Bai at Luoyang(洛阳), the eastern capital, when the latter had been bestowed on by the Emperor with gold and dismissed as an honoured subject but not given an office. They then visited Liang(梁) and Song(宋) in company, the towns Kaifeng(开封) and Sangqiu(商丘) of He'nan Province(河南省) today. The next year, they traveled together to Qi(齐) and Zhao(赵), the modern province Sandong(山东) and the region in the southern part of modern Hebei Province(河北省), the eastern part of Shanxi Province(山西省) and the northern part of the Luteous River

(黄河) in He'nan Province(河南省) today. They rode and hunted in company, composed poems together and commented on each other's works, loving mutually like brothers. In the autumn of that year, they parted at the county of Lu(鲁郡), now the *xian*(县) Yanzhou(兖州) of Shandong(山东) Province, when Du Fu wrote this poem. In it, our poet sighs at their common wanderings in uncertainty and failure to initiate the occult art of fairy *dao*(道), — "being ashamed for their inability to follow Ge Hong". The last two lines form a counsel to his friend as well as a warning to himself, so, how heart-felt is the friendship between them!

The original 飘蓬 means literally the flying, fluttered raspberry, a weed with leaves like those of willows and little white flowers; in autumn, it withers and is blown about by gusts of wind. lt is often compared to those whose residences are uncertain because of unstable occupation. Li Bai(701—762) and Du Fu(712—770), the former senior to the latter by eleven years, were both unlucky in their officiary careers. Taoists thought cinnabar could be forged into elixir for attaining longevity and making one immortal. Ge Hong(葛洪, 284—364), theoretician of Taoism, medical authority and alchemist of East Jin(东晋,317—420), called himself Baopuzi(抱朴子) and went up to the Luofu Mountains(罗浮山) for turning cininabar into elixir. Li Bai aspired fervantly for fairyhood; he had tried his hand at such occult practice; at Qizhou(齐州), he was initiated by ceremony into the inner circle of faithful believers. By the time when this quatrain was written, Du Fu had crossed the Luteous River with Li Bai to go up to Wangwu Mounts(王屋山) to visit the Taoist priest Huagai-*jun*(华盖君), who was however already dead. Highly disappointed, they failed in their attempts to attain fairyhood. Our poet asks his friend "for whom are you so defiant and arrogant?"(飞扬跋扈为谁雄?) Li Bai was noted for his chivalrous temperament and sword wielding; he had stabbed several men in fits of indignation.

—— The above notes are taken from Xiao Difei's *Anotated Selections of Du Fu's Poems*(《杜甫诗选注》)

(277) This poem was written in the autumn of the second year of the Qian yuan Period(乾元二年,759) during Su *zong*'s(萧宗) reign, when our poet was in his wandering stay at Qinzhou (秦州). Du Fu had four younger brothers, named Ying(颖) Guan(观), Feng(丰) and Zhan(占); at the time the youngest one of whom was with him, the other three being at Shandong(山东) and He'nan(河南). Herein are expressed his longings for his brothers and his native soil, pining at their being drifted elsewhere and his and their common home having vanished on account of the war of rebellison. Under the current martial law, when the night watch drums were struck, no pedestrians were allowed to walk on the streets. Wild geese usually fly in ranged files. To say one solitary brant is screaming in its flight over the border is symbolizing his own state of mind, which is missing the company of his three younger brothers. The night when this poem was written, it happened that the autumnal White Dew Period(白露节, one of the 24 climatic periods of the lunar year) commenced that

night, which was September 8 or on the Gregorian calendar. The turning of the season all the more deepens the feelings of our poet. The moon shines everywhere with the same lustre. To say that it glows particularly bright at home is of course due to his yearnings for home. With his brothers scattered elsewhere, if he still has a home at his native land, he could yet know their well beings or ill hap by writing to their common old home; but now that there is no more that old home, he has nowhere to inquire of whether they are still living or dead. And it is further to be grieved that the campaign to suppress the rebellion must be carried on indefinitely long.

(278) This poem was written by Du Fu in the summer of the first year of the Shang-yuan Period(上元元年,760) of Su-*zong*'s (肃宗) reign after four years' driftings from Tongzhou(同州) via Mianzhou(绵州) to the western suburb of Chengdu (成都), where, as it was not yet ravaged by the war of rebellion, by the side of the Brocade-washing and Flowery Runnel(浣花溪,濯锦江,百花潭), our poet, with the aid of his good friend Yan Wu, put up his thatched cot and began to lead a long-wished-for life of peace. The poem, showing the tranquillity of the writer's mind, is uncommon in his works. But in the last two lines our readers are reminded by the poet that he is not completely carefree: he has to depend on the kindness of a friend in helping him with a small portion of his office rice.

(July 12, 1984.)

(279) This poem was written by Du Fu in the summer of the first year of the Shang-yuan Period(上元元年,760) during Su-*zong*'s(肃宗) reign of the dynasty Tang. It first describes closely the exquisite state of his thatched cot, and then turn - ing the tip of the brush, proceeds to his destitute living, and at last, holding fast to his integrity, declares that he has not waived his fortitude to flatter power or debase himself.

(280) Ten-thousand-*li* Bridge(万里桥), a little stone one, is outside the South Gate(南门) of Chengdu(成都), where, during the Three Kingdoms Period(三国,220—280), Zhuge Liang(诸葛亮,181—234), the great statesman, strategist and chancellor of Shu-Han(蜀汉) saw Fei Hui(费祎,? —253) off as imperial emissary to Wu(吴). Du Fu's thatched cot was in the west of the Bridge.

(281) The original 百花潭 (Hundred Flowers Deep Pond) is purposely translated into its present form to avoid mentioning two names both with numbers, which in the Chinese original appear not monotonous but a desired verbal parallel. The Multiflorous Deep Pond was in the south of the thatched cot, which was situated in the north of it. Flower-washing Pool(浣花溪), also called the Brocade-washing River(濯锦江); Du Fu's thatched cot was situated in the north of it.

(282) Canglang Stream(沧浪江) is a tributary of the Han River(汉水), celebrated for its limpidity in ancient history. It was mentioned earliest in the chapter *Yu Gong*(《禹贡》) of *Shang*

Shu(《尚书》*The Book of the Past*), written by Confucius (551—479 B.C.) himself. In *The Analects of Mencius*(《孟子》), it is recorded that a boy sang a snatch of folk song about it thus:

沧浪之水清兮,
　可以濯我缨;
沧浪之水浊兮,
　可以濯我足。

When the water of Canglang is limpid,
　I could wash with it my hat's chin strips;
When the water of Canglang is turbid,
　I could wash with it my twain soiled feet.

(283) This alludes to his old friend Yan Wu(严武,726—765) Duke of the State Zheng(郑国公). When our poet first came to Chengdu, Yan helped him amply with his sovereign grants of office remuneration. But as these friendly gifts petered out, he, without his own resources, and his family had to suffer from starvation. His ill-fed children appear sallow and dismal in complexion.

(284) And yet he was not at all cowered by poverty, but was as ready as ever to express his uncommon, independent views on matters of the state and the society, though that might get him into trouble and hasten his death.

(285) He is prouder of and laughs at himself, the older he becomes, regardless of what the world thinks of him.

(March 14, 1986.)

(286) The poet's own note on this seven-charactered *lü* octave is "Pleased to have His Honour the town sheriff Mr. Cui's (崔明府) call on me." The tone of this poem is full of heartiness and candour.

(287) This poem was written in 761 as a cry of the poet in his wretched circumstances for the urgent but vain wish that poor scholars like himself be supplied with ample provisions of food and lodging, so as to enable them to carry on their intellectual pursuits for the benefit of society.

(288) In 756 A. D., Dang-xiang-qiang and Tu-yu-hun (chieftains of these tribes in ancient China) made constant intrusions into the territory of the Tang Dynasty. The Tang army being unable to put up an effective resistance, could only ride roughshod over the common people. Their atrocities are strongly condemned by the poet.

(289) These two quatrains, rendered here into English as two octaves, were written by Du Fu in late spring when he had returned to his thatched cot in Chengdu. After his tortuous and aimless wandering for three years, when he had seen Yan Wu (严武, 726—765), Governor and Duke during Su-*zong*'s reign and Du Fu's friend and superior, off to the court, our poet was struggling along in poverty at Zizhou (梓州) and Langzhou (阆州). Now that he is in more comfortable cir-

cumstances, he feels all the more poignantly the beauty of his natural surroundings. Yet, facing all such scenic delights, he cannot but be stirred up with nostalgic thoughts.

(February 5, 1986)

(290) Du Fu wrote this poem in Zhongzhou(忠州) in the year Yong-tai(永泰,765) of Su-*zong*'s(萧宗) reign. Yu's temple was in the south of Linjang *xian*(临江县), two *li* from the river Min(岷江).

Great Yu of Xia(夏禹), the first king of the dynasty, was the grandson of Zhuanxu(颛顼), who was said to have ruled for 78 years and was himself the grandson of the Luteous Emperor(黄帝轩辕氏), the earliest legendary *Di* of the Han(汉) majority of the Chinese race. Yu was ordained by *Di* Sun(帝舜) to be his imperial successor for his splendid achievements in conducting the deluge of the flooding Luteous River(黄河) that ravaged its banks for eight years from 2286 to 2278 B. C. to the eastern sea. It was common knowledge among China's school boys and girls before the middle of this century that Great Yu passed thrice the entrance of his homestead in eight years without entering it, while he was engaged in the expulsion of the flood. This great benefactor of the Han majority of the Chinese race ruled only eight years on his throne. He died in his inspection tour in 2197 B. C. at Kuaiji (会稽). The lunar Xia calendar inaugurated by Yu on his ascension to his throne is still partially in use in China today.

(291) According to the chapter *Yi and Ji*(《益稷》) of *Shang Shu*

(《尚书》, *The Book of the Past*), Yu said "I ride the four vehicles." These are explained in Sima Qian's *Chronicles*(司马迁:《史记》) as cart for conveyance on land, boat on water, sleigh(橇) on muddy terrain and palanquin(樺梮) for ascending elevations.

(November 30, 1983)

(292) According to the primal studies in the earliest anthology of ancient Chinese poetry entitled *Poetry*(《诗》), now known as *The Classic of Poetry*(《诗经》), the 305 poems collected in that anthology early in the dynasty Zhou(周,1122—255 B. C.) are capable of being specificed into six categories according to their nature, namely: popular ballads or folk songs garnered in its early halcyon days(风), lyric poems composed by its intellectuals(雅), odes on happenings of state magnitude(颂), expansions on themes of memorable affairs or occasions(赋), similitudes or comparisons between notable happenings of the past and the present(比), and musings or contemplations on the past, present and future of oneself and the state(兴).

Eight Octaves on Autumnal Musings (or Meditations) are a series of seven-charactered *lü* poems(律诗) composed by Du Fu at Kuizhou(夔州) in the first year of the Da-Ii Period(大历元年,766) of Dai-*zong*'s(代宗) reign during the dynasty Tang(唐). They are the product of broodings on autumn, hence Autumnal Musings. From the second year of the Qian-yuan Period(乾元二年,759) of Su-*zong*'s(肃宗) reign, when Du Fu left officialdom to reside at Qinzhou(秦

州) till now, he had spent in all seven years, leading a wandering Iife. During these years, the war to suppress the rebellion went on ceaselessly. Now, as the clime was desolate, our poet could not but be sorely moved by his deep concern for the current rule as a loyal subject, from which his personal dejection and self commiseration also arose. The lines "I use to yearn for the capital neath the Great Bear" in the second octave and "I think of my native soil as an absentee" in the fourth are the key statements of all these verses.

The structure of these *Eight Octaves* could be divided into two portions, with the fourth one as the transitional stanza. The first three dwell on Kuizhou first and then think of Chang'an(长安) the capital, while the last five think of Chang'an first and then reflect on Kuizhou; in the first three, the musings shift from reality to reminiscence, and in the last five, the musings flit from reminiscence to reality. And between the stanzas, the starts and ends are well connected, not interchangeable, the eight forming a concerted whole. *Eight Octaves on Autumnal Musings* thus form a featly executed masterpiece of Du Fu, either imbuing sentiments in scenic aspects, or motioning past events to signify the present, or stating current happenings without disguise, or stopping short just on the point of speaking, — the readers must peruse carefully to catch the illusive poetic essence.

(293) The first octave writes about the autumnal scene and the poet's feelings of wanderings and nostalgic thoughts for his native soil. The atmosphere of the Wu Mounts and Gorges around

the Great River is desolate and depressive. Du Fu was at Yun'an(云安) last autumn and is here at Kuizhou this one; so, from the time he left Chengdu(成都), chrysanthemums have flowered twice, with his tears also shed twice. He commits his hopes of returning to the capital to a single boat. Thinking of the pressing need of winter garments for the oncoming cold season everywhere and of the thick laundry clubbings before dusk in the high mountain town Baidi(白帝), meaning "the White Emperor," the poet is all the more overcome by nostalgia.

The ancient peopled center high on the mountain-side originally called Fish Belly Town(鱼腹城) was in the east of the present Fengjie *xian*(奉节县) of Sichuan Province(四川省). Its name was changed into Baidi(白帝), meaning the Town of the White Emperor, by Gongsun Shu(公孙述,? B. C.—36 A. D.) during early East Han(东汉,25—188 A. D.) who declared himself the supreme ruler bearing that title for twelve years.

——The above and following notes and comments are culled and translated from Prof. Xiao Difei's(萧涤非教授) thorough studies.

(294) In this second octave, the poet writes on the desolate sight of dusk at Kuizhou and his yearning for the capital Chang'an(长安). Every night, he relies on gazing at the Big Dipper to yearn for the imperial city, which he could not see, but was, as it is, now called Xi'an, just under the Big Dipper. Ursa Major, a constellation in the region of the north celestial

pole, near Draco and Leo, containing the seven stars that form the Big Dipper, is called the Big Bear in the West. According to Notes on *The Water Classic* (《水经注》) by Li Daoyuan(郦道元,466 or 472 ? —527) of North Wei(北魏, 386—557), a fisherman's song had

Amongst the gorges three of Ba-*dong*,
The Gorge of the Wu Mounts is long;
At the sad wailings of gibbons thrice,
One's tears drip down to wet his gown.

("巴东三峡巫峡长,猿鸣三声泪沾裳"). It is said in Zhang Hua's(张华,232—300, of West Jin,西晋,265—419) *The Record of Strange Strands, Rare Things and Unusual Events* (《博物志》) that old traditions have it that the Heaven's River(天河, or Silvery Stream,银河, i. e., the Milky Way) could be reached by the sea, that of late years there have been people who live on islets in the sea, every year in the eighth moon there were floating rafts coming in time regularly, people getting on the rafts with food supplies went away for some ten odd days and reached Heaven's River. Also, according to *The Daily Records of Things and Events in Jing and Chu*(《荆楚岁时纪》) by Zong Lin(宗懔) of Liang(梁,502—558), Emperor Wu-*di* of Han(汉武帝,140—88 B. C.) ordered Zhang Qian(张骞, ? —114 B. C.), the great general, to trace the Luteous River(黄河) to its source; taking to the raft, he reached the Heaven's River at last after a number of months. Line 4 above is making use of these two allusions to indicate the poet's relations with the court, likening Zhang Qian to Yan Wu(严武) and Zhang's reaching the Heaven's

River to Yan's returning to the court. Before Du Fu wrote the *Eight Octaves*, he as a counselor(参谋) to Yan Wu, was a member of the Imperial Secretariat(尚书省,检校工部员外郎). He had formerly entertained the hope of returning to the court in the retinue of Yan Wu. But Yan's death had dashed his expectation of going back to Chang'an — "toward heaven to repair".

In the Secretariat Ministry (书省 = 尚书省), according to *The Official System of Han*(《汉官仪》, Han, 206 B. C. — 8 A. D.), written by Ying Shao(应劭, *circa* 160—220) of Late Han(后汉, 25—220), now nonextant, the walls of the main official halls were plastered with white lead powder and painted with figures of ancient sages and heroic women. When the imperial secretaries attended their offices, they were waited upon each by two attendant ladies holding an incense burner. During Tang, the practice still held as in Han, Du Fu had in the past served in the office of Left Gleaner(左拾遗), which belonged to the Ministry of Attendance and Counsellorship(门下省). He was demoted for his untimely counsel to Emperor Su-*zong*(肃宗) to pardon Fang Guan(房琯) the chancellor for the smashing defeat of the imperial troops under his command by the rebel forces at the Battle of Chen-tao Marsh(陈陶泽), with 40,000 men completely wiped out. As a subordinate to Yan Wu(严武), Duke of the State Zheng (郑国公), Du Fu was recommended to the office of Overseering and Examining in the Department of Imperial Works(检校工部员外郎), which belonged to the Secretariat Ministry. Yan's death and the poet's own illness prevented him from attending the secretariat at Chang'an.

And at the limed parapet of Baidi's mountain town tower, he listens to the sad Tartar pipe vaguely moaning in the distance, which means the war of quelling the rebellion is still going on. The last two lines show that after the sun turning west in the first line, the poet has stood ruminating so long that the moon has already cast its sheen on the wisteria over the stones and the white rush flowers of the isle.

(295) In the third octave, the poet writes of the morning scene of Kuizhou and sighs on his good parts unappreciated and of no avail. The mountain town is that of Bai-di(白帝城). All around the storeyed riverside house, there was the undulating verdant mountain tops and vales — the expanse of rolling green. Nightly, the fishing boats float along carefree, in contrast to his enforced stay. The early autumn swallows, soon to migrate southward, seem to insinuate to him by their flitting about, that he could not go south to Chang'an the capital. Kuang Heng(匡衡), a noted scholar of Confucian classics in West Han(206—6 B. C.), was a chancellor of Yuan-*di*(元帝,48—33 B. C.) and was ordained Marquis of Le'an (乐安侯). Often dissenting from his emperor's views on matters of state, he was used to quote the classics in support of his own opinions. While his prototype Kuang Heng got encouragement from his sovereign Yuan-*di* of West Han for his dissenting counsels, Du Fu's own efforts to ask pardon from Su-*zong*(肃宗) for the chancellor Fang Guan's(房琯) smashing defeat by the rebel forces of An Lushan and Shi Si-

ming(安禄山,史思明): sustaining a total loss of 40,000 men at the Chentao(陈陶) Battle, resulted in the loss of his own post as the left Gleaner(左拾遗). Liu Xiang(刘向,77—6 B. C.) was also an eminent scholar of Confucian classics and a literati as well as a notable bibliographer of West Han. His son Liu Xin(刘歆,? —23) continued his heritage as an eminent scholar of the classics, a distinguished bibliographer and an astronomist to boot. Du Fu's grandfather Du Shenyan(杜审言,? —after 705) was a noted poet before him, but certainly not such a great one as he was. Here, our poet is polite in underestimating himself, speaking of the failure of his own aim. In these two lines, our poet tells his readers what he is thinking of in his solitude beside the longings for his sovereign and the court. And finally, he goes on to reflect on his erstwhile fellow students, who have all become darlings of Fortune now. In the original, the Five *Ling*(五陵) of the dynasty Han(汉,206 B. C.—220 A. D.) — Chang *Ling*(长陵), An *Ling*(安陵), Yang *Ling*(阳陵), Mao *Ling*(茂陵) and Ping *Ling*(平陵), the five settlements of rich families removed from all over the country to the capital to reside in — are spoken of to signify with irony the well-favoured families of the present with their light, fur-lined robes and fat horses (轻裘肥马).

(296) This fourth octave is the turning point — while the previous three dwell on Kuizhou, this and the following four expatiate on Chang'an. The capital, after its capture by the rebels, its tribulations and recovery, bears no more the complexion of its

past. Du Fu speaks of "these hundred years" in the original second line as a gross number to exaggerate their length, whereas actually the revolt of An Lu-san and Shi Siming broke out in 755, only eleven years before the first year of the Da-li Period(大历元年) when these octaves were written. My rendition is nearer the reality. The homes of nobilities, after the capital's fall and the tribulations have all changed their masters; also, after the rebellion, the newly entitled and fresh crop of notables are engaged in setting up their new mansions, vying with one another in luxury and magnitude. At that time, Su-*zong*(肃宗) and Dai-*zong*(代宗) both entrusted their state affairs in eunuches, giving them great power in military and political matters. Courtiers were divided into cabals and cliques, vying with one another and intriguing with the eunuches. There was also a group of illiterate enlisted chiefs, waiting at the "Hall of the Viruous"(集贤院) and known as scholarly courtiers. Such phenomena were unknown in the past, hence "none of years ago". The beating of drums (击鼓) and the clanging of gongs(鸣金) were orders of onward attacking and backward retreating in the army, meaning that warfare was rife. "The messages of westward campaigns," with birds' tail plumes stuck in them means the report is urgent for suppressing the rebellious forces and repelling the penetration of Tu-fan(吐蕃) hordes. The first six lines speak of Chang'an and affairs of the state, while in the seventh line our poet comes back to himself in Kuizhou. Like fish and dragons, he is submerged here as if in the autumnal river water cold; and here, he is full of feelings and reflections of his vicissitudes.

(297) This octave dwells on the magnificence of the capital's sights and atmosphere, and the notable state of the court. It is thus what is thought of in the first place by the poet among other things as a zealous courtier. The Penglai Palace, meaning that of the fairies, was on the Dragon Head Plain(龙首原) in the north-east of Chang'an, facing southward the Utmost South Mountains(终南山). The Golden Pillar was a stem 200 feet high supporting a big basin of seven embraces in circumference, the whole thing made of brass, with a "fairy's palm" in the basin for collecting dewdrops, which, when taken with gem particles, were suposed to give infinite longevity to a person. The structure was ordered to be fabricated by the Han emperor Wu-*di*(汉武帝,140—86 B. C.), a stalwart believer in fairyhood, and erected in the west of the Jianzhang Palace (建章宫) of Han's imperia! group of structures. During the Tang Dynasty, though the capital was still Chang'an as in West Han, there was no more the dew-collecting basin and its stem. Du Fu simply makes use of its fictitious or merely historical existence to give a halo of magnificence to the Tang capital. Dame Wang of the West(西王母) was a fairy lady inhabiting by the Gem Pool(瑶池) on the Kunlun Mountains (昆仑山). According to *The Chronological Book of Bamboo Strips*(《竹书纪年》), *King Mu*(穆王,*1001—946 B. C.*) *of the dynasty Zhou*(周,*122—256 B. C.*) *rode up the Kunlun Mountains*(昆仑丘) *in the 17th year*(*1017 B. C.*) *of his reign* to visit the fairy Dame Wang and was cordially enter-

tained by her. Here and in the next line, our poet imagines a legendary saying and a traditional lore to be connected with Chang'an to give it importance.

Lao-*zi*(老子 604? —531 B. C.) — reputed the earliest great thinker of the Chinese race, the senior sage of the Spring and Autumn Period(春秋,722—481 B. C.), elder contemporary of Confucius(孔丘,551—479 B. C.) and official compiler of the chronicles in the regal library of the Zhou Dynasty(周朝守藏室之史), of whom Confucius once asked instruction of ceremonials, — whose name is known to be Li Er(李耳) and whose tract *Lao-zi*(《老子》) or the *Dao-de Classic*(《道德经》) consists of 5000 odd characters on the conformity of human thinking and acts to the law of Nature, is here extolled by Du Fu in alluding to his going from Luoyang(洛阳) in the east westwards through Hangu Pass(函谷关), riding a cart drawn by a bluish dark ox, when the Pass-keeping governor Xi(关令尹喜) observed in advance a purple aura moving westward from the east, signifying the approach of a sage, and on his arrival at the Pass, he was requested by the high official to set down his metaphysical deliberations in the occult tract now known to us as *The Dao-de Classic*(《道德经》). The large fans mounted on poles and made of pheasant tail plumes were ceremonial means or appendants in the court hall, employed to cover up the emperor's sight from the looks of the attending courtiers before he sat down. When he had sat down above facing the kneeling courtiers or retired from their sight under the cover of the fans, these were taken away and put aside. During the

Tang Dynasty, the ceremonial court rite for the emperor to sit at the imperil assemblage was early before daybreak; so the first beams of dawn on the figure of the monarch would show his complexion. And then, the reader is told of how the poet finds himself, being fatefully struck down, lying beside the Great River, coming to, all of a sudden, so late in the autumn (as well as during his declining years, for he is fifty-five years old now). In the last line, he wonders how many times (seldom rather than often) he was summoned at the roll call by the portal(青琐,which was incised with designs of interlinked rings that were filled with bluish green pigment) of the yard of court hall to appear before the imperial majesty of Su-*zong*(肃宗) as his Left Gleaner(左拾遗).

(298) In this octave, our poet recalls the past festive splendour of Xuan-*zong*'s imperial visits to Zigzag River Pool(曲江池) in the southeast of Chang'an(长安) the capital. It is what is thought of by Du Fu in the second place, as he pines on the chaos caused by the rebellious uprising of An Lushan(安禄山) and Shi Siming(史思明). Du Fu, now staying at Kuizhou(夔州) which is in the west of the Qutang Gorge(瞿塘峡), the first one of the Three Gorges of the Long River (长江), is harking back at the good old days when he was at Chang'an(长安). The site of Zigzag River (this being its first, original name) Pool(曲江池) bank, today in the southeast of Xi'an(西安), the chief city of Shanxi Province(陕西省), was named Spring-befitting Grove(宜春苑) during Qin (秦,221—207 B. C.), called Pleasure-roaming Plain(乐游

原) in Han(汉,206, B. C.—219 A. D.), changed into Hibiscus Garden(芙蓉园) in Sui(隋,589—618) and excavated during the Kai-yuan(开元) years(713—741) of Tang(唐, 618—907) and renamed Zigzag River Pool(曲江池). As a spring pleasure resort, it was in the south of Chang'an and east of the Vermillion Bird Bridge(朱雀桥) and in the vicinity of the Pleasure-roaming Garden(乐游园), Apricot Garden (杏园) and Maternal Love Monastery(慈恩寺). During the An-Shi(安,史) revolt when Chang'an was occupied by the Tartar satrap and his deputy's troops, the scenic spot was in the main ruined. More than sixty years after the An-Shi rebellion was suppressed, efforts were made to rejuvenate the architectural beauty of the scene in Wen-*zong*'s (唐文宗) reign (827—841), but the destruction was too overwhelming and attempts at restoration proved to be of no avail. And then, toward the end of the Tang Dynasty, after the capital was taken place of by Luoyang(洛阳), the River water stopped to flow thither, so the Qutang Gorge mouth and Zigzag River bank, far away from each other, are exaggerated here to be ten thousand *li* apart in the original. In this autumnal season, war fires have linked them together. Xuan-*zong* had orderd to be built the "Tower that has Flower-and-seplas Mutually Shining on Each Other". In the 20th year of the Kai-yuan Period(开元二十年,732), a high-walled passage was built leading from the "Flower-and Sepals-Shining-upon-Each-Other Tower"(花萼相辉楼) to Zigzag River Pool bank for His Majesty to pass through unobserved by his subjects. To Hibiscus Garden, went the sad news of border war combustibles of An

Lushan's rebellion. The Zigzag River Pool bank in this octave is full of palaces and towers; in line 5, a swan alighting there would find itself lost among those structures, and in line 6, flying gulls would be frightened by such a host of masts and riggings on the Zigzag River Pool. These four lines, from the third to the sixth, describe the flourishing state of the Zigzag River Pool and its bank in the past. But alas! the thriving atmosphere and glamorous sights of the bygone days are no more to be found. And in the last line, the reigning soverign and his successors are reminded with warning that this old terrain "within the Pass" has been from ages past the domain of our memorable emperors and kings, "those of you who follow in their steps should remember their illustrious deeds and examples; you should not divert from their straight, upright paths to indulge in dissolution, ill deeds and wanton policies, in order to avoid this goodly domain fallen into battlefield ruins."

(299) Kunming Lake(昆明池), twenty *li*(6.214 miles) south-west of Chang'an and forty *li*(12.428 miles) in circumference, was dug in the third year of the Yuan-shou Period(元狩三年, 120 B.C.) of Wu-*di*'s(武帝,140—86 B.C.) reign of Han (汉,206 B.C.—8 A.D.) by imperial decree for drilling fleet fighting. No more existent today, it was there in the south-western suburb of Tang's capital as our poet remembers it here. In the Pool, two stone effigies were erected, the Cowherd(牵牛) in the east and the Shuttle Girl(织女) in the west to represent the stars Altair and Vega, south and north of

the Silvery Stream(银河), the Milky Way. In Chinese mythology, the couple meet each other only once in the seventh night of the seventh moon every lunar year when the Maid crosses the bridge formed by magpies linking one another by beaks and tail plumes to meet her lover. The stone figures still existent, are buried underground. The Shuttle Girl does not weave in moonlight night perhaps because then the star could not be seen with naked eyes. The jade whale was said to be agitating its tail and fins during thunderstorm; it is now preserved in the Provincial Museum in Xi'an(西安). In lines 5 and 6, the poet's thoughts wind on what he sees in imagination in the plants, zizania and lotus cupules, on the Kunming Pond. In the last two lines, he comes back to the inaccessible distance between the court of his sovereign and himself, and finally, to his lone and forlorn state as a solitary fisherman.

(300) In this the last one of the *Eight Octaves*, Du Fu dwells on his enjoyment of the scenic beauty of Meipi(渼陂), which consists of the fourth topic of what he thinks of in these strains. In the previous three stanzas, he recalls the Penglai Palaces (蓬莱宫), Zigzag River Pool(曲江池) and Kunming Lake (昆明池), all of which are affairs of the court. But in this last stanza, he is reminiscent of his personal enjoyment of the relevant scenic beauty. Kunwu(昆吾) and Yusu(御宿) were two spots in the south east of Chang'an, anciently in the extensive Imperial Park(上林苑) of the Han Dynasty(汉). To go from Chang'an by the circuitous way through Kunwu and Yusu to Meipi, one reached finally Meipi the Lake scene, the

source of which water was the Zhongnan (ultimate Utmost South) Mountains(终南山), today in the west of Hu *xian* (户县) of Shanxi Province(陕西省). When Du Fu was in Chang'an, he in the company of Cen Shen(岑参), Gao Shi (高适), Chu Guangxi(储光羲) and Xue Ju(薛据), took a trip to Meipi and all composed poems on the occasion. Du Fu wrote his *The Lay of Meipi* (《渼陂行》). Purple Pavilion Peak(紫阁峰) is a peak of the Zhongnan Mountains, deriving its name from the fact that early in the morning, the glow of sunrise shining on it casts a purple halo thereto to make it look like a pavilion. In the original 香稻啄余鹦鹉粒,碧梧栖老凤凰枝, there are syntactical inversions for the sake of tonal reasons in the make-up of characters. These two lines describe the beauty of the products of Kunwu and Yusuo. "Fairy companions"(仙侣) are meant for the companies enjoying their spring trips to Mei-pi, the beauty of which is like that of the fairyland, hence the expression. Du Fu here refers to his submitting two pieces of *fu*(赋) to Xuan-*zong*(玄宗) the Emperor, in the ninth and tenth years of the Tian-bao Period(天宝九载,十载,750—751) of his reign, attracting the previous emperor's attention. He was deprived of the office of Left Gleaner(左拾遗) by the present emperor Su-*zong*(肃宗), for his attempt to ask pardon for the chancellor Fang Guan(房琯), who had suffered a smashing defeat and lost 40,000 men under his command, slaughtered in the Battle of Chentao(陈陶) with the rebellious forces of An Lushan and Shi Siming. The last two lines turn back to himself as a summary: the upper one recalls his favourable notice by Xuan-

zong for his literary merits, the lower one says that though poverty-stricken, trod by luck, habituating himself to a lone, strange town in his old age, he is still fervently cherishing his dear native soil and harking back for the welfare of the state.

(301) This poem was written by Du Fu in the winter of the first year of the Da-li period in Dai-*zong*'s reign(代宗大历元年,766) when he was staying in the night at the west Pavilion(西阁) of Kuizhou(夔州). Spending his wandering days in this desolate, remote mountain town, the poet, overlooking the magnificent night scene in the Gorges and hearing the sad, heroic horns and drums, became filled with overpowering feelings. The poem is deeply plaintive in tone. Writing here far away from home, he calls it "the horizon". The screeching horns and pulsating battle drums tore the broad silence of night air. The Milky Way is commonly known in China as the Starry or Heavenly Stream. Thousands of families mourning and wailing in the wild for the loss of their sons refer here to the war of rebellion; the wood-cutters and fishermen of the minority groups singing their folk songs are thought of, together with the mourning families, by our poet in his rumination of sleepless night. "The Lying Dragon" means Zhuge Liang(诸葛亮,181—234), great statesman, strategist and premier of Shu-Han(蜀汉) of the Three Kingdoms(三国,220—280). The "Galloping Horse"(跃马) refers to Gongsun Shu(公孙述,? —36), a prefecture governor general(太守) of Shu (蜀郡) during the Pretender Wang Mang's(王莽) usurpation (9—22), who declared himself emperor at the end of

Wang's reign and was crushed by Emperor Guangwu(光武, 25—58) of East Han's(东汉) forces in the 12th year of his reign and killed. Both Zhuge Liang and Gongsun Shu had wielded activities at Kuizhou in their own times and both had left their memorial sites there. So, Du Fu, thinking of them, comes to the conclusion that after all, all is futility. And then, he pines on his own social relations and tidings of state affairs — they are now all severed from him. What can he do about them? Nothing now; so, let them be of their own accord.

(Feb. 18, 1986.)

(302) The second year of Da-li(大历), the name of the reign of Dai-*zong*(代宗) of Tang, was 767 A. D.

(303) In Kuizhou(夔州), called Fengjie *xian*(奉节县), Sichuan Province(四川) today, there was the official residence of the county governor or sheriff(刺史), in whom was invested the highest authority in civil as well as military affairs of the region. Yuanchi (元持) was the deputy governor(别驾).

(304) The fifth year of Kai-yuan(开元) during Xuan-*zong*'s(玄宗) reign was 717 A. D., when our poet was a child of six years only. In the prose introduction to the poem of some current texts, we have 开元三载, the character 三 of which is a misprint. In the third year of Kai-yuan, the poet was only four years old, too small a child to be a spectator of the dance. Du Fu was born in 712, the last year of Rui-*zong*'s(睿宗) reign

and a year before Xuan-*zong* ascended his throne; in the fifth year of Kai-yuan, 717, he was six years old, or eight years old according to the lunar calendar of Xia(夏历) and calculated in the customary Chinese way.

(305) The two troupes of danseuses Yichun(宜春) and Liyuan(梨园) were instituted within the enclosure of the court walls. There were troupes of *danseuse* and men-dancers formed outside the court walls. The numbers of dancers male and female totalled several hundreds; to say, as in line 15 of Du Fu's original poem, that there were "eight thousand waitng maids of the late emperor", is an exaggeration.

(306) Sage-artistic and Holy-militant Emperor(圣文神武皇帝) was a title of Xuan-*zong* offered to him for adulation by his courtiers in the 27th year of his reign Kai-yuan(开元).

(307) Zhang Xu(张旭), noted for his wild *cao*(狂草) mode of calligraphy, flourished during the Kai-yuan(开元) and Tianbao(天宝) years (713—755) of Xuan-*zong*'s reign. Li Bai's poetry, Pei Wen's(裴旻) sword dance and Zhang Xu's *cao* calligraphy were known as the Three Supremacies(三绝) of the time. Zhang said his art pranced forward by leaps and bounds after his having enjoyed the spectacle of Gongsun's sword dance.

(308) According to legendary lore, Yi(羿) the great archer and *Di* Yao's(帝尧) courtier shot down nine out of the ten suns for

their scorching and withering the green vegetation, thus saving all plant life and the human world.

(309) For fifty years, from the fifth year of Kai-yuan(开元五年, 717) to the second year of Da-li(大历二年,769), the rebellion of An Lushan(安禄山) and Shi Siming(史思明) had almost overthrown the Li(李) house and its dynasty Tang (唐).

(310) Li the Twelfth Lady of Linying(临颍第十二娘) is the "one bright star still sparkling". She performed her sword dance in November 767(大历二年十月).

(311) Xuan-*zong*, the emperor our poet has in mind here, died in 762 and was buried the next year on Jinsu-*shan*(金粟山), Golden Millet Mount, in Pucheng *xian*(蒲城县), Shanxi Province today. The trees planted before his mausoleum five years ago have grown tall when this poem is written.

(312) "The stone-walled town" alludes to White *Di* Town(白帝城); wherefrom the Linying Lady comes; it is in the vicinity of the Qutang Gorge(瞿塘峡) "The grasses are bare".

(313) Watching the excellent sword dance with high spirits for having seen the acme of graceful dancing of Lady Gongsun during the early Kai-yuan years still vibrantly alive in her disciple's performance, the poet yet pines with sad thoughts on the calamitous happenings to Emperor Xuan-*zong*, the rul-

ing house and the people at large. He lingers on what has just passed and refrains from stepping forth into reality and reminiscent miseries.

(314) The three-storied Yueyang Tower(岳阳楼) is a structure over the western gate of Yueyang's city wall overlooking the Dongting Lake(洞庭湖). It was built by the poet Zhang Yue (张说,667—730) of Tang(唐) when he was demoted from his original high post as the Imperial Secretary(中书令), Duke of Yan(燕国公), in the central government and banished to Yueyang as its governor.

(315) Dongting Lake(洞庭湖) was anciently known as the Xiang Stream(湘水). In the *Classic of Streams*(《水经注》), the waters of Dongting Lake are described to be over 500 *li* in girth and the sun and moon seem to rise from and fall into it.

(316) It is said that "In the third year of the Da-li Period(大历三年,768) of Dai-*zong*'s(代宗) reign, Guo Ziyi(郭子仪) commanding an army 50000 strong stationed at Fengtian(奉天) to guard against Tu-fan(吐蕃), and his generals Bai Yuanguang(白元光) and Li Baoyu(李抱玉) led divisions to attack the foe."

(317) Zhuge Liang, or Kong Ming(诸葛亮,孔明,181—214), a native of the Langya(琅琊) County of Lu(鲁), was the renowned statesman and strategist of Shu-Han(蜀汉) during the Three Kingdoms Period(三国,220—280). He was thrice

visited by Liu Bei（刘备，161—223）in his thatched cottage on the Longzhong Hills（隆中山），when he was a youthful anchorite only twenty-seven years old farming in Deng *xian*（邓县），at present Xiangyang（襄阳）*xian* of Hubei（湖北）Province，before he could be met with to consult on matters of the general political situation of the time. When Cao Pei（曹丕，187—226），the son of Cao Cao（曹操，155—220）usurped the Han throne in 220 as Wen-*di* of Wei（魏文帝），Zhuge counselled Liu Bei to declare himself the legitimate successor to the Han throne and was made by Liu his chancellor in 221. After the decease of Liu Bei，he upheld with might the prince Liu Chan（刘禅，207—271）in his weak reign till his own untimely death.

By the side of Liu Bei's temple in the western part of Chengdu（成都），the chief city of Sichuan Province（四川省）today，is located the Memorial Hall of Zhuge Liang，in the front of which is a giant cedar said to be planted by the Chancellor himself. The western portion of Chengdu was the ancient Town of Brocade-gowned Officials（锦官城）. According to *The Life of Zhuge Liang*（《诸葛亮传》）in Chen Shou's（陈寿）*Chronicle of the Three Kingdoms*（《三国志》），the Chancellor led in person the state's dispatch of troops via Xiegu（斜谷），to occupy Wugong（武功）and Fifty-feet Plain（五丈原）to face in opposition to Sima Yi（司马懿）the Wei（魏）general of Cao Cao at Weinan（渭南）. He remained at his post as commander for more than three months，till his own death in the camps.

(318) The original "空" when translated literally is "in vain".

(July 28, 1983)

(319) This poem was written by Du Fu as a captive in Chang'an(长安), the capital of Tang(唐), after it was occupied by the rebellious Hu(胡) satrap An Lushan's(安禄山) troops as the result of the smashing defeat of the imperial army commanded by the chancellor Fang Guan(房琯) at Chentao Incline(陈陶斜) and Qingban(青板), with tens of thousands of casualties.

(320) Gourd shell was used for holding food - stuffs and tea, and mug for wine.

(321) In the sixth moon of the fifteenth year of the Tian-bao Period (天宝十五年,756) of Xuan-*zong*'s(玄宗) reign, the rebellion broke out that was to last for more than seven years. In the seventh moon, our poet left his family at the village Qiang (羌村) of Fuzhou(鄜州) for Lingwu(灵武), where the prince royal had ascended the throne as De-*zong*(德宗). He was captured on the way by the rebel forces and taken back Chang'an. The next spring he composed his *Spring Prospects* (《春望》).

(322) The literal meaning of this line in the original is "(I) sit sadly (and) write (with my hand) in the air (strokes of the characters) '咄咄怪事' ('Huh, huh, what a strange thing!')". This is an allusion to an anecdote in the book *The World's*

Tales and Anecdotes Newly Related(《世说新语》) written by Liu Yiqing(刘义庆) in the Song Dynasty of Liu(刘宋, 420—479): Yin Hao(殷浩), when he was relieved of his office, sat alone and wrote in the air the four characters "咄咄怪事"(Huh, huh, what an oddity!) the whole day.

(323) In the first moon of the Yong-tai Period(永泰元年,765) of Dai-*zong*'s(代宗) reign, Du Fu resigned from his office under Yan Wu(严武,726—765). In the fourth moon, Yan died. In the fifth, Du Fu left his thatched cot in Chengdu(成都) with his family to sail east-wards. When his ship passed Yuzhou(渝州), called Chongqing(重庆) today and Zhongzhou(忠州), now called Zhong *xian*(忠县), he wrote this octave. He was then fifty-two years old.

(324) In this line, the poet means to say that he is noted not merely as a man of letters, but also as a figure notable in political affairs. In the next line, he insinuates that he was forced to resign his office out of displeasure. And in the last two lines, he pictures himself in irony as a man badly belittled.

(December 6, 1983)

(325) dhyana: in Hinduism, Buddhism and Jainism, meditation, especially an uninterrupted state of mental concentration upon a single object; higher contemplation.

(326) bonzary: the monastery of bonzes (bonze: a Buddhist priest in China, Japan, etc.)

(327) repair: go.

(328) covert: half-hidden; covered; concealed; sheltered.

(329) secluded: quiet; solitary:

(330) grove: group of trees; small wood.

(331) rare: thin; not dense; also, unusually good.

(332) aura: atmosphere surrounding a person or object and thought to come from him or it.

(333) the mind's ups and downs: alternations of good and bad fortune (figurative) in men's minds.

(334) hubbub: confused noise of many voices; uproar.

(335) spell: words used as a charm, supposed to have magic power.

(336) clang: loud ringing sound.

(337) Li Bai(李白 701? —762) is meant here, whose nickname "the exiled faery"(谪仙) was give him by He Zizhang(贺知章), a contemporary poet, on reading his poetry. Li and Du Fu(杜甫), his good friend, were the two greatest poets of the illustrious Tang Dynasty(唐). Han Yu, the writer of this

poem, lived some three generations later than Li and Du and was a great poet as well as a master of prose, an eminent scholar and a fearless political figure.

(338) King Xuan of Zhou(周宣王, 827—782 B. C.) is renowned in Chinese history for his revival of that dynasty from its enfeebled state during the reigns previous to his, to the state of its glorious beginning in the times of King Wu(武王) and King Cheng(成王). Thus, King Yi(夷王), his grandfather, crowned in 894 B. C., broiled his vassal Duke Ai of Qi (齐哀公) in a big bronze tripodal two-eared sacrificial vessel. And King Li(厉王), his father, crowned in 878 B. C., when threatened by an uprising of his subjects in 842 B. C., fled from his capital to Zhi(彘) and afterwards died there. These two monarchs of Zhou are noted for their violence and cruelty, as well as King Xuan's son, King You(幽王), who was killed by foreign invaders in 771 B. C. Xuan-*wang* was a ruler quite different from them. Two years after he ascended his throne, he dispatched large-scale campaigns against the Western Rong tribes(西戎) in the northwest and two years later against the Yan-yun tribes(严允) in the north, which in the times of Qin and Han(秦, 汉) were the Xiong-nu tribes (the Huns, 匈奴). In 823—822 B. C., he ordered marches against the Jing-man, Huai-yi and Xu-rong tribes(荆蛮, 淮夷, 徐戎) in the south and the southeast, and conquered them all. The Stone Drums were expressly fabricated to commemorate the occasion of his triumph when a royal hunting expedition was undertaken to celebrate it, according to the poet and

many others. These Drums are over three feet in diameter, the script being carved in large *zhuan*(大篆), the type of old calligraphy created by Shi Zhou(史籀), Grand Curator of History and Astronomy(太史) of Xuan-*wang*. Some other scholars attribute the date of these monuments earlier to the reign of King Cheng. Still others think they were executed as late as in the Qin Dynasty(秦). Ouyang Xiu(欧阳修), a great scholar, historian, poet, prose master and political figure in the middle of the Song Dynasty(宋), states in his *Antique Remains*(《集古录》) in the latter half of the 11th century that he had seen only 465 characters of these Drums. The earliest extant rubbing now in the collection of old, rare books in the Tianyi-*ge*(天一阁) Library in Zhejiang Province has only 462 characters. Poems and *fu* on the same subject were written by Wei Yingwu(韦应物), early Tang poet, Su Shi(苏轼), great Song poet, prose master, calligrapher, painter and political figure, and others besides this piece by Han Yu. In short, apart from the political importance of the historical record, the type of large *zhuan* calligraphy of the notation is unique buy itself, as distinguished from the small *zhuan*(小篆), originated with Li Si(李斯).

(339) Qiyang(岐阳), the town in the south of the Qi Mountains, is at present Qi-*shan xian*(岐山县), Shanxi(陕西).

(340) *Li shu*(隶书) is a type of calligraphy posterior to small *zhuan*(小篆) and prior to *zhen shu*(真书). It was devised by Cheng Miao(程邈) in the Qin Dynasty(秦). *Ke*(蝌) is an

abbreviation of *ke-dou*(蝌蚪), an early type of Zhou calligraphy resembling the tadpole.

(341) The water-dragon(蛟) is actually a nonentity supposed in folklore to be the cause of flood gushing forth from mountains. The *ling-tuo*(灵鼍) was said to be a crawling amphibian of the crocodile family with four claws, over twenty feet in length and fearful in its barkings and growlings. It was a peculiar wild brute of some of China's rivers and lakes. Its skin could be used for making big drums. It was also called the *tuo*-dragon or hog-dragon. The images in these five lines are descriptive of the calligraphic virtuosity of the large *zhuan* characters on the rubbing.

(342) Poems and ballads were collected extensively from the country-side as well as from the court and the ancestral temple of the royal family by a special organ of the government during the earlier reigns of Zhou. The inscription of the Stone Drums was neglected by the "ribald scholars" in their collection of *ya* poems, which were short lyrics only, the poet says here. It was Confucius who made the selection of the 305 pieces from the mass, that has formed *The Classic of Poetry* (*Shi Jing*《诗经》) — the *Book of Odes*, the rest having been lost during the centuries. The two *ya*, great and small ones(大雅,小雅), are poems "written by courtiers about court affairs with the intent of exhortation, the feelings of loyalty and filial piety and the compassion relevant to these, signifying what is good and disapproving the ill, earnestly related and clearly

expressed so as to make the hearer deeply touched. ”

(343) In his travels through various states late in the Spring and Autumn Period(春秋,770—477 B. C.) of Zhou to find a master worthy of himself, Confucius did not go far westward to enter Qin(秦), perhaps more for the reason that Qin was “a state of tiger and wolf” than that it was too far west. The next statement is figurative rather than literal, for he had nothing to do with picking departing souls for raising them to be stars. In ancient times, people of great eminence were believed to be transformed into stars when they died. The line means to say that even Confucius was not vigilant of a thousand and one things: he might miss one or two inadvertantly. Xihe(羲和) was the legendary driver of the Sun chariot and Ehuang(娥皇) was the queen of Emperor Shun(帝舜) of Yu(虞), daughter of Emperor Yao(帝尧) of Tang(唐).

(344) Han Yu was ordained a doctor of the Imperial College(大学) to lecture on literature by the authorities concerned in the first year of Emperor Xian-*zong*'s(宪宗) new reign named Yuanhe(元和,806 A. D.).

(345) The Drums, first verified in Tang at the time of the poet after they had been long forgotten, were located in the wilds of Chencang(陈仓), a *xian* now known as Baoji(宝鸡), Shǎnxi, which was in the right (western) vicinity of the capital Chang'an(长安), as one looked southerly.

(346) The bronze tripodal two-eared vessel *ding*(鼎), symbol of political sovereignty, placed in the ruler's ancestral temple, of the ducal state Song(宋), in its capital South Gao(南郜) is implied to be a war spoil when that city was captured, according to the *Spring and Autumn Annals*(《春秋》). This particular trophy, then, has taken on a general connotation here, and therefore means simply any such trophy in the Imperial Ancestral Temple of Li Tang(李唐). The importance of this vessel could be traced back to the nine *ding* cast by King Yu of Xia(夏禹), the great benefactor of the indigenous Chinese race and the first of the Three Kindly Kings(三王), who saved the people from extinction by conducting the deluge to the sea and set the lunar calendar now still in partial use, to name two of his great deeds.

(347) Evidently, an exhibition of the classics, presumably Confucian in substance, brushed on scrolls during Han, Wei, Jin and the Six Dynasties(汉,魏,晋,六朝), was held sometime before this poem was composed, at the shire town Hongdu newly founded(洪都新府) during early Tang. The city is today known as Nanchang(南昌) of Jiangxi Province. Hongdu was made famous by the great early Tang poet Wang Buo(王勃) in his splendid *fu*(赋), *Proem to the Teng-wang Pavilion*(《滕王阁序》).

(348) Wang Xizhi(王羲之), the great calligrapher of Jin(晋), whose *li*, *cao and hang* types of *shu*(隶,草,行书) are matchless throughout the ages, was said to be fond of watc-

hing white geese. Once he came upon a flock of them and offered to buy them from a Shanyin taoist priest(山阴道士). He was asked by their owner to brush on some sheets of paper the *Dao-de Classic*(《道德经》) of Lao-*zi*(老子, not *Huangting Classic*,《黄庭经》, also written by Lao-*zi*, mistakenly attributed by the great poet Li Bai to be brushed by Wang Xizhi for winning him the geese) and the geese were gladly presented to him in change.

(349) Confucius and Mencius. Their original names in Chinese are Kong Qiu(孔丘) and Meng Ke(孟轲).

(350) The tone of this quatrain in the original is one of desolation and time's mutability. The Cinnabar Bird Bridge(朱雀桥) was built during the Xian-kang(咸康) years(335—342 A. D.) in the reign of Cheng-*di*(成帝, 326—342 A. D.) of East Jin(东晋, 318 — 419 A. D.) as a buoyant bridge on the Qinhuai River(秦淮河). The site of the Black Coat Lane(乌衣巷) is in the south of the Qinhuai River at Nanjing(南京), Jiangsu Province(江苏省). The locality had served during the Three Kingdoms Period(220—280 A. D.) as the barracks of the Black-Coated (Doublet) Battallion(乌衣巷) of the state Wu(吴), hence the lane's name. Wang Dao(王导) and Xie An(谢安) were premiers of East Jin; their families were notable during the Six Dynasties and so were their residences. They have passed away long ago and nobodies have taken their places now in these premises. The third and fouth lines could be rendered thus:

The swallows ’fore the former notable houses
Now fly into the common folks homestalls.

(351) The ancient site of the Stone-walled City is around the Qingliang Hills(清凉山) of Nanjing today. During the Warring States Period(战国,403—247 B. C.), it was the city Jinling (金陵) of the state Chu(楚). During the Three Kingdoms Period(三国,220—280), Sun Quan(孙权), king of the state Wu(吴), rebuilt the city and called it the Stone-walled City(石头城). “The tides” in the second line mean those of the River Yangzi which beat the desolate old city and lonelily ebb again and again. Huai Stream means the River Qinhuai (秦淮河), which flowed past the city, very prosperous during the Six Dynasties (212—588) “the old time” and still flows as of old. As the beams of the old-time moon crosses the low parapel to shine on the west, the scene appears very desolate indeed.

(352) Liu Zongyuan(773—819), whose informal name is Zihou (子厚), was a native of Hedong(河东), at present Yongji *xian*(永济县) of Shanxi(山西) Province. He passed the imperial examination of *jin-shi*(进士), the candidate qualified for being elected to high officialdom during De-*zong*’s(德宗) Zhen-yuan(贞元) years(785—804). During the reign of Shun-*zong*(顺宗), he and his friend and fellow scholar of the examination Liu Yuxi(刘禹锡) together with Wang Pi (王伾), took part in Wang Shuwen’s(王叔文) Reform Movement group against corruption, tax extortion of the sub-

jects and compulsory contributions from local officials, oppression in general and the eunuchs cabal. The eunuchs plotted a coup d'État forcing the emperor to be dethroned and inherit his sway to the imperal prince. Wang Shuwen was executed. Liu Zongyuan was degraded in his banishment to Yongzhou(永州) as a country official and later therefrom to Liuzhou(柳州). when he was exiled to his second post, he heard Liu Yuxi was exiled to Bozhou(播州), which is Zunyi (遵义) of Guizhou(贵州) Province today. The latter town was a most miserable spot for human habitation. Besides, Liu Yuxi had an aged mother in the capital, who could not go to stay at such an impossible border town. For his friend's sake, Liu Zongyuan implored to go himself to Bozhou and let Liu Yuxi go to Liuzhou instead. Fortunately, some influntial court officials begged for mercy and succeeded to have Liu Yuxi exiled to Lianzhou(连州). Our poet's nobility of character as shown in this affair alone has ranked him an illustrious figure in China's literary history. His prose writings have made him a celebrated co-master of the "Old Prose School" (古文派) with Han Yu(韩愈) of the Tang Dynasty(唐) and Ouyang Xiu(欧阳修) and Su Shi(苏轼) of the Song Dynasty(宋). His prose pieces in recording his trips to various scenic spots round Yongzhou and Liuzhou are notable for their lucidity and scintillating picturesqueness.

In his *Preface* to *Poems Written by the Fool's Runlet* (《愚溪诗序》), our poet says, "In the north of Guan Stream(灌水) there is a runlet flowing eastward into Xiao Stream(潇水). Someone said that a certain Ran(冉) family resided there; so the water was named the Ran Runlet(冉溪). Someone else said that the water could be used for dyeing; so it was once named the Dye Runlet(染溪). I have committed the grave offense with my folly and was exiled to the Xiao Stream Valley. I love the runlet. Following the currents for two or three *li*, I have found an excellent spot to make my dwelling. In ancient days, there was the Foolish Sire's Valley(愚公谷). Now I build my abode by the runlet and, for lack of a proper name to be given to the water, as my neighbours contend that I must change a new name for the old one. I call it the Fool's Runlet(愚溪). Above the Fool's Runlet, I have bought a hillock which I call the Fool's Hillock(愚丘) from which walking northeastward some sixty steps, I come to a spring I have also acquired and named it the Fool's Spring(愚泉). The spring has six mouths, all issuing from the flat land by the side of hills and flowing together tortuously southward to form what I call the Fool's creek(愚沟). Then I dug out and heaped up clay, studded with rocks, to excavate my Fool's Pond(愚池). Towards the east of the Pond, I have erected the Fool's Hall(愚堂), in the south of it the Fool's Arbour(愚亭) and in the middle of the water I have piled up the Fool's Ait(愚岛) with fair trees and quaint rockeries on it. All these are spotlighted picturesque gems of the landscape, but all bear the shame of folly for my sake."

(353) The poet draws in this poem his spiritual self-portrait in his exile thousands of *li* away from Chang'an(长安), the imperi-

al city, to Yongzhou(永州) way down in the south.

(354) This is an excellent satirical poem with its thorns hidden under the obviously plain statements regarding the common knowledge about the beauty of the third elder sister of the imperial concubine, the Queen of the State of Cuo(虢国夫人), who was exclusively allowed by special permission of the Emperor himself to ride into the palace gate at early morn, which was strictly forbidden to the chief courtiers, even the chancellor himself, right before or after the period of formal court attendance. She was in Xuan-*zong*'s "supreme favour". Priding herself on her natal beauty, she declined to resort to cosmetics, rouge and eyebrow pencil for enhancing her looks. The promiscuous relations between the emperor and her were an open secret at the court and to the public, and her similar relations with her so-called cousin Yang Guozhong (see Note 213 of Du Fu's poem *The Lay of the Belles*) were also well known at the court and to the populace, except perhaps the sole person, Xuan-*zong*.

Jiling Terrace was on the Li Mounts(骊山) for paying homage to the gods. The Li Mounts were where the Li Tribesmen(骊戎) had been inhabiting during the Spring and Autumn Period(春秋,722—481 B. C.) of the Zhou Dynasty (周,1122—256 B. C.). The Li Mounts are today in the south-east of Lintong *xian*(临潼县), connceted with the Lantian Mounts(蓝田山) of Lantian *xian*(蓝田县), of Shanxi Province(陕西).

(355) The Clear-and-Bright Feast(清明) of spring has been a veligious festival in China from time immemorial. On this day in mid-spring, April 5th or 6th, people visit the burying places of their ancestors to do obeisance or pay homage and sweep the tombs. It is the 105th or 106th day from the winter solstice(冬至).

(356) According to *the Book of Sovereignty Homage* of the *Han Chronicle*(《汉书·郊祀志》), the wizards say, in the time of the Luteous Emperor(黄帝), Twelve Storeyed Houses were built in Five Walled Expanses(五城十二楼) to greet the faeries, called ' Welcoming the Year '(迎年). Ying Shao's(应劭) note on this is: "In Yuan-*pu*(玄圃) on the Kunlun Mountains(昆仑), the Twelve Storeyed Houses in the Five Walled Expanses are where the faeries permanently reside."

(357) A gifted poet of late Tang, Wen Tingyun's name is often accompained by Li Shangyin, who however excels him in imaginative quality. In the collection *Among the Flowers*(《花间集》), Wen is the foremost composer of *ci*(词), an outgrowth of *shi*(诗) rising during middle Tang, characterized by being sung and tuned with musical instruments. He was a frequent visitor to houses of singing girls and his life career was unhappy as a result of offending the powerful. His style is sometimes decorative. The title means "sad songs played on the ancient harp adorned with gems." According to *The world's Records*(《世本》), said to be compiled by chroni-

clers during the Warring States(403—221 B. C.), "the harp was first made by Bao Xi(庖牺) our earliest ancester, with fifty strings and placed on a wooden frame when being plucked. The Luteous Emperor(黄帝,2694—2597 B. C.) made it an intrument of twenty-five strings."

(358) The Gladdening Uplands were an elevated plain forming the spacious southern precinct of Chang'an(长安), the capital of the Tang Dynasty. They were a pleasurable park region overlooking the splendid, populous part of the imperial city.

(359) During the dynasty Zhou(周,1124—247 B. C.), Ba(巴) was a feudal state paying homage to the king of Zhou, the Son of Heaven. Qin(秦,246—207 B. C.) annexed it and made it a county of its empire. At the end of East Han(东汉, 25—219 A. D.), two more counties were instituted from it by the count palatine of Yizhou(益州牧) Liu Zhang(刘璋), named East Ba and West Ba, called in all the Three Ba(三巴). The dynasty Tang(唐,618—905 A. D.) blotted the two later names and gave them new ones. North Zhou(北周, 557—581 A. D.) of the North Dynasty(北朝,396—581) began to call the capital of old Ba *xian*(巴县). The Three Ba regions of ancient Shu(蜀), the present Sichuan Province(四川省), are a mountainous district. This Poem was written by Li Shangyin to his wife Lady Li-Wang during his visit to the Ba-Shu regions in the autumn of the second year of the Dazhong period(大中三年,848) in Xuan-*zong*'s(唐宣宗) reign of the dynasty Tang. Its tortuous circumstances and the

poet's relevant feelings are of notable nostalgic beauty. When he was writing these lines, it was raining in the hilly Ba-Shu district outside of his house; he was not sure when he would sit with her below the western window of their home, clipping the candlewick to make the flame shine brighter, and talk to her of his feelings for her this night.

(360) Chang'e(嫦娥) of exquisite beauty, originally called Heng'e (姮娥), was the queen of Hou Yi(后羿), the king of Dynasty xia's(夏,2205—1767 B. C.) tributary state Youqiong (有穷). Yi obtained the immortal herb from the fairy lady West Wang Mother(西王母). Heng'e stole the immortal herb of her husband, ate it and fled to the moon. She had to reside there alone through eternity. Hou Yi, a great archer, was reputed in legendary lore to have shot down eight out of nine suns in his time. He set up a dictatorship, ruled Xia for 49 years (2188—2139 B. C.) till he was killed by his own henchman Han Zhou(寒浞).

(361) The Cold Repast(寒食) was a feast held for three days from the 105th day to the 107th after the previous year's winter solstice. It usually commenced on the 4th or 5th of April, or the previous day to the Clear-and-Bright Feast(清明) in the third moon of the lunar year. The feast has been observed for centuries to memorize Jie Tui(介推), a faithful follower of Duke Wen of state Jin(晋文公) in the Spring and Autumn Period (722—481 B. C.), who accompanied the young prince in his flight to the state Qi(齐) but was forgetten to be

rewarded when the prince came back to be installed as the head of the state. In anger, Jie Tui left the court and retired to Mount Mian(绵山) as a recluse with his old mother. The young duke, soon aware of Jie's absence, sensed his own fault and dispatched men to induce Jie back to court to compensate him, but the messengers failed to locate Jie. An order was given to burn the weeds on the mount with the hope that the spreading wild fire would drive Jie down. In wrath at the young Duke's ingratitude, Jie clasped a tree trunk and was found burnt to death. The remorseful prince did penance to Jie Tui in sackcloth and ashes, ordered that thereafter no brushwood should be cut from Mount Mian and a feast of three days should be set up as Cold Repast(寒食), during which no fire should be lit to cook food. The feast is still partially observed today, for during the occasion people eat cold green dumplings stuffed with mashed red beans, though the practice of prohibiting fire to cook food has long been ignored out of memory. Most people are wholly ignorant of the origin why they eat cold stuffed dumplings on certain days in the spring at present.

(362) Su Shi was a great Song(宋) poet, a master of prose, an eminent calligrapher and painter and a fearless political figure. Besides his ceremonial name Shi(轼) and that of common usage among his friends Zizhan(子瞻), he called himself Dongpo(东坡), sometimes together with the appellation *Jüshi*(居士), that is, Eastern Slope Recluse, during his late years in his pursuits purely literary and artistic, for after he

was banished to Huangzhou(黄州) in 1080, the third year of Emperor Shen-*zong*'s(神宗) reign of Yuan-feng(元丰) for his opposition to Wang Anshi(王安石), the then premier, he built himself a house called Snow Hall(雪堂) at the Eastern Slope. His father Su Xun(苏洵) and younger brother Su Zhe (苏辙) were also of literary note. He lived through the four reigns of Ren-*zong*(仁宗), Yin-*zong*(英宗), Shen-*zong*(神宗) and Ze-*zong*(哲宗). Passing the high examination and winning the title *jin-shi*(进士) during Ren-*zong*'s reign of Jia-you(嘉祐), he was appointed a scholar of the Literary Cabinet(翰林学士) and in Ying-*zong*'s years was a curator of the Hall of History(史馆). Before that, he had submitted his weighty, eloquent "Responsive Proposal" to the Imperial School in Quest of the Sagacious and the Virtuous, the Square and the Upright, Outspoken Advices and Earnest Counsels(贤良方正直言极谏制科), for which he was elevated to the court by recommendation of the great poet, prose master and scholar Ouyang Xiu(欧阳修). Later, he presented his momentous counsels to his sovereigns again and again, culminating in his last and longest one to Shen-*zong*, coming finally to grief. He was once entrusted with the port-folio of the Lord of War(兵部尚书). He stayed in his banishment at Huangzhou and elsewhere for six years, being recalled from his exile at last in 1085. His prose achieves speed and grandeur, his poetry and *ci*(词) bear an ethereal, fairy-like strain.

(363) See the introductory remarks on the *fu* in my version of Song Yu's *A Fu on Gaotang*(宋玉《高唐赋》).

(364) There are three heights or highlands so called, all in the province Hubei(湖北). The first range is in the northeast of Jiayu *xian*(嘉鱼县), by the riverside. It was below them that Zhou Yu(周瑜) and Liu Bei(刘备) smashed Cao Cao's(曹操) army of 830000 strong by burning their warships interlocked with one another. The second range is outside the chief town of the *xian* Huanggang(黄冈), also called Chibi-*ji*, that is, Red Nose Islet(赤鼻矶). Our poet mistook it for the former range. The third one is seventy *li* southwest of Wuchang(武昌), also called the Red Islet or the Red Bank — Chi-*ji*(赤矶) or Chi-*qi*(赤圻).

(365) Ren-xu(壬戌) was in 1082, the fifth year of Emperor Shenzong's reign of Yuan-feng. This *fu* was written during the poet's exile at Huangzhou. China's lunar years since time immemorial are named by a combination of two characters from two different sets of symbols, the heavenly *gan*(天干), ten in number, viz. 甲, 乙, 丙, 丁, 戊, 己, 庚, 辛, 壬, 癸, and the earthly *zhi*(地支), twelve in number, viz. 子, 丑, 寅, 卯, 辰, 巳, 午, 未, 申, 酉, 戌, 亥. Legends had it that *gan* and *zhi* were devised by the Heavenly Emperor(天皇氏) himself and were first coupled one to the other at the time of Huang-*di*(黄帝). Such combinations were used in the remote past to indicate and differentiate the years, months, days and moment periods of the day correspondingly from one another. Sixty makes a cycle. At present, only the lunar years are indicated by them.

(366) Su-*zi*(苏子) means gentle scholar Su. The poet speaks of himself in the third person in this fore piece, although he resorts to the first person in the hind piece. I prefer to keep the concise original form intact instead of using the explanative title.

(367) The Long River (长江) or the Yangzi-*jiang*(扬子江).

(368) It refers to the poem, two lines of which are recited below by the guest, composed by Cao Cao(曹操) before his armada was destroyed by Zhuge Liang(诸葛亮) and Zhou Yu(周瑜) in the year 208.

(369) The first poem of *The Book of Odes*, the beginning stanza of which runs like this:

"Guan Guan," doth cry the osprey
  On the islet of the river;
Our virgin maid debonair,
  The virtuous youth would match her.

(370) There are four rhymes interspersed among the prose passage of the original, marking the ends of these three sentences and the first section of the last one.

(371) I take the liberty to alter the "orchid" of the original into this, for whereas "orchid oars" appears quite natural in the poetry of Qu Yuan and his school, meaning simply that they are fragrant like orchids, symbolic of the poet's personality, it

would become a forced metaphor, I think, to a western reader, especially if he is not a poet.

(372) "The Beauty" here should not be taken literally. She is symbolical of a sovereign like Ren-*zong*, the most benevolent as well as intelligent ruler of the Song Dynasty. The poet could not express his feelings more explicitly than in such a riddle, for he had been impeached by Wang Anshi's followers at the latter's instigation for the critical allusions in his poetry to the monarch and the "innovations" instituted by Wang. He was right now suffering from his dauntless difference with the premier who happened to be his former friend.

(373) There are in these three sentences in the original five rhymes interspersed among the passage and, besides, four other onomatopoeic concurrences with the rhymes.

(374) The next two lines of the quatrain run like this:

They wind around the trees three times,

But find no branches to perch on [perdie].

It has been said in literary comments later that this is an ill omen in Cao's own poem to his crushing defeat.

(375) Xiakou(夏口), a site in the west of the present Wuchang *xian*(武昌县), on the (Yellow) Swan Mountains(黄鹄山). It had been a town founded by the state Wu(吴) in the Three States Period(三国,199—264). The present city of Hankou (汉口) was also called Xiakou; now it is the chief city of the

xian Xiakou; it is on the southern bank of the River. From the context, it can be seen it was not meant by the guest here. The swan, pure white in its plumage, was called in China "the yellow swan" on account of the yellow protu-berance at its beak, although there are black swans in Australia.

(376) Wuchang (武昌), now the provincial capital of Hubei (湖北).

(377) Jingzhou (荆州), chief city of a county, the governor of which had been Liu Biao (刘表). Cao Cao fought Yuan Shao (袁绍) at Guandu (官渡), a town at present in the northeast of Zhongmou (中牟) *xian*, He'nan (河南) Province, asking help of Liu. Liu promised but did not send his forces of aid in time.
When Yuan was beaten, Cao led his troops to attack Liu, who died of carbuncle on the back before he was assailed.

(378) Jiangling (江陵), a well-known city by the River, was founded in the Spring and Autumn Period (春秋, 770—477 B.C.) of Zhou and was the chief borough of a *xian* during Han (汉). In the Tang (唐) and Song (宋) Dynasties, it was the principal city of a county and a district.

(379) The original 釃 means 酹, to splash libation.

(380) These two sentences in the original are each made up of three statements ending with a rhyme, thus forming two triplets of

rhymed prose sections.

(381) Confucius, standing on the bank of the Luteous River, asked, "Is what is vanishing like this, going on day and night?", — meaning that, is Time's passing away immutable just like the waves of the River, flowing on forever? Su-*zi* is alluding to that question, but turning it into an affirmative by omitting the interrogative 乎.

(382) In this dialogue with his chief guest, the Eastern Slope Recluse stands his own ground. Not at all regretful for his disgrace, he is optimistic and confident of his state and personality as a poet and a scholar, paying no regard to worldly success and political prominence whatsoever. What was in his mind and bosom was "only the clear winds on the River and the bright moon round the mountains". He rather despised and scorned Cao Mengde and his kind. Some twenty odd years earlier, in his *Responsive Proposal* to Ren-*zong*'s *Imperial School in Quest of … Outspoken Advices and Earnest Counsels*, he wrote, "*Tianxia*(天下, the world, or rather the country under the emperor's rule) is not the personal property of the sovereign; only it makes the sovereign act as its master." How democratic thoughts shown in such an assertion illuminate his name, we can feel palpably and keenly by.
The dialogue has the nature of the poet's soliloquy. Only his theme is quickly and clearly resolved with simplicity.

(383) Jin and Tang (晋, 唐) people (sometimes) used feathered

beakers(羽觞), oblong in shape and feathered or winged with two wings, as their drinking vessels for wine, while Song(宋) people used rather large, open-mouthed dishes (盏) as evidenced here. They are all yellowish to bluish gray in tint. I had collected quite a few samples of both, two of the former and seven or eight of the latter.

(384) Su Dongpo built his Snow Hall(雪堂) and wrote an essay on it. Its site is in the east of Huanggang *xian*, Hubei Province. He planted a plum tree before the structure, which did not wither until after Emperor Shi-*zong*'s(世宗) reign of Jia-jing (嘉靖) in the Ming Dynasty(明), living over 484 years.

(385) Lingao(临皋) is a locality in the south of Huanggang *xian* by the river-side. Our poet wrote to his friend Zhu Kangshu(朱康叔) in a letter, "I have moved to Lingao Pavilion(临皋亭) by the River." He had probably given this name to his new dwelling, as it was more to his liking for here he could feel the pulse of the great River.

(386) Huanggang, a range of hills in the east of Huanggang *xian*, is called by the poet here the Yellow Clay Incline(黄泥之坂). It was the Eastern Slope adopted as his literary name.

(387) These three sentences in the original are rhymed.

(388) There is in the temperate middle part of China a species of white perch(鲈) with black spots, big in head, stiff in fins,

wide-mouthed and tiny in scales, — a large one measures some two feet long. Its flesh is tender and delicious. It was called the silver perch(银鲈) or jade flower perch(玉花鲈) in olden times. The perch of Song-*jiang*(松江之鲈), on the other hand, is a quite different fish. It is also called the four-gilled perch(四鳃鲈) of that town, with two large extra gills, pink in colour, protruding out of its regular ones and wrapping on both sides of its body. It is only five to six inches long. It is a rarity and is of course also delicious, at its best about the winter solstice. Our good poet has probably confused the two entirely different sorts.

(389) Fengyi(冯夷), a god from heaven.

(390) There are three rhymes interspersed in this sentence in the original.

(391) There are three rhymes interspersed in these two sentences in the original.

(392) There are three rhymes interspersed in this sentence in the original.

(393) Robes of feathers were supposed to be worn by fairies.

(394) The orginal 揖 is to have one's hands held together, with arms extended and crooked a little, with head nodding twice or thrice and the joined hands and extended arms waving up

and down, at the same time, also a few times, to extend a courtesy or show respect.

(May 24, 1974)

附录 Appendix

孙大雨
(Sun Dayu)

Some Specific Thoughts on Rendering Ancient Chinese Poetry into English Metrical Verse

—— Two Tang Poems Translated by Herbert A. Giles and Witter Bynner Criticized, Etc.

Of late I have had the occasion to read in a current journal the English translation of two celebrated Chinese Tang poems made by Giles and Bynner very much praised and recommended for adoption in our English textbooks[①]. I feel their understanding of our ancient poetry is open to criticism and their competence to put their knowledge into English metrical verse form is questionable.

The following is a five-charactered octave, the *lü*(律诗) form of "late" or "modern" verse(近体或今体诗), by our early middle Tang(唐,618—907) poet Chang Jian(常建,circa 703—770), traditionally said to be a native of the then imperial city Chang'an(长安):

① Cf. 朱炳荪《读 Giles 的唐诗英译有感》,《外国语》,*pp*. 43—44, #2,1980 年.

题破山寺后禅院

清晨入古寺，
初日照高林。
曲径通幽处，
禅房花木深。
山光悦鸟性：
潭影空人心。
万籁此俱寂，
但余钟磬音。

The scenic spot sung of in the poem was a Buddhist monastery Po-*shan*(破山, the name of a famed prior, meaning "Broken Mountain") or Xingfu(兴福) Bonzary(寺) in the *xian* Changshu(常熟县) at present, Jiangsu Province(江苏省). The English version of the poem by Herbert A. Giles(1845—1935), the well-known British sinologist and professor of Chinese literature at Cambridge University was first published in his *Chinese Poetry in English Verse*, 1898. His rendition runs as follows:

Dhyana's Hall

At dawn I come to the convent old,
While the rising sun tips its tall trees with gold, —
As darkly, by a winding path I reach
Dhyana's hall, hidden midst fir and beech.
Around these hills sweet birds their pleasure take,
Man's heart as free from shadows as this lake;
Here worldly sounds are hushed, as by a spell,
Save for the booming of the altar bell.

The title of the poem in translation should be "Dhyana Hall", not "Dhyana's Hall" as Giles has it. "Dhyana" , according to Webster's *Third New International Dictionary of the English Language*, 1961, pronounced "dē'änə" was originally a Sanskrit word "dhyāna" from "dhyāti", meaning "he thinks". In Hinduism, Buddhism and Jainism, it means meditation, especially an uninterrupted state of mental concentration upon a single object, or higher contemplation. In the 15th — edition of *The Encyclopaedia Britannica*, 1974, it is said that the Dhyana (Chinese, *chan*; Japanese, *zen*) School of Buddhism(佛教禅宗) emphasizes meditation as the way to immediate awareness of ultimate reality, an important practice of Buddhism from its origin in India, and derives its name from the Sanskrit term for meditation, *dhyana.... chan*, with its special training techniques and doctrines and its Taoist influence, however, is generally considered a specifically Chinese product. It, the word "dhyana," is therefore a common substantive, meaning simply the practice of meditation or contemplation to realize religious illumination. To put "'s" after "dhyana", giving it a possessive signification, is altogether wrong, although the word may conceivably be capitalized to mean the particular school of Buddhism to which the premises were dedicated.

The rhymes at the end of the even lines in the original of Chang Jian become couplet rhymes in the translation. The verse of Giles is a mixture of tetrameter and pentameter lines. It is too often and improperly rhymed, producing a jingling effect not intended by the poet in the original. 曲径通幽处 (winding paths lead to secluded spots) and 禅房花木深 (the dhyana hall is embowered amidst trees and flowers) are improperly rendered into "darkly, by a winding path I reach Dhyana's hall, hidden midst fir and beech." 山光 is not understood by Giles and is thus skipped by him. The next line 潭影空人心 is altogether misunderstood by him, for he takes 影, reflections or images of the trees and peaks in the rock pools, as dark shadows, and says "Man's heart as free from shadows as this lake [*sic*]", aggregating in all three mistakes in one line, for the comparison between the shadows in the "lake", erroneously so rendered, and those in man's heart is nonexistent in the original. Actually, one of the two pools called the Heart-purging Pool(空心潭) today is only four to five feet in diameter; how could it be immeasurably extended in size to a lake for the sake of a couplet rhyme? The two lines 山光悦鸟性 and 潭影空人心 are in fact a parallel of plain statements serving to enhance the feeling of lightness and transparency in the birds' and men's minds, the latter expression meaning that reflections or images in the water of the pools have purged away all the anxieties and worldly cares from one's mind ("heart") to make it, as it were, limpid or empty. 磬 in a Buddhist bonzary is a bronze, half-global bowl some ten inches to a foot or more in diameter and about half an inch thick, to be struck with a short wooden rod of four to six inches, at rather long intervals of chanting the Buddhist psalms. If there is no ready word for it in the English vocabulary ("gong", too flat and large, is too noisy), it should be coined by transliteration. From his version, we could see that Giles is not only insufficiently studied in Chinese classical poetry and so having no deep genuine feeling for it, but also fails to turn regular metrical Chinese classical verse into English measured language of an equal number of rhythmical units, feet, in the lines.

The renowned five-charactered quatrain by Li Bai(李白), the most illustrious of our Tang poets, entitled《静夜思》(*Thoughts in a Still Night*), is as follows:

床前明月光，
疑是地上霜。
举头望山月，
低头思故乡。

In a popular anthology of the early middle Qing(清) Dynasty *Three Hundred Tang Poems*(《唐诗三百首》), the title of this poem is corrupted into《夜思》, and in the third line, the original, authentic reading 山月 is debased into 明月. Witter Bynner's English version in his The *Jade Mountain*, 1929, is as follows:

In the Quiet Night

So bright a gleam on the foot of my bed —
Could there have been a frost already?
Lifting myself to look, I found that it was moonlight,
Sinking back again, I thought suddenly of home.

In all the Song(宋), Ming(明) and early Qing(清) editions of noted anthologies and complete works such as Guo Maoqian's(郭茂倩) *Garner of Tunes Anthology*(《乐府诗集》), *Tome of Complete Tang Poetry* ,1707(《全唐诗》), *the Collected Works of Li Bai*,1717(《李太白文集》,康熙五十六年缪曰芑刻本) and the *Collected Works of Li Bai*,1758(《李太白文集》,乾隆二十三年王琦刻本), the authentic readings "静夜思" and "山月" are kept intact[①]. The poet most certainly wrote these lines in a house or cottage with a southern expo-

① In fact, the old authentic text of the first line 床前看月光 (The sight of the moonshine before my bed) is to be found in all these editions, but we would not be too much involved in details of textual criticism here.

sure. Looking out of his window, which was of course covered with no glass panes, but probably screened with a network of flax fibres with a paper scroll rolled up on the top, he could see in the distance a range of hills or further mountains. The season was winter and the moment quite late, perhaps approaching midnight. Just then the moon rose up the range of hills or distant mountains to cast its frost-like beams on the ground before his bed. Earlier, the rising moon was covered from sight by the hills or distant mountains, hence 山月. At the moment, all the bustles and noises of the town and the neighbours must have vanished: so the title tells us it is *Thoughts in a Still Night* (《静夜思》), not just *Night Thoughts*(《夜思》). 床前(before or in the front of my bed) of the original is wrongly rendered into "on the foot of my bed" by Bynner. Our Tang forefathers sat on mats, or on rugs over the mats, on the ground in day-time and slept in beds quite different from ours. These lay flat on the ground consisting of wooden planks, cushioned on the top with a thick layer of dried bulrushes or straw, wrapped over with a hemp, flax or silk(帛) coverlet, for there was probably not yet cotton for weaving the fabric we are accustomed to use as sheets. Chang'an(长安), now called Xi'an(西安), about 34 degrees in latitude north of the equator, has and had a temperature similar to that of Xuzhou(徐州) and slightly lower than that of Nanjing in winter. If the poem was composed in the imperial city by Li Bai, the bed was most probably not spread on an elevated brick structure called "kang"(炕), under which smouldering fire was lit to give warmth in regions much further north. So, 床前 here is actually "before the bed" and on the ground, not "on the foot of my bed," as Bynner has it, for the poet's bed had no wooden or metal legs. The moonshine on the ground is suspected by the poet to be the frost.

The sentence is an affirmative statement of his doubt. There is no necessity to turn it into an interrogative sentence in the English version. And to add the word "already" is wrong, for when Li Bai wrote this poem, it might have been the winter, not late autumn, as Bynner supposes. "Lifting my head" in the original 举头 is rendered into "Lifting myself", which is quite another matter. The authentic 山月 of the original (popularly corrupted into 明月) is turned awry even from the debased state, as "moonlight". The last line 低头思故乡 (I bow down to think of my homeland) is rendered into "Sinking back again, I thought suddenly of home": "sinking back" is mistaken, "again" is mistaken and "suddenly" is the third time mistaken. Bynner's version shows that he neither understands the Chinese literary language, nor could wield skilfully his mother tongue: his translation is a pair of tetrameter and a pair of hexameter lines.

Yet, finally, in spite of all the derogatory words I have said against Giles and Bynner in regard to their insufficiency in erudition and understanding of the Chinese language and lack of skill in turning two rare gems of our ancient poetry into English, l would still pay, nevertheless, my compliment to their ardour, love for Chinese culture and hard work in trying to master it that was so alien from their own. Compared to the fruits of some other sinologists, theirs are perhaps by no means to be depreciated too lightly.

OTHER VERSIONS OF THESE TWO POEMS FOR REFERENCE

Ⅰ.1 The Hall of Silence

Where the sun's eye first

Peers above the pines,
On the ancient temple
Early daylight shines.
To retirement guiding
Leads the winding way:
Round the Cell of Silence
Flowers and foliage stray.
Hark! the birds rejoicing
In the mountain light!
Like one's dim reflection
On a pool at night.
Lo! the heart is melted
Wav'ring out of sight.
All is hushed to silence.
Harmony is still.
The bell's low chime alone
Whispers round the hill.

— W. J. B. Fletcher

I. 2 A Buddhist Retreat Behind Broken-Mountain Temple

In the pure morning, near the old temple,
Where early sunlight points the tree-tops,
My path has wound, through a sheltered hollow
Of boughs and flowers, to a Buddhist retreat.
Here birds are alive with mountain-light,
And the mind of man touches peace in a pool,
And a thousand sounds are quieted
By the breathing of a temple-bell.

— Witter Bynner

Ⅱ.1 The Moon Shines Everywhere

Seeing the Moon before my couch so bright
I thought hoar frost had fallen from the night.
On her clear face I gaze with lifted eyes:
Then hide them full of Youth's sweet memories.

— W. J. B. Fletcher

Ⅱ.2 Thoughts in a Tranquil Night

Athwart the bed
I watch the moonbeams cast a trail
  So bright, so cold, so frail,
    That for a space it gleams
Like hoar-frost on the margin of my dreams.
  I raise my head, —
The splendid moon I see:
Then droop my head,
And sink to dreams of thee —
My fatherland, of thee!

— L. Cranmer-Byng

Ⅱ.3 Night Thoughts

In front of my bed the moonlight is very bright.
I wonder if that can be frost on the floor?
I lift up my head and look at the full moon,
  the dazzling moon.
I drop my head, and think of the home of old days.

— Amy Lowell

Ⅱ.4 On a Quiet Night

I saw the moonlight before my couch,
And wondered if it were not the frost on the ground.
I raised my head and looked out on the mountain moon,
I bowed my head and thought of my far-off home.

— S. Obata

Ⅱ.5 Still Night Thoughts

Moonlight in front of my bed —
I took it for frost on the ground!
I lift my eyes to watch the mountain moon,
Lower them and dream of home.

— Burton Watson

My versions of these two poems are as follows:

Ⅰ The Rear Dhyana Hall of Poshan Bonzary

Chang Jian (circa 703—770)

| Whēn āt dáwn | Ī rēpáired | tō thē bón | zārȳ óld, |
(anapaest)

| Thē fírst beáms | ōf thē rís | īng sún shóne | ōn treés táll. |
(bacchius)

| Wíndīng páths | lēd tō cóv | ērt, sēclúd | ēd gróves |
(amphimacer) (iambus)

| Whēre lúsh thíck | ēt ānd flów | ērs ēnclósed | th' dhyānā háll. |
(paeonquartus)

| Th'ráre áurā | ōf thē móunt | pleásed thē ná | tūre ōf th' bírds; |
(antibacchius)

| Ímāges in | róck pít póols | fréed thē mínd's | úps ānd dówns. |
(dactyl) (molossus)

| Áll thē húb | būbs ōf mén | wēre húshed ās | bȳ ā spéll; |

| Thēre wās nóth | īng léft būt | thē béll's ānd | *chíng*'s cláng s. |
(spondee)

Ⅱ Thoughts in a Still Night

Li Bai (701—762)

| Thē lú | mīnōus | móonshíne |
(pyrrhic)

| Bēfóre | mȳ béd |

| Īs thóught | tō bē | thē fróst

| Fállēn | ōn thē gróund. |
(trochee)

| Ī líft | mȳ héad | tō gáze |

| Āt thē | clíft móon, |
(spondee)

| Ānd thén | bów dówn | tō múse |

| Ōn mȳ dís | tānt hóme. |

The first poem above is an octave of anapaestic tetrameter lines and the second an octave of alternate iambic trimeter and dimeter lines, with variations of rhythm in the relevant feet.

Mr. Burton Watson's "I lift my eyes" is very much different from my "I lift my head", a precise rendering of the original "举头," in that the former implies the "mountain moon" being not very high, while the latter implies the "clift moon" so very high that the poet has to raise his head, not just eyes, to observe it arisen from the back of the range of mountains. This difference of the heights of the mountains has much to do with the title of the poem and the circumstances under which it was composed: the moment was then drawing towards midnight and the atmosphere was very quiet, hence the title *Thoughts in a Still Night*(《静夜思》).

Reading Professor Fan Cunzhong's(范存忠) erudite article *Chinese Poetry and English Translations* on the fifth number of *The foreign Languages Journal*(《外国语》), 1981, I find Giles's English version of Li Shangyin's following seven charactered quatrain, the *jue* (绝句) form of "late" or "modern" verse(近体或今体诗), praised in glowing terms by the modern eminent biographer Lytton Strachey:

夜雨寄北

李商隐

君问归期未有期,
巴山夜雨涨秋池。
何当共剪西窗烛,
却话巴山夜雨时。

You ask when I'm coming: alas not just yet...
How the rain filled the pools on that night when we met!
Ah, when shall we ever snuff candles again,
And recall the glad hours of that evening of rain?

Although Strachey is a radiant prose master of the Bloomsbury School and Giles not without his merits in some others of his *Gems of Chinese Literature*, *Verse*, yet I find his version above of Li Shangyin's poem mistaken and faulty. Here is my rendition of the poem, my notes on it and my comments on Giles's translation.

Lines Sent to the North.
Written during Night Rains

Li Shangyin (813—858)

Bēīn̄g	ásked	fōr mȳ hóme	cōmīng dáte.
Ī tēll thée	I'm̄ nōt súre	whēn thāt'll bé,
Ās níght ráins	ōn thē móunts	ōf Bá fáll
Ānd aútum̄n	póols āre brímmed	frōm thē léa.
Thēn wē sháll	bȳ thē wést	wíndōw sít,
Clíppīng	thē cándle-wīck	in̄ sōme níght,
An̄d tálk ōf	thē níght ráins	ōn th'Bá móunts,
Whīle Ī thínk	ōf thée wīth	múte dēlíght.

The Three Ba(三巴) region of ancient Shu(蜀), the present Sichuan Province(四川省), is a hilly district of the eastern part of Sichuan today. This poem was written by the poet to his wife Lady Liwang during his visit to the Ba-Shu region in the autumn of the second year of the Ta-zhong Period(大中二年,848) in Xuan-*zong*'s(唐宣宗) reign of the dynasty Tang. Its tortuous circumstances and the poet's relevant feelings are of notable nostalgic beauty. When he was writing these lines, it was raining in the hilly Ba-Shu district outside of his house; he was not sure when he would sit with her by the western window of their home, clipping the candlewick to make the flame shine brighter, and talk to her of his feelings for her this night. Giles's version of the poem mistakes the present for the past and expects, in the words of the poet as Giles thinks, to meet her and talk of that past, whereas actually the poet, writing of the present, is thinking of some future time when he would sit with her by the western window of their home and talk of the present, the circumstances in which he writes this poem. Candlewick was clipped to make the flame shine brighter; it was not put out, to make the room dark and for the couple to go to bed. Although "snuff" may mean either to trim the charred part of candlewick to make the light brighter or to put out the light, yet to prevent dubiety and make the meaning unmistakable, I think "clip" or "trim" is the better word. Besides, "the mounts of Ba", twice mentioned in the short original poem, are so full of pleasant associations in the poet's mind with the night rains, the brimming pools, his love and longing for his wife and his expectation of seeing her in some uncertain future night that to blot out their existence altogether in the English version cannot but be a grave defect in the translation. It is true we cannot fully revive and recapture the poet's associations. But we can at least make slight amends by getting a tithe, a fraction of a tithe, of the poet's associations by resorting to a note on the Ba Mounts. However, the deletion of the name altogether from the text of the English version makes an explanatory note out of place.

Next I read in Mr. Fan's article Louise Strong Hammond's rendition of Jia Dao(贾岛,779—843) five-charactered jue poem:

寻隐者不遇

贾岛

松下问童子,言师采药去。
只在此山中,云深不知处。

Which I have happened to have also put into English verse. Hammonds's version of *Seeking the Hermit in Vain* runs like this:

"Gone to gather herbs" —
So they say of you.
But in cloud-girt hills,
What am I to do?

"Evidently, much has been left out." My attempt at turning this five-charactered *jue* poem into English perhaps does not leave out much:

A Call on the Recluse Without Meeting Him

Jia Dao

| Ī ásked | thē bóy | bēnēath thē | píne trée, |
(tribrach)
Whō sáid,	Thē Más	tēr's góne hérbs	tō píck;
Hē múst	bē sóme	whēre róund	thēse clíffs
Cōncéaled	ūnséen	in thē	clóuds thíck.

The poem in the original is the writer's plain statement of the call on his recluse friend. his simple question put to the attendant boy and the boy's breezy reply. We can readily and should imagine the recluse is living alone in solitude with his boy in a cabin on the mountain heights. Abiding away from the world, he is interested in plucking fairy medicinal herbs that would perhaps give him perpetual longevity or immortal life. At the moment, he is hidden from sight in the thick clouds round the cliffs. In Hammond's translation, the boy has become "they"; we are told of the poet's disappointed feelings of not finding his friend and his being at a loss what to do. The disappointment and perplexity are not to be found in the original, and to bring in "you," for the sake of thyming with "do", gives a faint note of blame on the part of the poet for the recluse which is also not at all to be found in the original.

And then I came across another specimen of Hammond's rendition of the first of Li Bai's three poems composed to celebrate the beauty of Yang Yuhuan(杨玉环), the imperial concubine of Xuan*zong* of Tang(唐玄宗), in the aloes-wood arbour facing the blossoming peonies:

清平调词

李白

云想衣裳花想容，
春风拂槛露华浓。
若非群玉山头见，
会向瑶台月下逢。

Hammond's version runs like this:

Cloud-like garments, flower face,
Lattice which spring breezes trace.
Such are seen on Jade Hill Heights,
O'r some moonlit, mystic place.

"Again, a lot of things are left out, as they must be, in order to translate in accordance with the principle of 'one word in Chinese, one syllable in English'", which I think too mechanical and unnecessary. This telegraphic account of the glamorous original strikes the reader as a bare skeleton, a mere wreck, a vague shadow of the graceful. rich and vivacious poem in classical Chinese — an unworthy sacrifice for the mistaken tenet. My version of this poem is like this:

For Qing-ping Tunes

Li Bai

Tínged cloud	lēts āre lík	ēned únto	hēr ráimēnt
Ānd thē flów	ērs ūntō	hēr míen.
Spríng zéph	ȳrs ālóng	thē bál	ūstráde
Géntlȳ brúsh	thē crýstāl déws 'shéen.
If nōt séen	ōn thē wón	drōus Móunt	ōf Géms
Āt sóme	ēnchánt	ēd stránd,
Shē cóuld	bē mét wīth	ōn thē Mág	ic Tówēr
Īn thē móon	līt fáir	ȳlánd.
(Hybrid of iambic and anapaestic measures.)

This and two other poems were composed to be attuned with musical instruments, the melody being named by the poet to be Qing-ping Tunes(清平调). The original 花 (flowers) means the peony, with its round, large, gorgeous, pink (red, white or light green) flowers. The first two lines may have a variant reading like this:

Tinged cloudlets are thought of as her raiment
And the flowers as her mien.

The Mount of Gems(群玉山) and the Magic Tower(瑶台) are supposed to be in the fairyland of Dame West Wang(西王母). According-ing to *the Life of King Mu*(《穆天子传》), who reigned from 1001 till 946 B. C. in our Zhou(周) Dynasty, he took a long voyage to the fairyland in the west and was cordially entertained by the Dame as her guest. The book in bundles of bamboo strips, comprising six chapters, was unearthed from King Xiang of Wei's(魏襄王) mausoleum in the second year of the dynasty Jin's(晋) Tai-kang period(太康二年,281 A. D.) by its subject Buzhun(不准), as a spoil of plundering the regal tomb.

Last but not least, let me take the ballad from time immemorial for discussion, as it has been translated into English. The original is said to be hummed by octogenarians and nonagenarians in the times of *Di* Yao(帝尧) of Taotang(陶唐), who is said to have ruled ancient Cathay from 2357 to 2257 B. C., according to Huangfu Mi's (皇甫谧) *The Records of Di and Huang*(《帝皇世纪》), when they amused themselves by throwing clogs for fun. Pieces of wood were shaped like clogs for foot wear, broad in front and tapering towards the round end, one piece being laid on the ground and the player taking another piece and walking away for thirty to forty steps to throw it at the first piece. Those who could hit the first piece were the winners of the game. Ezra Pound, the noted American imagist poet, has rendered the ballad into English free verse thus:

Sun up; work
Sun-down; to rest
Dig well and drink of the water
Dig field; eat of the grain
Imperial power is? and to us what is it?
— Canto XLIX

The original of this ballad and my version of it are as follows:

击壤歌

日出而作，
日入而息，
凿井而饮，
耕田而食。
帝力于我何有哉？

Song of Clog-throwing

— an Ancient Ballad

Wórk āt	súnrīse;
Rést āt	súndōwn.
Díg wéll fōr	dŕinkīng;
Tíll fiélds fōr	eátīng.
Di's pówēr,	thóugh gréat, —
Whát's it tō	mé ānd ús?	(Trochaic dimeter.)

The thought of this primordal popular song smacks of Lao-*zi* and Zhuang-*zi*(老,庄). Ezra Pound's English version I take from Mr. Weng Xianliang's(翁显良) article *My Pipe Views of Translating Poetry*(《译诗管见》) in *Translator's Notes* (《翻译通讯》, No. 6, 1981). Pound's rendition of this ancient Chinese ballad gives one no inkling of its title, nor the circumstances under which it was sung, but simply brands it as number XLIX of his *Cantos*. To a common English-speaking reader ignorant of its historical and social background, it would perhaps appear to be an inscrutable, inert matter —

an expressed piece of primitivism at most, to an intellectual.

August, 1982

吴起仞　译

关于以格律韵文英译中国古诗的几点具体意见

近来,有机会在一份时下的刊物里读到两首驰名中外的唐诗的英译文。译者是素来为人称道的翟理斯(Herbert A. Giles)和宾纳(Witter Bynner);他们的作品有人推荐选作英文教材读物。[①] 我觉得他们两人对我国古诗的理解还有待评议,再则,他们以格律韵文的形式英译中国诗的能力也存在问题。

第一首是中唐前期(618—907)诗人常建(约公元703—770)的近体或今体五言律诗。相传作者是当时的京都长安人。

题破山寺后禅院

清晨入古寺
初日照高林。
曲径通幽处,
禅房花木深。
山光悦鸟性,
潭影空人心。
万籁以俱寂,
但余钟磬音。

这首诗歌咏的是破山寺的景色(破山系一位有名的方丈的法名)。破山寺即今江苏省常熟县的兴福寺,诗的英译文首次刊载在

① 见朱炳荪《读GILES的唐诗英译有感》,载1980年2月版《外国语》第43、44页。

1898 年出版的《韵文英译中国诗》。译者是著名的汉学家、英国人翟理斯(公元 1845—1935),当时任英国剑桥大学中国文学教授。译文如下:

Dhyana's Hall

At dawn I come to the convent old,
While the rising sun tips its tall trees with gold, —
As, darkly, by a winding path I reach
Dhyana's hall, hidden midst fir and beech.
Around these hills sweet birds their pleasure take.
Man's heart as free from shadows as this lake;
Here worldly sounds are hushed, as by a spell,
Save for the booming of the altar bell.

诗的题目应译为"Dhyana Hall",而不是翟理斯的译文"Dhyna's Hall"。据 1961 年第三版《韦氏新国际英语大辞典》,"dhyana"的音标为"dē′änə",自梵文"dhyāti"演化为"dhyāna",意即"他思索"。依印度教、佛教及耆那教,意为"参禅"(或禅思),专指对某一事物持续的、集中的精神活动或超脱凡尘的禅思。据 1974 年第十五版《大英百科全书》"Dhyana"条解(此词的汉语、日语的英译为 chan、zen,意均为"禅"),佛教禅宗认为参禅可使生灵顿悟天地万物之真谛。"参禅"是佛教修炼的重要功课,附带独特的修炼法及戒律,发源于印度;其中带有道家色彩的成分则为中国影响所致。而"禅"系出自梵文的"思"字:dhyana……即禅。由此可见"dhyana"一词从文法上分析是普通名词,意思不外乎从"静思"或"参禅"去寻求宗教的启示。在 dhyana 后加上"'s"使它成为所有格显然是个大错。当然,把"dhyana"的词首字母大写,使变成专有名词再加"s"来指明这后院系属佛门禅宗,也未始不可。

常建的原诗二、四、六、八行押脚韵；而译文用的是双行骈韵。从格律上看，翟理斯的译文是四音步和五音步诗行的混合体。过于频繁、不适当的韵脚造成了单调的叮当声效应，违悖了原诗作者的意趣。“曲径通幽处”①和“禅房花木深”②的译文为“darkly, by a winding path I reach Dhyana's hall, hidden midst fir and beech.”至少是欠妥的，与原文不符。“山光”一词因译者不明白其为何物而略去。下一行“潭影空人心”则完全理解错了。“影”的原意是树木和山峰在一潭清如明镜水中的反射或倒映，而译者却认为是黑影子，把这句译成了

Man's heart as free from shadows as this lake

“lake”（湖）中的影子原本是译者的误解，所以他在译文中把“湖”中的影子与人心中的影子作比拟是杜撰，原诗决无此等涵义。这样，在一行译文中就一连出了三处差错。事实上，破山寺现在还有两个小潭；其中之一名“空心潭”，直径仅 4—5 英尺。译者为了押双行韵竟将小小水潭的面积无限制地扩展为湖泊，那怎么行？“山光悦鸟性”，“潭影空人心”这两行诗实际上是一组平铺直叙的对仗句，前一句写的是（如此景色）在人，甚至鸟心中都添增了轻快、明朗的感觉；后一句的涵义是潭水的倒映或反射的映象涤尽了人心中所有凡俗的忧虑和垒块，使心境变得澄澈通明，无牵无挂。寺庙中的磬用青铜制成，状如钵，半圆形，直径有的 10 英寸，有的一英尺或更长些，壁厚约半英寸，是念经或礼佛时用的法器，用一根 4—6 英寸长的木棒敲

① 雨译：winding paths lead to secluded spots

② 雨译：the dhyana hall is embowered amidst trees and flowers

击；每次击磬间歇较长。如果英文里一时找不上匹配的词（因为锣显得太大，也太扁些，而且音量也过大），可以借助于音译。通览翟理斯的译文，可以看出，他不但对中国古典诗词的研究不够深入，缺乏真情实感，而且在把中国古典格律诗译成英文韵文方面（如在形式上使各行的音步数与原稿一致的问题上）也远未成功。

第二首是题为《静夜思》的脍炙人口的五言绝句。作者是大名鼎鼎的唐代大诗人李白。原诗如下：

床前明月光，
疑是地上霜。
举头望山月，
低头思故乡。

清代中前期的那本通俗诗选《唐诗三百首》把原诗的题目讹减成《夜思》，把原诗第三行的“山月”改为“明月”，败坏了原来的诗文。维脱·宾纳在1929年出版的《玉山》中的英译文如下：

In the Quiet Night

So bright a gleam on the foot of my bed —
Could there have been a frost already?
Lifting myself to look, I found that it was moonlight,
Sinking back again, I thought suddenly of home.

宋、明以及早期清朝的各部闻名的选集或全集的版本如郭茂倩的《乐府诗集》、1707年的《全唐诗》、1717年康熙五十六年缪曰芑刻本《李太白文集》以及1758年乾隆廿二年王琦刻本《李太白全集》都保留了原诗的本来面目；题目为《静夜思》，“明月”为“山月"[1]。诗人极可能是在一所窗户朝南的房屋或草屋中写就这首诗的。当时的窗自然不是玻璃窗;可能只是在窗棂上蒙上一层亚麻纤维织物,有纸帘卷在窗顶上;向外可望见窗外景物。作者就是从这种窗口望见远处的小山或大山峦的。时令是冬季的夜晚,接近半夜了。就在此刻,明月升起,在这远山的山峦之上,把银霜似的一片光芒洒满了作者床前的地上。而在此刻之前,月亮还未升上山冈,给挡住在山后。这就是作者用"山月"两字的背景。其时,城中及邻里之间的一切纷扰、喧嚷均已平息。此所以诗题告诉我们这不只是夜思而是静夜思。原诗的"床前"宾纳误译为"on the foot of my bed"。在唐朝,我们的祖先白天就在草荐上席地而坐,至多在草荐上再添一条毯子。晚间所睡的床也与今天我们的床迥异。那时的床就用木板铺在地上,板上加一厚层干芦苇或柴草作垫子,垫子又蒙上一层大麻、亚麻或丝织物(帛)做面子。当时恐怕还没有棉花,所以也不可能有像我们用的棉织品床单。长安现名西安,地处北纬34°左右,气温与徐州大体相似,较低于南京。李白这首诗如写就于京都,这床就绝不可能铺设在高于地面的土炕之上:烧炕取暖的地区一般还要往北些。故此,床前就是指的床前地上,并不是宾纳所译的"on the foot of my bed"。诗人的床既无木腿,更没有金属腿。诗人怀疑地上的月光像霜,该句就是这种疑惑的陈述句,英译时毋须改为疑问句。"already"一词也添得不对,因为李白写诗时可能正是冬天,并非译者假定的深秋。原诗的"举头"给译成了"lifting myself",意思并不一样。原诗在善本中的"山月"(虽则在通俗本中已误改为"明月")译文成了"moonlight",比讹传的"明月"离得更远。最后一行"低头思故乡"(I bow down to think of my homeland)译成了"Sinking back again, I thought suddenly of

---

① 事实上,在这些版本中还可以见到原诗真正的第一行为"床前看月光"(The sight of the moonshine before my bed),但我们不愿在这里对版本校勘作过细的评议。

home”。“Sinking back”是不对的；“again”也不对；“Suddenly”就再一次不对。宾纳的译文说明他不很懂得中国的文学语言。宾纳的译文是一对四音步诗行和一对六音步诗行。从英文韵文的格律看，这样处理也说明他在驾驭其本国语言方面也尚显得才疏力薄。

最后，尽管我们用了不少贬义的文字指出了翟理斯与宾纳的学识之不足，他们对中国文字理解之粗浅以及他们英译我国古代诗歌中两颗稀世珍宝时在技巧上的贫拙，但我还是要对他们表示我的赞赏。我赞赏他们两位对中国文化的一番挚情和热爱；赞赏他们不惧中国文化与他们相距如此之远而仍试图去掌握它；赞赏他们在这方面所作出的辛勤劳动。与其他一些汉学家相比，他们的贡献显然不能过于被轻视。

以下罗列这两首诗的其他一些译文，以资参改：

OTHER VERSIONS OF THESE TWO POEMS FOR REFERENCE

Ⅰ.1　The Hall of Silence

Where the sun's eye first
　Peers above the pines,
On the ancient temple
　Early daylight shines.
To retirement guiding
　Leads the winding way：
Round the Cell of Silence
　Flowers and foliage stray.
Hark! the birds rejoicing
　In the mountain light!
Like one's dim reflection

On a pool at night.
Lo! the heart is melted
Wav'ring out of sight.
All is hushed to silence.
Harmony is still.
The bell's low chime alone
Whispers round the hill.

— W. J. B. Fletcher

Ⅰ.2 A Buddhist Retreat Behind Broken-Mountain Temple

In the pure morning, near the old temple,
Where early sunlight points the tree-tops,
My path has wound, through a sheltered hollow
Of boughs and flowers, to a Buddhist retreat.
Here birds are alive with mountain-light,
And the mind of man touches peace in a pool,
And a thousand sounds are quieted
By the breathing of a temple-bell.

— Witter Bynner

Ⅱ.1 The Moon Shines Everywhere

Seeing the Moon before my couch so bright
I thought hoar frost had fallen from the night.
On her clear face I gaze with lifted eyes:
Then hide them full of Youth's sweet memories.

— W. J. B. Fletcher

Ⅱ.2 Thoughts in a Tranquil Night

Athwart the bed
I watch the moonbeams cast a trail
  So bright, so cold, so frail,
    That for a space it gleams
Like hoar-frost on the margin of my dreams
    I raise my head, —
The splendid moon I see:
    Then droop my head,
And sink to dreams of thee —
My fatherland, of thee!

— L. Cranmer-Byng

Ⅱ.3 Night Thoughts

In front of my bed the moonlight is very bright.
I wonder if that can be frost on the floor?
I lift up my head and look at the full moon, the dazzling moon.
I drop my head, and think of the home of old days.

— Amy Lowell

Ⅱ.4 On a Quiet Night

I saw the moonlight before my couch.
And wondered if it were not the frost on the ground.
I raised my head and looked out on the mountain moon,
I bowed my head and thought of my far-off home.

— S. Obata

Ⅱ.5 Still Night Thoughts

Moonlight in front of my bed —
I took it for frost on the ground!
I lift my eyes to watch the mountain moon.
Lower them and dream of home.

— Burton Watson

下面这两首诗是我的译文：

Ⅰ The Rear Dhyana Hall of Poshan Bonzary

Chang Jian (circa 703—770)

| Whēn āt dáwn | Ī rēpáired | tō thē bón | zārȳ óld, |
(anapaest)

| Thē fírst beáms | ōf thē rís | īng sún shóne | ōn treés
(bacchius)

táll, |

| Wínding páths | lēd tō cóv | ērt, sēclúd | ēd gróves |
(amphimacer) (iambus)

| Whēre lúsh thíck | ēt ānd flów | ērs ēnclósed |

Th' dyȳānā háll. |
(paeonquartus)

| th' ráre áurā | ōf thē móunt | pleásed thē ná | tūre ōf th'
(antibacchius)

bírds; |

| Ímāges īn | róck pít póols | fréed thē mínd's | úps ānd
(dactyl) (molossus)

dówns. |

| Áll thē búb | būbs ōf mén | wēre húshed ās | bȳ ā spéll; |
(amphilbrach)

| Thēre wās nóth | īng léft būt | thē béll's ānd | *chíng's* (spondee)
clángs. |

Thoughts in a Still Night

Li Bai(701—762)

| Thē lú | mīnōus | móonshine | (pyrrhic)
| Befóre | mȳ béd |
| Īs thóught | tō bē | thē fróst
| Fállēn | ōn thē gróund. | (trochee)
| Ī líft | mȳ héad | tō gáze |
| Ā thē | clíft móon, | (spondee)
| Ānd thén | bów dówn | tō múse |
| Ōn mȳ dís | tānt hóme. |

第一首是抑抑扬格八行诗。第二首是抑扬格八行诗,单行是三音步诗行,双行是二音步诗行。两首诗在音步上均有相应的韵律变化。

伯顿·沃森(Burton Watson)的译文"I lift my eyes"与我的译文"I lift my head"是截然不同的两回事。"I lift my head"不仅从原文措辞"举头"上讲是准确的释译,这与"山月"的意境有关。渥曾的译文意似这"山月"(mountain moon)并不高,而我的译文根据原诗则表明"山月"(clift moon)从山岗后面爬上来是很高的,以致诗人感到光靠往上转动一下眼球还不够,必须抬起头来看。这山的高低之分对于诗的命题以及引起诗人灵感的环境关系甚大。不妨再提一下:是接近夜半的时候了,周围异常宁静,所以诗题是《静夜思》。

在1981年第五期《外国语》中读到范文忠教授的博学文章:《中国诗歌及英文翻译》。文中提到近代杰出的传记作家历顿·史屈莱契(Lytton Strachey,1880—1932)对翟理斯英译李商隐的一首近体或今体七言绝句,曾作过热烈的赞扬。

夜雨寄北

李商隐

君问归期未有期,
巴山夜雨涨秋池。
何当共剪西窗烛,
却话巴山夜雨时。

翟理斯的译文为:

You ask when I'm coming: alas not just yet...
How the rain filled the pools on that night when we met!
Ah, when shall we ever snuff candles again,
And recall the glad hours of that evening of rain?

史屈莱契虽则是布鲁姆丝布莱学派(Bloomsbury School)的一位才华横溢的散文大师;翟理斯在他的《中国文学之瑰宝一诗》中有些译品也有所建树,但是翟理斯对李商隐这首诗的译文是有问题的、错误的。我的译文、注释及对翟理斯的评点如下:

Lines Sent to the North Written during Night Rains

Li Shangyin(813—858)

| Bēīng ásked | fór mȳ hóme | cōmīng dáte, |

Ī tēll thée	I'm̄ nōt súre	whēn thāt'll bé,
As níght ráins	ōn thē móunts	ōf Bár fáll
Ānd aútum̄n	póols āre brímmed	frōm thē léa.
Thēn wē sháll	bȳ thē wést	wíndōw sít,
Clípping̅	thē cándle-wīck	īn sōme níght,
An̄d tálk ōf	thē níght ráins	ōn th' Bá móunts,
Whīle Ī think	ōf thée wīth	múte dēlight.

古代处于蜀地的三巴即今四川省东部丘陵地区。这首诗是作者在唐代宣宗大中二年出游巴蜀地区时写给他妻子李王氏的。诗中描述的曲折交错的情景以及作者的感受引起人们对思乡之情的极为美妙的憧憬。诗人在写这首诗时,正当巴蜀山区的夜晚,屋外下着雨,他无法断定何时才能回到家中和妻子一起凭西窗而坐,剪烛拨亮烛焰,把一片思念之情向她尽情地倾吐。翟理斯的译文把现在的事误认为是过去的情景。译者认为诗中描写的是作者期待着和妻子会面可以畅叙这“过去的情景”。实际上诗人写的是即时的此情此景,诗人向往的是将来他回家之后能和妻子一起坐在西窗下欢叙这段引起他诗兴的“此情此景”。烛芯要时时修剪,使烛光明亮些。剪烛并不是把烛火熄灭,夫妻上床。“snuff”一词可以指把烛芯的枯焦部分(俗称灯花)剪去而拨亮烛火,也可以指把烛花熄灭。为了避免模棱两可的弊病,准确地表达命意,我认为用“clip”或“trim”较好些。此外,“巴山”一词在短短二十八字的原诗中出现两次,足以说明它曾激起诗人满怀联翩浮想:“巴山”使他联想到夜晚的雨声,想到涨满雨水的池塘,想到诗人对妻子的眷恋和思念,想到诗人是何等急切期待着能在不久将来的一天夜晚和妻子相会,却又因为这日期定不下来而怅惘不已。然而翟理斯在译文中竟根本把“巴山”抹掉了,这不能不叫人认为是一大败笔。诚

然,我们没法叫诗人的联想和感受重新再现让人体验一下,但是,对"巴山"作个注释至少或可做些补偿,即使能让人再领受到诗人十分之一的激情或者哪怕是部分的十分之一也是好的。可惜,由于译文把"巴山"一词一笔勾销,作注释就成了无本之木了。

下面我们再讨论范文中路伊斯·史屈朗·海孟(Louise Strong Hammond)对贾岛(779—843)的一首五言绝句的翻译。原诗如下:

寻隐者不遇

松下问童子,
言师采药去。
只在此山中,
云深不知处。

海孟的译文如下:

Seeking the Hernict in vain
"Gone to gather herbs" —
So they say of you.
But in cloud-girt hills,
What am I to do?

"显而易见,好多意思漏译了"。我也恰好译过这首诗,我的译文恐怕漏译不多。

A Cail on the Recluse without Meeing Him

Jia Tao

| Ī ásked | thē bóy | bēnēath thē | píne trée, |
(tribrach)

| Whō sáid, | "Thē Más | tēr's góne hérbs | tō píck; |

| Hē múst | bē sóme | whēre róund | thēse clíffs |
| Cōncéaled | ūnséen | īn thē | clóuds thíck." |

本诗描写的是诗人拜访一位隐居的朋友的情况。全诗是借助于诗人向童子的问讯以及童子轻灵的答话得以表现的。读此诗,我们一下子就会想到,也应该想到,这位遁世之士带着小童子就隐居在这山上的一所小屋里。他远离尘世,一心只想采集仙草以求长生不老。这时,他正在山顶上,藏身于浓厚的云雾之中。海孟的译文中,童子变成了"they"译文表达了诗人访友不遇而怅然若失、不知所措之感,而原诗中却丝毫见不到这类失望或困惑。为了与第四行的"do"叶韵,在第二行引用了"you",这一下给人的印象是诗人似乎对这位隐士稍有责备之意,而这种含义又是原诗中所没有的。

我还见到海孟所译李白的三首盛赞杨贵妃美貌诗中的第一首,即唐玄宗与杨贵妃在沉香亭观赏牡丹:

清平调词

李白

云想衣裳花想容,
春风拂槛露华浓。
若非群玉山头见,
会向瑶台月下逢。

海孟的译文如下:

Cloud-like garments, flower face,
Lattice which spring breezes trace.
Such are seen on Jade Hill Heights,
O'r some moonlit, mystic place.

“和前一首一样,又漏译不少。这是为了遵循‘一个汉字顶一个英文词音节’这原则的必然结果。”我认为这太机械了,没有必要这样做。看原诗多么令人心旷神驰,而译文却像一则打电报的文字;原诗是如此的曼妙、富丽、丰满、生动,对比之下译文只是一具枯槁的骨骼,一副残骸,一抹淡漠的影子。为了坚持一种不正确的主张,作出偌大的牺牲,太不值得。我的译文如下(译文是抑扬格和抑抑扬格混合格律):

For Qing-ping Tunes

Li Bai

Tínged clóud	lēts āre lík	ēned ūntō	hēr ráimēnt
Ānd thē flów	ērs ūntō	hēr míen.
Spríng zéph	ȳrs ālóng	thē bál	ūstráde
Géntlȳ brúsh	thē crýstāl déws'shéen.
Īf nōt séen	ōn thē wón	drōus Móunt	ōf Géms
Āt sóme	ēnchánt	ēd stránd,
Shē cóuld	bē mét wīth	ōn thē Mág	īc Tówēr
Īn thē móon	līt fáir	ȳlánd.

这首诗和其他两首都是准备配乐的,诗人把曲调定名为清平调。原诗中的花即牡丹花。花朵丰硕圆润;粉红、大红、净白或淡绿的色泽,多么雍容华贵。开始两行也可译成:

Tinged cloudlets are thought of as her raiment
　And the flowers as her mien.

群玉山和瑶台传说在西王母的仙境。《穆天子传》(穆天子,周朝的一位君主,公元前 1001 至 946 在位)一书中有穆天子远游西方寻访仙境,被西王母待为上宾之说。《穆天子传》的竹简册子共六章,晋太康二年(公元 281 年)由其臣民不准从魏襄王陵墓中掘得。不准犯了盗王陵的罪,这册书成了赃物。

最后我还想讨论一首上古的民歌,其年代已无从稽考了。这首歌已被译成英文。相传它是陶唐帝尧时八九十岁的老人们击壤作戏时哼唱的。据皇甫谧《帝皇世纪》,帝尧于公元前 2357—2257 年是古中国的君主。壤形似木鞋,像现代的木屐,前部较宽阔,往后渐收狭,跟作圆形。击壤者先把一只木鞋似的木块放在地上,击壤者手拿另一块壤走三四十步远就向地上的木块掷去,击中者获胜。美国知名的意象派诗人厄泽拉・庞德(Ezra Pound)以自由韵文把这首歌译成英文如下:

Sun up; work
Sun-down; to rest
Dig well and drink of the water
Dig field; eat of the grain
Imperial power is? and to us what is it?

— Canto XLIX

原诗及我的译文如下:

击壤歌

日出而作,
日入而息,
凿井而饮,
耕田而食。
帝力与我
　何有哉?

Song of Clog-throwing

— An Ancient Ballad

Wórk āt	súnrise;
Rést āt	súndōwn.
Díg wéll fōr	drínkīng;
Tíll fiélds fōr	eátīng.
Dis pówēr,	thoúgh greát, —
Whát's it tō	mé ānd ús?
(*Trochaic dimeter* 扬抑格二音步)

这首上古时期民谣思想颇有点老、庄的味道。庞德的译文是我从翁显良先生1981年第六期《翻译通讯》中《译诗管见》一文内见到的。庞德在译文中竟丝毫不提这首歌谣的题目,也不谈哼这首歌谣的情境,而只是注上了他诗集的号码XLIX,对于普通的讲英语的读者来说,因不明白民歌的历史和社会背景,译文便成了一篇简直是令人费解的、味同嚼蜡的文字;对西方的知识阶层说,至多也不过是一篇显示先民生活风尚的诗歌而已。

1982年8月

图书在版编目(CIP)数据

古诗文选英译:英文/孙大雨译.
—上海:上海三联书店,2022.8
(国学经典外译丛书.第一辑)
ISBN 978-7-5426-7806-5

Ⅰ.①古… Ⅱ.①孙… Ⅲ.①古典诗歌—诗集—中国
—英文②古典散文—散文集—中国—英文 Ⅳ.①I211

中国版本图书馆 CIP 数据核字(2022)第 144871 号

国学经典外译丛书·第一辑

古诗文选英译

译　者　孙大雨

责任编辑　钱震华
装帧设计　徐　徐

出版发行　上海三联书店
(200030)中国上海市漕溪北路 331 号 A 座 6 楼
印　刷　上海颛辉印刷厂有限公司

版　次　2022 年 8 月第 1 版
印　次　2022 年 8 月第 1 次印刷
开　本　700mm×1000mm　1/16
字　数　580 千字
印　张　43.75
书　号　ISBN 978-7-5426-7806-5/I·1780
定　价　99.00 元